When Love Perseveres

Charles W. Innocenti III

This book is a work of pure fiction. References to real people, events, establishments, or locales are intended only to provide a sense of authenticity and are used fictitiously. All characters, and all incidents, and dialogue are drawn from the author's imagination and are not to be construed as real.

DEDICATION

To my daughters, Jessica and Rachel, and to the women of the United States Army.

Table of Contents

ACKNOWLEDGMENTS

This book would not have been possible without the help I received from numerous people, all very dear friends of mine. But most of all, I want to thank my wife, JoAnne, for her unyielding support, and my children, Will, Jessica, and Rachel, for making me smile, laugh, and for supporting my efforts. You all are the greatest gifts God has ever given me.

QUOTE

Failure does not come from not succeeding; it comes from not ever trying. For when one gives all in trying, they become immortal. Their spirit joins the long line of those who have come before and after who build the platform upon which those who succeed stand. Without those that tried, there is no effort, no success, only fear. And those that succumb to that fear will never know the power of endeavor, conviction, faith, and honor and will forever live in the darkness of fear, hollow and empty, simply awaiting death.   Bill

Dying is easy. It takes courage to live.

PART ONE

AN ANGRY YOUNG WOMAN

Chapter 1

SEPTEMBER 2025 "What?" John exclaimed, not sure if he correctly heard what Sara said.

Sara answered with a shaky voice, "I said, I want to join the Army and be an infantry officer like you,".

"Oh, hell, NO!" John screamed.

"Why?"

"Are you crazy, Sara? You can't be an infantry officer! You have no idea what you're asking!"

"Yes, I do!" Sara screamed back. In addition to her temper, Sara also inherited Lisa's strong aversion to being told no, and John had just crossed the line.

"Why, Sara? Why an infantry officer?"

"Because I want to make a difference in this world. I want to do the things you did? I want to . . "

"Do the things I did? Sara, you have no idea what the hell you're talking about! Look, if you want to join the Army, we can talk about it. There are lots of things you can do that will set you up in the civilian world. But you're not going to be in the infantry!"

"Why?"

"Because I said so!"

"That's not a good enough reason!"

"Sara, you're sixteen years old! You have no clue what you want to do. You have your whole life ahead of you yet."

Growing red, Sara's face demanded a more detailed answer.

"Look, Sara. Infantry is an extremely demanding branch, both physically and mentally. I mean, you're a girl. You just don't have the strength that men do."

Sara's eyes bulged at John's comments. "I don't have the strength! Are you kidding me? You think all the hard work I've done for dancing all these years doesn't take strength? You've got to be joking? I've got more endurance and can do things most guys can't even dream of doing. I can . ."

"It's not the same!"

"I . "

"I said NO! That's enough! I don't want to hear any more about this! We're done!"

Sara was beside herself with John's stubbornness. She couldn't believe the man who repeatedly told her she could do anything in the world was now forbidding her to do what she deeply felt she wanted to do. She was on the verge of screaming at him, but knew it would only make him more adamant.

Sara forcefully sighed, turned, and stormed off to her room.

The next thing John heard was the door to her room slam shut so hard it seemed the walls shook.

"Watch the damn door!" John yelled, but it was more for his benefit to release his anger than for Sara's sake.

Just then, John's cell phone rang, and he grabbed it. "Hello!" he answered, his voice still on edge from the argument with Sara.

"Well, hello, John. Is everything alright? You sound upset," Mary asked.

"That's because I am upset. Your niece has gone crazy. I don't know what has gotten into her these past couple of days. She's a freaking raw nerve."

"John, she's sixteen. She's trying to figure the world and herself out. You know what that was like."

"Well, I wasn't that crazy!"

"Oh, really?"

"Look, Sis. Now is not the time. What do you need?"

"I thought I would invite you and Sara to have lunch with me today. Jason is out of town, and with the boys gone, this old woman gets lonely sometimes. How about you two come into town for lunch, and maybe we can do something this afternoon?"

"Well, I was hoping to try out that new gym that opened in the old shopping strip center near your house this morning. It's time to get off my ass and hit the weights again and get back into shape."

"OK. Why don't you drop Sara off at my house on your way in? You can clean up at my house when you're finished, and we can grab lunch and visit after that."

"That sounds like a good idea. Maybe you can talk to her and see why she's so moody these days."

"Sounds good. I'm sure we'll have lots to talk about with you gone. It's been a while since we've had a good niece and aunt visit."

"Great. I'll see you in an hour."

After hanging up the phone and waiting a few minutes to let Sara cool off from their argument, John told her about his plans for them to visit Mary. To his great surprise, Sara did not resist the invitation. He sensed that she wanted to talk to someone about their argument, and Mary was just the person for Sara to confide in.

As soon as John dropped Sara off at Mary's, she began venting to Mary about what happened earlier that morning.

"I don't know what's gotten into him these days," Sara complained to Mary as they both sat at the kitchen table peeling potatoes. "One minute, it seems he's depressed. Then the next, he's all better. Then, he's yelling at me for telling him about paperwork I got from a college program I asked about."

"Sweetheart, you know how your father gets around this time. Every year when it's the day that your mother passed away, he gets depressed. It doesn't get easier for him."

"I know, Aunt Mary. I was with him at the cemetery the other day. He was so distraught that he fell on his knees and started crying. He scared the hell out of me!"

Mary stopped peeling potatoes and seriously looked at Sara. "Was your father alright?"

"Yes, he was. I ran over to him, and once he stopped crying, he was OK."

Mary put her potato and peeler down and said, "Sweetheart, your father, and mother loved each other very much. But for some reason, it wasn't easy for either one of them. It took a while for them to get together, and even then, it still wasn't easy. Just as they got a chance to settle down and finally have a family, your mother got sick. That was very hard on your father."

"I know. I can see it in his eyes whenever he talks about her. I know he loved her very much. But the problem is I never knew her, and I really don't know much about her."

"But certainly, your father has told you about Lisa."

"He told me that she liked to dance, and she wanted me to learn how to dance. He told me she was pretty and that they got together when he was in the Army and that I look like her. But he doesn't talk about her much other than that. I don't know why they waited so long to get married. Grandma tells me stories about my mom as a little girl, but no one tells me anything about what kind of woman she actually was. What did you think of her, Aunt Mary?"

Mary was afraid Sara was going to ask her that question. Painfully, she remembered how harshly she treated Lisa when Lisa and John started to reconnect and how she had not told Lisa about John being wounded. Although Lisa had forgiven Mary for all of those things, Mary had not forgiven herself. In Mary's mind, she owed Lisa. It was one of the biggest reasons Mary helped John raise Sara, although she quickly fell in love with Sara as if she was her daughter. Mary knew about Lisa's life between the summer she met John and when she reconnected with him and the poor decisions she had made. But that was the old Lisa and not the one that reunited with John. That Lisa helped John recover from his wounds, loved him very deeply, and made him happier than Mary had ever seen John in his life. That was the Lisa Mary wanted to make sure Sara knew, so she decided she needed to be careful in what she said.

"She was a wonderful woman, sweetheart. She was beautiful, smart, funny, and very outgoing. And she loved your father very much."

Sara eyed Mary for a moment. She had heard the things Mary said before, but to Sara, they lacked substance. Sara knew her mother was beautiful. She had seen pictures of her. But to Sara, those words did not delve down below the surface of what kind of woman Lisa truly was. She had found a couple of rather risqué pictures of her mother that seemed to be before she and her father married, and those pictures often brought questions no one wanted to talk about.

Sara did not ask any more questions and an almost uneasy silence hung in the air. Not believing Mary would tell her what she wanted to know about her mother, Sara decided to stop asking any more questions.

Mary sensed Sara's frustration and decided to change subjects. "So, what did you tell your father about college that got him so upset?"

"I told him I asked Texas A&M about their ROTC program."

"OK. I don't know why your father would get very upset with you about that."

"Well, I told him I wanted to be an infantry officer like he was."

Mary restrained herself from flinching when she heard what Sara said and did her best not to show any surprise. She did not want to make the same mistake John made and overreact.

"Well, Sara, that's usually not a job many women in the Army do. Why do you want to join the Army and be in the infantry?"

Sara thought before she spoke. "I want to do something special with my life, Aunt Mary. I look around at most of the girls I know my age, and they are just so shallow and fake. They live off of their daddy's money with no real ambition. All they think about is what they look like, and lots of them already have fake boobs and plastic surgery to look good, at 16! Then they just use people. They are always trying to get something from the guy they are with. Lots of guys are like that too.

Most of them are just trying to sleep with you. They could not care less about having a true relationship. I don't want to be around people like that. I just can't stand them! I want something different in life."

Mary listened patiently. "OK."

"Well, I remember some of the people that were with Daddy in the Army. None of them were like that. They were all genuine. I also remember all the people that told Daddy how much they learned from him. You know lots of them still call him today. You should see how happy it makes him when they reach out to him. He smiles the whole time he is on the phone with them. I want to be able to help people like that. I want to be a part of something like that."

"OK, Sweetie. You could do all that and still be in the Army. But why be in the infantry?"

"I guess because I want to be where the real action is. I want to have a direct impact on what's happening. I just feel if I did some other job in the Army, I would be on the sidelines. I know that sounds crazy, and I know it would be very hard. But I know I could do it. I want to prove to myself I can do it. At least I want to try. I know I would regret it if I never tried."

Listening to Sara, Mary's mind wandered back to when John talked to their parents about joining the Army. She would swear that these were almost the exact words John had told them when their father objected to John's desire to join.

When Mary did not say anything after Sara finished talking, Sara figured she must have sounded foolish. "I know, Aunt Mary. I sound crazy."

"No. I wouldn't say that. I'd say you sound like your father."

"Then why did he get so upset with me?"

"Sweetheart, you know what your father went through while he was in. I know he doesn't talk about it a lot, but you know he deployed several times and got wounded other times besides the time when his leg was hurt so bad. If it wasn't for your mother, I'm not sure he would have walked again. Don't you think he would have visions of all those bad things happening to you? Don't you think that would make him upset?"

"I guess so."

"The only reason he got upset is because he loves you so much and doesn't want those things to happen to you."

"I know. But that shouldn't stop me from doing what I want to do with my life. If my father was willing to join and do things like he did, why can't I?"

Mary could not argue with Sara's logic. Looking at her, Mary saw Sara was serious, and knowing both John and Lisa could be stubborn at times, she did not doubt Sara's dedication. Inside she was shaking her head. *Sara, you definitely take after both your father and mother.*

Mary leaned over and put her hand on Sara's. "Sweetheart, you are a very smart and beautiful young lady. You have your whole life in front of you, and you can do anything you want if you put your mind to it. I know you can."

Sara bashfully smiled. "Thanks, Aunt Mary."

"Just have patience with your father. If you want to join the Army, I'm sure he'll come around to the idea."

"I hope so."

Then Sara asked, "Do you mind if I go and wash up a little before we eat? I know I have flour all over my face and hair."

"No, sweetheart. I've got everything I need to start cooking. Take your time."

Sara thanked Mary, and then went to the back bathroom to clean up.

Mary then proceeded to start cooking the food they had prepared. A few minutes after she started cooking, her cell phone rang. It was Mary's friend Jennifer from down the street asking her if she had some old cookbooks Mary talked about.

"Hi, Jen! Yes, come on over, I've got those books I've been promising to get to you," Mary told Jennifer. Jennifer Mason had moved into the neighborhood a block away a few years ago. During a chance encounter, while walking, they discovered their mutual interest in wine and quickly became friends. Jennifer was an attractive, 48-year-old, blond-haired, green-eyed beauty from Florida, who had moved to Texas to be near her parents after her divorce. She worked as a real estate agent and made a good deal of money. Since her divorce, Jennifer was in no hurry to marry again and took the time to enjoy the men she met on her timetable. She and Mary had become close friends, and Jennifer would invite Mary and Jason over to parties at her house filled with exciting people and fellow wine connoisseurs.

A few minutes later, Jennifer walked into the kitchen and found Mary digging out several cookbooks she had promised her. "Hi, Mary!"

"Hi, Jen! Come on in. I've found the cookbooks I promised to give you and that bottle of wine I was bragging about."

As they talked, Sara had finished cleaning up, and when she heard someone in the kitchen talking, she thought it might be John. She walked down the hall and saw Jennifer when she turned the corner to the living room. The instant Sara saw Jennifer, she took a dislike to her. Something in Jennifer's mannerisms and attire screamed insincerity and instantly reminded Sara of the kind of girls she spoke about earlier and loathed. Jennifer's spray-on tan highlighted by a pair of white shorts and

7

her finely detailed manicure were key indicators to Sara about her suspicions.

"Hey, Sara. I'd like to introduce you to my friend, Jennifer. Jennifer, this is my niece, Sara," Mary said as she faced the two."

Sara begrudgingly made her way over to Jennifer as Jennifer turned around to greet her.

Jennifer cheerfully said, "Hi, Sara."

Sara stood in front of Jennifer and eyed her before she put her hand out. With a less than enthusiastic tone, she finally said, "Hello, Ma'am."

Jennifer picked up on Sara's behavior that she was not enthused about meeting her but remained polite. "Mary's told me a lot of nice things about you, Sara, but she wasn't lying when she said how pretty you are."

Sara forced a smile and said, "Thank you, Ma'am."

Mary, too, picked up on Sara's cold manner and tried to warm things up. "Sara's sixteen. She's a sophomore at West High School this year and is on their drill team."

"That's awesome, Sara!" Jennifer said.

An awkward pause ensued until Sara spoke up and said, "Well, it's very nice to meet you, Ma'am. If you'll excuse me, I need to make a phone call before lunch."

When Sara turned the corner to go into the hall, Jennifer turned and looked at Mary with a confused look on her face. Then, she quietly asked, "Did I do or say something wrong?"

Mary was as confused as Jennifer. "No. I'm not sure what the problem was. She's usually a very happy girl. I'm sorry, Jen."

"Don't worry about it, Mary. She might have something on her mind. I remember what it was like to be a teenager."

As Mary and Jennifer were visiting, John was driving back from his workout at the nearby gym to meet Mary and Sara for lunch. He was feeling great. His body felt invigorated after the wonderfully restful night. The gym played some classic hard rock during his workout, and John pushed himself. He loved the testosterone-laced high he got from working out hard and that pumped feeling as blood filled his muscles. Although he still felt the pump, he was now enjoying the glacial calm that always followed his strenuous workouts as the endorphins ran rampant through his body. He often imagined he could calmly walk through an active L-shaped ambush kill zone when relaxing after a workout. He also felt particularly satisfied that two reasonably attractive women in the gym seemed to sneak a few peeks at him during his workout. He laughed to himself as he thought, *Ah, I still got it!*

He pulled into Mary's driveway and wiped the sweat from his brow as he walked into the house.

When Mary and Jennifer heard the front door open, they turned to see John walking in. He was bathed in sweat, wearing a compression T-shirt that outlined a well-toned and muscular upper body, shorts, tennis shoes, and a towel in his hand.

Entering the living room and looking toward the kitchen, the first thing that caught John's eye was a nicely shaped set of tan legs highlighted against a pair of tight white shorts on a blonde-haired woman visiting Mary. Finally looking up, John realized Mary and the woman were both looking at him.

When John entered the kitchen area, he was embarrassed by his appearance. "Hey, Mary. I didn't know you had company. I'm sorry, I didn't mean to interrupt you."

"No, problem, John. I'd like to introduce you to Jennifer. She's my neighbor down the street." Mary then turned to Jennifer and said, "Jennifer, this is my brother, John, Sara's father." That Jennifer was staring at John with her mouth slightly open was not lost on Mary.

John looked straight at Jennifer and was immediately struck by the rest of her curvy body and beautiful face. For a split second, John saw her eyes widen just before she broke into a broad smile. "Hi, Jennifer. I'd shake your hand, but I'm pretty sweaty from my workout. It's very nice to meet you."

Jennifer's momentary loss of consciousness quickly left as she maintained her beauty queen-worthy smile, and she extended her hand and softly said. "Hi, John. That's quite alright. I'm very happy to meet you."

John shook her hand and swore there was a bit of an electrical current momentarily exchanged between them.

"Do you live in town? I'm surprised we've never met before."

"Well, we've only been in Victoria a little while since we moved from Killeen."

"I see," she said, still smiling.

Looking at John, Mary made a disgusting expression on her face and put her hand to pinch her nose shut. "You need to take a bath, stinky brother. And soon!"

John rolled his eyes and laughed as he said, "Yes, stinky sister!" He then turned back to Jennifer. "I better go clean up. It was nice to meet you, Jennifer."

"Nice to meet you too, John."

John turned and walked to his room, thinking, *Damn! That woman is hot! Hmmm. Maybe? No, she's probably not interested. She's a lot younger than me too. Still.*

As John walked away, Jennifer's eyes tracked his every movement. As soon as he was out of sight and earshot, Jennifer turned to Mary and quietly yet excitedly said, "You said you had an older brother, not a younger one!"

"He is older than me. John will be 57 this year."

"No way! I'd swear he was 47! What's his secret? Does he work out all the time?"

"Well, since his wife, Lisa, died, and he left the Army, he's been working out a lot. He says it relaxes him."

"I'm very sorry to hear that about his wife," Jennifer said. Then her eyes grew big again, and she said, "Mary, you've got to set me up with a date with him!"

Mary laughed, "What?"

"Not a what. I said a date."

"Jennifer!"

"I'm serious, Mary!"

Mary paused. She was excited that Jennifer found John attractive enough to try and get a date with him. But she was afraid Jennifer did not understand what she was walking into. "OK, Jen. Before you get any ideas, I have to explain a few things. First, John loved Lisa a lot. I'm not sure he's ever gotten over her. He still visits her grave periodically. And second, he was a Soldier and saw a lot of combat. He's not a typical guy. He's different. I mean, in a good way, just different when it comes to having a good time."

"He was a Soldier?"

"Yes, he was a colonel when he retired, and he was an exceptional officer."

Jennifer's smile turned into a look of pure carnal desire. "You just get me that date and leave the rest to me, sister-in-law."

Mary gawked at Jennifer and said, "Oh, my God, girl!"

Later, as John, Sara, and Mary ate lunch, John started asking questions about Jennifer. He did his best to pretend to be neutral in his enthusiasm, but Mary sensed he was interested in her.

"You seem to be asking a lot of questions about Jennifer," Mary teased.

"Oh, I was just curious. That's all. I don't know many of your friends in town. Just curious," John answered, still trying to hide his curiosity.

"She seems kinda fake if you ask me," Sara said before taking a drink from her glass. Her tone was meant to tell John she disapproved of Jennifer, but he was not paying much attention. However, Mary got Sara's message.

"Well, Sara, you just haven't been around Jennifer. She can be a lot of fun."

When Sara finished lunch early and went outside, John asked, "So, Mary, what exactly does Jennifer do?"

Mary finished putting her plate in the dishwasher and sat down at the table with John as she broke out into a grin. "OK, John. Before you ask any more questions, let me just tell you something right now."

"Oh, OK." *Yeh, she's married. I should have known,* John thought.

"The moment you left the room, Jennifer asked me to set her up with a date with you."

"Come on, Sis! You're pulling my leg now."

"Nope. Totally serious."

"Bullshit! She's got to be in her thirties. Why would she be interested in an old man like me?"

"She's 47. She is currently unattached. She is loads of fun. And to answer one of the questions on your mind. Yes. They're real."

John's eyes exploded. "Jesus Christ, Sis!"

Mary laughed. "I just want to provide my brother with the best intelligence possible before he conducts any offensive operations."

Laughing, John said, "OK, you've definitely been hanging around me way too long."

As if almost on cue, Mary's cell phone rang. It was Jennifer. "Hey, Mary. Guess what. I finally found that bottle of Pinot Grigio I've been after. I was wondering if you, John, and Sara would be interested in coming over next Friday and having supper with me and enjoying opening it. Oh, of course, if you and Sara can't make it over, I totally understand, Wink. Wink."

Mary laughed. "Let me see, dear." Then she turned to John and mischievously said, "Well, John. Someone would like to invite us over to supper next Friday. It's a shame Sara and I are tied up for the evening. Would you be interested in going over by yourself?"

John stared at Mary and mouthed the words, Jennifer.

Mary nodded her head.

John pondered the invitation. *I don't know. Am I really ready for something like this? Maybe I should just pass. Still. Damn, she looked good in those shorts! No. Well. Fuck it, John. Come on. Start living your life. Quiet living like some fucking monk. Do it!* He smiled. "Tell her I'd love to."

11

"OK, Jennifer. Well, Sara and I can't make it, but John would like to take you up on that invitation," Mary told Jennifer, trying her best to keep a straight face.

"Great! Send that hunk of man over around seven, sister-in-law," Jennifer said.

Mary rolled her eyes and shook her head as she hung up her cell phone.

John looked at Mary, eagerly awaiting Jennifer's response.

"Well, your date is arranged. Be over at Jennifer's around seven."

Grinning, John felt the boyish mischief slowly build within him.

Then Mary said, "John, I don't know if you picked up on it, but Sara does not like Jennifer. I don't know why, but I definitely got the angry female vibe from her earlier when she met Jennifer and while we were eating lunch. I'm just letting you know."

"I tell you, Mary. She's been a raw nerve this past couple of weeks. I just don't understand."

"She's becoming a young woman, John. She's sixteen. There's a lot of things going on inside her right now."

"I guess so."

"How did your talk with her about taking the pill go?"

"Oh my God! It was a cluster fuck from the word go."

"Well, I told you you needed to be careful about that discussion."

"Yeh, I got that. I tried to tell her I was not giving my consent for her to sleep around, but I knew she would be tempted, and I just wanted her to be careful and not make any mistakes she would regret later. I don't know what the right answer is, to take it or not. But I really wanted to talk to her about it."

"Well, what did she say?"

"She just blew up. Said I didn't trust her to make good decisions. Asked me what kind of girl did I think she was."

"Well, what did you say to that?"

"I said, I know how kids her age are. I know what goes on. I was young once."

"John, that probably wasn't the best way to address her concerns."

"It's just hard for me to talk to her about that kind of stuff, Mary! Do I need to remind you I've never raised a daughter before? Especially without a mother! God, how I wish Lisa were here to help me with her."

Mary was about to say something to John but paused. She knew Lisa was always a sensitive subject with him, and she needed to be cautious about what she said. Finally, she said, "Maybe you should just tell her about how you and Lisa got together?"

John thought for a minute, then said, "I can't tell her that Lisa was on the pill without her parents knowing and all the mistakes she made with men back then." He then lowered his head and sighed.

Mary wasn't sure if John was ashamed of what he said about Lisa or sad. She reached over and touched his arm. As John looked up at her, she tenderly said, "I don't mean that. I mean about you and Lisa and the start of your relationship and the young love you two shared that summer. She should know how you two got started. I think she'd learn some good lessons about what true love is."

John lowered his gaze again. It had been a while since he thought about those days, and when he did, he always wished he could go back. "It's . . It's hard for me to talk about Lisa like that to her. I can't do it, Mary, without tearing up."

"She needs to know how exceptional a woman Lisa was even if she made some mistakes in the past. I think Sara would appreciate the stories you could tell her about Lisa."

As John and Mary were talking, Sara had decided to walk back into the kitchen to get something to drink. When she heard Mary mention Lisa's name, she stopped just before leaving the hallway and tried to listen in. When Sara heard John saying her mother was on the pill and about her mistakes with men, she quickly turned around and went back to her room.

I can't believe this! Sara thought. *My mother sleeping around at my age so much she needed to be on the pill! Is that the kind of woman she was? No wonder all those men were around her in that picture of her in that tiny bikini! How could my father marry someone like that? Is that what he thinks of me? I'll just be another tramp like my mother?*

Sara closed her eyes and tried her best to suppress the combination of hurt and rage in her. *That can't be true. I know my father is a good man. But here he is now all google-eyed over some sleazy woman! If I only knew the truth about my mother, what she was really like!*

Chapter 2

From the moment John arrived at Jennifer's house, he sensed those old familiar feelings. Once again, he felt that nostalgic anticipation of being on a first date, although the experience from being a 57-year-old retired Army colonel removed his youthful awkwardness.

Jennifer captured his eye immediately when she met him at the door. She was comfortable dressed in a deep plunging V neck, white sleeveless top with a center knot that was tight around her narrow waist, and a pair of dark jeans that accentuated her full figure. Her long blonde hair hanging just past her shoulders highlighted her alluring emerald eyes and flawless skin.

John often found it hard to look away from Jennifer. It had been a long time since he had been in the company of such a beautiful woman. However, her easy-going manner relaxed him, and soon they began cracking jokes with one another as if they were old friends.

Jennifer's sensual and deliberate movements reminded him of Lisa, and he tried his best to put those thoughts aside, even though it pained him at times. He had resolved long ago he would never forget Lisa. But tonight, John felt he needed a break from the heartbreak of loneliness, if only for a while.

Jennifer had cooked steaks and served John a meal that looked like it had come from one of those expensive, fancy restaurants he and Lisa would go to sometimes. They took their time eating and chatted about Jennifer's house and work.

She was pleased John took a genuine interest in her instead of talking nonstop about himself, like most men she knew. His compliments were honest, and the more they talked, the more Jennifer enjoyed his company.

After the meal, Jennifer asked John if he would like to move to the living room with a glass of wine to continue their visit.

John agreed. After helping her take the dishes to the sink, he went to the living room and sat on the end of the couch.

Jennifer brought two glasses of wine and said, "This is the wine I was telling Mary about. I think you'll love it."

She then handed him a glass and asked, "Do you mind if I put some music on in the background?"

"No. Not at all."

"I've got a playlist of some old 70s songs I love to listen to. I just love the old Eagles albums. Do you like them?"

"Oh, I love their music!"

Watching Jennifer start the music, John thought, *I wonder if Mary told her I love music. Hmm. I wonder what else is programmed for the evening?*

The Eagles' "Best of My Love" started to play, and John was pleased. *Oh my God, woman! Perfect song for the evening!*

Jennifer returned and sat down on the couch next to John, a little closer than he would have anticipated. "Do you like this wine?"

"I haven't tried it yet. I have to tell you, Jennifer, I really don't know anything about wine. I rarely drink any alcohol. This one glass alone will probably make me a bit dizzy."

"Well, I promise not to take advantage of you if you find yourself feeling faint," Jennifer teased. The gentle tone in her voice sent a slight shiver up John's spine, and he grinned.

"You haven't told me tonight about you, John. Mary said you were a colonel in the Army. What did you do, exactly?"

"I was an infantry officer."

"I see. Did you have to go overseas?"

For the first time during his visit, John's face went solemn. "Yes, I did several tours in Afghanistan and Iraq."

Sensing the change in John's mood, Jennifer gently placed her hand on his forearm. "I understand. Not a subject for discussion tonight. Whatever you did over there, I know it wasn't easy. My brother was a Marine for 12 years and did two tours in Iraq. I know what you guys went through. I also know not to ask any more of those questions unless you want to talk about it."

The ends of John's mouth slightly turned up, believing her words were genuine. He found comfort knowing she was not oblivious to what he had been through.

"Thanks. No, it wouldn't make for good conversation tonight. We probably need to talk about something else. How about you tell me more about you? What's a nice girl like you doing in Victoria?"

Jennifer laughed. "Nice line." She then took a sip from her wine glass.

WHEN LOVE PERSEVERES

The moistness of Jennifer's lips enchanted John's eyes, and the movement of the liquid sliding down her throat brought his attention to her beautiful long neck. *Easy, boy!*

Jennifer started telling John about her divorce several years ago, her decision to move to Victoria to be near her parents as they grew older, and how she started her business. Her stories reminded him of Lisa. Jennifer had some hard knocks along the way in her life, but she was a woman as strong as she was beautiful, a combination John felt very attracted to.

Listening to Jennifer talk, John finally took a sip of wine, found it delicious, and eagerly drank the rest of his glass.

When Jennifer refilled his glass, she took the opportunity to sit closer to John and asked questions about his life.

The soft music of some of John's favorite 70s groups, his alcohol-induced lightheadedness, and Jennifer's sincere attention put him further at ease. Before long, he was talking about subjects he'd found difficult to talk with others about, like his relationship with Sara.

"You know, Jennifer, I've tried to raise Sara right as a daughter, but I just don't think I've done a good job."

"She's beautiful, John, and Mary says she's very smart. She's well-mannered and polite, even if she doesn't like me. So, what are you worrying about?"

"Well, she has her mother's looks, that's for sure. And she is very smart. But I'm talking about being a young woman. I don't know anything about that stuff. Sometimes, I think I could have done a better job, but I'm just lost sometimes. I just wish . ." John stopped. He realized he had been dominating the conversation and mentally chastised himself for doing so.

"I'm sorry, Jennifer. I wanted to hear more about you, but it seems I've been talking about myself a lot suddenly. Please forgive me."

"There's no need to ask for forgiveness. Honestly, I'm flattered."

"Why are you flattered?"

"Tell me. Who else have you told these things to?"

John lowered his gaze and thought. "No one, really."

"That's what I thought. And that's why I'm flattered; that you feel comfortable enough to talk to me about these things."

John turned back to Jennifer and stared at her. He could feel her kindness. She was not the shallow woman he had feared but an interesting one with sincere empathy. "You're a good listener."

Jennifer smiled, accepting his compliment. "Thank you. But it's easy to listen to you," she said, as her green eyes magnetically pulled him to her.

He hesitated as her beautiful face encompassed his whole attention. Before long, he blinked and came out of his trance. He then happened to glance at his watch and realize it was after eleven. "Wow, I had no idea how late it is. I hope I haven't overstayed my visit. I don't want to keep you up if you have a big day ahead of you tomorrow."

Staring at John, Jennifer's expression conveyed the prelude to the deepest of passions as she seductively whispered, "Don't go yet."

Her request captivated him. Her warm body next to his and her hand now resting on top of his thigh excited him. John felt his pulse react as a beautiful pair of green eyes, and two moist red lips beckoned him.

Slowly, he leaned toward Jennifer as her eyes closed, welcoming his advance. Once their lips joined, he closed his eyes and slowly began his exploration.

John took his time as if sipping another glass of wine. When she parted her lips, his tongue tasted the remnants of the sweet nectar in her mouth, and his mind filled with images of coming attractions. He could feel the stirrings of an unquenchable desire from within. It had been so very long, he had almost forgotten the sensations he was experiencing, yet the memories and feelings came rushing back.

Jennifer responded to John's movements slowly, deliberately, allowing him to set the pace. Then, easily, she unbuttoned his shirt's top two buttons, slipped her hand inside, and gently rubbed his chest with her fingertips.

Flushed with the scent of her provocative perfume, the savory taste of her mouth, and her sensual touch, John wanted more. His growing yearning removed the last remnants of restraint, and John put his arms around her and pulled her into him. He felt her breathing deepen, and he responded by moving his kisses to her neck.

Jennifer moaned, and John's heartbeat exploded. He leaned back on the couch, pulling her with him so he could feel her body pressed against his. Suddenly he felt a warm moist feeling on his thigh.

"Oh, my God, John! I'm so sorry!" Jennifer anxiously said as she sat back up on the couch. She had spilled the wine from the glass she was still holding onto his pants.

John heartedly laughed. Feeling a bit lightheaded, he remained lying back on the couch with his head on the armrest. "So, was this your plan to get my pants off? Spill wine on them and then tell me you have to wash them while I wait?" he joked.

Jennifer returned his laugh. "Honestly, no. No devious plan." But then she gave him a sultry look and whispered, "But it does seem to have happened at just the right time. Don't you think?"

John arched an eye and smiled.

"But seriously, why don't you take them off and let me wash them quickly before it does stain?"

John grinned. The alcohol had removed his inhibitions, and a mischievous thought came to his mind. "Nope!"

Jennifer playfully frowned. "What do you mean, nope?"

"You take yours off first. Then you can have mine."

Jennifer's eyes widened with surprise. His sexy, playful flirting had caught her off guard, and she loved it. She now had him exactly where she wanted him.

She seductively narrowed her eyes. "OK. If you insist."

Jennifer then stood up and slowly started to unbutton her pants while eyeing John the whole time. With a sultry sway of her hips, she let them drop to the floor and then stepped out of them. Then she casually unbuttoned her blouse, looking directly into John's eyes the whole time, and slipped out of it.

John lay on the couch, captivated by her sensual movements. His sexual desire grew with each piece of clothing that fell to the floor.

There was little left to the imagination when Jennifer finished, and John shook his head in anticipation. He was impressed. When he saw the tan lines near her breasts, his heart raced.

Jennifer then slowly crawled on top of John bringing her face to within inches of his, and whispered, "I think it's your turn now."

"All in good time," he replied as he pulled her into a kiss. Feeling her soft body on his, John felt feelings he hadn't felt in years. That carnal desire from within was bursting, but he fought back haste to savor the moment.

Jennifer's kiss was unhurried, soft, and sensual as she took one hand and ran it through John's hair.

He could hear her breathing deepen and feel her legs entangle with his.

Despite both of their attempts at control, passion got the better part of them, and before long, they were in Jennifer's bedroom, filling their mutual cravings for one another, a night they would both remember.

Early the next morning, John's cell phone started to vibrate on the nightstand next to the bed he was in. The years of sleeping in a war zone made him a light sleeper, and the sound quickly awakened him.

He looked over on the stand and grabbed his phone, too sleepy to see who was calling. "Hello," he said with a tired voice.

"Where the hell are you?"

John rubbed his eyes and tried to clear the lingering mental fog in his mind. "Sara?"

"Yes, it's me! Where are you? Why didn't you come home last night? I called you, but there was no answer."

Taken aback by his daughter's demanding tone, John replied, "I decided to stay over at someone's house last night. Are you alright? Is something wrong?"

"The only thing wrong is that my father is out galivanting around like some teenager!"

Fully awake now, John's anger started to rise. He'd had enough of Sara talking to him like some young Army recruit. "Look here, young lady, I'm not some damn teenager! I'm just fine! I'll be home in a while, and we'll talk about this then. Out!"

John quickly hung up the call before Sara could reply and laid the phone back on the nightstand. Then he lifted his head a bit from his pillow and looked around. He was in a bedroom, alone, that was most certainly a woman's. *Where the hell am I? I was with Jennifer. Couple of drinks. Her house. Sex! Oh, fuck!*

He then looked under the covers and saw he was naked. Then he looked around to see if he saw his clothes. He was trying to decide what he should do when Jennifer walked in the bedroom wearing a short, loose-fitting robe showing off a lot of bare legs.

"Good morning," she said as she sat on the bed.

"Good morning," John bashfully replied.

"Who was that on the phone you were talking to?"

"That was my daughter, Sara. She wanted to know where I was. She said she called me last night, and I didn't answer, but I don't ever remember getting a call."

Jennifer tilted her head. "I think I did hear your phone ring once, but we were a little busy at the time."

John grinned as he remembered their nighttime activities. *Oh, man! This woman was incredible! But I wonder what she thought of me?* He leaned toward Jennifer, resting against his arm on the bed. With an unsure tone in his voice, he said "To be honest, Jennifer, I haven't been with a woman since I was with Lisa last. You . . .You are incredible."

Jennifer's face softened. "Thank You. That was sweet of you to say. And you, sweetheart, are an incredible man."

John felt a wave of relief come over him. *So, I did OK last night. Thank God! Maybe it's time to really move on. Maybe there's a real possibility here with her for a future.* "So, you had a good time?" he asked. But this time, he was surer of himself.

"It was great! Up until the point when you came, and you called me, Lisa."

"What?" John blurted out, fearing he had heard her correctly.

"You called me Lisa last night. Two times, in fact," Jennifer coldly said.

John's eyes got big, and then he closed them as he rubbed his temple. *Fuck! Why did I do that? She must really think I'm a jerk. Why? Come on, John. You know why. You miss Lisa, and if you say anything otherwise, she'll know you're lying.* "I'm sorry, Jennifer."

"Is the photo in your wallet a picture of Lisa?"

"What?"

"Your pants got a bit messy last night when I spilled the wine on them. I put them in the washer and finished drying them this morning when I got up. I took your wallet out, and it opened up to a picture of a woman. I assume it was Lisa, your wife."

John lowered his gaze. Of all the times to be confronted with his feelings for his departed wife, this was the most awkward. "Yes, that's a picture of her."

There was a moment of silence as John did not know what to say, and Jennifer waited for him to talk. Finally, when John did not speak, Jennifer said matter of factly, "She was a very beautiful woman. I can see why you fell in love with her. She must have been very special to you."

"She was," John said, then paused before he quietly continued, "is."

John didn't know what to say. He couldn't decide if Jennifer was angry with him or just trying to make conversation. Either way, this was not how he had envisioned the morning after his first sexual experience since the last time he was with Lisa, and he was in no mood to talk about it. *John, you're fucking STUPID! What the fuck! Stupid! Stupid! Stupid!* "I probably need to get dressed and go home to calm my daughter down."

Without hesitating, Jennifer got off the bed and started walking out of the room. "Sure. Let me get your pants from the dryer. Your underwear and other clothes are on the chair. I'll be right back."

John sighed. He was sure she was angry with him now. He got up and started to put his clothes on.

Soon, Jennifer brought his pants and then went into the bathroom to get dressed.

When John finished dressing, Jennifer was still in the bathroom. Embarrassed by what he had done, he was tempted to leave without talking to her. But he decided that would not be appropriate and nervously waited for her to come into the living room. He felt he owed her some sort of parting remark.

After a while, Jennifer came into the living room wearing a tight pastel T-shirt and shorts.

John did not see her initially, but Jennifer saw the embarrassment and worried look on his face as he continued to rebuke himself over what he had done. She called to him to get his attention. "John."

John anxiously looked at her. He couldn't make out the look on her face but assumed she was ready to be rid of him. He figured he would apologize and not bother her anymore. "Jennifer, I'm sorry. Please. I . ." But before he could finish, she walked up to him and placed her right index finger on his lips to silence him.

She squinted her eyes at him before speaking. "I should be angry with you. I've never had a man make love to me before and call out another woman's name. Considering that I think I'm a good partner in bed, that was very embarrassing to me. But, to be fair, Mary warned me about you. She told me about Lisa and how beautiful she was and how much you loved her. I just figured once I got you in bed, I could make you forget all about her. I see I was wrong."

Then her face relaxed into a sad smile. "I'm not angry with you, John. No, not really. What I am is envious of Lisa. Even being gone as long as she has been, she still has you. I wish one day I could find a man who loves me that much."

John looked at Jennifer and nodded to let her know he understood. She was tactfully admitting defeat to a memory of a woman who John's heart would never forget. Her kind words had removed the awkwardness of the moment, and he appreciated that.

"I'm sorry about last night. I didn't mean for it to end like this." He then hung his head, trying his best to find some appropriate words to say.

But before he could speak, Jennifer gently placed her hand on John's cheek and got him to look at her. The look of desire she had for him last night reappeared. "I know I might not be up to Lisa's standards and may not have made a good first impression on you, but you definitely made a good one on me last night, despite your faux pax in bed. So, if you ever find it in your heart to give me another chance sometime down the road when you've been able to put Lisa behind you, I'd like to try again."

Jennifer then put her arms around John and pulled him in for a kiss.

John closed his eyes but was surprised when he felt her soft lips on his cheek instead of his lips.

Jennifer released him and longingly smiled at her loss.

Her kind words and expression melted John's heart, and he concluded she was indeed a remarkable woman. But she was right. He was not over Lisa just yet. But looking at her, he felt a closeness to her, a yearning. She had patiently listened to his fears and was genuine in her concern for him. And she had felt so good in his arms.

Hearing Jennifer's words of regret, John regained his self-confidence and decided he would not let her simply slip away so easily. He deeply looked at her and then gently pulled her back to him. Confidently and passionately, he kissed her lips as he held her tight in his arms and did his best to let her know it was Jennifer he wanted then and not Lisa.

Jennifer was surprised, but soon John felt her arms around him holding him as tight as he held her.

They kissed until John felt the need for air. He released her, and Jennifer took a deep breath as she met John's eyes searching deep into hers. She had gotten his message.

John softly said, "Thank you for understanding." He then smiled and said, "Would you wait for me?"

Jennifer smiled back at him as her eyes ran around his face, taking in his enticing sexy look that had fully captured her heart. She teased, "I'll give it serious consideration."

John chuckled and replied, "You do that."

He then released her and left her house.

As he started his car, fresh memories of making love with Jennifer floated into his mind, and he shook his head. *Yeh, that woman is incredible. But am I ready for this? And if not, will I ever?*

Chapter 3

As soon as John walked into the house, Sara marched right to him and heatedly asked, "Where have you been, and why didn't you answer my calls?"

Even though John understood her valid point of not informing her he would not be home for the night, something he demanded of her, he was in no mood to be talked to like a child. He angrily shot back, "I've already told you I decided to sleep over at a friend's house, and I didn't get any of your calls. Yes, you're right. I should have called you. I'm sorry about that."

"Why didn't you get any of my calls? Did you cut your phone off? That's not very smart!"

"What the hell, Sara! I'm 57 years old! I'm a damn retired colonel with more time in a war zone than you've got on earth, almost. I think I can take care of myself!"

Sara drew her index finger and pointed it at John like a foil. "You're running around like some damn teenager! You need to call and tell me when you're not coming home and where you're staying overnight."

"Say what?"

"You heard me! You had me worried like hell about you when you didn't answer the phone!"

John was on the verge of completely losing his temper until he took a moment to look at Sara. The expression on her face, the tone in her voice, the finger, the anger, and her overall demeanor were pure Lisa when she was angry. He was amazed at the resemblance and started laughing.

"What's so funny?" Sara angrily asked.

"Look at you?"

"What?"

"Do you know who you look and sound exactly like? Do you?"

"Who?' Sara demanded, her anger growing.

Suddenly, John grew somber and said, "You look exactly like your mother."

To Sara, John's words seemed flippant and added gasoline to a raging fire. The snippet of conversation she overheard where John said Lisa was on the pill at a young age without her parents knowing and the recent photo she'd found of her mother in a revealing bikini surrounded by men immediately came to her mind. For Sara, who was trying to figure out what kind of woman her mother was, the evidence did not paint a good picture and the rage she felt fed her worst fears.

"You mean like someone who was on birth control pills at my age like some whore?" Sara blurted out without thinking.

Instantly, Sara felt a sharp sting across her face. Her eyes watered from the pain as she looked back at John.

His face was red with rage, tensed as if he was about to explode, his hands shaking.

Sara was shocked. John had never slapped her before, and he'd rarely ever spanked her. She had never seen him this angry, and a streak of fear shot through her.

"Don't you ever talk about your mother that way again!"

Sara burst into tears, ran to her room, and locked the door as John called out to her. She threw herself on her bed, pulled her legs into her chest, and wept.

After several minutes and still lying on her bed, she was able to stop crying.

For the next hour, silence filled the room as a cacophony of thoughts revolving around her mother and father filled her mind. She repeatedly tried to reconcile the fears of who her mother truly was with what she knew. Her father had always spoken well of her when he did, although he sometimes appeared guarded in his words. She often wondered what he was holding back. When Sara weighed what she knew against what she did not, she realized the large gap between them.

Hearing nothing outside her door, she wondered what John was doing. He had not come to her or called for her like he usually did when she was upset. She thought about the rage in his face she had never seen before and wondered if she had crossed a line that had changed their relationship forever. She wasn't sure what she should do if she had.

Then, out of nowhere, there was a light knock at the door. "Sara? It's Aunt Mary. Can I come in?"

Sara slowly got out of bed and pulled herself together. She was glad it was Mary and not John. She did not know what to tell John or if she should be ashamed of what she did or continue to stand her ground.

She unlocked the door, and Mary slowly came in, holding an old cardboard box in one arm.

Sara put her arms around Mary, and a few sobs escaped from her eyes as she tried to release some of the raw emotion still lingering within. She desperately needed to let it out and be held by someone she trusted, and Mary was probably the only person other than John she trusted that much.

"It's OK, baby," Mary calmly whispered as she held Sara in her arm and rubbed her back.

Sara was still too upset to speak.

After a moment, Mary said, "Sara, honey. Let's sit down on the bed for a moment."

After Sara sat on her bed with Mary sitting beside her, Mary continued, "Your father told me what happened. Are you OK?"

Sara sniffled a few times, and Mary rubbed her back. Sara then said, "Aunt Mary, I've never seen Daddy act like that towards me. He's never struck me before. Maybe I shouldn't have said what I said. I don't know."

"Sara, you have to understand. Your father loved your mother very very much. She was his whole life when they finally got together."

"Aunt Mary, like I told you before. I don't know my mother. No one has ever really told me about her past. A few weeks ago, I cleaned out one of the closets, and I found an old box with pictures. There was a photo of my mother and several men. She was in a pretty small bikini. And I heard Daddy tell you about her being on birth control pills without her parents knowing about it when she was young. Why did she do those things? Why would she keep a picture like that? I just want to know the truth about my mother. What did you really think about her? Please tell me the truth."

Hearing Sara's question brought many memories back to Mary, several of which were not good ones. She felt disappointed in herself for how she had treated Lisa for so long before they reconciled. And that reconciliation was short-lived before Lisa fell ill and died. Mary found herself deep in thought for an instant, and then when she returned, she placed the box she had brought on her lap. "Sara, your mother was a good woman. She had her faults; we all do. She did make some mistakes in her past. But there is one thing I know for sure. She loved your father as much as he loved her. I can tell you that the two of them went through some tough times together, but their love for one another never faltered. But I don't think you should take my word for it."

Mary then placed the box sitting on her lap onto Sara's. "Your mother packed this box before she died and sealed it. No one knows what's in it. She wanted you to have it when you graduated high school. I know it's a bit early, but your father wanted me to give it to you now."

Sara looked down at the old box. The tape used to keep it shut had yellowed, and it still had some dust on it. However, in impeccable handwriting written on the lid were the words, "To my dearest, Sara." She continued to stare at the old box as her mind raced with curiosity and excitement. *This is from my mother to me!*

Mary brushed Sara's hair with her hand and said, "I need to leave you two alone for a while."

Sara silently nodded, and Mary got up. Just as Mary was about to close Sara's door, she said, "I don't know what is in that box. But I think when you finish going through it, you will find the answers to your questions."

Mary then closed the door.

Sara continued to stare at the box for a while, trying to imagine what could be in it. She hesitated opening it as she reflected that her mother had specially prepared whatever was inside just for her. Then, suddenly, she felt a warm connection to a woman she had no memory of.

Slowly, she broke the tape and opened the cardboard folds. Inside was a collection of photographs and what looked like old letters and long pages of handwriting. But in the center was a letter in an envelope with the inscription "To my most precious daughter." She opened the envelope, pulled out the letter, and began to read it.

My dearest Sara. I can only imagine the wonderful and beautiful young woman you have turned into as you walk across the stage on graduation. It is my deepest regret that I could not be there with you on that day and along your journey. I know that by now, you probably have lots of questions. Some of those are probably about me, your father, and how we came to be. I am so sorry I was not able to answer those questions you may seek, and knowing your father as I do, he may not have told you all the things he could. Please do not hold that against him. You just have to understand the kind of man he is, one of deep feelings who holds those things very dear to him close to his heart. So, to try and answer the questions you may have about him and me, I have placed inside this box some things from our past that will hopefully give you a picture of who we were.

Your father is the most extraordinary man I've ever met in my life. He is a man of passion, thoughts, strength, and convictions, and because of that, he is a man who has endured deep pain. I was one of the causes of that pain, and when I finally could, I tried to give him the love he so rightly deserves and make up for those things I did to him. I made lots of mistakes in my past, and there are lots of things that I'm not proud of.

26

But the one thing that made all the difference in my life was your father and the love we shared. I want you to know what we shared because when you do, you know where you came from and the love that produced such a wonderful child. And if you don't already know it, you will see what an exceptional man your father is. I hope what I have put in this box will show you all these things.

I love you, Sara, my precious baby girl, and now my beautiful young daughter. From the moment I felt your first kick inside me to the last moment I held you in my arms, I have loved you. I prayed with all my heart that I could be there with you to help and see you grow up, but God had other plans. But I know that your father will take care of you because I know the only person in the world who loves you as much as I do, is him. After you have a chance to go through all the things in this box, I ask that you do two things for me. First, please take care of your father. His life has been a full one, but in many ways, it has also been a hard one. I know he can be difficult at times, but have patience with him, and always remember how much he loves you, even if there are times when he may not say it. Finally, know that no matter where you go in your life, who you are with, what you are doing, or what you are about to do, I love you, and I will always be with you, my precious. Sara. It was signed, *your loving mother.*

When Sara finished reading Lisa's letter, the tears had already rolled down her cheeks onto the paper. It had been as if she had heard every word Lisa had written.

For the next hour, Sara went through the contents of the box. Inside were love letters written by both John and Lisa from the summer of 1989 and other letters written later in their lives. Lisa had written other pages that talked about her life separate from John, her previous marriage to Richard, and what she had done in her life she considered mistakes. Sara was amazed at Lisa's openness in her letters, but Lisa expressly said her intent was Sara would not make the same mistakes. Lisa also had pages written about John and all the things he did in the Army before and after he and Lisa reunited. There were pictures of Lisa throughout her life and others of her and John. Some were very old, unfocused Polaroids from that fateful summer. Sara was in awe of her mother's beauty and the smiles of joy on John and Lisa's faces in all of their pictures together.

There were pictures of John as a young man on the back of a motorcycle. Those seemed to be later, after that summer. Her father was young, and his hair was long. Sara had never seen John with long hair before. She thought he looked very dashing and handsome. It was easy for her to see what had caught her mother's eye about him. He appeared happy in most of those photos, but in some, he did not smile. There was a look in his eyes Sara imagined was the emptiness that had descended upon him with Lisa's departure that summer.

Lisa had included pages written about her illness and what John had done for her. When Sara found a picture of John at his promotion to colonel, she looked closely at the woman standing beside him. When she realized it was Lisa, she then understood the terrible toll cancer had taken on her mother and how much Lisa and John both must have suffered then.

After reading many of Lisa's letters, Sara picked up a picture of Lisa holding her as a young infant. It looked like it was only a few days after Sara's birth; she was so small. Looking at the photo, Sara felt a closeness to her mother she had never felt before. She saw the joy on Lisa's face as she looked down on the infant, the smile of a mother in love with her child. Sara placed her fingers on the photo as if she was trying to touch Lisa's face. A single tear fell as she murmured, "Momma." She closed her eyes and put the photo against her chest, trying her best to imagine Lisa's arms around her.

Finally, Sara looked up and saw she had read letters and looked at pictures for over an hour. She still had much to go through, but she knew she needed to find her father before she could continue. The more she reflected upon what she had read, the more Sara felt she needed to talk with him. She looked down and picked up an old Polaroid photo of John and Lisa from their first summer together.

Sara opened her door and went in search of John. Looking through the window to the patio, she saw him sitting in a chair, deep in thought.

She gazed upon him and thought of the pain he had endured. Lisa's letters told of his time in combat, his nightmares, his injuries, and of his deep depression when she left him after that first summer and later after their reunion. Lisa had held nothing back in her letters, and Sara appreciated it. She finally had a good grasp of who Lisa was, and what John experienced during his life that made him the man he was. Looking at her father, Sara felt pride, sympathy, love, and shame. Shame for how she had treated him and for the words she had called Lisa.

Sara gently opened the patio door and walked over next to John.

John was so deep in thought he did not realize she was there. But, then, he looked up and calmly said, "Hey."

Sara looked at him with puffy eyes. She sat in the chair next to him, and they sat in silence for a minute before she said, "I just didn't know, Daddy."

"Know what, Baby Girl?"

"About you, and Momma, and so many things. Aunt Mary gave me a box this afternoon."

John simply nodded but did not say anything. Then he saw a photo in Sara's hand and asked, "What's that?"

She handed it to him.

When John looked at the old Polaroid, his mind locked on to the memories of that magical summer with Lisa. He stared at the picture of the woman who changed his whole life—the woman who his heart could never forget. For a second, he was back in time, a young man having found the woman of his dreams and discovering she loved him. He could still feel the warmth in his heart from then. He saw Lisa smile at him and could hear her call his name, his hand in hers as they walked to get the mail in his parent's mailbox in the country.

"Momma loved you very much," Sara softly said.

Her words brought John back to the present. The spell was broken, and Lisa was gone. The love of his life had been gone for many years now. He would never hold her in his arms again.

John closed his eyes and bowed his head. It took every ounce of will to keep from crying until he felt Sara's soft hand on his forearm.

"I'm sorry, Daddy."

Now it was John that looked at Sara with wet eyes. Then he said, "She loved me very much. But the one person in the world she loved as much, if not more than me, was you. She was so proud of you, Sara. She spent every single minute she could with you. She loved you so much."

Sara smiled sorrowfully. "I know that now. Tell me about her, Daddy. Tell me about Momma and you and that summer."

John took a breath and then proceeded to tell Sara about the summer he and Lisa met and many of the things that had happened since those days. At times, John's face lit up with joy. At others, Sara saw he fought to hold back tears. For the first time, Sara believed he finally opened up to her regarding her mother.

After they had talked for a good while, the conversation slowed, and John sensed they needed to return to the discussion about Sara wanting to join the Army. From the stories he'd just shared, he hoped she would see her decision in a new light. "Sara, about your desire to join the Army and be an infantry officer. Please understand. I promised your mother on her death bed I would take care of you. I can't let you go and do those things. If something was to ever happen to you, I don't know what I would do."

Sara listened to what John said, but his stories had only confirmed for her the things she wanted to experience and do. She remained adamant in her decision. She softly said, "Daddy, I know you may not understand why, and I know why you feel like you do. But you have to believe me when I say this is something I truly want to do. I've thought about this for a long time. I want to do something special with my life. I need to prove myself to me. I need to know that I can be something else beyond what everyone else thinks I should be, and the only way to do that is to push myself beyond my limit. I know what I will face, but I have to try. There will come a time when I have to go out on my own, and if I don't try, I'll never know how far I can go. Please. You of all people must understand what that feels like."

Staring at Sara as she spoke, it wasn't Lisa John saw in her now. He saw himself. She had spoken almost the exact words he had told his parents years ago when he decided to join and try to become a Soldierr. But Sara's statement also contained the words Lisa had told him about why she couldn't marry him that summer. She needed to prove herself. He understood what she was saying and concluded that inside Sara was the unquenchable desire for life that had filled both him and Lisa. Looking at her, he felt a sense of pride but also fear. Fear of what she was opening herself up for.

"It will be very hard, especially for you. Not just because you are a woman, but because you are a beautiful woman. You will be challenged because of that your entire career."

Sara smiled at John. "Then teach me, Daddy. I can't think of a better person than you who can show me how to overcome those challenges."

"And your mother? What will I tell her when she asks me why?"

Sara became melancholy hearing John talk as if her mother was still alive. But after learning what she had from reading Lisa's letters in the box, she understood. "You will tell her that we will make her proud of me."

John looked away for a moment. He thought about all the training she would have to go through. Not only would she have to pass, but she would have to excel. He thought about the problems she would encounter as a woman, even now, in the Army of the 21st century. And he especially thought about what could happen if she ever went to combat. A deep fear shot through him for a microsecond as the image of his daughter mangled or dead appeared in his mind. Even if she did not suffer physically, he feared the demons that had haunted him would come to her.

But his pride in Sara also grew. He admitted to himself now something he had always thought but never spoke aloud; she was a woman of destiny. There had always been something about her that made her stand out amongst all others. She was a born leader. He'd seen it in her many times. He should have known she would want to do something like this.

It was now in his hands, and she was waiting for an answer from him. Finally, he said, "OK."

Sara's face exploded into a huge smile, and she got out of her chair and threw her arms around him. "I promise you, Daddy. I won't let you or Momma down."

John could only imagine what Lisa was thinking now.

The following day, Sunday, at 5 a.m. sharp, Sara's bedroom door flew open as John came in, beat the walls, and screamed, "Get up! Come on! Time for our morning run! Let's go, Soldier!"

Sara shot up in bed and excitedly looked around. "Oh, my God! What's wrong? What's wrong?"

"Nothing's wrong. You need to get your ass out of bed, and let's go for a run!"

Sara blinked her eyes, trying to clear her mind of the sleep and the adrenaline that just forced her awake. "What run? What are we doing?"

"You said you wanted me to help you learn how to become an infantry officer, so we start today."

"It's 5 o'clock! It's still dark outside! Can't we start a little later? And can you please stop that yelling?"

"Nope, we need to start now! Get dressed! Let's go!"

"Daddy, come ON!"

"Look! You want to be a Soldier? Then get your ass out of bed, NOW!"

"OK, OK! Give me 15 minutes."

"You got five. Meet me outside in the front yard. Get going!"

"OK!" Sara yelled.

Sara then lazily got out of bed, yawned, and stretched her arms.

"You got four minutes!" John shouted from the hallway.

Sara rolled her eyes. She hurriedly got dressed in a T-shirt, shorts, and some running shoes. Then she went outside.

When she found John in the front yard, he said, "OK, let's go."

"Wait. Aren't we gonna stretch first before we run?"

"I've already stretched. You're late."

"But dad, I need to stretch so that I don't hurt myself."

"That's your problem, not mine. Let's go!"

Sara bit her lip. John's rude tone was starting to get on her nerves. She was about to say something back to him but figured this was some game of his, and she would not let him upset her. She was going to keep her cool and show him what she was made of.

John took off, running down the gravel driveway to their house, and Sara fell in behind him. When they reached the road in front of their home, John turned right and kept running.

"It's still pretty dark, and we're not wearing any reflective gear. Aren't you worried we might get run over?" Sara asked as they started their run.

"Nope!" John flippantly said.

John set a quick pace, but Sara kept up, although she was already struggling a bit.

"How far . . . How far are we going?"

"This is your first day, so I think about 5 miles."

Is he crazy? Sara screamed in her head. "Well . . . good because . . . . I can easily do that."

"Good. Then we should make it 8. I don't want to start too slow with you."

Sara said nothing. She already had it in her head to kill him before the run was over.

By the time John finished the first half-mile, he was starting to feel some pain in his leg. When he turned back to look at Sara, she was breathing hard but still behind him. *She's doing better than I thought. I sure hope she's not serious about doing 5 miles.*

When they reached a mile, John decided to pick up the pace.

Sara kept abreast of him for the first minute but then slowly started to fade back. John could hear her breathing getting harder and decided he would pick up the pace a little more.

"Come on, Sara! I'm a damn old man! Certainly, you can keep up with me!"

Sara did not say anything. She was doing her best just to keep running at this point, and every time John taunted her, her anger rose. *He is crazy! He just wants to break me. But . . I can do it! I can . . . . do it!*

John continued running yet slowed a bit to stay ahead of her but not lose her in the darkness. Then he heard her yell out, "Ouch!" as she continued to run.

"What's wrong?"

"I stepped in a hole . . . on the side of the . . . road. . . . I can't see!"

"That's not my problem. Look, if you can't hack it, then just stop and go home now. You're a girl anyway, so it's not a problem."

Now he was making fun of her for being a girl, something he had never done in the past. Sara said nothing, but she was beet red angry.

Soon after, the sun started its ascent, and the early morning gave way to the Texas heat. Between Sara's hurt leg, lungs aching for air, her sweat-covered body, and John's constant taunting, she was seconds away from her limit.

"I bet you thought all of that dancing would get you in shape. You're in terrible shape. I've already had to slow down to just stay near you. Come on! Put at least a little effort into it," John said.

"Hold it right fucking there!" Sara yelled at the top of her lungs.

John stopped and turned around. Sara very rarely cussed and never to him. He figured he had her where he wanted her.

Sara had stopped running and yelling out took every bit of breath she had left. She bent over for a second to catch her breath, and when she stood up, she had fire in her eyes, and her whole body tensed as she raised her hand and pointed at him. "I don't know what the fuck you think you are doing, but this is all bullshit! You are treating me like crap, and I'm not going to take it anymore!" Sara screamed at him.

John knew he had her exactly where he wanted. He had to press his lips to suppress a smile. How many times had Lisa looked precisely like that as she unleashed on him, and Sara looked exactly like her mother?

John walked over to Sara and calmly said, "Sara, there will be days when you are leading Soldiers, and everything seems against you, and it looks like there is no hope. Their lives will depend upon you, and they will look to you to lead them. You can never give up. When the time comes, you must make your stand and always try. There is no dishonor in failure, only in not trying. Learn how to take the rage and energy you feel right now and use it to do whatever must be done for the mission, for them, and yourself. Remember this moment when those times come. Do you understand?"

Sara was still breathing hard, and her rage focused her attention on John. She had expected him to continue to taunt her. But John's composed tone surprised her. She contemplated his words as she caught her breath.

John patiently waited as her breathing slowed, and she relaxed. Finally, she quietly asked, "Do you think I have what it takes?"

John smiled. "Yes."

Sara looked into John's eyes and saw his pride for her, and her young heart beamed. For the first time, she believed she could be a Soldier like him. "I promise I will make you proud of me, Daddy."

"I know you will, sweetheart."

The smile on Sara's face grew even bigger as she felt his commitment to helping her live her dream. Inside, she swore she would never let him down.

John put his arm around her and said, "How about we walk home, Baby Girl?"

"I think I'd like that."

Sara would never forget this moment, and in the future, when there were the days John spoke of, she reflected upon his words. But mostly, she remembered her promise to him. A promise she swore she would never break.

PART TWO

THE LAST MISSION

Chapter 4

14 AUGUST 2027. John kissed Sara on the forehead and wished her well on the eve of her first college semester, unaware that his own remarkable new journey would also start that day.

Having finished saying goodbye, he watched Sara walk from the parking lot to her new college dorm. Neither one was sure who was more excited, nervous, or sad. Many colleges had gone to being strictly online with no required campus attendance, but both John and Sara agreed it was time for Sara to be on her own, away from Victoria for a while. So when Sara received her approved submission to attend Texas A&M in College Station, they were both thrilled. College Station was only about three hours from Victoria, far enough for Sara to be on her own, yet close enough to come back home on the weekends if she wanted.

While Sara was excited about starting a new life and finally being on her own, she was sad about leaving her father. Since learning about Lisa's past, she had a clearer understanding of why her father was the way he was, strengthening the father-daughter bond between them that had strained with her maturing. She also finally understood the depth of John and Lisa's love. Sara did not feel good about leaving her father alone.

John, too, was sad to see Sara leave. They had become a team in doing so many things. But he knew it was time for her to be on her own, which meant a necessary separation. He knew she would do well and was excited to see how far she would go.

Just before she opened the door to her dorm, Sara turned and waved goodbye to John one last time.

He smiled and waved back.

When she entered the building and John could no longer see her, he felt a cold chill enter his body, reminiscent of the days when Lisa was no longer with him after their first summer together. He wondered how much Sara would change before the next time he saw her again.

He glanced up at the sky and saw a line of rain clouds with a magnificent blue hue on their underbellies, reminiscent of Lisa's beautiful blue eyes. He imagined Lisa standing with him, her hand in his, and quietly said to himself, "Well, sweetheart, our little girl is on her own now."

John closed his hand, hoping by some miracle to feel Lisa's hand, but instead, he felt nothing but his fingers. She had been gone a very long time, and with Sara now gone, he was very much alone again. That three-hour drive back home was going to be a long trip.

He turned and started walking toward his trusty 4Runner when he saw a man standing a few yards in front of him. Something looked familiar about him, so he paused and then exclaimed, "Jim!" It was his old friend, Jim, whom he had gone to the Infantry Officer Basic Course with when they had both joined the Army to become officers. After graduating, they remained very close throughout their respective careers. Since Lisa's funeral, John had not seen Jim, although he had talked to him on the phone a few times.

Jim had a massive grin on his face as they both walked toward each other and gave each other a heartfelt hug.

"It's great to see you, John."

"What the hell are you doing here? I didn't know you had kids that went to college here."

"I don't."

"Then what are you doing here?"

"I came to see you. Do you have some time to talk?"

Intrigued, John replied, "Sure. I've got all the time you need this afternoon."

"Great. Let's go grab a cup of coffee somewhere for me and a big glass of sweet tea for you."

John laughed that Jim still remembered he liked sweet tea. "Lead the way, my friend."

The two of them ended up in a fancy coffee shop near the college and sat in a far corner to visit after ordering some drinks.

Jim's career had been very successful, and he retired a three-star general, which did not surprise John. Jim's father had been a colonel, serving in Vietnam, and from day one, Jim wanted to follow in his father's footsteps. In addition, he was an excellent leader who John held in the highest regard.

However, John was surprised when Jim retired as he was sure he would earn a fourth star and possibly become the senior Army general. It was something John wanted to ask him about one day.

After a few polite exchanges, Jim got right to the point of his visit. "John, I started a security contractor business after I got out and have been running it for the past three years. We handle a lot of security assistance missions and operations around the world, and some are for some very important government clients."

"Do you mean like the old Blackwater company? Mercenaries for hire?"

"Yes. Very similar, but we're not a bunch of cowboys running around with guns. My folks are professionals."

"That sounds exciting. I always saw you doing something like that once you retired, especially being a general with all your connections. Is there a particular reason why you're telling me all this now?"

"I'd like you to come to work for us for a particular project we've got. It's a critical mission, and I need someone I can trust to run it. You would be perfect."

"You want me to go play infantry Soldier again? Is that what you're asking me to do?"

"In a way, yes. But you would oversee the mission, planning, and training for it. You wouldn't necessarily be the guy who would go and do the mission."

John sat back and heartily laughed. "Jim, are you serious? Look at me, old buddy. I'm going to be 60 next year. I'm a fucking old man! I can't do that kind of shit anymore."

Jim did not laugh. He eyed John and asked, "How much do you bench press?"

"What?"

"I said, how much do you bench press?"

John squirmed a bit before he said, "280, but it ain't pretty."

"Ah uh. A 59-year-old man who can still bench press 280 lbs. Come on, John! I know you work out like a horse every day. You look like you're ten years younger than you are, and you're probably in better shape now than when you were in the Army in lots of ways. You are far from being an old man yet."

John rubbed his chin and said, "Look, Jim. Even if I was in half-ass shape, which I'm not, I've got other priorities now. I'm past all that stuff."

"Like what? What are you going to do with yourself for the next couple of months while Sara is in college?"

"Well, I got lots of stuff," John quickly said but then paused as he tried to determine what that stuff was. "There's a lot of work around the house that needs to be done. I'm thinking about putting in a garden. And

I want to do some fishing. And, Mary asked me to help her with some things around her house. She's getting along in age, too, these days."

"You? A fucking gardener? Come on, John! Don't bullshit me."

"No, for real."

Jim leaned forward on the table closer to John so he could quietly talk. "John, I know you. Have you forgotten all the crap we went through, and who the hell you're talking to? I know you just dropped your daughter off to start her first year of college, and you don't have a damn thing to do for the next couple of months. And please don't give me that shit about being past all that stuff. Because I know that's bullshit. You work out to get that high of being on the edge because pushing yourself in the gym is the closest you can get to it right now. You and I did stuff they write books and make movies about. You don't do that and then just walk away. You think you did, and you fill your time with a bunch of crap you find as boring as watching the grass grow. You can tell yourself all the bullshit lies you want, but down deep inside, knowing you as I do, you'd kill to do one more mission given a chance. Am I right?"

John knew deep inside, everything Jim said was true. He was bored with his life. He did workout hard because it was the only way to keep his desire to challenge himself in check. But most of all, he had no clue as to what he was going to do the next few months with Sara gone. He rubbed his jaw with his hand, thinking. But John was still not convinced. "Look, Jim. Sure, I miss the action. Who wouldn't? But there is one thing I don't miss. I've had my fill of killing. If you know me, then you know I never liked that shit. I know you never enjoyed that part either. You know what I'm talking about."

"I do, understand. But this mission is not just killing. It's a hostage rescue situation."

"Well, why don't the guys who get paid to do this stuff go do the mission?"

"It's complicated. They can't get involved, but we can."

"OK, Let's just say that you have piqued my curiosity. Give me more info on what you're talking about, and I can think about it."

"No. I can't talk about anything like that here—no details whatsoever. But what I can do is fly you to our training facility, and we can go over the mission with you there. We will lay out the mission parameters, your role, and your compensation package."

"Compensation package? Does that mean I will get paid for this shit?"

"Yes, very well, I might add."

"Well, Jim. If you know me, then you know I don't care or need any money. That shit doesn't mean anything to me."

"Yes, I do know. But I also know you have a daughter in college who will go very far. Even if she gets all the scholarships she can, it would be nice to be able to have the money to give her a chance to do whatever she wants to do in life."

John sat and thought. "Can I think about it and let you know?"

"No, buddy. This is a very time-sensitive situation. I have to have your answer now."

John paused as he weighed the pros and cons in his mind.

Seeing John contemplating what he should do, Jim spoke again. "John, I know what I'm asking, and I know I'm not giving you a lot of details. But, this could be very important for the future, big time. I don't have to tell you about all the bullshit that's going down in the world right now as well as the past ten years."

John eyed Jim and understood he was dead serious. "Honestly, Jim, I can't really run anymore. I do good just to keep the pain in my joints in line most days."

Jim eyed John back. "I need someone who has had the training, experience, and has the fight in him to do this mission if we are going to succeed. I don't care if you can't jump hurdles or run a mile anymore. What I need is what's in here, but mostly here," Jim said as he first pointed to John's head and then to his heart. "I need someone I can implicitly trust. That's you. Like I said. I know what I'm asking and the risk involved. If I did not think this mission was so important, I would never have asked you. I need you, old buddy."

Looking at Jim, John thought back to the group of four men he attended the Infantry Officer Basic Course with when he first joined the Army. They had formed a tight group, and their careers crossed paths several times while they were in the Army. They had all done multiple tours in Iraq and Afghanistan. He had trusted them with his life at times, and they had done the same of him. There was nothing any one of them would not have done for the other. But now, there were only two of them left. Matt had been killed in a training accident, and Tom had remarried after he left the Army, only to live a few years and then die from cancer. It was just John and Jim left. Hearing Jim's words, John knew what his answer would be. The loyalty he maintained for those dearest to him gave him no choice in the matter.

John sat back in his chair and grinned. "You know you're going to owe me big, and I'm not talking about money."

"You still want a date with my sister?" Jim teased, relieved at John's hint of acceptance.

John laughed. "That just might be a start. What do you need me to do?"

"Tomorrow morning, we'll send you a ticket in the mail. Your flight will be the following morning. Just bring a change of clothes and your passport."

Still grinning, John asked, "Your sister still have a good figure on her?"

"She's dumping husband number three next week and will be back on the prowl. I'll put you in the queue," Jim said with a matching grin.

John laughed and shook his head, wondering what the hell he had just agreed to.

Walking into the ticket area at Houston's George Bush International Airport, John put his old Army backpack down and looked around. The driverless car sent to pick him up had dropped him off in front of the entrance to the United terminal and then went on its way. John could never get used to them. His current 4 Runner had auto-driving as an option, but he still preferred to drive himself. He enjoyed the feeling of driving his vehicle more than passively riding.

It was still early, and the airport wasn't crowded yet. His instructions said to wait at the United entrance, and someone would come and get him. His flight was in two hours.

A young man wearing a suit and tie and driving an electric cart stopped next to John a few minutes later. "Sir, are you, Colonel Bradford?"

"Yes, I'm John Bradford."

The young man eyed John and said, "Sir, do you mind if I see your passport. I was expecting someone a bit older."

John handed the young man his passport, and after he looked at it, the man said, "Great. I'm Barry. Please put your bag in the cart and have a seat. I'll take you to your flight."

John did as instructed, and off they went.

They drove for several minutes, winding through the bowels of the airport. "Don't I need to go through security and get my passport stamped?" John asked.

"No, Sir. We'll take care of everything."

After a long ride, they exited a large building and pulled up next to a small executive jet sitting on the tarmac in a distant corner of the airport.

"Sir, just climb aboard, and they'll take it from here."

John thanked the man, grabbed his backpack, and climbed the stairs to the jet's open door. He stuck his head inside, and a stunning young woman turned to greet him. "May I help you? Are you Colonel Bradford?"

"Yes, Ma'am."

She smiled and said, "Wow! I was expecting someone much older. Let me take your bag, and please take a seat."

John handed the woman his backpack and took a seat as she stored his bag. *What is all this crap about expecting someone older? And when did they put models as flight attendants? I don't know about all this. What the hell kind of cloak and dagger operation does Jim run? If she tells me her name is Pussy Galore, I know something weird is going on.*

"My name is Stacy. Can I get you something to drink?"

"I'm fine. Thank you. When will the rest of the passengers arrive?"

"Oh, you're the only passenger we have. We'll get going in about ten minutes. The flight should be a couple of hours, so you might want to catch some sleep after we're up."

"Thanks. Where exactly are we going?"

The woman just smiled.

Ten minutes later, they were taking off, and John laid his seat back for a nap.

Two hours later, the young woman brought John an early lunch. As he ate, he looked out of the window and saw they were over water, and from the direction of the sun, they seemed to be traveling east.

A few hours later, his jet landed at a small airport on a large island he assumed was somewhere in the Caribbean. The cool ocean breeze and abundant palm trees told John there were somewhere in the tropics.

Another man, dressed in what one would consider island clothes, picked John up as he got off the plane and took him a short distance to a helipad where a helicopter was waiting with its rotors spinning. John thought the aircraft looked like a souped-up modern version of an old Hughes 500. He'd remember the Special Forces guys flying around Baghdad on those when they conducted raids in the middle of the night. Those helicopters were so small the seats passengers sat on were on the outside of the aircraft.

John climbed in the back through the doorless opening, and the man helped him put his backpack in and then helped John put some headphones on. John found that a little strange. He thought he'd just be a passenger along for the ride, but at this point, he figured anything was possible.

To John's surprise, the man put John's safety belts on and pulled the straps very tight.

When John gave an inquisitive look to the man, he smiled and yelled out just above the noise of the running engine, "You'll thank me later. Good luck. You're gonna need it!" He then walked off away from the helicopter, laughing.

John did not have a good feeling.

Then, a loud, animated voice came on the intercom. "Johnyyyyyy!"

It had been years since he'd heard that voice. *No way!* "Fred? Fred, is that you?"

"Fuck Yeh!"

"Fred! What the hell are you doing here?"

"Same thing you are. Jim gave me some bullshit story. Needs a good pilot. Some secret squirrel mission shit."

"What the hell did he promise you to get you here?"

"That I could fly all I want and how I want. By the way, have you had an erection today?

John busted out laughing. "No, but something tells me you're about to give me one."

Just then, Aerosmith's "Sweet Emotion" started pumping through the intercom, and John knew exactly what was going to happen next. He started to shake his head just as the helicopter jumped straight up and made a sharp turn to the right, leaving John's stomach somewhere back on the helipad. They continued to turn hard right to the extent that John felt they were at a full 90 degrees for several seconds. He could feel his body pressed into the seat by the ever-increasing G forces until finally, they leveled off.

"Goddammit Fred! What the fuck are you doing up there?" John yelled over the intercom.

"Yeah, she's a little sluggish today. Must be that loose cable in the tail rotor. Hey, I need a little evasive maneuver practice. You don't mind, do you?" Fred asked.

Before John could answer, Fred had dropped to just below treetop level and proceeded to simultaneously swing from side to side and jump over the palm trees in his path.

The combination of laughter with the thrill of flying and seeing a dear old friend while his body was being tossed around like a rag doll strapped to a roller coaster made it hard for John to talk.

"Fred!" John choked out.

"Yeh, Johnny, it's been kinda boring around here lately. I'm glad you're here. Gonna liven up the place."

"Fred!"

"Hey what do you want to hear next? I got AC/DC or Blondie. Man, that Blondie chick had some legs on her back in the day. She was hot! I think we'll start with Dreaming."

"Fred!"

Dreaming kicked off, and Fred started to sing along.

"Fred!" John continued to yell into the intercom.

"Yeh, Johnny. What you got?"

"Dammit, Fred! Can we stop the roller coaster? My stomach can't take much more."

"OK, party pooper. Hey, you want to do some fishing?"

"I didn't bring any gear, but I'm sure you've got that covered."

Suddenly, the helicopter turned sharply to the left as it swung out toward the ocean. When Fred leveled off, John swore they were no more than ten feet above the water. He could feel the spray of the waves as the rotor wash hit the water.

Coming up fast, in the distance, was a large center console fishing boat a couple of miles off the coast.

"You know Johnny. You got to keep your eyes peeled. You never know what you're gonna see out here."

Seconds later, Fred buzzed the boat and suddenly pulled the helicopter straight up until it seemed to float in the air. John found himself lying on his back with a weightless sensation before the aircraft fell onto its left side and back into powered motion. Fred then circled the boat, giving John a full view of what had caught Fred's eye.

"Man, did you see the jugs on that chick in the back? Sweet baby Jesus!" Fred called out.

However, the boat occupants didn't seem happy with Fred's antics and responded with fists and one-finger salutes.

John's spirit soared as he felt the adrenaline pumping through his body. He was once again back in his nirvana of speed and rock music provided by his favorite crazy friend. He found himself goading Fred as he had many times before when they flew together. "Fred, I think you've gotten soft on me. We were only about 20 feet away from that boat. You're not turning into a pussy on me, are you?"

"Did you say you wanted to see pussy? Sure, I can do that!"

The helicopter then leaned forward as its speed increased. Suddenly, without warning, Fred pulled the aircraft into a sharp right turn. As they descended, John saw they were flying parallel to a beach, again, at an extremely low altitude.

"Get your camera ready, Johnny!" Fred called over the intercom as he tilted the helicopter to the left so John had a clear view of the beach through the open door. Unexpectedly, John's view filled with countless women on the beach. As he looked closer, he saw that most of them were not wearing bathing suit tops or any clothes for that matter, and they all seemed to be waving as the helicopter swiftly went by.

"Jesus, Fred! You hit the motherload!"

"Yeh! It's my second home! OK, enough of this bullshit. You got work to do, Johnny!"

"Come on, Fred! Just a little more!"

"No, no! Time to earn your pay!"

Fred swung hard left, and they continued to fly very low into the island's interior until they reached a compound with a helipad.

After landing and before John could get a chance to talk with Fred, he was whisked away to a small office and asked to wait for Jim to arrive.

Jim walked in with a massive smile on his face and slapped John on the back. "It's great to see you, brother! How was your trip?"

"Good. Right up until I caught a ride with Fred, Then it was great! You didn't tell me he was working for you!"

"Well, he was a hard sell. That is until I told him he could fly the latest stuff however he wanted. Then he caved like an ice cream cone on a super hot day."

John continued laughing. "So, when do we get started?"

"We're going to get you started today with your inprocessing and medical checkup. Then we'll assign you quarters. I'd like to get you briefed up on what we have later this evening. We really don't have a lot of time."

"Medical checkup?"

"Yeh, John. We need to put you through the wringer this afternoon. I'm not worried about your overall physical condition. But with all this virus crap we have been through the past couple of years, we can't take any chances—especially where you will be going."

"Why do I have the feeling I'm going to be a pin cushion for the rest of the afternoon?"

"Well, I do give the doc a bonus for every shot he gives," Jim joked. Then his face turned serious, and then he held out his hand to John. "I'm really glad you're here, brother."

The look on Jim's face and the tone in his voice told John Jim was dead serious, and John warmly shook his hand. "I'm glad to be here."

John was then taken to a building that looked like a small medical clinic where his prediction proved correct. By the time the doctor finished his examination, John had received five shots and a comprehensive exam.

As he was putting his shirt back on and the doctor looked over John's results on his tablet, John asked, "What the hell was that last shot for? It felt like you left that thing in me for about 5 minutes."

Without looking up from the tablet in his hands, the doctor casually replied, "It's an experimental drug for the latest virus that just hit Asia. You'll need it for the upcoming mission."

"Experimental?"

The doctor looked at John and smiled, "It's alright. The FDA just hasn't gotten around to finalizing their paperwork. The military gets first crack at that stuff. You don't need to worry. He then looked at his tablet again and continued. "Overall, you are very healthy for a man of your age. Very good in some aspects. But I can see you had your share of bumps and bruises from your time in the Army. That leg injury looked pretty extensive, but it healed very well. Does it bother you?"

"The past couple of years, the pain seems to be present more often than not. But honestly, there are days when every joint in my body hurts to some degree."

"Well, that comes with your age. Arthritis, Tendonitis, and a few other issues. What are you doing to treat it?"

'Nothing."

"Nothing? Do you have a primary care physician? What about the VA?"

"It's my fault, Doc, but I just haven't made all that a priority unless something serious happens, and nothing serious has happened in a while."

The doctor nodded. "OK, there's a couple of things I want you to do while you are here. First, they are going to issue you a set of a load-bearing exoskeleton. You strap that thing on, and it takes a lot of weight off of you that you will carry if you do any training. That will help immensely with the pain in your leg."

"Exoskeleton?"

"Yeh. It looks weird, but it works. It's basic issue to all infantrymen today. Get the folks at central issue to show you how to use it."

"OK. If you say so."

Then the doctor walked over, got two bottles of pills from a nearby cabinet, and gave them to John. "Next, I want you to take these pills in the blue bottle once a day. They will help you with your joint pain. When you leave here, I will write you a prescription for them. The pills in this orange bottle are stimulants. If you have to do some heavy physical activity, take one to get you through the next six hours, but no more than two a day. You'll need to sleep at some point, and I don't want you going nonstop with these things."

John looked at the orange bottle and said, "Look, Doc. I don't need to get hooked on any uppers while I'm here. You can keep these."

Before John could give the bottle back, the doctor replied, "I understand what you're saying, but neither one of us need to worry about that. You're an adult, and you'll know when you need them and when you don't. Besides, these are not addictive. But you also need to be aware that many of the bad people you will meet up with will be taking these, and you'll necd every advantage possible. I wouldn't give them to you unless I thought you might need them. You're in great shape, but you're still a 59-year-old man. You're gonna need them sometimes."

John concluded what the doctor said was right. His young days were long over. He nodded and kept the bottle.

"Also, I'd like you to come by, and let's talk about some other prescriptions for you after you get settled. Medicine has come a long way, and as I said, we get access to a lot of cutting-edge stuff."

John grinned. "You mean you just want me for more guinea pig tests."

The doctor returned John's grin and replied, "Oh, and one more thing. Roll up your sleeve. I've got one more thing we need to put in you."

"Again?"

"Last time. I promise."

John took his rolled up his sleeve and watched as the doctor took a strange-looking syringe and shot something into his arm. "Damn! That hurt like hell! What was that for?"

"Microchip."

"What?"

"I put a microchip in your arm. We use it for numerous things. For example, we can upload all your personal and medical information on it, track you during operations, monitor your health, and quickly identify you if you are killed. These are standard issue to all military personnel now."

Putting his shirt back on, John shook his head. "I'm definitely a guinea pig now."

The doctor then directed him to the small central issue facility to pick up his assigned gear.

When John walked into the small warehouse, it was totally unlike the ones he had been in before. The ones he remembered in the Army were large warehouses where the little old ladies in tennis shoes in the different stations along the way quickly grabbed the military gear and threw stuff into your duffel bag. This place looked more like another clinic with people in lab coats.

A woman took John's measurements, and a few minutes later, she brought him several uniforms and undergarments before thoroughly instructing him on their use.

John held up what looked like a long sleeve undershirt and long underwear pants and asked, "These things look pretty thick. I don't think I will need these for the tropical weather around here."

The woman replied, "You have a cold weather and hot weather set of these. Make sure you wear them appropriately. Not only will they make you comfortable in the hot or cold weather, they have a layer of blood clotting liquid that will help stop bleeding the moment you are wounded. Plus, they are compression-tight to help you with physical endurance and must be worn if you use any exoskeleton equipment. I'm giving you several pairs. But break open a brand-new pair when you go on a mission."

Then she picked up a helmet. "Now, here is your helmet. Slide these visors down to protect your eyes against debris and especially lasers, and slide these visors down for night vision. We will teach you some voice commands so information will appear on the heads-up display on your visor. The headsets are built-in so you can talk to anyone on your team as well as your higher headquarters with your helmet on. It's mostly non-line of sight comms going straight to a satellite. They also have noise reduction and sound amplification built-in. Turn this switch on, and the system will give you much better hearing, but automatically reduces extreme noise like gunfire and explosions."

"Nice!"

"Use this attachment in NBC environments. It's good for a full 24 hours."

John looked at the helmet and was impressed. "I almost look like Darth Vader."

The young woman looked at him questionably. "Who?"

"Darth Vader? Star Wars?"

The woman pleasantly shook her head, "I'm sorry, Sir. I must have missed that one."

"Probably a little before your time," John said. *Damn! Am I that old or is she that young!*

Once John completed his inprocessing, he returned to Jim's office, where Jim was waiting for him. He told John the next step was for his staff to brief him on the mission.

They then walked to a fully fenced-in building from Jim's office that looked like every high-security facility John had been in during his career.

Before arriving at the briefing room, John and Jim had to check in with an armed guard at the front door to the building holding their intelligence section, and then Jim had to punch codes into several doors to get to the final briefing area. John did not ask any questions as he followed Jim, but he was impressed with their security.

The briefing room was relatively small, with several large screens on the wall in front of the table. The U-shaped table had several stations for smaller computers and looked like it could be used as a command post if need be.

Jim introduced John to his three key intelligence experts, a retired Army, another retired Navy, and finally, a retired Air Force officer. They were all in their late 40s to early 50s and professionally dressed. John watched their interactions with Jim, and they seemed comfortable with one another, yet they were very respectful when talking with Jim. Clearly, these were people who had worked with Jim before, and knowing Jim as John did, he could safely assume they were the best in their respective areas.

After the introductions, the officer in charge, a woman Jim identified as a retired two-star Army general named Jaime, began the briefing.

"Good evening. I want to start this briefing by reviewing some key global developments and then focus on the middle east. Beginning from an international perspective, the United States, Europe, and the west, in general, have seen a period of decline in global power and standing. Two major movements have led to this development."

"First, the US withdrawal from the international scene in conjunction with the collapse of Russia has left China as the single superpower that is willing to flex its muscle internationally. China is now in a position to make major expansive moves around the globe, and President Xi's successor, President Zhang, has accelerated China's nationalistic policies well beyond what Xi was willing to tolerate."

"Second, although there have been advances in clean energy, most of those advances have only benefited the few major powers that can afford it. That means a significant number of countries still rely on oil. China controls much of the technology for clean energy, but it also still requires relatively large amounts of oil, which is now suddenly a cheap alternative fuel."

Jaimie then put up a map of the middle east on the large front screen containing information on each country's leaders. "The reduction of demand for oil on a global scale has robbed the oil-producing countries of their former wealth and status. OPEC is no more the powerhouse it once was. With the loss in revenue, most oil-producing nations have experienced severe civil unrest to the point their respective governments are barely holding on to power. Each of them has an extremist-led element either seriously vying for power or has already taken control in some form."

"Israel is no longer in a position to leverage any major power short of strictly guarding what borders they have left. Two years ago, the nuclear exchange between Iran, Israel, and Saudi Arabia left much of Israeli land uninhabitable. They've taken a beating. But they're not completely out. Their intelligence arm is still very effective and has been supplying us with some vital information. Iran and Saudi Arabia also took major hits to their infrastructure and are no longer the regional powers they once were."

Jim turned to John and said, "The bottom line, John, is the middle east has been reduced to every man for himself. They're just trying to survive right now and don't have any global leverage anymore. They're desperate to sell whatever oil they can to survive, which makes them fairly easy pickings for someone to come along and take control of the region. Enter our friends, the Chinese."

When Jim finished, he looked back to Jaimie. "As I stated earlier, the Chinese have gained a substantial amount of influence on clean energy because of their control of much of the significant pieces of technology required. If they can take control of the middle east, they will have a corner on the market for both clean energy and fossil fuel for the world. The ramifications of Chinese control of global energy are obvious."

"China has grown close to the regional disrupting extremist movements by providing them support in an effort to remove many of the governments that could or would resist China's expansion into the middle east. However, they face a major obstacle against their expansion by Egypt. Since the return of the monarchy as a result of the second Arab Spring, the king has successfully kept the Muslim extremists at bay in Egypt and has fought to support non-extremist Arab nationalists in the region. Consequently, Egypt currently represents the single biggest obstacle to Chinese control of the middle east. Should the current regime be exchanged for one much less critical and more accepting to the Chinese, this would be a major tipping point in the region and a severe blow to current US national interests."

Jaimie then paused and changed the big screen to individual pictures of one woman and two men. "Six days ago, the daughter, son, and senior advisor to the king of Egypt were kidnapped. Everything points to an inside job conducted by a Sunni extremist element. However, the operation was carried out too successfully. There is no doubt they had help, and we have a pretty good idea of who and why. The Chinese know they cannot directly take the King out, but if they could interfere with his succession, that gives them time and opportunity to shape his successor to their side."

Jaimie then looked at John, who had indicated he had a question. "Why kidnap them? Why didn't they just kill them outright?"

"We figure they want to see if they can leverage them to force the king to change his policies. The longer they have them, the longer they have leverage. As soon as they kill them, that leverage no longer exists, so there is a good chance they will keep them alive for a while to see what they can get for them."

"OK, well, assuming you are right and assuming it is the Chinese for the reasons you've explained, why doesn't Delta or the Seals mount a raid to find them. Are you telling me you are going in to get them out?"

Jaimie looked at Jim, who then slightly swiveled his chair toward John. "You know all the political bullshit that has occurred over the past couple of years. The US has turned completely inward. When Congress mandated all US combat operations in the middle east come to an end, and anything further had to be approved by them directly, that's when the whole place went to shit. Elections are coming up, and this administration doesn't want a major failed military operation that would start another entanglement in the middle east and especially in support of a country that does not have good relations with the US on its scorecard."

"Has the King asked for assistance?"

"Officially, no. Unofficially, yes. They have asked the United States via Israel if they could help. The US is interested, but they don't want to be directly involved. That's where we come in. After I left you, I flew to Egypt to meet with their Chief of General Staff. When I was the deputy CENTCOM Commander, we developed a pretty solid friendship. He knew of the business I currently run and asked if I could help. I had already received a phone call from the CIA on the flight asking if we were interested. As a private organization, we could do the mission, and they would arrange some support. If we succeed in rescuing these folks, everyone is happy. If we fail, we're just a bunch of mercenaries, and the US is clean."

"Whoaa, hold up," John said. "This is going to be a major operation. You're telling me we will receive no help from Uncle Sam?"

"No, not exactly," Jim answered. "We have been guaranteed access to intelligence, movement of our assets overseas, access to bases as launch points, and possible air cover. A lot of details have to be worked out. But they do want to remain in the shadows regarding the operation on the ground."

"So, when do we go?"

Jaimie answered, "We have an idea where they are holding them, but we don't want to tip our hand just yet. Besides, it looks like they are constantly moving them to guard against ambush. We have narrowed it down to three sites we are pretty sure they will utilize. If they go to one of these, we can position ourselves to attempt a rescue."

John then asked, "How long before they do that?"

"We're thinking a month at least."

Jim turned to John and said, "John, for planning purposes, assume you have one month of training to get these guys ready."

In John's mind, one month was ridiculously short to prepare a team of men who he knew nothing about for this kind of operation. However, he wasn't going to complain because he already knew the situation they were in. He'd have to do the best he could with whatever he had.

John asked a few more questions, and after a summary from Jim, the briefing ended.

Glancing at his watch, John saw it was after 9 P.M. It had been a long day, and he was mentally exhausted.

Jim walked John his quarters, and to John's pleasant surprise, it was a small bungalow near the beach.

"Damn, Jim! This looks like a cozy little place. And next to the beach too! Very nice."

"Well, nothing's too good for my buddy. But I wouldn't get too comfortable. You'll be spending very little time here. I'll send someone to get you at 0700, and we'll get started."

John thanked Jim and bid him good night.

He found his baggage and gear in the small bedroom and decided he would unpack later.

After changing into a T-shirt and pair of shorts, he laid down on his bed and looked out of the open window. The full moon's light brightened the tops of the waves just before they crashed in the surf, and the calm ocean breeze was just strong enough to keep the sweat away. It was the perfect end to the first part of his new adventure, with one exception. He was alone.

John turned away from the window and looked beside him.

Without any real thought, he reached out into the darkness and onto the bed beside him, only to feel empty sheets. He thought how wonderful it would be to share this tiny piece of paradise with someone.

But that thought went as quickly as it came. Tomorrow was going to be another full day, as well as all the rest for a while. However, he'd worry about that in the morning.

John closed his eyes and drifted off to sleep.

Chapter 5

The following two days, John discovered how much he needed to learn about the new military and how much he needed to teach the old ways.

A young man arrived at his door at 7 o'clock prompt and gave him a quick tour of the compound before being ushered to watch the ongoing team training. The large facility was a vast resort abandoned after two back-to-back hurricanes damaged it several years prior. Jim's company acquired it and rebuilt it into an extensive training and central command facility for their ongoing overseas operations. Various buildings were used for offices, housing, training, and equipment storage. There was a large dock for sizable boats and several smaller ones, a helipad, and a small airfield. The island also had a few square miles of undeveloped interior used for tactical training, and since the facility was on an island, overall security was very manageable.

Despite the facilities' primary mission being military-oriented, much of the former resort landscaping and layout remained. Numerous palms and other more vinelike trees thrived throughout, with the ocean breeze keeping them in constant motion. The sound of the waves never seemed far away.

The young man told John several of the key employees rotated in for about three months at a time, and the rest came for planning and training for specific operations before being sent out. He also said several much larger and more populated islands were about 30 minutes away from them, but most of the company folks stayed on this island while working. It looked like they had gone to some length to add pleasurable features to occupy folks off time. The stretch of beach in front of John's small bungalow seemed to be set aside for swimming and lounging, and John had seen a few men fishing in the surf.

When John's tour was over, the young man brought him to the area where much of the training was conducted. Many of the basic combat training aspects he observed remained the same from when John served. The team members conducted extensive individual physical exercises in addition to the physical portion of specific skill training like repelling. He was very impressed by how physically fit each man seemed to be, but he wondered if any of them took advantage of the stimulants the doctor had told him about.

However, several aspects of the training were new to John, specifically the virtual training. One of the very large buildings on the island had been converted to a virtual training facility where it served as the equivalent of a large simulator for ground combat operations. Almost any natural environment, urban area, or existing building could be replicated and used as the training setting. Partitions could be added and moved accordingly, but most of the training revolved around the participants wearing virtual reality headsets linked to the computers at the Training Facilitating Office or TFO as it was referred to.

The TFO was a large office room located well above the ground floor on the building's north wall. It housed the computers that created the training environment and served as a vantage point to observe the training. Several large monitors displayed the programmed training setting from an overhead perspective at the center of the room. In addition, the combatants' location was shown on the board, and what each individual could see could also be displayed as well as their physical status.

John watched as a fully equipped fire team entered the space to conduct a mission. Their weapons had modified laser boxes on them that allowed them to shoot at virtual targets and produced the same recoil as if they had fired a live bullet. Massive speakers surrounded the large space that could make any sound associated with the environment. Pipes hung just below the ceiling that could simulate rain and numerous lights that could be dimmed or turned off completely to simulate night. The facility was the equivalent of a giant flight simulator but for ground combat training.

While the fire team conducted their mission, their individual statistics could be displayed and recorded for analysis. The man in charge of the training facility was proud to spout off the percentages, probabilities, and other performance statistics to John. Further analysis showed individual tendencies, reactions to pain, and various stimuli reactions. But for John, everything was too artificial. This wasn't a training facility, he believed, as much as a giant laboratory where men were being artificially conditioned for artificially structured events.

After two days of observing the training, John had seen enough. He decided he needed to talk to Jim about his observations and recommendations. Upon John's request, Jim immediately set up a private meeting with John in his office.

"So, what do you think?" Jim asked.

"Jim, I don't want to come across too negative. There have been a lot of changes since I was in. I would have loved to have had some of the new equipment you guys have back in the day. That helmet system is fucking awesome. And all the high-tech training is pretty impressive, I'll admit. But I don't know."

Knowing John was trying to be diplomatic, Jim said, "Tell me exactly what you think, and don't sugar coat it, old buddy."

John got the message and said, "Your training program sucks. Too much bullshit. First, way too much virtual training. These guys need to be shooting real bullets in a hot, dusty, nasty mockup somewhere that constantly changes. Not in some airconditioned virtual training room. Plus, all this algorithm, most likely scenario shit. What the fuck is that? You know as well as I do, war is a big fat ugly collection of chaos in perpetual motion. You've got to expect the totally unexpected. We need battle drills honed to perfect execution, yes, but we need to be able to adapt at a moment's notice."

Jim listened intently. "OK. What else?"

"Where did you get some of these guys? They sit around all day and play video games. Yeh, I got it. They can do one-arm push-ups all day and run me into the ground, but we need more than just physical endurance. We need guys who can think on their feet, guys with initiative. Most of these guys don't have any real experience. And another thing. None of these guys cuss. What the hell is that all about?"

Jim laughed as he said, "I understand. Yeh, this is not like the days when we were in. A lot has changed, some good, some bad. The technology has come a long way, but not so far that you or I can't figure it out. And I understand what you're saying about the men. You need to remember what has happened in the past couple of decades. Starting with the COVID virus combined with all the virtual reality stuff, we've got a generation of folks who don't have the same experiences you and I do. They don't know what life is like without technological connectivity of some sort. They've grown up in an era of fear, and they dealt with that fear by living online, constantly connected, I guess you could say. I know I'm making some broad generalizations, but that's my take."

"The other thing is you need to understand what has been happening to us as a country on the international level. With all the internal divisions here in the states, we have significantly withdrawn from the international community. The wars in Iraq and Afghanistan did not help. We haven't committed troops to anything major since then. Yeh, there have been a couple of actions here and there, but nothing where you got a lot of guys getting experience extended over months and years like we did. So, they've substituted experience for algorithms and predictive intelligence that tells us what is most likely to happen down to the minute detail. Or so they think. Look, the guys and gals we have are not bad. Most just lack our experience."

Then Jim laid back in his chair and asked, "What do you recommend?"

"I want to make some major changes to the training. We do live training. We learn battle drills. We need to train for the totally unexpected, and I want to incorporate Fred's guys in all of this. And we need to do it immediately. I'm not sure if we even have enough time, but it needs to happen now."

"You're going to run into some resistance. This is going back to some of the old ways. But I like it! What else?"

"A question and a request."

"OK, Shoot."

"Why?"

"Why what?"

"Why are you doing this? I know it's not for the money; that's never entered my mind. But you have something pulling you to this mission."

Jim's smile disappeared as his mood turned pensive. "When I was the assistant CENTCOM Commander, I got to know many senior military leaders in the region, especially the Egyptians and Israelis. I formed some pretty strong friendships with those men. When the nuclear war with Israel came, and we didn't come to their aid, I had a lot of anxiety over that. I watched men I had worked with for years supporting us in covert operations beg me for help, and I could do nothing. That's not how warriors treat one another. You know that just as well as I do. I won't go into a lot of details. Let's just say this is part of my way of unfucking what we fucked up over there."

John nodded. "Ok. Fair enough. I just have one other thing."

"What is it?"

"I start training with the folks you have. I do everything they do; physical training, combat training, everything. And if they go in, I go in."

"I don't know about that, old buddy. I wasn't banking on you actually participating in the mission. It's going to be risky. Plus, you said it yourself. You're a bit old for all this."

"Look, you put me in charge of this cluster fuck, so that means I'm in charge. Jim, you know how I operate. I won't send Soldiers in to do anything I won't do. I can't work that way. Yeh, I'm sure I'll hate myself for committing to this, but it's the way it's got to be with me. If I honestly can't hack the training, I'll not go in. But that's my call."

Jim thought for a while, then finally asked, "What about Sara? What if something should happen?"

John glanced down for a moment. He had thought about that on the plane ride over. In fact, it had been the first thing he thought about before he committed to Jim. "When I gave you my word that I would do this mission, I had already thought about her. Like you, I won't go into details."

Jim knew he did not have to ask, but he needed to be sure. He believed John would never have committed to helping him without looking at everything from all angles, and once John had given his word, it was his bond. "You sure about this?"

"Positive. Either we do it my way, or you send me home. Your call."

Jim reflected long and hard for a while and then smiled and said, "This is exactly why I need you. Welcome aboard."

John returned Jim's smile. "Oh, and make sure you've got that date lined up for me with your sister as soon as I get back."

Jim started laughing. "It's in the bag, old buddy. Just remember I warned you."

They then discussed a few more details and agreed they would brief the team first thing in the morning.

Glancing at his watch, Jim said, "Well, our timing couldn't be any better. Come over here and take my seat. There's someone who wants to have a video chat with you, and it should start in about fifteen minutes."

"Who wants to talk to me at this late hour?"

"My friend, the Egyptian Chief of Staff, called earlier and asked to talk to you tonight. Let's change seats, and I'll get you set up."

John and Jim exchanged places as Jim set up the video chat. After showing John how to run the program, Jim sat next to John but out of the camera's field of view.

Soon, a call came over the computer, and a face came on the screen. It was a man in an Egyptian general's uniform who looked to be sitting at a desk. A voice came on and said in accented English, "Good evening. My name is General Fahmy. I am the Chief of the Egyptian General Staff. Are you Mr. John Bradford?"

"Yes, Sir, I am. It's very good to meet you, Sir."

"I am very pleased to meet you, Mr. Bradford. My friend, Jim, has told me many good things about you. I am very happy to hear you have agreed to help him with this mission."

"Thank you, Sir. I've also heard a lot of good things about you as well from Jim."

A gregarious grin broke out on the general's face. "Well, Mr. Bradford, Jim sometimes tells good lies."

"I'm sure all the good things he's said are true, Sir."

After a few more pleasant exchanges, the general asked John to wait. He was going to transfer him to a man who wanted to talk to him.

The next face on the screen was an older man whose face was dark with deep lines and gray hair from years of heavy responsibility. His expression exuded authority, yet his dark brown eyes betrayed a deep sadness.

John recognized the man from the pictures of the key leaders in the Middle East in his briefings to be the King of Egypt. Without speaking, John then slid a glance to Jim, who nodded his head in affirmation.

The man spoke in Arabic as an interpreter translated his words into English. "Good evening, Mr. Bradford."

"Hello, Sir. It is a great honor to meet you."

"Thank You.

"I know, Mr. Bradford, that you have been told what this mission is all about. I do not need to explain to you its importance to me. I'm sure you understand. This is not the way I wish to do things. I would much rather have my Soldiers conduct this mission. However, we do not have the capability to do so. Therefore, I must rely on you. I do not like this, but I am grateful there is at least a chance I may one day see my children again."

The king paused, and John felt it was necessary to confirm he had been listening. "Yes, Sir."

"Mr. Bradford, I have been a Soldier all of my life. Even though I no longer wear a uniform, I must still ask my men to do many things. When I do, I have to determine what kind of men they are. I have to know if I can trust them. The only way I know how to do these things is to look into their eyes. Over the years, I have found I can tell a great deal about a man when I look into his eyes. Mouths lie many times. Eyes do not. I find myself in the uncomfortable position of relying on you and your men, yet I exercise no authority over you. I have been told much about you. However, I still needed to know what kind of man is leading this mission. I needed to look into his eyes so I would know."

Again, the king paused, and although he was looking at John via a video chat from thousands of miles away, John could feel the king's eyes on him, searching him to find the answer to his question. More silence continued, and John again acknowledged he had been listening and waited.

Then in an emotional tone of broken English, the king said, "I have seen what I needed to see. Mr. Bradford, I sincerely ask you to do your best to bring my children back, but I beg of you with all my heart for one thing."

The interpreter stopped talking, and the king then said in his heavily accented English, "bring my daughter back to me, . . . please."

What John heard in the king's voice then told him everything he needed to know. From then on, he did not require explicit commander's guidance or a briefing on the geopolitical implications of his success or some locker room speech. All he needed was what he heard, a desperate plea from a father for his daughter, something John fully understood.

"I will, Sir. I swear to you."

"Thank You. Good luck, Mr. Bradford. May Allah go with you."

After the king spoke his final words, the video chat ended.

John turned to Jim, who had been listening.

"Well, you have your marching orders," Jim said.

Later, as John walked back to his small apartment on the beach, he wondered if he had made the right decision in accepting this mission and his plan to guide the training. But ultimately, it did not matter. He was committed now.

The next day, Jim called a meeting with the key staff, primary trainers, and current team leader. After announcing they were going to make some changes, Jim turned the meeting over to John.

"Jim, first, I'd like to say you guys have done an impressive job assembling this team and the facilities."

John paused for a moment as everyone around the table smiled. Then he turned and looked directly at Jim. "But you did put me in charge, and it's time for me to exercise my authority. We need to make some changes effective immediately."

Everyone but Jim stopped smiling as Jim said, "Sure, John. What do you want to do?"

"First, no more virtual reality bullshit. I want a real area to do primary training in, and we'll use the virtual reality room as soon as we have a final target. There's what looks like another abandoned part of the resort a few miles from here. We'll use that and then change every few days."

"Second, I may need to change Hanson and Wilbanks as squad leaders. They're too robotic. They can't adjust to change. Munoz impressed me as someone who could think on his feet. He's my first prime candidate."

"Third, you will issue me a full set of equipment, and I will train and do everything exactly as my men. The only way I can understand their limitations is to do exactly as them."

"Finally, when we do drills and practice operations, it will always be with live ammunition. No more fucking blanks."

"You mean you want them to shoot at one another?" one of the trainers exclaimed.

"I want them comfortable with hearing bullets around them. It's very crowded in a firefight, and they need to be used to it. It has to be second nature to them, in the real world, and not some sort of virtual reality video game." John firmly said

When John finished, everyone had a frown on their face, except Jim, who still retained his smile.

John saw the now-former team leader raise his hand and say, "Excuse me, Sir. But you're cussing again. We can't tolerate cussing. It's divisive for our well-being."

John turned to the man and looked at him as though lasers were shooting out of his eyes. "And last, but not least. Cussing is authorized. I don't give a flying fuck about your candy ass well-being! Every ass clown pussy in my outfit will be allowed to cuss and cuss excessively. Do you fucking understand?"

The man jerked back in recoil, and before he could respond, Jim jumped in and said, "We'll definitely work on that." He then turned to look at everyone and followed up with, "OK, I say these are all good recommendations. They're approved. Gentlemen and ladies, we have a lot of work to do. I recommend we start immediately."

Not asking for questions, Jim dismissed the meeting, and everyone got up to leave.

As John and Jim turned to leave, Jaimie, the senior intelligence officer and former general who had briefed him a few days earlier, stood right in front of them. She said, "Colonel Bradford, we have the next intelligence update briefing tonight at 1900 hours. Please make sure you are there." Then her face turned stern as she said, "I'm sorry. Let me rephrase that. You better have your goat smelling ass at my briefing tonight, Colonel, or your ass will be grass, and I'm the lawnmower." She then poked him in the chest and asked, "Got it?"

John, stunned, answered, "Ah . . yes, Ma'am."

Jaimie's stern face then grew into a huge grin. She said, "I think we'll get along just fine," and left.

Jim looked at John and said, "We used to call her the Iron Lady back at CENTCOM. You might want to go easy with her."

"Oh, I will!"

The following day, John, dressed in a black T-shirt and shorts, and fell out for physical training with his team. After a few stretches, they started on a two-mile run that would end in an obstacle course.

Even John was surprised at how in shape the team was. He plodded along as best he could, however before he finished the run, most of the others were halfway finished with the obstacle course. By the time John finished the obstacle course, all the other team members were headed to breakfast.

Breathing hard and moving slow, John finished the last obstacle and started limping toward the chow hall. Looking up, he saw Jim standing in his path. He had also run that morning, but not nearly as far or as fast as the team.

Slowly walking up to Jim and still trying to catch his breath, John glanced over at him and breathlessly said, "Don't say . . . A fucking . . . thing."

When John walked past, Jim laughed to himself and shook his head.

After breakfast, the next activity scheduled was close-quarters marksmanship. John separated himself from the team for a half-hour to zero his weapon and then joined them in the drills. He had bought an assault rifle and a few pistols soon after he retired that he shot from time to time on his land in Victoria and was happy to see his marksmanship was still excellent.

But while his marksmanship was good, once again, the constant quick movement had him breathing hard. John was thankful when it was time for lunch. He needed the break to recharge.

After getting his food, which today was a tasty-looking ground steak, he decided to sit with some of his team members and get to know them better.

"Mind if I sit with you guys for lunch?" John asked a couple of the men sitting at the table nearest to the cafeteria line's end.

"No, Sir. Please do," one of them answered.

John thanked the man and took a seat in an empty chair at the table. An awkward silence momentarily followed before John decided to speak. "I'm surprised at the selection of chow here. I figured being on an island, all we would get is fish, but the meat has been pretty good so far."

The two men sitting nearest to John smiled at him but did not stop eating, while the third man seemed to ignore him.

Seeing his attempt at small talk was not working, John figured he'd try again. "That was pretty good shooting today, Saunders. I see the Seals taught you well."

Sanders finished taking a drink from his glass and said, "Thanks, Sir. I spent some extra time at the range since I've been here to improve my shooting. Last time I did any serious shooting was in Afghanistan."

"When were you there?" John asked.

"From 2020 to 2021. The place is a shit hole! Just about froze my ass off. Jimenez was with me on that mission. He remembers."

The man on the other side of John then spoke up. "You can say that again. I wonder what is what like back when they first invaded?"

A memory of his first combat missions in Afghanistan flew through John as he replied, "It was a shit hole then as well."

Saunders looked over at John and asked, "You were in Afghanistan during the initial invasion?"

"No, but I went in for Operation Anaconda with the 101st. And I froze my ass off then too."

Saunders and Jimenez shook their heads and smirked.

Then John looked across the table to the third man. "I saw that you've been to Afghanistan also, Munoz. What did you think about it?"

Munoz continued to eat. After he swallowed his food and without looking up, he said, "They're all shit holes if you ask me."

There was an arrogance in Munoz's tone that caught John's attention, especially since Munoz had not even bothered to look at him when he spoke. John remembered Munoz had muttered remarks about John being too old for the mission earlier in the morning, and in the few interactions they had had so far, his attitude seemed to be one of disdain.

As the leader, John knew he would have to address Munoz's disrespect if it got much worse, but this was not the time or place, so he let it go.

Saunders asked John what Operation Anaconda was like, and John shared a few stories with him.

Jimenez listened and also asked a few questions, but Munoz never said anything or made eye contact with John.

Finally, Munoz finished eating, stood up, and looked at John. "Those are all great stories, Sir, but it's a lot different out there now compared to the stone age days. It's a young man's game with no room for error," Munoz said and then walked off.

John's eyes narrowed at Munoz's statement, but still, he held his tongue. While Munoz was about half of John's age, he was unsure how much combat experience he had, as most of the team's was limited, and his comment did not sit well with John.

Saunders saw the look on John's face and said, "Sir, don't pay any attention to Munoz's smart-ass comments."

"He doesn't seem to be a very happy man," John sarcastically said.

"He's not. It has to do with his family."

"What's up with his family?"

"He lost his wife and son to one of those pandemics that hit the US several years ago. He was in Afghanistan at the time when he found out they were sick. When he asked to go home, they denied his request. A month later, he was notified they both had died. He's been a pretty bitter man since then. He got out of the Army as soon as he got back."

"I'm sorry that happened to his family. Maybe I shouldn't have brought up Afghanistan."

"You didn't know, Sir."

Jimenez then said, "It really is a shame that he's the way he is. He's a great Soldier. I served with him in Afghanistan during that deployment. Pretty brave motherfucker. It's just that attitude of his."

"Well, thanks for the heads up, fellas. I need to stop by admin before we start the next set of drills. I'll see you on the range," John said, and then he picked up his tray to turn it in.

After putting his tray on the cart to be washed, John wondered what he would do with Munoz. From what he had seen, he was very skilled in his warrior tasks, but he couldn't allow his attitude to go uncheck and cause problems within the team. He figured he'd have to deal with it sooner or later.

By day's end, John was dragging his ass back to his private room, and doing his best not to show it. After closing the door, he slumped down in a chair in the small open space. He wanted to take his boots off but just did not have the energy to do it yet. He felt sore in almost every muscle in his body and knew by tomorrow, it would be worse. His previously injured leg did not feel as bad as he thought it would, but he feared the pain might get worse.

He laid his head back and sighed. It was time to begin to come to grips with reality. Despite the lies he told himself, old age was beginning to settle in. *So, this is what it is to get old. Dammit! I felt I was in better shape than this! What the fuck! I looked like damn some over-the-hill mercenary straight out of Soldier of Fortune. I heard what some of those guys said under their breath. "Fucking old man can't hack it anymore!" Maybe they're right. Perhaps I have bitten off more than I can chew this time. I wonder what Sara would say about me after seeing me today? But I can't fucking quit now. This is just the first day. I'm committed. I've got to see this through!"*

John took another deep breath and felt his eyes beginning to close. *Maybe if I get a good night's sleep, it will be better in the morning.*

No sooner had John begun to fall asleep there was a sharp knock at his door.

Who the fuck can that be? I'm too tired to get up. "Come in."

The door opened, and the doctor that examined him when he first arrived walked in. "Hello, Colonel Bradford. Mind if I come in for a minute?"

"No, Doc. Come on in and grab a seat. What brings you here?"

The doctor closed the door and sat on the small couch next to John's chair.

"I saw Jim at lunch today, and he asked I stop by this evening to check on you. How are you feeling?"

"I'm alive. That's about the best I can say."

"How's your leg?"

"It's OK, but I can tell it's going to give me trouble by tomorrow."

"Did you take any of those pills I gave you for it?"

Forgetting the doctor had given him medicine for the pain in his leg, John hesitated in answering. "Ahhh, those pills in that little blue bottle?"

"Yes. The pills in the little blue bottle."

"Ahh, no, I haven't taken them yet."

"Why not?"

John hesitated, knowing his answer was not acceptable. Then he said, "I forgot."

"I see. Tell me, Colonel Bradford, what would you tell one of your subordinates if you told him to do something and he told you he forgot?"

John sighed. "I would not be happy with that individual."

The doctor nodded but did not say anything.

"OK, Doc. I get the message. I will be more diligent with my medication."

"Good. So, from now on, you will not only take the medication I gave you, I want you to come by my office every three days for a quick check-up."

"Why? Do you think I'm sick or something?"

"No, you're not sick."

"Then why do you want me to stop by every three days?"

"Because we need to keep you healthy."

"Look, Doc. I am healthy! I don't need some nursemaid to keep an eye on me."

"Colonel Bradford. My job is to make sure everyone assigned to this mission is and remains in great shape. On one hand, you are healthy. As a 59-year-old male, you are in the high percentile of health for your age group. Your continued strength training has done that for you, and you are to be congratulated."

"On the other hand, you are a 59-year-old man, which means your days of acting like a 20-year-old are over. You've had a major injury to your leg, which by some grace of God, you made a remarkable recovery. You've had several blows to the head from explosions and other trauma. And your body, in general, has had several injuries. I'm surprised you're still alive. Nevertheless, I am your personal physician while you are here, and I will do my job. You, in turn, will do your job and follow your orders. You've been in the Army. You know how to follow orders. Or do I need to get Jim involved?"

"No, no. We don't need to get Jim involved. I promise to follow my orders, even though I think they're bullshit."

"Good. So may I ask you a question for my own curiosity?"

"Sure, Doc."

"How did you recover so well from the injury to your leg?"

The question brought John back in time, starting with the ambush that almost cost him his life, then followed by his lingering in the hospital on the verge of losing all hope. But a smile came to him, remembering when Lisa came to him and how she dedicated herself to his recovery, pushing him beyond what he thought he could ever do. He slightly shook his head, acknowledging to himself it was only through her efforts that he recovered as he did. But the smile left as the one thought that forever haunted John came to him. While Lisa had saved him, he felt he had not saved her from the cancer that eventually took her. He slowly bowed his head and, for a second, squeezed his eyes shut to suppress the tears that wanted to form.

The doctor watched as John's face reacted to recalling the memories of his injury and subsequent recovery. Seeing John bow his head, he momentarily became slightly concerned. In addition to reading about John's physical injuries, he also read the psychiatrist's report on John's PTSD diagnosis and remembered from his talk with Jim that John had lost his wife.

John opened his eyes and looked sadly at the doctor. "Let's just say I had an exceptional nurse and leave it at that. OK."

Seeing this was not a topic of discussion for John, the doctor decided to leave him to his memories. "I understand."

Then the doctor stood up and said, "Well, I'm glad we had this little talk. If you need anything before your first visit, please stop by my office."

"OK."

The doctor then walked toward the door and opened it.

When he opened the door, John called out to him. "Doc."

"Yes?"

"Thanks. I appreciate you coming to check on me."

The doctor smiled at John and replied, "You're very welcome, Colonel."

He then walked out and closed the door.

Suddenly, sitting in the dim light of the room, John was alone again. After a few minutes, he finally gathered the strength to shower and get ready for bed.

Lying in bed, John tried his best but ultimately found it impossible to concentrate on the next day's training. The distant sound of the waves hitting the beach drew him back to memories of Lisa. It had been a while since he thought of her, and the near silence filled him with a growing longing for her. From the day she committed herself to him in the hospital, she had been his strength. *If only you were here with me now, Lisa*, John thought just as he fell asleep.

When the doctor turned the corner in the hall to his room, he saw Jim waiting for him.

"John doing OK, Doc?"

"Yes. I needed to remind him to take his medication and told him to see me every three days so I can make sure he's doing OK. But he'll be fine. He is in great shape for his age. We just need to watch his old injuries, especially his leg."

"Good! I appreciate you taking care of him.

"How was he able to recover so well from that injury?"

"His wife was with him that whole time. From what he told me in the past, she pushed him hard to recover."

"I see. She must have been something else."

"She was, Doc."

Chapter 6

Despite his age limitations, within a few days, John showed improvement and began the road to gain the respect he needed to lead the team in combat effectively. The pills the doctor had given him and the exoskeleton he was finally used to wearing helped, although the other men were still in better shape than he was. What he lacked in endurance, he made up in strength. A few heads turned two days later when he made his way to the gym and knocked out several sets of heavyweight bench presses. His shooting accuracy greatly improved once he became comfortable with his rifle, and his experience began to show as their drills continued.

The more he watched his men going through training, the more he understood potential problems. None of them had his experience, and it showed. But the biggest issue he saw was a general lack of initiative by the team members at the level required to conduct the type of mission they were given.

John believed the team's expectation of perfect intelligence and implementation of a strictly controlled plan from higher robbed them of the ability to think on their feet. Having years of combat experience, he understood combat was an exercise in chaos, and a successful operation was just one small step below total confusion. War was an affair where change was constant, and adaptation was essential for survival. The ability to execute combat drills to perfection was always necessary, but never enough. One also had to know when to deviate from the plan and alter those drills accordingly, especially when contact with leaders was lost.

With very little time, John did his best to instill initiative into each team member and for them not to be afraid to deviate from the plan when required. However, it wasn't easy at first. Some resisted, while others timidly tried.

It was then John realized the one man on his team who had both experience and initiative was Munoz. Despite his ill manners, Munoz was a natural leader. The men seemed comfortable deferring to him when unexpected changes occurred.

During one evening, John took the time to read Munoz's file and was impressed. He had been a highly decorated non-commissioned officer in the Green Berets before leaving the service. Although not as extensive as John's, his combat experience was more than anyone else on the team.

But what else stood out in his file were several reprimands for resisting authority. However, those reprimands lacked the detail that explained to John the why of Munoz's actions.

Jim told John many times to keep in mind that today's Army had gone through some tough times resulting from a lack of leadership. John wondered if Munoz's resistance to authority resulted from a lack of leadership he experienced while in the Army. After watching Munoz work with his fellow team members, he started to conclude his suspicions were correct.

John believed if he could change Munoz's resistance to authority, he could leverage his expertise and initiative for the mission. He figured Munoz would be a perfect team leader on the ground. He'd seen it many times in his career, Soldiers who were troublemakers in garrison yet highly effective in combat. He just needed to figure out a way to affect a change in Munoz's attitude. Looking at the following day's training schedule, John saw what he thought might be an opportunity.

The next day while leading the training, John kept a close eye on Munoz. The drill was simple. Three men come to a small house with the front door closed. They would need to enter the house and clear the first room, a breached entry it was called. Although it sounded easy, the problem was an enemy Soldier was in the room waiting for them.

The first two teams, consisting of three men each, quickly arranged themselves beside the front door, busted it down, and rushed into the room. Each time, two of the three Soldiers were killed in the exercise. When the third team did the same thing, John was livid.

"Stop!" John yelled at the three team members once they entered the room and were all killed. "What the fuck are you doing?"

"Standard breaching drill, Sir," the team leader answered John.

"OK, so walk me through this. You know a bad guy is waiting for you, and you just bust the door down?"

"Basically, Sir. I mean, we're just sticking to the three basic tenants of Close Battle Combat, Surprise, Speed, and Violence of action."

"But if the result is everyone gets killed, then we need to do better," John said and proceeded to explain alternative ways of entering the room.

After watching several more breaches, John saw Jim walk up and wave to him.

"How's it going, John?"

"Good. I think we finally might be coming together."

"How's Munoz doing?"

"Well, he's still pretty obstinate, but I'm working on him."

"John, of all the guys we have, I'm telling you, he's a trouble maker. I've never liked his arrogant attitude. He's been a pain in our ass for a while. I'm just looking for one more slip-up from him to fire him."

"I know, Jim. But the guy is a natural leader. He has initiative and doesn't wait around to get directions when shit goes bad. I'll just coach him a little more. You know, do that leadership thing."

"OK. Well, he's your responsibility, then."

"Fair enough. Hey, how is Fred coming along with his pilots? I'd like to practice some mounting and dismounting drills."

While John and Jim were talking, Munoz turned to his buddy, Saunders, standing next to him and said, "Hey, bro. I'm headed over to the island tonight to see my girl. You wanna go?"

"You can't leave the island, Man. You know we got orders to stay put."

"Fuck that shit! I ain't got laid in so long that supply chick is starting to look good. I'm heading over to Sharkies to hook up tonight."

"You can't go, I'm telling you. If they find out, everyone is going to go ape shit, especially Bradford."

"Fuck Bradford! That old man scares you guys, but he doesn't scare me."

"How the hell are you going to go?"

"I gave the guy at the marina some dollars to let me borrow a boat for the night. One of those cigar jobs. I'll be at the island in less than thirty minutes and back before first light with plenty of time to spare."

Saunders shook his head at Munoz. "I wish you wouldn't do this."

When John finished talking to Jim, he returned to the team and said, "OK, Munoz, it's your turn now. Take your two guys and give it a try."

Munoz took his two men and talked to them for a second before getting into their starting positions. Once they were ready, they signaled John, and he started the drill.

When the three men moved up to the door, Munoz ran over to a nearby window and started shooting inside the room. When he stopped, the two men at the door busted the door down but quickly jumped to the sides as the enemy Soldier inside shot at them. This was enough of a distraction for Munoz to shoot the enemy Soldier, then enter the room through the window.

Once inside, he signaled the other two team men to enter, and all three completed the task alive.

John walked over to Munoz and glared at him. He asked, "Who told you you could use the window? The task was to go through the door. No one said you could use the window for the entry. How do you even know it's there?"

"Look, Sir, no one said I couldn't use the window, and from what I could see, it was there. It's stupid to just rush into the door when you know damn well someone is waiting for you on the other side. And I ain't stupid!"

John's glare transformed into a smile as Munoz had done as he expected him to, finding a better way outside the task's parameters. "That was good thinking on your part, Munoz. I agree. You did a great job."

Munoz grunted and walked away.

John watched him leave and thought, *Yep! That's the guy I need to be a team leader.*

Later that night, John was sound asleep when he awakened suddenly to the sound of someone pounding on his door. He sat up in bed, rubbed his eyes, and listened again to make sure he had actually heard a knock. A few seconds later, there was another series of knocks.

"Give me one second," John called out.

He glanced over at the clock on his nightstand. *Twelve thirty! What the fuck!* Then he suddenly thought maybe it was Jim with an update about the mission, and immediately he was up and out of bed. He threw some pants on and quickly walked to the door.

When John opened the door, Saunders and Jimenez were standing outside. "What's going on?" John asked.

"Sir, we need to talk to you," Saunders said.

"Has there been a change or an update about the mission?"

"No, Sir. Not that we are aware of."

"OK. Then what the hell is so damn important that you guys need to wake me at one-thirty in the morning to talk about."

Saunders turned his head and looked at Jimenez. From the expression on their faces, John determined their news was not good.

"Sir, it's about Munoz."

"What about Munoz?"

"Sir, he went over to the neighboring island for the evening."

"What! You guys know the rules. No leaving this island until the mission is complete or canceled! Why did he leave?"

"Sir, he said he had to go into town. You know, get laid, blow off steam. That kind of stuff."

"Goddammit! How the hell did he get over there?"

"He bribed the guy at the marina and borrowed one of the boats to get over there."

"That's just fucking great!"

Then Jimenez spoke up. "Well, Sir. It only gets better. He called about thirty minutes ago. He was drunk off his ass, talking about kicking some guy's ass at Sharkies. It's a low-class bar on the island. We tried calling him back, and he never answered. We're afraid something might have happened to him."

John was wide awake now, angrily shaking his head. "Goddammit, you guys should have stopped him!"

Both men hung their heads and were silent.

John thought. If Munoz opened his mouth about what they were doing, the whole operation could be compromised, and the only way he would know is if he personally went and found out what had happened to Munoz.

John looked over at Saunders and asked, "OK. Saunders, you were in Marine recon. Can you run a boat at night?"

"Yes, Sir. With the navigation equipment on board some of the fast boats at the marina, it would be easy."

"OK. You two get down to the marina. Wake up the bastard who runs that place, get a boat ready, and wait until I get there. The three of us are heading over to the island to see what the hell happened to Munoz."

Both men acknowledged John's orders and left for the marina.

As soon as John dressed, he called Jim and told him what had happened. As John figured, Jim was beyond angry. John explained what he was going to do, and Jim begrudgingly gave his approval.

John then ran down to the marina and found Saunders and Jimenez waiting in a boat, ready to go.

John was thrilled the sea was relatively calm, and there was a full moon as they raced to the nearby island. He wasn't excited about riding in a boat at night, but Saunders was very experienced and expertly navigated them to their destination.

They soon got to the island, and the bar Munoz had called his buddy from was nearby.

John opened the door to the bar, and the two men followed him in. Looking around, John thought if there ever was a scene that mirrored the bar scenes in those old noir and adventure movies, this was it. The dim lighting limited his vision and incited his nerves while the smoke-filled air attacked his lungs. Several tables were between the front door and the main bar, and from what John could see, each one was filled with various collections of dirty, semi-filled glasses, bottles of alcohol or beer, and a wide array of the lower end of the local residents. The floor was littered with peanut shells, old paper napkins, and various other items; cleanliness was apparently not a priority of the establishment. To the right was another set of tables next to some pool tables where several large men, dressed in sleeveless shirts and baggy pants, were playing. They glanced at John when he opened the door but then returned to their game. Several women lounged throughout the bar with clothing that left little to the imagination.

As John surveyed the large room from the entrance, the klaxon in his head was screaming. The stares looking back at him and his men ranged from imminent hostility to vampiric thirst. He could feel his pulse picking up. *This is not going to be good!*

Finally, he spotted who he thought might be Munoz at one of the tables in a far corner next to the pool tables. He was sitting in a chair slumped forward, laying on the tabletop, not moving.

John turned his head back to Saunders and Jimenez men and said just over the pounding heavy metal music playing, "Just wait here for me. I'll go see if that is Munoz in the corner. Don't make any aggressive moves. We just want to get Munoz and leave. I don't want any trouble at all. OK?"

Both men nodded and moved off to the side as John weaved amongst the tables toward the man he thought was Munoz.

As he walked by one of the tables, a woman reached out and grabbed John's arm. "Hey, baby! I haven't seen you in here before. Why don't you sit with me for a while, and we can visit?"

Even in the poorly lit room, John could see the leathery texture of her skin from too much time in the sun and the deep lines in her face caked with makeup trying to make her look much younger than she was. But unfortunately, the makeup wasn't doing its job.

John smiled at the woman and politely pulled her hand away from his arm. "Thank you, but I need to get a friend of mine. Maybe later."

The woman smiled back at John, and he noticed she was missing a few of her tobacco-stained teeth. Walking past, he felt a hand take its liberties with his butt. When he turned, the woman's smile was broader and accompanied by a wink.

John politely grinned back but kept walking toward the man lying on the table. It was Munoz.

When he stopped next to Munoz, the smell of alcohol just about knocked John over. Looking down at him, he saw several deep bruises on Munoz's face and a badly bloodied lip.

John bent down, gently shook Munoz a few times, and whispered, "Hey, Munoz. Wake up."

Munoz moaned, and after John shook him again, he sat back in his chair. He barely opened his black eyes and tried to look at John.

"Munoz. Get up. Let's go."

A deep voice yelled out from a nearby pool table, "Leave dat motherfucker lone!"

John looked up and saw a bald head attached to a very large man, who had been playing pool, now turned and looking at him. He not only stood at least four inches taller than John but probably outweighed him by a full 50 pounds. The numerous graphic tattoos covering his exposed arms and neck added to his menacing appearance. *Oh shit! OK, John, play it cool. Let's not provoke Godzilla.*

"This guy is my buddy. Looks like he's had a rough time tonight. I just want to get him back home. That's all."

"I said leave dat motherfucker lone! I'm not pinished wit him yet!"

"Hey, friend. I'm not here to start any trouble at all. I just want to get my buddy out of here."

"I'm not your motherfucking friend. Dat motherfucker tried to fuck my girl! No one fucks my girl but me! I'm in the middle of teaching him a lesson, and soon as I finish my game, gonna fuck him up some more. So just leave dat fucker lone!"

John couldn't figure out what accent the guy had or if he was drunk, and had a hard time understanding him. But he'd got the gist of the giant's request. Unfortunately, retreat was not an option here. *Goddammit, Munoz! You've gotten yourself in a hell of a shit hole. Easy, John!*

"I apologize for what my friend did. I promise he will not make any more trouble for you. I'll just get him out of here, and he won't bother you again. I promise."

"You don't fucking understand. I'm gonna kill him before this is all over. Now git the fuck out before I hurt you too!"

John's heartbeat spiked with fear, and he could feel that fight or flight moment coming. The last thing he wanted to do was get in a fight, but his options were narrowing. He glanced over at Saunders and Jimenez, who were watching him, and slightly shook his head, indicating for them to stay away. He wanted to minimize what might happen, and a full-out brawl was not a good plan at this time.

He then slid his eyes left and right and identified the two guys who might back up their large friend.

"You merican? Ain't you! Probably one of dose fucking pussy Soldiers from da island nearby."

"We're just in town on vacation. I don't know anything about an island with Soldiers."

"Yeah! Right! You one of dem pussy Soldiers. You and your two friends at de door don't scare me," the man said as he laid his pool stick on the table and scowled at John.

"Look, I don't want any trouble. OK? Just let me . ."

"To late pussy Soldier. You mericans all suck! You tink you fucking tough. I killed lots of you bastads in the stan back in the day. Then I fucked their whore wives when I got to the states."

For John, who had led Soldiers into combat in Afghanistan and seen many die mercilessly at the hands of the insurgents, the man's words struck a sensitive nerve. Even worse was an image of this man sexually assaulting the wives left behind. What had been fear instantly turned to hate, and John tightened his hand to stop the trembling that had started. *He's deliberately cornering me! All right you overgrown fuck! Now you're taking it too far.*

The man saw John's shaking hand and menaced, "You scared old man?"

John narrowed his eyes and calmly answered, "No."

"Huh, huh. We'll see."

Suddenly, the man lunged at John.

Anticipating his move, John quickly front kicked the man in the balls.

The large man bent down, screaming in pain, and in a flash, John grabbed a pool stick leaning on the wall near him and slammed it against the back of the man's head.

The man went down with a loud thump, and just as John thought, the two men at the pool table with him threw their sticks on the table and one yelled out, "You hurt my friend, you fucking bastard!"

As the man's friend ran toward John, John struck the man's nose with the palm of his hand, driving it back into his head.

The man yelled and blood splattered on the floor. John grabbed a glass beer bottle from Munoz's table, smashed it against the side of his head, and he fell to the ground next to the first man.

By now, the third man was upon John and caught him square in the face with a punch.

John tumbled over a table and ended up on the floor. He felt both pain and light-headed. As he tried to stand, the man grabbed John again and punched him again.

John fell backward over several chairs and again was on the ground.

Feeling even more pain and disorientation, John slowly stood up and tried to focus on the man who was just standing looking at him. He saw the man reach into his pocket and pull out a knife.

"It's going to feel good killing you, old man. Then I'll get to be the one to go fuck your wife and not my friend," he laughingly said right before he rushed toward John.

When an image of Lisa in danger from the man sprinting toward him flew through John's mind, he felt a lightning strike of adrenaline hit his body and a single thought jumped in his mind. *Kill him!*

John kicked one of the chairs near him into the path of the running man causing him to trip, and then he knocked him to the floor.

John then stomped on the man's hand holding the knife with his boot. The man screamed, released the knife, and John kicked it away.

In a flash, John jumped on the man and maneuvered him into a chokehold.

John was breathing very heavy now, but the imagery of dead American Soldiers and Lisa in danger fueled his hate, filling him with a strength that removed all the pain he should have been feeling. Holding the large man in the chokehold, John squeezed as hard as he could, and the man flailed and gasped for air. Hearing the gasps energized John even more.

John hissed, "Now you listen to me, motherfucker. I killed lots of you bastards too back in the stan. I loved killing you little fucks. And I'll kill you right fucking now if you don't leave my friends and me alone. Do you understand me?"

The man said nothing but continued to resist.

John shook his hold on the man, violently jerking his head, and yelled, "Did you hear what the fuck I said?"

Still gasping, the man tried to nod his head.

Suddenly, a gunshot rang out, and the entire bar went silent. Then, through the dim-lighted, smoke-filled room, a man armed with a shotgun walked into John's view and pointed the gun at him. "Let him go."

John fought to catch his breath and looked up at the man.

"I said release him. I've got three shells left, and that's enough to kill both of you," the man said.

Knowing he had no choice; John released his grip on the man.

As his opponent choked filling his lungs with air, John slowly stood up. He found himself staring down the barrel of a short-muzzled automatic shotgun. The man facing him was well built, wearing a sleeveless T-shirt that showed a few scars on his arms. By his gray hair, John figured they were both about the same age.

Then John looked over at Saunders and Jimenez and saw another man holding a pistol on them. They returned John's look in despair.

"Manny! Henry! Get over here!" the man with the shotgun called out.

When two larger men appeared, the man told them to pick up the guy on the ground John had been choking.

The two men reached down, pulled the beaten man up, and held both of his arms behind his back.

"Omar, I've told you and that fat fuck of a friend of yours on the floor three times now, I've had enough of your bullshit. Every time you fuckers come in here, you start a fight, and every time I have to clean it up. We're done with this. Don't ever fucking come in here again. Got it?" the man with the shotgun said.

When the beaten man gestured consent, the shotgun man signaled for his two friends to take the man outside.

All the while, John stood silently, still catching his breath.

When the shotgun man was talking to the beaten man, John noticed he had a First Cavalry Division patch tattoo with a large two in the center. Underneath it was written "Spring Break 04."

After the two men dragged the guy lying on the ground away, the man with the shotgun looked at John and coolly said, "I don't mind having trash like them in my place telling their bullshit lying stories as long as they pay. If they pay, I make a profit, and all is good. But all you've done is come into my place and rip it up. Who the fuck are you, and why shouldn't I kill you right now for payment for all the damage you've done?"

John looked at his tattoo and calmly replied, "I was with Black Jack in Iraq in 2004."

Squinting at John, the man asked, "What do you know about Iraq in 2004?"

"I know about a shit hole by the name of Sadr City. Ever been there?"

The man did not answer. He just silently stared at John and remembered. Sadr City wasn't a place for him but a time in his life when he believed each day to have been his last.

Finally, the man muttered, "Yeh. I remember Sadr City."

Then the man looked at Munoz, and then slid his eyes to Saunders, Jimenez, and then back to John. He sighed and said, "OK, friend. I know who you guys are. This is your one freebie. You take all of your friends and don't ever come back here again. Especially your lady's man over there on the table. Otherwise, I won't interfere next time, and if Omar and his friends don't kill you, I'll kill you myself. Is that clear?"

John shook his head, "Yes, Sir. We are clear."

He then nodded for Saunders and Jimenez to get Munoz.

As John and his three men made their way out, he thanked the man with the shotgun, who said, "Don't forget what I said."

When they got back to the boat, John felt the throbbing pain from his beating start. His whole face felt like one big bruise as he sat down and tried to gather his thoughts.

Saunders and Jimenez sat Munoz down in the seat next to John. Then, Saunders handed John a wet cloth and said, "Damn, Sir. Where did you learn to fight like that? We thought for sure you were a goner when that first big guy went after you."

John wiped his face with the cloth and replied, "Saunders, my head is pounding too hard to talk. Just get us home and take it easy."

Saunders then turned to Jimenez, and they started the boat engine and plotted the course back on the navigation system.

Munoz, who had sat in silence the entire time, turned to John and quietly said, "Sir, I just want to say thank you for coming after me. I don't . ."

"Just save it, Munoz! We'll talk about this tomorrow morning!"

Munoz hung his head and remained silent the rest of the trip back.

Forty minutes later, they were back at the dock, and when John was getting out of the boat, he saw Jim waiting for him.

"You OK, old buddy? You look like shit! Your lip looks like someone went crazy with a Botox injection, not to mention your new face coloring," Jim said as John came into the light and stopped in front of him.

"Yeh, I ran into some of the neighbors next door. Not the friendliest of folks in these parts."

"What happened?"

"Munoz decided he needed a night out to blow off some steam and must have hooked up with a woman with a very jealous boyfriend who beat the hell out of him. He and his buddies weren't too pleased with me when I tried to get Munoz out of there either, so we had a "discussion" over his indiscretions."

Visible upset, Jim asked, "Do you think the mission is compromised?"

"No, I don't think so. I took it that it's no huge secret to the locals what goes on over here, but there was no reason for me to believe they have any idea what we are about to do. I was thinking about that on the way home too and figured maybe it worked out well. Something like this might get people to think all is normal. Maybe too much secrecy might lead to folks asking questions."

"Maybe. I'll have Jaimie run an OPSEC assessment."

"Good idea."

"I'll have Munoz gone first thing in the morning."

"Well, how about if we wait on that?"

"Wait? What the fuck, John? This asshole has broken curfew and threatened the security of the entire operation, as well as has been a general pain in the ass for all of us. I won't have that kind of indiscipline in this type of operation!"

Raising his hands as if to absorb some of Jim's anger, John replied, "I know, I know. You're right. It's just . . well, you know the deal, Jim. Some of the best combat Soldiers we had were guys who were problem children back in garrison. But the moment bullets started flying, those were some of the main guys we relied on."

"OK, but this is supposed to be an elite team, not run-of-the-mill infantry Soldiers."

"Yes, you're right. It's just I see something in Munoz. I think maybe we turned a corner with him tonight."

Jim shook his head. "John, if we go in, we can't half-ass this operation. Too much is at stake. I'm not sure I can support your request."

"I understand, Jim. You're the boss and if you don't agree with me on this one, I won't push you."

Jim sighed. He knew John always loved his Soldiers and they knew it. That was why he was able to get them to go the extra mile and do things other leaders could not. "You're sure you want to try it with him one more time?"

"Just one more time, and if he slips up in the slightest, you can fly his ass out of here by the end of that day."

"OK. He's all yours. But I'll be watching him."

John smiled, but then grimaced as soon as he felt the pain from the bruises on his face.

Jim grinned and then glanced at his watch. "It's almost morning. How about you take a rest day today? I think you got enough combatives training for a while. Get some sleep, and when you get up, go visit the doc for a quick check-up and a few pain pills."

"Yes, Sir. I think I'll do that," John said, still trying to smile without flinching.

Chapter 7

John sat mesmerized, listening to the gentle roll of the waves hitting the beach with the soft caress of the ocean breeze that touched his face and washed his mind with thoughts and memories. After sleeping a few hours, he had walked in front of his bungalow and sat in one of a pair of white Adirondack chairs placed at the beach's edge to watch the sunrise. He needed time to think.

Soon, the sun slowly rose from the horizon like a bright orange ball bringing daylight, and beads of sweat appeared on John's forehead as the heat edged its way higher. But he did not mind the heat or the sweat. On the contrary, he liked the feel of the sun's warmth on his face and the sweat's relief from the heat. It was as if his body was lubricating itself for his manual labor that would follow.

John sat for hours, simply watching and thinking. Occasionally, he would watch a bird would swoop down to the ocean to catch his morning meal, or look at the water's edge and see the fiddler crabs dance along the path of the water's fringe as it reached for the sand and then quickly returned.

His mind mirrored the water's movement, rushing toward the shore, reaching as far as it could, and then receding; constant motion. He had come so far in life, only to find himself as if caught in a continuous circle since the time he had left home. Once again, he was to lead men into combat, and once again, living another day was questionable. His mind was a whirlwind of memories and thoughts; growing up in Victoria, his parents, the Army, Lisa, Sara, mental rehearsals of the mission. He tried to find a pattern to answer the question that ultimately always came to him. Why.

But eventually, he rambled to one subject he had not thought deeply about in a while, Lisa. Although she was never far from his mind, he did his best to keep her memory at bay in an attempt to live in peace. It had been 17 years since he had last held her hand, but when he thought deeply about her, it was only yesterday.

He took a swig of cold tea from his insulated container and closed his eyes, allowing his mind to grasp at random memories. It wasn't long, and one revealed itself.

John remembered an afternoon at home in Kentucky soon after taking battalion command. For some reason, he had the devil in him and was pestering Lisa. He was chasing her in the backyard when she'd reeled around and yelled at him.

"Dammit, John! I told you to stop!"

"Oh, come on, babe. I'm just fooling with you. Don't you like to be tickled? You know, I could get you if I really tried."

Lisa narrowed her beautiful blue eyes at him. "Huh! That's what you think! You know I don't like to be tickled, so just keep your distance."

Feeling she had just dared him, John replied, "Oh, really! Hey, I just did a combative training session for PT this week. I did pretty well for an old man. Think I'll try out a few lessons on you if you're not nice."

Placing her hands on her hips, Lisa stood her ground. "Don't you dare!"

Her resistance only enticed him more as John crouched down low and started slowly circling her.

She wagged her finger like a foil, and snarled, "John, I'm warning you!"

Suddenly he lurched out toward her, but as he reached for her, Lisa grabbed his hand and twisted her body, placing her hip next to his and expertly used his momentum to throw John directly on his back where he landed with a loud "thump!"

John opened his eyes and found himself looking up at the sky, trying to orient himself to what had just happened. "Uhhhh, shit."

Lisa bent down and looked at him. "Are you all right?"

All right! What the fuck, woman? Slowly, he struggled to get up. His back was feeling the impact with the ground, and it was not fun. "Yeh. I'm fine."

Lisa reached out with her hand. "Here, let me help you up."

But John ignored her offer. "I'm fine. I can get up." His voice lacked any emotion, and his playful attitude from moments ago was gone. He got up, wiped himself off, and slowly started walking toward the door.

"John?"

"I'm fine. I'm just going in the house for a moment." He lied, and Lisa saw through his lie instantly. His pride was hurt, but he did not want to show it. *I'm supposed to be the super Soldier, and my wife Judo body throws me like I was some kid. Just great!*

Lisa had an idea what John was thinking and decided to let him have a moment to himself. It wasn't like he was yelling at her or being outwardly angry, but she knew he was upset, probably with both himself and her.

John walked into the house, sat down on the couch, and surfed TV channels. He heard Lisa come into the house but did not say anything.

After an hour of not talking to her, Lisa decided she needed to fix the situation. She approached him from behind and slowly ran her hand through his hair. "You OK, sweetheart?"

John did not move and continued to watch TV. "I'm fine."

She bent down and put her lips to the back of his neck and slowly started kissing him.

"Lisa, please. I'm really not in the mood."

Now it was John who had thrown the gauntlet down for Lisa, and it was Lisa who could not back away. She was determined to break his pouty mood with the most devastating weapons she had. She momentarily left the room, then returned and gently sat in his lap as she put her arms around him and propped her feet up on the couch. She gazed into his eyes while John looked elsewhere, trying not to pay attention to her. She whispered to him, "Are you mad at me?"

John flashed a look at her and then looked back at the TV, but not before he saw she was no longer wearing a bra and her open shirt barely covered her breasts. Doing his best to remain impassive, he said, "No, I'm not mad."

Lisa slowly started to lightly kiss his cheek several times as she breathed in his scent, which was always a sexual motivator for her.

John knew his game was found out but decided to try and play hardball. He was not going to allow her to manipulate him. "It's not working, Lisa."

Lisa then transitioned to the corner between his neck and shoulder, rubbed her wet lips there, and kissed him. "Hmmm, what's not working, baby?" she seductively said.

John could feel his resistance beginning to break. Her lips against his bare skin were sending tingles down his spine. When Lisa was determined, he knew it was only a matter of time before she wore him down, and it seemed she was doubling her efforts. But he was adamant about trying a little harder. "I know what you're trying to do."

"What am I trying to do?" she asked, her voice dripping with desire.

Then she gradually moved to his ear and began to nibble away while her hand roamed through his hair.

John's nose filled with her sweet perfume, and his senses were in overload. Her tender nibbles were enticing his desire from within. He felt her ample breasts pushing against him, and his arms wanted to come up from his sides and hold her. His resistance to her was efficiently being reduced to a thin line.

Lisa quietly moaned in his ear. "Mmmmm, is it working now?" Then she started to slowly unbutton his shirt with her free hand.

At this point, she had broken him. He closed his eyes as his blood was already alerting his body to prepare for action, and his reply was simply, "Yes."

She whispered, "Good. Can we do something about it now? Because I'd really like to," with a sultry voice now captivating him.

The moment she started rubbing his chest and using her tongue to explore his ear, John reacted automatically. He picked her up and then laid her back down onto the couch, placing himself on top of her. "Dammit, woman! You're fucking driving me crazy! You know that!"

She laid back, her eyes and lips with a come-hither look that captivated him to no end. "That's exactly what I wanted to do to you," she said.

"Tell me something. Where the hell did you learn how to throw me like that?"

Lisa's look transitioned to a sad face knowing he would not like the answer, but she decided to tell him. "When I was married to Richard, he worried about me working late and made me take a judo class. My instructor had competed in the Olympics and was very good."

John looked at her. He felt stupid for his pouty fit and decided to ask for forgiveness. "I'm sorry, Lisa, for throwing a fit. Will you forgive me?"

She smiled with the glee of victory and then transitioned once again to an alluring, magnetic look. "How about you make it up to me?"

In an instant, John began his labor.

Reliving the distant memory, he felt the edges of his mouth curl into a warm smile. But the moment passed, and the realization Lisa had been gone for so long hit him. He felt a single tear escape from his closed eyes as he whispered to himself, "I miss you, Lisa."

Sitting by himself on the beach, John suddenly felt very alone. He needed to talk to someone, to air out the loneliness inside.

He went back to his place and changed. Then, John decided to walk over and talk to Fred, who he assumed was at the hanger. In addition to asking Fred a couple of questions about the upcoming air mission, he wanted to visit with someone he knew.

John walked into the hanger through a slit in the large center door, looked around, and saw one of the other pilots headed to lunch. He stopped the man and asked him where Fred was.

"He's over in the tilt-rotor aircraft in that corner. He's going through aircraft emergency procedures."

When John approached the aircraft, he heard what sounded like some kind of New Age mood music playing, slow and relaxing.

He looked inside the open cockpit door and saw Fred sitting in his seat surrounded by dials, switches, and displays. Red lights flickered, and the heads-up display flashed with simulated flight data.

John walked over and stopped just outside the door next to Fred who was absorbed in his concentration on the instruments. Maintaining one hand on the center control stick, he smoothly flipped switches and controls with his other hand while his eyes remained glued to the numerous lights and dials. He seemed oblivious to John's presence.

John looked down at Fred's phone sitting next to him. It displayed the music selection playing over the sound system. The album was named "Sex Music," and the selection was called "Sex on the Beach."

John looked back at Fred, who had still not acknowledged John.

"Fred."

Without flinching, Fred answered, "Yeh."

"What the hell are you doing?"

"Training."

"Uh-huh."

"Yeh. I'm reviewing the emergency procedures for power loss. Give me one more minute."

A minute later, Fred flipped the last switch that turned off the simulated drill and reached over and turned off the music. "What's up, Johnny?"

"How the hell do you do training to sex mood music?"

"Johnny, Johnny. I was reviewing the emergency procedures so they will be automatic if I need to do them. If I ever lose power, that can be a bit stressful. So, listening to some relaxing music helps me concentrate. Kind of records in my mind the checklist to a peaceful vibe. Helps me focus."

"But sex mood music?"

"I can't help it if flying is synonymous with sex to me. You want to borrow my album? Got some pretty good stuff in there. Some of that Kama Sutra stuff."

John laughed. "Thanks, but I'll pass."

"Damn, Johnny! Looks like you've been doing a little too much full-contact training lately."

"Yeh, I had a little problem with some gorillas on the neighboring island. But I think we got that all straightened out last night. Do you have a few minutes? I have some questions about the air mission I wanted to ask you about?"

Fred nodded, and John asked his questions. Fred was surprised at many of John's questions because the air mission was still preliminary until the actual target location and flight profile were established. He knew John knew that as well, but Fred tried to fill in what he thought.

"Until we finalize the target location, that's the best I can tell you. So, you answer a question for me."

"OK."

"What did you really come over here for?"

John tried to suppress the grin that eventually won out. He was amazed Fred saw through his façade and understood John's visit was more than just a casual conversation. In all the years they'd known each other, their relationship had been one of two kindred spirits attracted by their mutual love for music, speed, and living on the edge. However, they'd never had a deep discussion before. It wasn't that John thought Fred was not capable of deep thoughts. It just seemed both of them enjoyed the lightheartedness of their bond. However, today, John needed a deeper discussion. "Can I ask you a serious question?"

"Shoot."

"Fred, why are you here?"

"So, you're in one of those moods, are you?"

"Yeh. You could say so."

Fred turned to his instrument panel and pondered the question. Finally, he said, "I guess cause, in a way, I don't have anywhere else I can go. I felt as long as the Army would let me fly, I would stay. When they decided I didn't need to fly anymore, then I got out. I tried some civilian flying jobs, but that was so boring, I about fell asleep most of the time. I looked around, and I didn't know what I was going to do. I wasn't ready to drown myself in the mental masturbation of the lies we tell about ourselves to keep us occupied while we wait for the final fade to black. That's when we've given up on our passions for life, to live our lives in the arena, to push the envelope, and to do the things guys like you and me were meant to do. Instead, we give up. We don't venture into the arena anymore but are content to live our lives in the stands. We let age take over and allow ourselves to grow pessimistic, bitter, and fat while telling lies about how wonderful we are. But we aren't anymore. I wasn't ready for that, not yet. When Jim offered me this job, I couldn't wait to get back to real flying. This is where I need to be right now, Johnny."

John was intrigued Fred hadn't given him a flippant answer. He'd never heard Fred speak so eloquently before. "I see. You ever wonder about the day when you can't fly anymore, Fred?"

Fred was silent, and John thought maybe he'd asked a question he shouldn't have.

"No, I don't. I guess I just don't want to think about it."

John nodded.

"So, Johnny, let me ask you. Why are you here?"

"Jim came to me and said he needed me."

"Yeh, I got that. But why are you really here?"

John had been asking himself that very question all morning. "I guess I wanted to prove myself to myself one more time before I really got old, and Jim allowed me to do just that."

Fred's face turned devoid of its normal youthful elan as he asked, "Why do you need to prove yourself to yourself again, Johnny? You've checked those blocks more than most of us. You don't need to do that again. You've got a lot more years left in you. Don't waste them doing this kind of shit. Don't get me wrong. I'm damn glad you're here with us on this one, running those damn gorillas of yours. But you've got too much life left to live. There's too much risk for you here doing this kind of shit from now on. Of all people, you should let the past go and focus on the now."

"I know, Fred, but . ."

"No buts," Fred said, but then he stopped trying to determine what he truly wanted to say. "Are you running away from something by being here? From the pain?"

John was speechless as Fred's words squarely hit him. It was as if Fred had looked deep inside of him, through the chaff that filled his thoughts and feelings and maybe hit upon the essence of what John was searching for.

Fred was silent as he watched John sift through what he had said.

Finally, John said, "Maybe."

Then Fred said, "Dying's easy. It's living that's hard. That's what takes courage. And you got too much courage, my friend, not to live. Let's get this one behind us. Then when you're done, decide what the rest of your life is going to look like."

John appreciated Fred's uncharacteristic seriousness for a change. He wondered if Fred had given him what he was searching for. He smiled to himself, contemplating that of all his friends, Fred, who seemed to be the most lighthearted one, had the deepest of insight.

"OK, Fred. I'll think about that. But what about you? Shouldn't you do the same thing for the day when you can't fly anymore?"

Returning to his mirthful demeanor, Fred said, "Yeh. When I'm 90, I'll start thinking about it."

John smirked. "Of course. Certainly not before 85."

"OK, Johnny, if you don't have any more questions, I've got to work on reviewing my auto-rotation drill." Fred then pointed to his phone near John and asked, "Can you put on the song listed as "Orgasm" so I can get started?"

"Sure, Fred. Whatever you need."

John did as Fred asked and left him to his work.

He then returned to his small beach cottage to review some training notes.

Not long after he returned to his cabin, there was a knock at his door.

When John opened the door, he found Munoz waiting with the beating he'd taken that night still prevalent on his face.

"Sir, may I come in for a minute?"

John motioned for him to enter.

After closing the door, Munoz cleared his throat as his eyes wandered the floor, searching for his opening words while John patiently waited.

Finally, Munoz looked up at John and said, "Sir, I saw a lot of what happened the other night when you came to get me. And, ah, what I didn't see, Saunders and Jimenez told me. Ah, I wanted to say thank you. If you hadn't come to get me, well, I probably wouldn't be here."

Munoz paused. His eyes resumed their anxious exploring, again trying to figure out what to say next.

"Sir, I've got my bags all packed. I just wanted to say thank you. No one has ever looked out for me like you did, and I owe you at least that."

"Where do you think you're going?"

"Sir?"

"Are you quitting?"

"No, Sir, not exactly. But I understand what I did. There's no excuse I can give you for my actions."

"Tell me exactly what you did?"

Confused and without his usual arrogant pride, Munoz answered, "I've threatened the security of the mission. I broke curfew and disobeyed your orders. I've failed in my obligations to this company, just to name a few."

"You're Goddamn right you threatened the security of this mission! If word of what we're preparing to do here gets loose, the mission is scrubbed! Those hostages will pay with their lives for your stupidity!"

Munoz hung his head and whispered, "Yes, Sir."

John was silent.

"But, Sir, I swear I didn't say anything about the mission. And no one asked. You've got to believe me!"

John remained quiet, letting Munoz boil in his conscious for a while.

Then, believing his fate was determined, Munoz was ready to leave. He needed relief from the torment of John's silence. "Well, Sir. I said what I wanted to tell you. I'll find a ride to the big island and get out of here."

"Do you want to stay?"

"Stay?"

"Yes. Do you want to stay and be a part of this mission?"

Munoz didn't believe what he was being asked. "Yes, Sir. But, how?"

"I'm going to level with you, Munoz. You are a very tactically proficient operator. You have two critical things most of the guys around here lack, initiative and experience. But you are also an arrogant son-of-a-bitch who has a problem adhering to authority. I don't know why that is. Maybe it's in your nature. Or maybe it's because your leaders failed you in the past. Well, I can't fix the past, and this ain't the past. You're on my team now, and on my team, we all take care of one another. If we can't trust each other to take care of one another in combat while we do whatever it takes to get the mission done, then we can't be on the same team. In this case, that means you're out. Can I trust you to do those things without question?"

Munoz thought. John had gone up against three monsters to bring him back and undoubtedly saved his life. He'd put it all on the line for Munoz, despite the way Munoz had acted. No one had ever done that for him before, and especially no senior officer. Munoz couldn't say no. "Yes, Sir. You can trust me to do that."

"Then you stay."

"Are you serious? You'll give me a second chance?"

"Yes, I will."

Munoz's eyes danced with enthusiasm. "I don't know what to say."

"But know this. I'll be on your ass 24 hours a day. I will expect nothing less than perfection from you from here on out. If you as much as walk one inch out of line, your ass is out! No mercy, no questions."

"Yes, Sir!"

"We clear about that?"

"Crystal, Sir!"

John cracked a grin. "OK, then get your ugly ass out of here. I'll see you tomorrow morning at training."

"Yes, Sir!"

With a new lease on life, Munoz thanked John and rushed back to unpack.

No sooner had John closed the door behind Munoz, there was another knock on it.

"What the fuck!"

This time, Jim walked in. "I see someone is enthusiastically running back to their room. You had your talk with our problem child?"

"We came to an understanding. I think I just picked my new team leader."

"I see. Well, let's hope we've got that fixed. Oh, doc asked how your head was feeling?"

"It feels like Godzilla just finished round two on me. Does that answer your question?"

"That's what I figured. Well, you need to get better faster. I think we're going to get our break."

"Yeh? When?"

"We've got SIGINT intercepts saying they may be moving the hostages in the next two to three weeks to a location we can get to. Will you be ready?"

"Do I have a choice?"

"No."

"Then we'll be ready."

"That's what I need to hear." Jim patted John on the shoulder and said, "Good night, buddy."

John wished Jim good night and saw him out.

Standing in the doorway, John reflected on the day, his daydream about Lisa, Fred's words, Munoz's redemption, and the mission. Was he where he needed to be? He wondered.

Chapter 8

As John opened the heavy door to the exterior bulkhead and walked out onto the edge of the carrier flight deck, he felt the surge, knowing the time had finally come. The moment he walked outside, the strong wind hit his face, and he smelled the salty spray of the ocean. It was dark but light enough to see the unfolding operations as the flight deck crew darted about. He watched as each person deliberately moved in the closely orchestrated preparation for mission launch. He'd never been on an aircraft carrier before. It was huge.

He glanced at his watch, 22:40 hours. *Ten minutes to load time.*

John looked out past the edge of the deck and saw only darkness. He felt the slight balancing of the deck and the sensation that no matter how big this ship was, the sea was still its master.

Looking out on the flight deck, he saw three VL-25 tilt-rotor helicopters in the center. Directly behind those was a UH-70 with its counter-rotating rotors and push propeller already spinning. If any problems during take-off required the VL-25s to ditch, the UH-70 was ready for immediate rescue. It was only a matter of minutes now before it began.

As he stood waiting for the helicopter crews to man their aircraft and his men to link up with him, he stretched his right hand in his skin-tight glove, trying to release the anxiety he was feeling. The deck officer told him the flight deck would be loud and that wearing his helmet was mandatory once he exited onto the carrier's deck. But he'd already grown used to wearing it and the advantages of its combination of amplified hearing and noise reduction. So far, it proved to be a massive improvement over the old days when a Soldier carrying a radio for him shadowed his every movement.

He wore his clear visor down. His vest bulged with his protective armor plates, front and back, ammunition, grenades, knife, first aid kit, extra batteries, water camel on his back, and an old fashion compass and map stuffed in his cargo pockets of pants just in case. He trusted technology only so far. His rifle hung in front of him, cradled by his right arm and by a strap around his body.

John was glad he had his long insulated underwear on. The wind whipping underneath his visor onto his face had a bit of a sting to it. But despite the cold, he was sweating from the tension he felt growing within.

He laughed to himself as he reflected that the infantry's lot never changed even with all the advanced technology. He had tried to strip their average combat load down as much as possible, and the set of load-bearing exoskeleton that he wore helped with the weight a lot. But he still felt slightly worn with the equipment he had on. *I guess it doesn't matter what century you fight in; if you're infantry, you're going to carry a lot of heavy shit,* he mused.

But there was one thing he brought with him, no matter how much weight he carried. He touched the pouch on the top of his vest and poked his finger inside until he felt the envelope. It was there. Inside was the letter Lisa had written to him when he deployed to Iraq as a battalion commander. He'd kept it all these years inside that envelope and could still smell a hint of her perfume when he pulled it out. He remembered how close he felt to her after reading it. Whenever he had trouble sleeping while deployed or on a dangerous mission, he carried it with him. It made him feel as though she was beside him. If there was ever a time he wanted her near him, it was now.

Just then, he felt a hand slap him on the back. He turned, and despite the large flight helmet and bulky flight suit, he could still see that unmistakable smile with flawless white teeth.

"Johnny!" Fred cried out.

Despite John's anxiety, Fred's smile was contagious, and John felt one prance upon his face. "Goddammit, Fred! You scare the shit out of me when you do that!"

Fred laughed. "You ready?"

"About as good as I can be. I guess. How about you? How are you feeling?"

Fred's smile only grew more prominent. "On top of the world, my friend. Couldn't be better."

John shook his head. Fred was already in the zone.

John glanced toward one of the vertical lift aircraft. "What's that shit hanging under the wing of your bird?"

"Missiles. I might need those to bail your ass out tonight!"

"Well, how the hell you gonna shoot those when the props are forward?"

"Johnny, Johnny. Don't worry about that. Some rocket scientist has it all figured out. Besides, you just leave the flying to me."

John shook his head again and grinned. "OK, Fred."

"Can I give you a piece of advice for tonight, old buddy?"

"Sure."

Fred put his hand on John's shoulder, looked right at him, and said, "Try to enjoy yourself tonight, Johnny."

John stared at Fred as though he had lost his mind.

Then Fred patted John on the side of his arm. "Gotta get going. Hurry up and get those hairy assholes of yours on board. I ain't got all night. Got to get back early for this date I got with a hot lieutenant commander." Fred then turned and started walking to board his aircraft.

John laughed and yelled at Fred as he walked away, "You just get my ass there and back, Mr. Hot Date!"

Fred raised his right hand with a thumbs-up as he continued to walk. "Piece of cake, old buddy!" He then walked up to the tilt-rotor VL-25 aircraft, admiringly looking it over. The engineers had done well, he thought. She was the hottest rotary-wing aircraft in the air these days, and Fred had made her his. The smell of aviation fuel filled his nose, and the sounds of the engine prep gave him that familiar feeling he craved.

He crawled inside the cockpit and closed the door. His copilot was already strapped in and checking the instruments as he went through the lift-off checklist.

Fred strapped himself in and tightened the straps a little firmer than usual. He wanted to be a part of her on this trip, feeling every movement she made.

He plugged his helmet connections into the aircraft, and the radio came to life. He scanned the numerous lighted dials, buttons, and indicators. The various colored lights created a stunning array that spoke to him. Having memorized what each one was for, he looked them over and was satisfied with what they told him.

He took a cable connected to a small device in his thigh pocket and connected it to one of the auxiliary receptors on the center console. When the time would come, he'd need his music.

Fred reached out and gradually wrapped his hands around the control wheel in front of him. As his fingers closed their grip around the controls, he tightened his grip. It wasn't just the feel of the soft leather in the palm of his hands as much as the feel of the power it controlled, the anticipation of flight, and those sensations that defined what flying had always been to him. Freedom. Every fiber in his body instantly came to life. He felt his body drink the adrenaline pumping into it, begging for more to come as he let out a long deep breath, enjoying the rapture he was experiencing.

When his lungs emptied, a thought came to him. He'd run across it before and had put it aside. He couldn't change the past. But lately, he'd found the thought coming back more and more.

Fred reached in his pocket and pulled out an old photograph, and placed it in the clear map holder on his knee pad. He took a long look at the smiling young woman looking back at him. Her blonde hair, brown eyes, and happy expression brought back many memories from the distant past, mostly good but ultimately missed opportunity. *Yeah, sweetheart. I think I should have taken you up on your offer way back then. You were the one*, he reflected.

He felt his copilot poke him in the arm with the checklist and indicate all was ready, bringing Fred back from the past.

He took the checklist, looked it over, and flipped a switch. The big propellers started to turn, and soon they were blocking out all noise except for the radio transmissions inside Fred's helmet.

"Chief, we're clear to load," he said as he continued to flip switches and monitor his instrument panel. By now, he was relaying his status to the flight control and mentally going through his own checklist beyond the one on paper. His mind had forgotten all about the young lady staring up at him from his knee, reaching out from the past and asking a single question. Why.

By the time Fred was at the aircraft, John's team members had started to exit the bulkhead and line up near him as they waited for the signal to load.

Each man was equipped like John, and to the untrained eye, they almost seemed identical. But not to John. As in the days when he commanded Soldiers, John knew his men's characteristics and recognized each one simply by how they stood.

He then began what, for him, was a ritual. He walked up to the first man standing near him, patted him on the arm, and said, "You ready, Frank?"

"Yes, Sir."

"OK, remember. Report the moment you have contact."

"Yes, Sir."

John gave him a good luck squeeze on the arm and went to the next man. It was the same. He asked a question so when the man responded, he could gauge his mood, give encouragement if needed, and provide last-minute guidance. As he walked the line, his mind wandered back to that first combat mission in Afghanistan. He could still feel that morning cold so long ago and see the looks in the eyes of those young men. He'd forgotten many of their names years ago, but not their faces and especially, not their eyes. Those images he could never forget.

Finally, he came to the end of the line. "How do you feel, Munoz?"

"Nervous, but good. I'm ready for this, Sir."

John did not doubt it, as Munoz stood confidently. But he knew even in the most confident men lurked a fear of the unknown. To be otherwise would be foolish.

"Good. Violently in and swiftly out. Nothing more, nothing less. And, the moment you think you need help, let me know."

"Got it, Sir."

"And one more thing," John said as he looked directly at him.

"Yes, Sir."

"Be careful. OK?"

John's tone told Munoz his concern was genuine. He smiled. "You too, Sir."

"Thanks."

Then a deck crewman walked over. "OK, let's line up on the flight line edge opposite your bird. We will load in three minutes."

The team members then moved to their assigned locations.

John was walking to his position when a man came up to him.

John smiled as soon as he recognized Jim.

"How do you feel? Nervous?" Jim asked.

"I don't think you ever get used to this part. I'm sure my stomach will be in my throat until the moment we land back here on the deck," John said, unconsciously flexing his right hand again into a fist.

Seeing John's hand out of his peripheral sight, Jim nodded. "Everything is set from this end."

"Sounds good."

"Sir! We're loading," Munoz yelled out to John.

John waved to let Munoz know he had heard him. He then turned and stuck his hand out to shake Jim's hand.

Jim ignored John's hand, pulled him into a hug, and quietly said. "You take care, brother."

John squeezed Jim's back with his free hand and quietly replied, "Thanks, brother."

Jim released John, and John turned and started to walk to his aircraft. Suddenly, as if he had forgotten something, he quickly turned back to Jim and opened his mouth to say something.

But before John could speak, Jim already knew what he was going to ask, and spoke before John. "Sara won't want for anything. I swear I'll take care of her."

John smiled. Jim knew him well. Sara would be in good hands should anything happen to him, and with Jim's reassurance, John released her from his mind. It was time to focus totally on the task ahead.

He turned back and walked up to the aircraft. As he got closer, he felt the buffering of the prop blast from the spinning blades as the engine noise got louder but still manageable because of the noise reduction qualities of his helmet. Each step brought both confidence and anxiety, as each breath brought relief and fear.

The crew chief met him at the aircraft door and ushered him inside.

John made his way through the crowded dark aircraft, finally lowering himself into his seat. He grabbed the strap buckles and quickly connected them to strap himself in.

He heard the door shut, and the darkness deepened as he leaned back and settled into his seat. Soon he felt the seat vibrate as the engines repped up to take off. It wasn't long now.

But as John sat in his seat, anticipating the aircraft's lift-off, a thought occurred to him. He was exactly where he needed to be. He felt as if everything he had done in his life, all of the training, combat, and experience he had accumulated, had somehow prepared him for this moment. It wasn't that the fear in him went away, but a feeling that all the twists and turns in his life had brought him to this time and place to do what he was about to attempt. John had never felt this way before and wondered why he felt this way now.

He brought his hand to his chest and placed a finger inside his pocket until he felt the edge of the envelope.

He closed his eyes. *Lisa.*

Chapter 9

When the aircraft ramps dropped and the team members departed into the darkness, the race to rescue the hostages quickly began. The aircraft John was on, and a second one had come in low, landed, exited the team, and were gone in seconds. A third VL-25 flew nearby. The carrier's distance from the mission location was so far apart that any requirement to replace one of the aircraft carrying the mission team would take almost hours at best. Hence, a backup aircraft was part of the original mission package.

John sat with two other team members who formed a small reserve as he received updates from the men on the ground and relayed any critical assessments to Jim and the command crew back on the carrier.

The more the operation unfolded, the more John felt his excitement rise. It had been almost 20 years since he had participated in a combat operation, and as much as he hated to admit it, he missed it. His mind had been trained to a fine edge, to receive information rapidly, process it, and make instant decisions in uncertain situations. But, since he had retired from the Army, he had done nothing like that.

Now, he was in overall command of a desperate rescue mission far from any friendly presence with lives hanging on to his every decision. It surprised him how quickly he had regained his mental agility and rapid decision-making process during the training, and by now, it was second nature to him again. The adrenaline flowing through his body was tempered by years of experience. Knowing he had trained his men hard also offset a lot of additional worry in addition to having Fred as his wingman. Fred's experience and expertise made a huge difference, allowing John to focus on the ground mission. John trusted Fred like very few other men. He was the perfect wingman for a mission like this one.

From the moment they approached the mission location, John's confidence grew, and he felt he was where he needed to be. For a second, he remembered Fred's words back on the carrier to "enjoy himself" and wondered if that was what he was doing.

The moment the troops hit the ground, they moved quickly, taking the terrorists by surprise. The initial action had been quick and violent as John's team converged and attacked from several directions. Within minutes, the team killed most of the terrorists, and the few remaining fled or were too disoriented to fight back. Now came the search for the hostages.

John monitored what he could of his team from the video feed of two circling drones on his helmet visor's heads-up display. After being on the ground for a full fifteen minutes, he had not heard anything from Munoz regarding finding the hostages.

Soon, he started to feel a little nervous. He needed to get the team back on board shortly. The extreme distance had pushed the VLs to their range limit, and the time allotted for the ground mission was no more than forty minutes, so they would have enough fuel to make it back. Yet, John remained confident they would find the hostages. He had come to trust Jaimie's intel analysis, and if she was convinced the hostages were here, then he was too. It was only a matter of finding them.

"Tactical net," John said to automatically switch his microphone to the radio frequency to talk to the team on the ground. "Raider 5, Raider 6. Have you found the packages yet?"

"Negative 6. Still looking."

"Look, we're starting to run out of time here."

"Roger 6. We're checking out the last building now. Stand by, Raider 2 is heading this way."

John held his breath, hoping Munoz had good news.

"Raider 6, Raider 5. We got them!"

"Awesome, 5!"

"Wait. Stand by."

John held his breath again.

"6, this is 5. We got two of the packages. Both male. Negative on the female."

Fuck! John thought. They could recover the two they had and claim mission success. But John's insides twisted. He knew what the terrorists would do to the woman if they failed to recover her, assuming she was still alive. He couldn't let that happen, but he was running out of time, and the longer they stayed, the more he put his team in danger.

"Raider 5. Is there any other place you can look?"

"Negative 6. We've covered all of the buildings here. Negative info on any further leads."

"Roger. Stand by."

Then John heard Jim from back at the carrier say over his radio, "Raider 6, this is Guardian. We've monitored your conversation with Raider 5. Great job! We need you to begin exfiltration now. Over."

Great. Now I got the guys back at the carrier listening to my tactical comms. Dammit! I'm one short! But I have nowhere else to look. "Roger, Guardian. Stand by."

John thought hard about last-minute options but came up short. With nothing else he could do, he decided to order the recovery to begin.

"Raider 5, Raider 6. Begin immediate movement to PZ. We'll be on the ground in ten mikes."

"WILCO 6."

As John sat back, he didn't have a good feeling at all about leaving behind the third hostage even if he had no idea where she could be."

Fred came over the radio and said, "Raider 6, Warbird 6. John, take a look at the video feed from Nightstalker 2. Tell me what you see."

John quickly switched the video feed in his heads-up display to the second drone. He saw a building about a mile away from the compound they had just raided. Several persons were getting out of an SUV and seemed to be forcible taking someone out of the back seat and making them go inside the small building. The video footage was not entirely clear, but there was little doubt in John's mind some of the terrorists had managed to take someone from the raided compound to a safe location nearby. He began to get excited about what he and Fred had found.

"Aircraft Intercom," John said so he could switch his frequency to talk directly to Fred on the aircraft internal communications link that no one outside could monitor.

"Fred, what do you think that was?"

"That was whoever the hell managed to escape Munoz and your boys taking someone who didn't want to go to a place far enough away that we might overlook it."

"That's what it looked like to me."

"Well, shit, John. That's your third hostage."

"Fuck! I think you're right. But we're running out of time, and you're running out of gas."

"Bullshit. I ran the mission parameters before we left for the third time. We have enough fuel for an additional twenty minutes on station."

John rapidly considered options. He was glad Fred was piloting the aircraft he was on. "Fred, what if we sent the backup bird and bird two to the PZ while we make a detour to get the third hostage? That guarantees the team is picked up and frees us up for an attempt for the third hostage? What do you think about that?"

"Exactly what I was thinking, old buddy. Let's do it!"

John didn't think twice. He told Fred to relay the change in plan to his aircraft while he coordinated with the guys back at the carrier.

"Command net," John said so he could talk directly to the command center on the carrier. "Guardian, Raider 6. We see a possible location for the third package from the video feed from Nightstalker 2. I'm ordering Warbird 2 and 3 to pick up Raider 5 and party while we swing down to check out this last location."

John finished his transmission and started telling the two guys on board with him about the mission change while he waited for a reply.

Back at the carrier, and unknown to John, the senior CIA officer, a man named Branson, who oversaw this mission, was on board. Having been the man who hired Jim's team to conduct this mission, he was essentially Jim's boss. Branson was in the carrier's operations center monitoring the mission progress with Jim.

Branson turned to Jim after hearing what John said and asked Jim, "What the hell is your guy doing? We're not going to stay there all night running around on some wild goose chase. We got what we need. Get those guys back now."

"Sir, I've been monitoring Nightstalker 2's video. Mr. Bradford is correct. There's a very good chance the third hostage is at the location he mentioned," one of the navy crewmen monitoring the UAS video station said.

Jim listened to the crewman and then turned to Branson. "If that's the case, we need to get that woman out of there. At least he can check it out. We owe it to the king to have tried everything to bring back his daughter."

"I'm not worried about the daughter. We have his son and the nephew. That is enough to accomplish the mission. We will tell him she was unlocated and assumed dead."

Jim stared at Branson. Jim never liked his condescending tone, nor did he ever like Branson, who he considered to be an arrogant ass. He could not believe what he was hearing and gave Branson an expression that said so.

Jim's demeanor made Branson angry, and he said with a firm tone, "Do I need to remind you the CIA is in command of this mission? Not you. Initiate the recall and deny the change of mission request. That's an order."

Jim hesitated. They had come so far, and he disdained Branson's callousness. But he was right. The CIA was in charge, not him.

He picked up the microphone and said, "Negative Raider 6. You are ordered to return now. The allotted mission time is up. No change in mission is authorized."

John heard the transmission, but it was too late. He had already made up his mind. He pictured the female hostage's family coming to him afterward and asking him why he had not recovered their daughter despite having an idea where she was. He imagined if that woman was Sara and how he would feel. His mind was made up. Before John replied, he had already given instructions to Munoz regarding the change.

"Negative Guardian. I've run this past Warbird 6. He approves the change. We're executing. If we run into trouble, Warbirds 2 and 3 will depart on schedule," John replied to Jim.

Hearing John's reply, Branson exploded. "Goddammit! I told you to tell that son-of-a-bitch the mission was over!"

Jim's patience with Branson was coming to an end. "He is the ground commander, and ultimately he is just trying to accomplish the mission we gave him. If the air commander on the scene has approved his change, we need to let them try. They have better situational awareness than we do."

"That's fucking bullshit! I am in command here, and you bastards work for me!" Branson yelled out. "Give me that fucking microphone!"

Branson grabbed the microphone from Jim and screamed into it. "Listen here, Bradford. You get your ass back to this location immediately, and I don't want to hear about any more changes. Do you understand?"

John's mind was focusing on implementing the changes to the mission, knowing his time remaining was precious. Hearing Branson lambasting him about his decision only strengthened his commitment. "Look! I don't know who the hell this is, but I'm not leaving here until I get that third hostage! I'm not leaving that woman with those animals down there! Do you understand? I'm the commander on the scene! Me and the air commander will handle this! Out!"

"Bradford! I'm the man ultimately in charge of this mission! Not you and not Jim! Get your fucking ass back here, now, or I will personally fuck you over!"

That was it. John had had enough. "Don't threaten me! I'll deal with you when I get back!" he yelled and then cut off his link to the command net.

"Bradford!" Branson screamed. When no reply came, he screamed again. "Bradford!

"He's cut the comms link, Sir," the seaman manning the communications station reported.

Branson threw the microphone to the ground, looked at Jim and yelled. "You are responsible for this! I hold you personally responsible for this cluster fuck!"

Jim said nothing. He simply stared back, and then a hint of a grin appeared on his face.

Jim's reaction surprised Branson. Then it came to him. "You knew he would pull this kind of shit! Didn't you? That's why you got Bradford. Isn't it?"

"I got Bradford because I knew he would do whatever it took to accomplish the full mission and not pull off something half-ass."

Branson fumed.

Back over the mission area, Fred spoke to John over the intercom. "OK, we've lost the element of surprise here, so I'm going to set down in three locations for a few seconds. The first and last time will be false insertions. You and your guys jump out on the second one. It's the closest to the target with the most cover and concealment to the building. We'll confirm a PZ after you grab the hostage."

John replied, "Don't hold up Warbirds 2 and 3 after they pick up the team if we're running late. They need to get out of here. If we fuck this up, I don't want them to pay for our mistake."

"There won't be any mistake, Johnny. You just handle the ground mission and leave the flying to me."

"OK, buddy. You got it."

"Give me five minutes, and we will do the first false insertion."

John felt the big aircraft bank right a little quicker than he thought possible. Fred was deep in the zone now.

In the operations center onboard the carrier, a civilian who accompanied Branson and had been monitoring a laptop computer near him said, "Sir, I just got an ELINT hit. The SAM system is definitely there and now operational."

Jim turned to the civilian, "What SAM system?"

The civilian looked at Jim and then looked at Branson.

Jim asked again, but this time forcibly. "I said what SAM system? Is there an operational SAM system down there?"

Branson answered, "Yes. There's a HQ-14 missile system down there that has just turned on and is operational."

Now it was Jim who exploded, "Where the fuck did that come from? You said there was no SAM threat with the very low possibility of maybe some shoulder-fired launchers. You never said anything about a major SAM system being present!"

"We concluded it was a very low probability it was there. The only way that system could be involved is if the Chinese are operating it.

102

Well, we were wrong, and that confirms for us they backed this whole operation. That's why I wanted fucking Bradford out of there already."

Jim shouted, "Why didn't you tell us this from the start? We don't have anything to counter that kind of SAM threat loaded as part of this mission package. There's no way they can fly away from that kind of threat! They're sitting ducks out there!"

While Jim and Branson were discussing the new threat, Fred was about to land at the first false insertion point. He then called to John. "Well, buddy. This shit just got more complicated. I got an ELINT hit on my warning system. Looked like one of those high-speed Chinese systems."

"What? Holy Fuck, Fred! No one said anything about a SAM system being here! Do we need to abort the mission change?"

"Negative! But I've got to take this thing out. The moment we gain altitude, they will nail us all, and the ECM we have loaded is for shoulder-fired heat-seeking missiles, not the big radar-guided stuff. You jump out at the next insertion point. Follow through on the ground as we planned. I've got an idea I'm going to try."

"Fred, can't we just stay low off the ground and fly out?"

"Can't do, old buddy. Ground fire could surely take us out at that altitude. Plus, flying that low, we won't have the fuel to make it home. Just get the final hostage, and I'll get you. And also, I'm throwing my copilot out. He'll help you coordinate the PZ after you're mission complete."

"I don't know about this, Fred. This new threat was not part of the plan."

"Johnny, what did I tell you in the beginning? Just relax and enjoy yourself. This is just like being back in the stan again."

John shook his head, but Fred was right. John had to trust his judgment for the air mission. He might be a crazy flyer, but he had pulled off miracles when they were both deployed to Afghanistan with the 101st Air Assault Division back in 2002. The only thing John didn't understand was why Fred was putting his copilot on the ground with them. He had an idea, but there was no time to argue. The mission was evolving so fast that he had to trust Fred to handle the air part while he took the two men left with him and now Fred's copilot to get the final hostage. "WILCO."

Just then, Jim called to John. "Raider 6, Guardian. We've got a SAM system in your AO. You need to abort now and return."

Hearing it was Jim's voice on the radio, John decided to answer. "Negative, Guardian. We have to take that target out to get back.

103

Warbird has a plan. Will continue with mission change. I'm dismounting in three mikes. See you back at the ranch. Out."

Jim was about to radio back to John his concerns but knew it was useless. It was all in John and Fed's hands now. Jim whispered to himself, "Good luck, brother."

When John finished his transmission, Fred said over the intercom. "I'm setting her down now. You got 10 seconds to get off my bird. GO!"

The back ramp was already down, and John felt the bump as Warbird 1 touched the ground. Instantly he ran out the back of the aircraft, followed by the two other men from his team and the copilot.

Waiting for John and his team members to disembark, Fred reached down and flipped a switch to the small box containing his music that he had plugged into his console. The Eagles' opening chords of "Take It To The Limit" started. *Perfect selection*, he thought.

Then Fred glanced down at the beautiful face looking up at him from the photograph strapped to his knee. Remembering what he had done and wondering where she was, he felt that old pain sting him again and questioned if this would be the last time.

He then jerked the collective up, and as the aircraft rose, he turned it sharply toward the next false insertion site. He didn't have a lot of time left.

John looked at his heads-up display on his visor and saw their position was perfect. It was directly behind a small hill so no ground fire from the building could hit the landing aircraft.

He crouched behind a bush and took a moment to get oriented. The night vision from his visor was a drastic improvement from what he worked with previously. While it still had a green tint, it was almost as clear as daylight.

The copilot came up behind John and touched his shoulder. "I'm going to make a quick survey and see if this will be OK for a PZ. I'll stay in contact with Warbirds 1, 2, and 3 and monitor your tactical ground net. Call me when you are ready, and I'll relay PZ instructions."

Despite whispering, John's helmet's sound amplification picked up the copilot's words, and he clearly heard them. He acknowledged the copilot's instructions and began moving forward with his two men toward the small building.

He heard Fred flying to the next false insertion point, and was confident the aircraft noise was drowning out any movement noise. However, he knew whoever was waiting for them had heard something possibly land nearby and would be looking in their direction, so he maintained caution.

"Jimenez, take the right flank and Saunders, stay on the left. We'll move abreast and let me know the moment you see anything," John told them over his radio.

The two men acknowledged, and they all deliberately moved forward.

Glancing constantly to his left and right, John maintained visual contact with the man on each side of him, ensuring no one got out in front if firing started.

It wasn't long, and he saw the building, which was not more than an old shack and an SUV parked nearby.

John crouched and froze the moment he saw someone run from the SUV to the shack. He took his time and closely scanned the area. He then saw what he thought were two heads looking over the SUV hood in their direction. He was pretty sure they could not see him from their lack of movement, but John was taking no chances. He remained motionless.

"Sir. Don't move. I can take the guy on the left out," Saunders said over the radio to John.

Then Jimenez said, "I'll take the guy on the right. On the count of three."

"Roger," John whispered and remained still.

"One, Two, Three." The moment John heard the word three over his radio, he saw two small, silent explosions as the heads of the two men jerked from the impact of the bullets. Their bodies sunk behind the SUV.

John waited to see if any movement would indicate any other terrorists in the area, but he saw none. He then stood back up and started to move toward the shack slowly. "Jimenez, stay in overwatch. Saunders, move forward with me."

He had just given his orders when he heard what was undeniable a woman's scream over his amplified ear system coming from inside the shack. The shout startled him, and he worried if the female hostage died in the next few seconds, their effort would be wasted. "I'm going in. Saunders, get up here!" John shouted over his radio as he broke into a run. He was not waiting any longer and prayed he still had the element of surprise on his side.

Running as fast as he could, he lowered his shoulder into the door and burst into the shack. John's vision blurred for a second from the transition from his night vision system turning off to accommodate the room's dim light. He looked around and saw a woman tied to a chair with two men standing on either side of her. For John, the next five seconds flew by as the men's heads turned with surprised looks on their faces, followed by their bodies turning until they both fell from shots from his rifle.

The woman screamed again, and John immediately turned all around, looking around to see if anyone else was in the small room. There was no one else.

He turned back to the woman and walked toward her. The woman's eyes were enormous with a horrified look upon her. She shook her head and seemed to be pleading to John in Arabic.

As he approached her, he flipped his face visor up and waved with his hand. "It's OK! It's OK! I'm not going to hurt you. It's OK. I'm here to help you."

The woman stopped screaming, but her wide eyes remained glued to John, her body shaking with fear as he approached her.

John knelt beside her and tried again to calm her with a gentler tone. "It's OK. I'm here to rescue you. Do you understand me?"

Still shaking, the woman seemed to understand and nodded.

John pulled out his knife to cut the zip ties that bound her arms and legs to the chair, but the moment he brought it to her arm, the woman jerked back in fear. "It's OK. I'm just going to cut your zip ties. I promise I'm not going to hurt you. I swear."

The woman indicated she understood, and he cut her loose.

As soon as she was free, John heard firing outside the shack, and Jimenez said over the radio, "Sir, we got company. We need some help out here. If you and Saunders can pin the guys on the other side of the road down, I can quickly move and take them out."

"WILCO. I got the package, but I'm making her stay here in cover until we can clear the outside. Don't leave her if I don't make it. I'm moving now."

"WILCO."

John then looked at the woman. "Get down and stay here. I'll be right back."

The woman started to shake her head. "No! No! I go wit you," she said in broken English.

"No. You can't. Stay here. I'll be right back."

"No! No!" she said again as she grabbed him.

John held her by the side of the arms and told her, "Listen to me! Listen."

The woman calmed down and starred back at John.

"I promise you. I will come back and get you. OK? Trust me. I promise. OK?"

The woman shook but did not say anything. John knew she did not believe him.

"You have to trust me. We came this far to get you. I won't leave without taking you back. If you go out there now, you won't have any protection. I promise you! I will come back!"

The woman's eyes never left John's as she tried to decide if she could trust him. She had trusted men before, and they had all failed her, except her father. They had lied to her, cheated on her, and betrayed her. Only her father had protected her, and even that was not enough to keep her safe. And now, this total stranger who only moments ago freed her from her captives and from the living hell she had endured for weeks was her only hope. But there was something she saw in this man. His touch was firm but protective, his tone directive yet empathetic. Finally, she silently nodded.

John pushed her down onto the floor, pulled down his visor, and moved to the door. "I'm ready to head outside. Where do you need me?"

"Sir, take up a position on the other side of the SUV and orient toward the wall across the street. That's where they are. They've got Sander's pinned down by the trash heap behind the house," Jimenez said across the radio net.

John knocked out the lamp on the table as he moved toward the door. After he heard Jimenez's instructions, he ran out of the door toward the SUV and listened to the unmistakable sounds he had heard countless times of bullets flying near him.

He took a position behind the SUV and moved toward its rear.

He peeked around the corner of the bumper and, through his night vision, could see five men on the opposite side of the wall alternating shooting towards Sander's direction.

He calmly raised his rifle and leaned against the bumper of the SUV to steady his aim. He waited until two of the men raised and pulled the trigger. Both men lifelessly fell, and none of the others raised their heads. "I've got them pinned down. Get moving Saunders!"

"WILCO!"

He turned and saw Saunders run to the flank of the wall to get behind them and finish them off.

Suddenly three shots rang out, and John jerked back as he heard them hitting the metal of the SUV. They had discovered his position.

He crouched back behind the SUV and moved toward the front bumper to reposition himself so he could take a couple more shots before Saunders could get behind them.

When he got to the front bumper, he raised up just above the hood to see if there were any more targets along the wall. He saw four men rising from behind the wall.

WHEN LOVE PERSEVERES

He aimed at one and pulled the trigger. The man fell, but just as John moved his rifle to line up his next shot, there was a bright flash followed by a stream of light that led straight to the SUV. Seconds later, when it reached the SUV, there was a tremendous explosion.

John felt the concussion and heat from the explosion violently throw him to the ground. He felt his head hit hard against an object, and his body twisted with a burning sensation in his lungs. He began to lose consciousness as the sound of close battle instantly went silent. He felt himself on his back as the darkness grew. Sara flashed before his mind. She would be alone now. His last thought was his end had finally come. The life force from within seemed to fade away with his vision. Then, nothing.

But just as nothingness engulfed his world, he became aware of his breathing. His world remained black, but he was breathing.

Then a soft hand caressed his cheek, and he smelled a sweet fragrance and searched his mind for the familiar scent.

He opened his eyes and found himself staring into a pair of breathtaking blue eyes he hadn't seen in years. Lisa! Almost as if to convince himself she was there, he reached out and touched her face. His fingertips rejoiced with the feeling of her soft skin once again.

He cautiously called out, "Lisa?"

The ends of her lips slowly curled up into a sad smile, her eyes never leaving his. "I've missed you so much, baby. But it's too soon. It's not yet your time," Lisa cooed to him.

"What do you mean, it's not my time?"

She closed her eyes and pulled him in for a kiss. When her lips touched his, John felt a forgotten warmth in his heart, and felt all the pain in his life disappear. How long they kissed, he did not know.

Then, Lisa reluctantly pulled back and looked at him with the love he had desperately wanted since she died. "I'll be here, John. Remember, I will always wait for you." And then she was gone.

Then John felt the sensation of lying on his back again. The sweet fragrance was gone.

His eyes slowly flickered open as he tried to regain consciousness in the world he thought he had left permanently. The noise of the ongoing battle once again filled his ears, and smoke irritated his nose and lungs. His body ached. He slowly moved his hands and felt his body to determine if he was wounded. He touched his helmet and discovered it was severely damaged. His visor was cracked, and neither the radio nor the noise amplification feature worked.

He felt what he thought might be shrapnel embedded in his front vest.

He raised his head, looked around, and gradually sat up as the cobwebs from his mind finally began to clear. Then he remembered. Lisa! Where was Lisa?

He called out, "Lisa?"

There was no answer other than the sound of the fighting.

He anxiously looked around, and now he screamed her name. "Lisa!"

But again, no answer.

Then it hit him like a thunderbolt. She was not there. He was not dead. He had been taken from her, once again. The woman he dreamed of and missed for years, his soulmate had once again been taken away, and he was alone again. Her kiss had reignited the love he had remembered and longed for for so long. Yet it was not to be. It was only a reminder of what once was, but what was no longer. He felt the anger in him building, the hate, the indignation of being denied her love.

In a fit of rage, he screamed as loud as he could to try and release the pain inflicted on his soul. "Lisaaaaaa!"

His mind searched desperately for who had done this? Who had denied him her love once again? It was those who had tried to kill him. They were too incompetent to have completed their task, which would have reunited him with his lost love, and in his rage, he was determined to kill as many of them as possible. He fumed that they were too stupid to figure out how to kill him, but he was very capable of killing them.

With the energy of a madman, John jerked up.

He turned and looked at the doorway to the shack where the woman hostage was just as two men entered it, and he heard her scream out again.

He had no thoughts in his mind other than to kill.

He looked around for his rifle in what was barely enough moonlight to make out outlines and picked it up. He felt the barrel was damaged but picked it up anyway. Then, ignoring the pain he felt, he ran toward the shack.

He entered the shack and swung his rifle as hard as he could into the side of the first man's head. He heard a dull crack, and the man flew off to the side.

The second man was turning around and raising his rifle at him as John grabbed the rifle barrel with one hand and pointed it away from his body. He then quickly grabbed the man's neck with his other hand.

They briefly struggled until John slammed the front of the man's head against a column in the wall, and he felt the man's resistance weaken.

He then slammed it again and again until the man stopped moving and fell to the ground.

The woman, who had been hiding in the corner of the room, came out and clung to John. "We go now! I'm not leaving you again!"

John bent over to catch his breath. His pain was still held at bay by the adrenaline running through his body.

As he caught his breath, he looked at the woman and tried to assure her between breaths. "I told you . . . I was coming back . . . for you."

Despite the darkness, John saw the woman smile at him.

He then looked on the ground and picked up a rifle from one of the dead men lying on the ground. He pulled the charging handle back, and the gun successfully loaded another round. He then beckoned the woman to follow behind him.

She grabbed the back of his protective vest with one of her hands and held on.

When they came to the doorway, John stayed to one side and listened. The sounds of the fight were suddenly gone. It was almost silent.

He heard footsteps outside the door. They moved a few paces and then stopped.

John raised his rifle. He stopped breathing as he waited for the man to step into the doorway.

"Colonel Bradford," Saunders called out.

"Saunders. It's me."

John then exited the doorway, and Saunders and Jimenez were standing on the opposite side of the door.

"You OK, Sir? We saw that RPG hit the SUV and wasn't sure if you made it when you didn't answer your radio."

"Yeh. I'm beginning to feel like shit, but I'll make it back. What's the SITREP?"

"Munoz has linked up with the two birds. They're loaded, and they're waiting to fly over here and pick us up. That copilot has an LZ marked out about 300 meters from here across the way near the hillside. Warbird took out the SAM, so we need to get out of here ASAP."

"Why doesn't Warbird 1 just come and pick us up?"

There was an initial silence that told John something had happened.

"Sir, Warbird 1 got hit by the SAM site."

"What?"

"Yes, Sir. Looks like he got in their engagement arc so he could get them to light up their radar and take them out. He fired just before they fired, and they took each other out."

For a second, John did not believe what he was hearing. *Not Fred! No! He can't be gone! No way!*

But his mind jumped back with the realization they were still in enemy territory, and his first priority needed to be to get everyone out and back to the carrier. The mission was far from over.

"OK. Radio Warbirds 2 and 3 and tell them to meet us at the LZ."

John then turned to the woman behind him. "Here. Go with them, and I will follow you."

"NO!" she vehemently said. "I will only go with you!"

John didn't have the strength to argue. "OK."

He then turned back to Jimenez. "OK. Take the point, and I'll follow. Just remember I don't have my night vision anymore."

Jimenez acknowledged, and he and Saunders started moving forward.

When they arrived at the LZ, the aircraft had landed and were waiting for them.

John was the last man to load. Right before he loaded up, he asked Fred's copilot, who had set up the LZ and was waiting for them, "Are you sure Fred did not make it out?"

"Yes, Sir. He was telling me what he was doing as he did it. I saw the explosion as his aircraft got hit in midair. No way he could have made it out alive."

John was silent in disbelief as he felt the deep pain of losing his dear friend. Trying to think of what else he needed to do, exhaustion began to rob him of his focus. Finally, he concluded the only thing to do now was load up. Once they were airborne, there was nothing more he could do. Their fate rested in the hands of the pilots.

John boarded the aircraft and shuffled to one of the webbed seats in the dim red light of the cabin. The young woman he had just rescued still clung to his vest and sat beside him as he took his seat.

He glanced at the woman, and her face was still filled with fear. Nevertheless, he figured he had gained her trust, so she was sticking close to him no matter what.

When John felt the aircraft tremble as it took off, he tried his best to relax. But the memories of what had just happened flooded his head. The mission, his men, Fred's death, seeing Lisa, his almost death, it all rushed to him. He felt the anxiety and fear take him as it had many times before. His right hand began to shake despite his best effort to stop it.

Then he felt two small, soft hands take hold of his shaking hand.

In the dim red light, John turned and saw the young woman holding his hand with both of hers and looking at him. She smiled and whispered, "It is OK, my friend."

John was captured by a pair of eyes that gazed upon him with empathy. He returned her smile, then listened to his helmet radio for any traffic between the pilots and the mission command center. But as he sat and thought about her compassionate gesture, he squeezed her hands to say, "Thank You."

She continued to hold his hand until they landed safely on the carrier.

When John felt the aircraft make its soft landing, he finally relaxed for the first time since he started the mission.

The aircraft ramp lowered, and men slowly made their way out. John grabbed his gear and stood up. Every muscle in his body screamed at him as he walked down the ramp and toward the assembly area on the carrier flight deck.

All of a sudden, he grew dizzy. He stopped walking and took a knee to prevent himself from falling.

The woman, who John had rescued, ran over to him, bent down next to him, and put her arm around him. She asked in her accented English, "Are you OK?"

John took a breath and shook his head. "Yeh. I just got dizzy for a moment." He took a few more breaths, and then he stood up as the woman helped him. "Thanks," John told her.

Seeing something shiny had fallen on the deck next to John, the woman bent down and picked up a pair of dog tags. She looked at John to give them back to him.

He blinked his eyes and turned to look at the woman. It was the first time he had gotten a good look at her in the light. He was amazed.

A pair of beautiful dark eyes stared directly into his. Her hair was deep black, and her full lips were a lush shade of red, even without the benefit of lipstick. Beads of sweat slid down her olive skin that was otherwise clear of any blemishes. John blinked a few times to make sure he saw clearly. As disheveled as she looked, she was still a stunning woman.

She put the dog tags in one pants pocket, pulled a cloth from another, and patted his lower lip. "You're bleeding a little."

It took a moment before John could shake himself loose from her gaze. "Thanks again."

A dark-looking man dressed in a traditional Arab robe flanked on either side by two huge men wearing western-style suits walked toward them and stopped. The man spoke to the woman in Arabic, and the woman answered. It sounded to John as though they wanted her to go with them. The woman did not turn to face the men. After the man asked two more times with no reply from the woman, she quickly spun around and sharply spoke to him. All three men stiffened and then bowed their heads to her. It was clear to John the woman was someone of great importance.

She turned back to John and once again took him into her gaze. "What is your name?" she softly asked.

"John. John Bradford."

Hearing him answer her, she slowly raised her hand to him and wiped away the sweat from his face with her cloth. Her eyes never once left his. Then she slowly closed the gap between them and gently kissed him on his lips.

John stood still, unsure what to do but feeling his body relax as a wave of peace came upon him.

The woman then placed her arms around John and tightly hugged him as she whispered into his ear, "I shall never forget you, my prince."

She held him for a long time. When she finally released him, she kissed his hand and walked away with the three men.

As John watched her walk away in silence, he felt numerous emotions churn within him. He reflected upon his earlier feelings right before the mission when he thought his whole life had prepared him for this particular mission. Finally, only a single question remained in his mind. Why?

Chapter 10

John leaned forward against the deck railing at the rear of the carrier, watching the churning of the ocean from the massive propellers that mirrored the feelings within him. After waking up from a long-needed sleep, he needed a moment to breathe, to escape the confines of his cabin, reflect upon what had happened, and try to contemplate his future. The open ocean view before him was the perfect canvas for his thoughts. The familiar smell of the sea brought childhood memories of precious weekends at the Texas bays with his grandparents that served as a milestone to show him how far he had gone.

Only twenty-four hours prior, John and his team had returned from their rescue mission. Immediately after returning, he received a medical check-up from the team doctor to address any injuries, followed by a thorough debriefing of the mission. He told Jim and the doctor he just had a few bruises, but they both insisted on a medical check-up after hearing about the explosion that John survived.

When the debriefing ended, John finally got a chance to sleep. He slept a full ten hours, and when he woke up, he felt the muscle soreness in his body that told him it had gone through hell. He understood then he had pushed his body beyond its current limits and needed to take it easy for a few days.

He felt mixed emotions about the mission. First, it had been a huge success, and Jim was ecstatic. Even the grumpy CIA boss shook John's hand as well as many others. Before he left the flight deck to go to his check-up, an impeccably dressed Arab-looking man told him the Egyptian king had personally told him to relay to John he was forever in his debt for the safe return of his children. Having a daughter himself, the simple knowledge that the king would not have to suffer the loss of his daughter gave John his greatest reward.

However, Fred's death hit John hard. If there was one man to John that seemed always to defy the odds, it was Fred. While he was not as close to Fred as he was to Jim, Matt, Tom, or Jack, John shared a different kind of closeness with Fred. He was the one man who completely understood and shared John's love for combining the sensation of speed and music that brought an intoxicating invigoration. And if there was one man John saw as fearless, it was Fred. Now with Fred gone, John felt a deep emptiness within him. But that emptiness was tempered, knowing Fred would not have wanted his death to be any other way. He knew Fred lived to run against the wind. Fred was not a man who would ever go quietly in his sleep. Jim told John they would hold a memorial service for Fred, but John told Fred goodbye as he looked out onto the waves from the big ship's wake.

However, despite Fred's loss, John felt good about the mission and what he had done. He had taken the reigns of a dedicated group of young men and put his impression upon them. His training and gut feeling about each of his men and the mission had paid off. His instincts to take a chance to find the last hostage succeeded in bringing them all back alive. Even the complication over the surprise over the SAM system did not keep them from success if one could accept Fred's death. Knowing Fred as John did, he could hear him saying, "it was just my time to go and the price for success – no big deal."

Reflecting on his short encounter with the king's daughter, an Arab woman of obvious importance, John hoped he could visit with her after he woke up from his rest. After getting dressed, he asked about her and was told they flew her and the two male hostages off the carrier while he was asleep.

The young woman made a strong impression on John when she held his hand as it started to shake on the flight back, and he felt a deep sense of loss at not seeing her again. He wanted to thank her for her compassion and make sure she was OK. For some strange reason, he could not forget the simple kiss she gave him and the words she said as they walked off the aircraft together. The look in her eyes and her touch was reminiscent of Lisa many years ago. As absurd as it sounded to him since he was three times her age, he felt a compulsion to look into her eyes once more. But she was gone, and John felt sad.

Then John realized he had not felt an emptiness the whole time he was focused on the mission and working with his team. He also remembered he was not nervous when he boarded the aircraft for the mission as he had always been before previous missions. Instead, he felt then he was exactly where he needed to be. He wondered if perhaps this feeling was the key to his future.

At that moment, a voice behind him said, "I thought I might find you here. Did you have a good sleep?"

John turned around and said, "Hey, Jim. Yeh, I did."

"Good. I made sure no one bothered you. How are you feeling?"

"A little sore. Got a few bruises here and there. You know. The usual. But, hey, I got to sleep in a warm bed afterward, so I'm not complaining."

Jim knew John was referring to their time in Afghanistan when they were company commanders and went days without rest.

After a short pause, Jim said, "I wanted to take a moment just between you and tell you a few things. First, I'm sorry about Fred. I know you and him were close."

"Thanks, Jim. I guess I was as close as someone could get to Fred. He really never let anyone get very close to him, I think. He just had that air about him. You know, fly by the seat of his pants aura, a bit of a loner. But that guy could fly."

"I know what you mean. Fred had great respect for you. I remember I was talking to him before we got with you about someone to get the team in shape and possibly lead the mission. Without blinking an eye, he said, 'If you're truly serious, you need Bradford. He's the best."

Humbled, John nodded and turned to look toward the open ocean. "Well, I'm going to miss him. But honestly, that's how he wanted to go when his time came. If the day ever came he couldn't fly, he wouldn't have lasted long, so I know that was the best way for him to go."

"You're right. That crazy bastard wouldn't have wanted it any other way."

With a half-hearted laugh, John said, "No, he wouldn't of."

"John, I want to tell you how thankful I am for everything you did for us. We couldn't have pulled this operation off had it not been for you. We all owe you a great deal."

Embarrassed at the compliment, John dropped his gaze for a second and replied, "Thanks. You've got some great people working for you. I enjoyed working with all of them."

He then looked at Jim and joked, "It'll all make for a great book that I can write one day."

Jim arched an eye and said, "Oh, no! No book."

"I know. I know. None of this ever happened."

"Well, the Chinese know by now what we did, but we still have plausible deniability in the eyes of the world. At least for now, and we need to keep it that way."

"OK. But you owe me! I mean besides your sister's phone number and introduction."

Jim laughed. "OK. What exactly did you have in mind?"

"I've done some thinking. I want to come and work for you permanently. I'm sure you will have another operation going on before long. I'd like to be involved in them. I've got a few years still left in me. It's like you said when you recruited me to come along. This is where I belong, not sitting at home, wasting away. How about it?"

Hearing the enthusiasm in John's voice, Jim was sad about what his answer would be.

When Jim did not immediately respond to his offer, John felt uneasy. "What's wrong? You don't think it's a good idea?"

"John, that's the last thing I needed to talk to you about. I can't do that. As much as I'd love to bring you onboard permanently, I just can't do that anymore."

"What do you mean, anymore? Why not? Hell, you practically begged me to do this job."

"It has to do with your health. We were going to have the doc talk to you about it, but I might as well be the one to break the news. Doc got the results back from your MRI they did on your head when you returned. He could talk to you about it in medical terms of your brain and the plaque and tangle buildup in your neurons, but I'll just speak in English. You have had one too many concussions. It's to the point if you have any more, you may start ending up with permanent brain damage. We can't risk that, and neither can you."

"Wait a minute! I feel fine!"

"I know, and we want you to stay that way. I want you to stay that way."

"Come on, Jim. Don't pull the medical card on me now. Let me make that decision about the risks involved."

"I won't do that, John. I care about you too much. And beyond you, I care about Sara. I have to admit I had a few sleepless nights thinking about what it would be like to tell her her father was killed in some operation, and she was now without any parents."

"So, it's a big deal now, but not when you recruited me?"

"Look, I'll admit I probably pushed you pretty hard to get you here. I felt we needed you that bad, all things considered. When you got your MRI when you inprocessed, Doc mentioned possible future problems, but everything was OK then. I know he talked to you about it. But he was pretty adamant when I saw him a few hours ago. You can't afford any more blows to the head. Considering what happened this time, you're damn lucky to be alive, much less to have all of your marbles."

John knew Jim was right. He should have been killed by the explosion that knocked him down. But he already knew the reason why he wasn't - Lisa. But John wasn't going to say anything about that to anyone. He figured they would think he was crazy for sure if he did. "Well, what about if I worked for you but didn't go on missions?"

"We both know how you are. I could probably do that, but then you'll still find some damn way to go on those missions, one way or another. Tell me I'm wrong."

John sighed heavily. Jim was right. He could not send men to do things he would not or could not do. It was just in his DNA. Maybe he might grow into it one day, but not anytime soon. It was useless to argue with Jim.

But as John thought over what Jim said, that feeling he'd fought for so long crept in. He was old. Much too old and beat up to do the things he'd done in the past. Those days were finally over. Whatever spark of life that was in him suddenly left, and his life felt empty. The world had seemed at his fingertips just over 24 hours ago, preparing to go into battle once again. And for the first time, he felt he was truly ready. But now, that moment seemed like a lifetime ago.

"You OK, buddy?" Jim asked.

Snapped out of his trance by Jim's question, John looked at him. "Yes. No, you're right. I understand."

Then John put his hand out to Jim for a shake. "I owe too, Jim. I appreciate everything you've done for me, giving me another chance to be like we were. You had faith in me to let me run the show. I don't want you ever to think I am ungrateful."

Jim shook John's hand and said, "Sure, buddy. Anytime. And by the way, we got you set up to make a few phone calls back to the states if you want to call Sara and maybe Mary, so they don't worry about you being mysteriously gone. Just call the ship's operator, and they will hook you up with a line."

John smiled. "Thanks. I think I'll hang around here for a little while longer and then head to my cabin to make those calls."

"OK, buddy." Jim then patted John's shoulder and left him to his thoughts.

Turning back to the open ocean waters and looking at the large ship's wake brought John back in deep thought. *Where do I go from here?* he pondered. Looking back at his life, he would have a hard time imagining the young man that grew up in the small town of Victoria, Texas, would end up having spent his life as he did. The initial chance at love, the birth of a young officer in the Army, his growing into a combat proven leader of men, a renewed chance at love, facing death as often as he did, a young daughter that wanted to follow in his footsteps, the loss of his beloved, and a last chance of glory all ending on the back deck of an aircraft carrier was beyond what he had dreamed.

However, none of that reflection brought any answers to his original question of where to go from here. Sara was well on her way, and it was time for her to find her path. No need to babysit her anymore. Mary was doing fine with her family and new grandchildren. What would he do from now on?

He closed his eyes and turned to the person he always went to at times like this, his beloved Lisa. How he loved to do nothing more than lay in bed with her snuggled against him, her hand on his chest, during these moments of solemn thought, for her touch always reminded him he was never alone. He wished she was with him now. John then remembered what she'd told him on her deathbed, to do whatever he needed to do to be happy in his life and not worry about her. She'd always be waiting for him.

Then a thought came to him. *What did Fred say? Dying is easy. It takes courage to live. Hmmm.*

With that thought, an idea came to him. *Yep! Time to make a few phone calls.*

An hour later, John was finishing up his phone call to Sara. She was fine, filling his ear with stories about college and the new friends she'd made. She was looking forward to his next visit.

After he finished hanging up from talking to Sara, John scrolled through his numbers on his cell phone's contact list, hoping he still had her number. Finding it, he pushed dial and anxiously awaited to see if she would answer.

"Hello."

"Jennifer, this is John Bradford. How are you doing?"

"John! I saw you're name pop up on my phone, but I figured it had to be some mistake."

"Well, I hope you're not disappointed it's actually me."

"Of course not, silly! I was hoping it was you."

"Really?"

"Yes, really. Where are you? Are you in Victoria?"

"Ah, no, I'm not in Victoria. But I'll be back there in a week or so."

"Good. So, what have you been doing with yourself lately? Out saving the world again?"

John chuckled, "Something like that. Hey, I got a question for you."

"OK."

"What are you doing in two weeks on that Friday?"

There was silence on the other end of the line, and John felt a knot in his stomach grow. Maybe he had waited too long. Then, finally, she answered, "Nothing too important. Why?"

"How about you let me take you to dinner? If that fancy restaurant on top of One O'Connor Plaza is still open, how about we make a reservation for, say, seven?"

"Are you sure about this? I'd love to see you again, but you remember what happened the last time. My terms still stand."

"I'm sure, and I'm ready to meet your terms."

"OK, then, yes, that restaurant has reopened. Seven would be perfect, but there is one other thing that I would ask."

"What's that?"

"Is this the kind of date where you would consider breakfast at my house the next day?"

John laughed. She hadn't changed. "Well, that depends on how dessert goes."

"I have a feeling it will go just fine," Jennifer said with a sultry voice that got John's full attention.

"Sounds good. I'll call you as soon as I get to Victoria."

"Before you go. I really missed you, John."

"I'll see you soon. Goodbye."

When John hung his phone up, he felt like a high school kid anticipating a big date. But more importantly, he was a man waiting to start the rest of his new life.

PART THREE

SARA BEGINS HER JOURNEY

Chapter 11

MARCH 2030. Sara rolled over and awoke to the sound of the rolling waves occasionally hitting the beach and the slight whisper of the wind as it hit the screen on the open window. She opened her eyes feeling the soft silk sheets caress her bare body with the perfect combination of temperature and texture.

She blinked a few times, slowly outstretched her arms, and smiled as she basked in the afterglow of a full night of making love in the arms of a man who knew his craft well. The memory of the ecstasy she experienced made her close her eyes and take a deep breath as her body slightly trembled.

Sara raised her head and looked around for her lover. He was not in the room, but she did not worry. She wanted a few minutes to enjoy the morning alone. It had been just over a month since she had finally given in to the charms of a young man she initially despised.

James Beachman's reputation as the great-looking, bad boy, spoiled rich kid on campus preceded his first attempt to ask Sara out for a date. His candy red Ferrari always seemed to have the accompanying full-bodied blonde in the passenger seat whenever she saw it around the school. So, when he caught up with her in the student union and asked her out, she thought he was joking. She turned him down three times before finally accepting. Although she did not like his reputation, she secretly found his bad-boy antics enticing and had even snuck a few peeks at his handsome looks.

What she found on their first date was nothing she expected. Instead of dazzling her with an expensive, over-the-top evening, James bought her a hamburger meal, and they sat under a tree in the local park visiting and enjoying each other's company. No fancy dinner, no outrageous venue, no social media photos, just simple conversation that quickly turned into laughter. To Sara's great surprise, he didn't even try to lay a hand on her for the first couple of dates.

Soon, they had developed a trust between them, and James told Sara things he said he had never shared with anyone. From his tone and behavior, she believed him. Despite having had no intention whatsoever, she soon found herself falling in love.

Looking outside the large bay window, she saw a breathtaking ocean scene just beyond a pristine white sandy beach. In the distance, offshore fishing boats left in search of their prey. The seagulls glided across her view, and the palm trees waved in the breeze.

In the two days since she had arrived, Sara hadn't had a chance to look around too much. James had brought her to this Bahama paradise and occupied much of her time in the sheets.

Sara wondered what it would be like married to a man who could afford anything for her to live the rest of her life in luxury. Her wildest wish to be his command to fill; a large house, travel abroad, cars, clothes, whatever she wanted. But of course, she would reward him for his diligence.

She laughed to herself, thinking, *Oh my God, Sara! Listen to you! What would daddy think of me thinking like this?*

But Sara knew better. The things money could buy she did not care much for, although she had to admit she was tempted. No, a man who loved her above all else is what she craved.

Her thoughts were interrupted as James, dressed only in a towel around his waist as not to obscure his sculpted abs, walked into the room holding a tray of breakfast. "Good morning, beautiful! I hope you slept well."

Sara embraced him with her eyes as she replied, "The little sleep I got was good. But I see you are up early."

James placed the tray on the nightstand, sat on the bed's edge, and leaned toward Sara with his arm on her opposite side. "I got up and asked Daniella to make us some breakfast. I didn't want to disturb you."

Sara laid back on her pillow and stared into his captivating blue eyes. "That was awful nice of you. It's not every day I get to wake up in a tropical paradise with the ocean just outside my window and a handsome man bringing me breakfast."

James smiled. "It's the least I could do. It's not every day I get to spend the night with a goddess of love."

Sara chuckled. "How many times have you used that line before?"

The smile left James, replaced by a look of seriousness, love, and lust. "Never, because it's never been true before."

Seeing the seriousness on his face, Sara felt her heart skip a beat. "For some reason, I actually believe you."

"I hope you do, Sara, because it's true. I've never been with someone like you before. You are incredible."

Suddenly, Sara felt her guard slip away. From the moment she met him, he had broken the mold of all the previous young men she had met. Exceptionally bold, yet patient, caring, and tender were just some of the words that came to her mind as she looked at him. *Certainly, this Adonis would not settle for someone like me*, she had told herself many times.

Yet he had gone out of his way to pay her attention, treating her like a queen since they met. His invitation to spend the weekend at his family's Bahamas resort house came as a complete surprise to her. Despite her initial reservations, Sara accepted, and since her arrival, she felt like royalty. It all seemed like a dream of hers when she was a little girl. An actual prince charming had found her. But were his words true?

Even though Sara inherited her mother's beauty, Lisa, she always questioned herself about meeting her mother's high standards for looks. It wasn't that physical beauty was paramount to her, but down deep inside, she shared some of the insecurity John had always had about himself in those matters. In the back of her mind, those insecurities fueled the fear she was not worthy of someone special in her life. Hearing his words took those insecurities and fear away as no one else in the past had done.

"Do you really think so?" Sara bashfully asked.

"Yes," he said, his eyes never left hers.

Sara softly smiled back, her confidence returning. "Thank You." *He is telling the truth! He does find me attractive and desirable. He does really love me!*

"Are you ready for breakfast?"

Sara's expression transformed to a seductive look as she rubbed his arm beside her with her hand. She purred, "I was hoping we might start breakfast in a different way this morning."

The young man's eyes widened for a moment, then narrowed with lust. He took his free hand and slowly pulled the sheet down from Sara's neck, exposing her bare breasts.

Sara patiently waited as he began to lower his lips slowly.

Then a cell phone began to ring, and by the sound of the ring tone, James knew who it was. He raised his head with a disappointed look on his face and sighed. "Give me one second," he asked as he got up and went to the dresser to look at who was calling.

As soon as he looked at the caller ID, he ensured he was facing away from Sara so she would not see the scowl on his face. He then declined the call and shot a message to the caller, telling them he was in a meeting.

He then placed the phone back on the dresser and returned to Sara's side of the bed. "Now, then. Where were we?" he asked with a goofy look on his face. "Ah, yes! I remember now!"

Sara laughed at his antics just before round six started.

Walking up to Sara, who was standing outside her dorm, John hadn't had a chance to say anything before she yelled out, "Daddy!" and smothered him in a hug.

"Hey, Baby Girl! You OK?" John asked as Sara squeezed him hard.

Sara released him, flashed a broad smile, and replied, "Yes! Everything's wonderful!"

"Good. You seem to be in an exceptional mood today."

Still sporting her giant smile, Sara said, "Of course I am! I get to see my wonderful father, who I haven't seen in several weeks!"

John grinned. "You need some money, don't you?"

"No! I don't need any money. I'm just feeling super wonderful today," Sara said, placing her open hand on her chest as she addressed herself.

Then John saw it. "Whoa! What's that on your finger?" he asked as he held up and gazed at the massive diamond ring on Sara's finger.

Sara giggled. "Do you like it? My boyfriend gave it to me?"

"Boyfriend? What does this guy do? Go to college on the side while he manages some huge stock portfolio."

"No. He's a full-time student. His name is James Beachman. I've been seeing him for the past two months."

Looking at the huge smile on Sara's face, John knew she was smitten. Then he thought. "That wouldn't be Beachman of Beachman Electronics, would it?"

"Yes, Daddy. It is. He's Mr. Beachman's grandson."

"I see." John paused, picturing some wealthy playboy in his mind. But he knew Sara had a good head on her shoulders and was not easily impressed by simple good looks. He figured by her behavior she was in love. He didn't want to be pessimistic, but he still did not feel good about this. Before delving into the subject more, he decided it would be best to get settled in a quieter environment. Then he would press for more details.

"I want to hear all about it. But first, how about we get some lunch. I'm starving, and I thought I'd treat you to that new Italian restaurant that opened just off campus."

"Mario's Italian House! Oh, I'd love to go there! I haven't been yet! Let's go!"

Sara grabbed John's arm and practically drug him to his car.

Twenty minutes later, they were seated and had placed an order. Just after taking a sip of his sweet tea, John asked, "So, how long have you two been going together exactly?"

"Just over two months now."

"So, you two have been going together just two months, and he gives you a ring like that. This sounds like it's pretty serious?"

"Yes. I think so. Two weeks ago, I went with him to the Bahamas and stayed a long weekend with him at their private island there. Oh, Daddy, it was fabulous!"

"Bahamas? Sara, you left the country and didn't tell me about it?"

"I know. It was kind of last minute. It was only for the weekend. I was back late Sunday evening. We flew on their private plane."

"Was it safe?"

"Of course! They own the whole island. There was no threat of any kind of virus or anything like that. Everything is tightly controlled, and it's only for their family."

John blinked his eyes a few times, trying his best to calm down. *I can't believe this, Sara. You leave the country with some guy to go to some secluded compound, and you don't tell me? What the fuck?* Inside, alarms were going off, but he did his best to remain calm. He knew he had to handle Sara differently. She was not a child anymore. Still, he felt very protective of her. "Sara, I know you're an adult now. But please, in the future, please tell me before you leave the country like that again. OK?"

"I told you it was safe."

"I know, sweetheart. But if something ever happened to you . . . " John didn't finish his sentence. Thinking about the possibility of losing Sara rendered him momentarily speechless. The memory of the young woman he rescued on his mission and what she told him the insurgents did to her filled him with anxiety. *Sara doesn't understand what the hell can happen and how bad things can get. She just doesn't have a clue!*

Sara sensed John's uneasiness. Despite not wanting him to fear for her safety, John's protective attitude gave her a feeling of security. She understood these were not idle words. She knew if anything ever did happen to her, John would not stop until she was safe. Additionally, Sara knew if John felt that way about her, she could only imagine what he had felt towards Lisa. That devotion to the ones he loved made John the kind of man she wanted as her husband. The warmth of his concern for her softened any worry about being treated like a child.

"I understand, Daddy. I promise not to do that again without checking with you first."

John sighed and decided he had made his point. His tone softened, and he asked, "So, when do I have the pleasure to meet this young man that seems to have stolen my daughter's heart?"

Sara had watched John and saw the range of emotions going through him. She was very good at reading what he was thinking. She had expected the onslaught of questions but was happy when it did not appear.

"Daddy, I'd love for you to meet him! I've told him all about you, and he was impressed with everything you've done!"

"What are his parents like? How were they when you visited their island?"

"Well, they weren't on the island when we stayed the long weekend. I haven't met them yet."

Once again, the klaxon in John's head went off.

"So, you two stayed that whole weekend at their island, and they weren't even there?"

"Yes, Daddy. It was just the servants and us."

John tried to figure out the best way to talk to her about a subject he knew she would be sensitive about and get her to take things slow. "Sara, I know you've got a good head on your shoulders, so I won't preach to you. I . "

"Daddy, I know all about the birds and the bees! Remember, we had that talk a long time ago with the book and the pictures."

John laughed, remembering how nervous he was. "Yes, I know. I'm not talking about that." He paused again, trying his best to measure his words, but finally just gave up. "Look, dammit. I don't want my baby girl to get hurt here!"

"I know. But James is different. He's kind, sweet, considerate, smart, mature, and handsome, and just not at all like you would expect such a rich young man to be. He's different than any other guys I've been with. Being with him is a whole different world."

Fearing Sara was being swayed by not just his charm but also his wealth, John got even more concerned. He thought back to his discussion with Lisa at the Sonic that Christmas they met. He remembered her words clearly. *"I did all the things that society told me to do to be happy, but I never was."* Was Sara about to make the same mistakes as Lisa?

John was silent for a moment. He knew Sara knew about Lisa's past. Lisa had not held anything back from Sara in the letters she left in the box for Sara. His heart tugged at him as he thought about bringing up Lisa's failed past. But John understood Lisa would not want it any other way. She would not want Sara to fail in the ways she had.

"Sara, I know your mother told you in her letters what she did when she was younger. She would be the first to tell you the bright lights blinded her in her past. I'm not saying you're about to make that mistake. But I know the last thing Lisa would want would be for you to repeat her mistakes. I only say that because I know she would want me to."

When John finished speaking, he stared at Sara with concern. *I want to believe everything she's telling me, but I just don't know. Dammit, John! Are you just jealous because this guy is rich and can offer Sara the world at his fingertips? Would Lisa not want those things for her? No, Lisa would want her to find a man that loves her. That's what she would say. Sara is a smart girl. You need to trust her.*

Sar thought for a second. Then she looked up and saw the questions still in John's eyes.

She reached out and touched his hand and softly said, "Daddy, I understand what you and mom went through. I also know what you meant to one another, and I just want to find the same love you had for mom from someone for me. I think James could be the one. But I appreciate your concern for me and why. I wouldn't want it any other way." She closed her statement with a smile that tugged at John's heart.

When she looked at him like that, there was nothing he wouldn't do for her. "OK, baby girl."

Sara's smile grew, and before she or John could say anything else, the waitress had brought their food.

They then spent the rest of their lunch talking about things other than Sara's boyfriend.

When John finished his visit and waved as he drove back to Victoria, Sara reflected on his words about Lisa. He was right. Lisa had written several letters about her past mistakes, and Sara had been too overwhelmed by James to consider those things. But suddenly, it was as if Lisa herself was asking her many of the questions John had asked. Was James the kind of man she wanted to marry?

Chapter 12

MAY 2030 Strolling along the campus sidewalk in her uniform on a perfect afternoon allowed Sara to revel in the fantastic news she'd just gotten. She had just come from a meeting with the senior ROTC instructor. When she got word to go to his office, she was afraid she'd done something wrong, but soon after her meeting started, she realized she was wrong.

Sara heard the pounding of feet come up behind her and turned as her friend and fellow cadet, Jim, dressed in his PT gear, slowed down his afternoon run to jog alongside her. With a crooked grin and a little out of breath, he asked, "Well, how did it go?"

Sara couldn't contain the smile on her face as she replied, "Very well."

"Well, come on, Sara! Don't give me some BS answer. Give me the details."

Her smile grew. "Well, he said they've been very impressed with my performance, and depending upon how I do in Advanced Camp this summer, they're looking at putting me in a senior commander position for my senior year!"

"Aha, didn't I tell you!"

"But how did you know?"

Jim smiled and then took off running as he yelled back, "Cause I know things, Ms. Soon-To-Be Colonel Bradford!"

Sara shook her head. She thought Jim was a crazy guy, but she liked him. Thinking about what he said, she couldn't contain her excitement. *Colonel Bradford, Senior Corps Cadet! Oh, WOW! That would be so great! And dad would be so proud of me!* She couldn't be happier.

It was the end of her junior year, and she had advanced in rank and was doing exceptionally well within the Texas A&M Corps of Cadets. Her close cadet friends, like Jim, had been telling her the past couple of days she was in line for a big promotion, but she didn't believe them.

Now it was official, and just the thought she was being considered for the senior cadet leadership position in her senior year thrilled her.

But her excitement soon met with concern. The past two years she hadn't done much outside of her studies and ROTC. However, since she met James, that had changed, and she started to worry.

Every weekend was a new adventure with him, it seemed. Although Sara tried to focus on her studies and ROTC during the week, James had a penchant for dropping by and taking her out. It seemed studying was not a priority for him, which gave him a lot of free time. Unfortunately, her extracurricular activity had resulted in her not doing as well as she thought she should have on two recent tests. Naturally, Sara wasn't happy about that, but it was hard to tell James no when he flashed her that sexy smile of his.

As she walked along, the dialogue in her mind seemed to take over. *I love my ROTC time, and already I can feel myself doing things I didn't think I could do! I love the time I spend with my fellow cadets too. There are some great folks in the Corps. But I have to wonder if I'm doing the right thing. It's just being with James is a whole different universe, it seems. He's treated me so well these past months. When he first told me he loved me, I wasn't sure, but I am now. I can tell just by how much time he wants to spend with me. I think he could be the one. But what does that mean? What do I do if he asked me to marry him? Do I give up on an Army career? Come on, Sara! You have already come so far. No, I don't want to do that. I wonder what James would say if he asked me to marry him and I told him I wanted to still be in the Army? Maybe I'm selling myself short by only looking at an Army career? I just don't know.*

Sara's line of thought was suddenly interrupted by the high-pitched whine of a sports car coming up behind her she had heard many times before.

She stopped and turned around as the red Ferrari pulled up alongside her with the top down and the driver's arm outstretched over the top of the passenger's seat. "Excuse me, but I was looking for this super-hot chick I know. She usually walks this way to her dorm. Have you happened to have seen her?" James nonchalantly asked.

"Well, could you give me a better description, and maybe I could tell you if I saw her," Sara playfully replied.

"Sure. She's medium height with long, gorgeous legs. Long beautiful brunette hair when she wears it down. Dreamy blue eyes. Perfect lips. Oh, and a nice rack and super tight ass!"

Sara's eyes widened a little after his description. "No, I haven't seen anyone like that around."

"I see. Well, how about you get in the car with me, and maybe you could help me find her?"

Sara batted her eyes, put her hand to her chest, and said, "You mean little old me, get in that fancy car with a handsome man like you? Oh, I couldn't do that. I'm a Soldier. I have to walk everywhere I go."

James laughed and replied, "I think it will be OK just this once. I promise not to tell anyone."

"Well, if you insist, I could make an exception just this once," Sara said and then opened the door and got in.

After she got in, James reached over and gave Sara a quick kiss. "Hey, babe."

Sara smiled at James and said, "So nice rack and tight ass, huh?"

"Oh, yeh!" James said as he reached over with both hands and tried to pull Sara closer to him.

Sara brushed his hug off. "How about you keep both hands on the wheel, and I'll just sit here and look pretty?"

James gave an exaggerated pouty face and replied, "Oh, alright. Party pooper."

Sara laughed, and they took off.

"Why are you wearing that uniform and those boots?"

"I needed to wear it for my meeting with the senior ROTC instructor this afternoon. Why? What's wrong with my uniform?"

"It just looks so bulky. You need to wear something sexy."

"To show off my nice rack and tight ass, huh?"

"Yeh!"

"James, officers don't wear sexy clothes while they're on duty."

"Are you really going to do that? Be an officer?"

"Of course, I am! Why else would I be in ROTC if I wasn't?"

"I don't know. I thought you were doing it just for the scholarship. You should do something else."

"Like what?"

"Like be a model."

"A model! James, are you crazy? Even if I wanted to be a model, I don't even come close to being that pretty."

"I wouldn't sell yourself short, Babe. I've seen what's under that uniform. You could do it in a heartbeat."

Listening to James's single track of thinking since he picked her up was beginning to annoy Sara. "I've told you before how important being an officer is to me. I can't believe you're questioning me about it. Just a nice rack and tight ass. Is that how you see me??"

"Of course not! I was only joking, sweetheart."

"I want to do something with my life, James. I want to do the things the Army will allow me to do, like being a leader."

"Hey, I'm sorry. I didn't mean to get you upset."

"Besides, even if I could be a model, I don't want to be one."

"Sure, I understand. Hey, why don't you go inside and change, and I'll take you out to an early diner? We could stop first and get a few drinks and then go to a restaurant."

"I wish I could, sweetheart. But I've got to study for my chemistry test on Friday."

"Just skip it tonight. You'll do fine."

"I can't do that! I don't want my grades to drop. My ROTC instructor won't like it if he sees another bad grade in chemistry this semester. Don't you need to study?"

"Sometimes, but not tonight."

Just as James finished his last sentence, he arrived at Sara's dorm and parked directly in the no parking zone in front of the building. "Madame, we have arrived."

Seeing his antics had not made a good impression on Sara, James then said, "Sweetheart, I'm sorry if I annoyed you tonight. Please forgive me."

When he asked for forgiveness, Sara couldn't resist James's blue eyes; they always melted her anger. Believing James was genuinely sorry, she gave him a reassuring smile.

"Oh, I forgot to tell you. My parents are having an open house to celebrate their thirtieth wedding anniversary in two weeks. I'd love it if you came by the house to meet them. They live about an hour north of here. How about it?"

Despite all the time she'd spent with James, this was the first time he'd asked her to meet his parents. Sara wondered if this was the beginning of an eventual proposal.

"Sure! I'd love to come."

"Great! I can't pick you up and bring you. I have to be at the house for pictures before the event. I'll text you the address and make sure they know you're coming. I'll meet you once you get there."

"OK. I'll see you there."

James reached over and gave Sara a gentle kiss that tempted her to have supper with him after all. But she jumped out of the car and waved goodbye to him to stop her temptation.

As James sped away, Sara wondered again, *What am I going to do if he asks me to marry him?*

"Sara," Sara's cadet friend, Sandy, called out for the third time.

"What? What was the question again?" Sara replied after bringing herself back to the present.

"I asked, name the key commanders for the north and south at the Battle of Vicksburg. Remember. We're supposed to be studying for our history test next wcck." Sandy answered.

Sara thought as she stared out of her apartment window. The raindrops hitting the glass pane made it hard for her to concentrate as they lulled her back to her sullen mood.

When Sara didn't answer, Sandy turned off her tablet that contained her textbook and said, "OK, we're done."

"I'm sorry, Sandy. I'll pay better attention. Give me another question, and we can come back to this one."

"Your mind has been somewhere else all evening. What's going on with you?"

"Nothing. I'm just tired. That's all."

"I don't believe you. You've been down for days now. What is it? Is it James?"

The mention of James's name felt like a pin pricking a sore spot to Sara. Something seemed to be going wrong with their relationship, but she didn't want to talk about it. "No, nothing's wrong with James."

Sandy knew that was a lie. "Then why hasn't he been by to see you lately?"

Sandy got up and sat down next to Sara on her bed and said, "Come on. I know better. Tell me, what's going on?"

Sara bowed her head. Sandy was her best friend at school and hearing the concern in her voice, Sara decided to open up. "OK, it is James."

"I knew it!"

"It started two weeks ago when I went to his parents' house for their anniversary celebration. He didn't bring me, and I had to meet him there. I was really looking forward to meeting his parents. I thought this might be the start of something special between James and me. But the whole time I was there, he barely paid any attention to me. There were several times when I found myself standing alone, in fact."

"Did you meet his parents?"

"Yes. I met his dad first. He seemed really nice. Then later, I met his mother. She asked a lot of questions like where I went to school, where I grew up, what my father did . ."

"OK. Was that bad?"

"Yes! The whole time I talked to her, I felt like I was being interrogated. She had this fake smile on her face while we were talking, and she kept glancing over at James when I would answer her questions."

"Well, what did James say about it?"

"Well, every time she looked at him, he seemed to turn away, almost like he was embarrassed. So later, when we were alone, I asked him if I had passed her test. He said she was just that way sometimes, that I shouldn't worry about it."

"Maybe she was just trying to be overprotective of her son."

"Oh, but it gets better. Toward the end of my visit with his mom, she asked him if he had seen Crystal yet. That she was looking for him."

"Who is that?"

"His former bleach-blond, girlfriend, that's who."

"What?"

"Yes! And she looked right at me after she asked him that!"

"What a bitch! Did you ask him about that too?"

"Yes, and he just blew it off. But I saw her at the party. She was cozying up to his dad. Then I later saw her talking to his mom."

"That's bullshit, Sara!"

"I know! And the week after that, James rarely called me or came by, and I haven't heard from him at all this week!"

"Have you tried to call him?"

"Yes, but my calls keep going to voice mail. I went to his rent house yesterday, and a guy there said he'd gone home early for the weekend. Something is just not right."

Sandy feared for Sara. Although she did not know James personally, she had heard a lot about how he treated women from others who knew him, and she didn't like it. She'd had tried to talk to Sara about it when she first went out with him, but Sara wouldn't listen. Soon after, it was evident to Sandy Sara had fallen deeply in love with James. But she was afraid Sara was about to get her heart broken. Although Sandy didn't want to see her friend hurt, she did want to prepare Sara that James was probably breaking up with her. She tried to step lightly on the subject, but there was no easy way to say it. "Sweetheart, maybe James has decided to move on. I mean . "

"No! He wouldn't break up with me like that!"

"Sara . "

"No, Sandy! I know what you think of James, but he's not like that. When he's with me, he's kind and gentle and genuine. No, something else is going on, and I'm going to find out what it is!"

Sandy watched as Sara got her cell phone and called James. When yet again she got no answer, Sandy saw the pain etched in Sara's face, and she worried about her friend even more. She didn't understand how someone as smart as Sara could have fallen for someone like James. As is usually the case, she concluded that love had blinded her.

When Sara hung up her cell phone, she said, "That's it! I'm going to drive up to his parents' house tomorrow and find him."

"Do you want me to go with you?"

"No. I need to do this by myself."

"Are you sure?"

"Yes. I'll be alright. But thanks."

Having made up her mind, Sara decided to call it a night and go back to her room.

Sandy wished her goodnight, hoping Sara would get some sleep because she feared tomorrow would be a long day for her.

The next day, Sara felt nervous standing in front of the massive ornate wooden door of the Beachman mansion. Something inside of her told her this was not going to be a good visit. During the hour drive to James's parents' house, she'd gone over in her mind what she might find and how she would react to each contingency. It was as if her military training was starting to kick in as she wargamed the various options open to her.

By far, the biggest mystery to her was why James had stopped talking to her. Their last conversation, while relatively short, had given her no indication he was breaking up with her.

James had lamented to her several times about the Beachman dynasty and the power his mother wielded, many times to his detriment. She wondered if maybe his mother was somehow interfering with him. Sara never did have a good feeling about her after she attended the anniversary party.

Finally, after waiting several minutes after ringing the doorbell, a nicely dressed woman, who Sara remembered seeing at the anniversary party, opened the door and asked Sara, "Yes, Ma'am. May I help you."

"Hello. My name is Sara Bradford. I wanted to see if I could talk with James."

"Yes, Ma'am, I remember you from the other weekend. Unfortunately, James can't be seen right now."

"I see. Is something wrong? Is he sick, or has something happened to him?"

"No, Ma'am. James is well."

"Then may I ask why I can't see him."

"He's asked not to be disturbed."

"Well, can you just tell him I'm here? I'm sure if he knew I was here, he would want to see me."

"I can't do that right now, Ma'am. But I can deliver a message if you'd like."

Sara began to get frustrated and knew for sure something was up. Finally, she said, "Ma'am, I've traveled a long way to see James, and I'm not going to leave until I see him."

Hearing Sara's determined voice, the woman realized Sara would not take no for an answer. "Very well. May I ask you to wait here just inside the door for a moment while I make a phone call?"

"Certainly." Slightly relieved she might finally get to talk to James, Sara stepped inside and waited as the woman closed the door and walked out of sight into a nearby room.

The woman returned a few minutes later and said, "Ma'am, please follow me." She then led Sara a short distance to a room that looked like a small sitting room.

"Please wait here, Ma'am," the woman said, and before Sara could ask a question, the woman was gone.

While Sara waited, she looked around at several pictures on the wall and was drawn to a large painted portrait of a stunning young woman. Looking closely, she recognized it was a picture of Mrs. Beachman at a much younger age. Even as a young woman, an aura of power emanated from her face. Sara found it interesting that there were no pictures of Mr. Beachman or other family members.

Just then, Sara heard the door open, and to her disappointment, Mrs. Beachman walked into the room stylishly dressed and effortlessly wearing a look of authority.

With a less than genuine tone, Mrs. Beachman said, "Hello, Sara. Is there something I may help you with?"

"Hello, Mrs. Beachman. I'm here to see James. I haven't been able to get in touch with him, and I wanted to make sure he is alright."

Mrs. Beachman smiled at Sara and said, "He's doing fine, my dear. No need to worry."

"I see. Well, can I see him then?"

"I'm afraid not. He's very busy these days."

Sara waited for Mrs. Beachman to expound on her answer, but she said nothing further.

After a moment of awkward silence, Sara said, "Well, what exactly is he doing? I really would like to see him for just a second, and I'm sure he would want to see me."

Still smiling, Mrs. Beachman replied, "I'm sure that's not possible, but I'll make sure to mention to him that you stopped by."

Sara's started to grow angry at the vague answers to the questions she had been asking from both the woman earlier and now Mrs. Beachman. However, she felt she needed to temper her anger because of who she was talking to. However, she was determined to understand why everyone was deliberately trying to keep her from seeing James.

"Ma'am, I don't mean to be rude, but it seems every time I ask a question about James, I get ambiguous answers. Would you please tell me exactly why I cannot talk with him?"

Again, there was a moment of silence before Mrs. Beachman slightly cocked her head and said, "I'm sorry, Sara. James does not wish to share your company any longer. You know how these things go. A young man's fancy comes and goes these days."

Surprised, Sara belted out, "What do you mean he no longer wishes my company? And if that's the case, why doesn't he tell me himself?"

"I can understand you being upset. Please forgive his rather rude manners at this discretion. Unfortunately, you're not the first young lady James has done this to."

"Ma'am, I know James very well. This is not like him at all. I don't understand."

"Yes, James can be very sweet when he wants to. He really is a fine young man. He just needs to mature a little more. But honestly, this is for the best. Certainly, you understand his place and yours."

At first, Sara thought she misunderstood Mrs. Beachman's last comment. "What do you mean, understand his place and mine?"

"Sara, you and James come from different worlds. An extended relationship between the two of you would not be feasible in the long run."

"Are you saying I'm not in the same class as you all? Are you seriously saying that?"

"I didn't say that, but you're certainly getting the picture. I'm sure you are a wonderful young lady. You're very pretty, and I'm sure you will experience great success in your future endeavors. However, your future does not lay with the Bachman's.

Sara was beside herself, and whatever restrain she'd previously had was gone now. "Excuse me, Mrs. Beachman, but I'm not just some simple acquaintance of James's. He loves me. Now I demand you tell me where he is or let me see him right now."

"Sara, let's get a few things straight since you don't seem to be able to take a hint. First, James will not see you again. He's not interested in you anymore. Second, you will never take that tone of voice to me again. And third, if you don't leave the premises in the next 5 minutes, I will call the police and have you removed. Are we clear, my dear?"

Sara glared at Mrs. Beachman, but Mrs. Beachman did not flinch. They stood staring at each other for a few seconds as Sara's mind tried to come to grips with what she had just been told. But despite her anger, she realized she had no leverage in the current situation. Although she doubted James no longer wanted to see her, she had no recourse but to leave.

Sara did her best to keep her pride and calmly said, "Very well. I will leave."

"Good. I believe you know the way out," Mrs. Beachman replied.

Knowing it was best to say nothing more, Sara turned toward the door. Behind her, she heard Mrs. Beachman say, "I'm sorry this happened this way, Sara. But look at it this way. It wasn't a total loss. You got some nice jewelry out of it."

Hearing Mrs. Beachman's last words, Sara froze as her anger level spiked. Suddenly, she felt her right hand begin to shake. Then, calmly, yet deliberately, she turned and took a single step toward Mrs. Beachman. She stopped the moment she saw Mrs. Beachman take a slight step back and a sudden look of concern race over her face before Mrs. Beachman regained her aura of authority.

But Sara wasn't fooled. Mrs. Beachman had been afraid, and something inside of Sara gave her a feeling of satisfaction at having temporarily cracked Mrs. Beachman's façade of superiority. She displayed the subtlest of a satisfactory smile on her face to let Mrs. Beachman know she was not afraid of her despite her threats. Then she turned and left the room.

Walking back to her car, Sara felt a tsunami of emotions, from anger at what had just happened to fear that possibly James had broken up with her to confusion over the entire situation.

When Sara returned to her apartment and closed the door, she was mentally exhausted. The pain of losing James was hitting her hard. She had given all of herself to him, and she feared maybe she had been wrong about him. But her heart kept telling her that was not the case, and she continued to have faith he would come for her, and this was not the end.

She had just sat down when she heard a knock at the door. She figured it was Sandy coming to check on her. She was in no mood for visitors but decided she owed Sandy a short explanation about what had happened.

When she opened the door, to her great surprise, it was James.

Sara threw her arms around him and squeezed him with all her might, and did her best to hold back her tears.

"Easy, baby. It's alright. It's OK," he said as he hugged her and gently rubbed her back.

Once James felt Sara calm down, he pulled away to look at her. Then, seeing the tracks of her tears, he took his hand and softly dried her face with his thumbs.

"James, I went to your house looking for you."

"I know. I heard all about what happened. I'm sorry you had to go through all that."

"I don't understand! How can your mother say those things?"

"It's just the way she is. Are you alright?"

By now, Sara had calmed down. James was here, and she knew everything would be alright now. She smiled at him. "I am now that you're here."

"Good. Everything will be alright."

"I know it will, sweetheart. I just hate to think about what's going to happen when you tell your mother we're still together."

Suddenly, James was silent, and his knitted brow betrayed concern.

"Is everything OK, babe? You are going to tell her, aren't you?

When James still didn't answer, Sara grew concerned. "James?"

"Look, babe. We need to talk about this. OK?"

"What is there to talk about, James? You do still love me. Don't you?"

"Of course I love you! You've got to believe me! You're unlike any woman I've ever known. I never lied to you about that."

"Then what is it?"

"Sara, please. You've got to understand."

"Understand what?" Sara asked, praying that his answer was not the one she expected.

James hesitated to answer. His mouth tried forming words, but nothing came out.

"Understand what, James?" Sara asked again, but this time with force in her voice.

"Understand that the Beachman lineage is something of great importance to my parents, especially my mother. The money is all in my mother's name. She'll fucking cut me off," James blurted out.

Sara stared at James and said nothing, unable to believe what she heard.

"Look, babe. We could still be together. We just can't make it public. Why don't we just cool it for a little while?"

Sara continued to look at James in disbelief. *Are you choosing money over me? Do you not have the balls to stand up to your mother for the woman you say you love? Is your lifestyle more important than me?* Her mind flooded with questions, and none of the answers she came up with brought any comfort, and then it hit her. She had been warned. Several of her friends had asked her about her relationship with James. They'd relayed stories of infidelity and his shallow behavior. Her father had questioned her, despite deferring to her thinking. But she had ignored them all. She'd even ignored herself. She'd put aside his minimizing her desire to serve in the Army and blindly rationalized it away. But she couldn't ignore the words he was saying now. The few he'd said already said way too much to overlook, and the pain started to pulsate deep within. *How could this be? How could I have been so wrong? I can't believe this! No! this can't be!*

"Look, you don't need to worry about anything. In a few months, we can get back together, and they'll never know about it. Then we can be together. Just like before. I promise," James continued.

But when he went to hug Sara, she stiff-armed in the chest and pushed him away. "Don't touch me!" she said.

"Come on, babe. Please! I need you!"

Sara tried to calm herself and decided she needed to make sure she understood what he was saying. She decided to give him one more chance. Fearing what the answer might be, she gathered her strength and asked, "James, will you tell your mother you love me regardless of what she thinks and decides to do? Will you do that for me?"

James didn't answer.

With her voice now trembling, Sara asked again, "James?"

"Sweetheart, you have to understand. I can't do that right now. I can't . "

"Stop!" Sara firmly said. She didn't want to hear anymore. He'd said all she needed to know. She didn't want the man she loved so dearly to expose his true self anymore. It was just too painful for her to bear.

Sara struggled to maintain her composure as she gathered her dignity. But despite her effort, tears began to fill her eyes. She pulled his ring from her finger and placed it in his hand. "Please leave."

"Babe, please. Don't do this." James pleaded, yet Sara remained adamant.

"No, James. You don't need me. You need your money and your lifestyle. Please leave, now."

James stared at Sara for a moment, and Sara prayed he might have a change of heart. But when he dropped his head and walked off, her last hope faded away.

As emotion pulled her in every direction, Sara closed the door and remained standing near it. The one man whose hands she had solely placed her heart was not the man she believed him to be, and in that instant, their relationship was over. She was frozen as she replayed what James had just told her and now ashamed at how wrong she had been.

She pulled out her phone from her pocket and deleted his number. But deleting him from her heart would not be so easy.

Chapter 13

AUGUST 2031 When John entered the front gate at Fort Benning, Georgia, his whole mood brightened. The Sergeant manning the gate saluted him smartly after seeing his ID card listing John as a retired colonel, and John felt pride saluting him back.

He loved the thick pine trees lining the entrance drive, and already the memories of many cold and hot days and nights spent in the local training areas on post started to emerge. He seemed to shiver for a second as he drove, vividly remembering waking up one morning and discovering a blanket of snow had covered him as he lay in his sleeping bag.

As he entered the main post, he saw that while many of the buildings were new, a few old ones remained. He had some initial difficulty navigating his way, but eventually, he saw the landmark that always told him where he was, the Airborne School Jump Towers. Constructed in the 1940s, the towers stood over 250 feet high and could be seen from almost any angle on main post. They were used to train Soldiers to drop in parachutes before their actual drop from an aircraft. They had not been in use for many years, however they still stood as giant metal sentinels watching over the base.

John decided he would take a short detour and drove over to the street they were on. The offices for the Infantry Officer Basic Course or IOBC as it was abbreviated, where Sara was enrolled were nearby.

He pulled into the Airborne School parking lot, got out, and stood beside his car to stretch a bit. The stiffness in his legs reminded him how long it had been since he had last been here. From this strategic spot, he surveyed the three primary places on post that played essential roles in his career.

First, he looked up at the ominous towers and remembered the day he went up one for his airborne training. He was the first of his class to be tested, and he couldn't have been more nervous. They raised him to the top of the tower as he dangled below an open parachute. He remembered how small the ground got and how he could see the entire post below him. As soon as he reached the top of the tower, there was a jerk that released his parachute. From there, it was up to him to guide his descent and safely land. He remembered the excitement of successfully landing with all limbs still intact. But even that could not compare with the thrill of his first jump from an old propeller-driven C-130 or jet engine C-141 transport aircraft.

He then decided he would start his walk down Riordan Street. Walking down the sidewalk, he looked to his left and saw what had been his introduction to being an officer in 1989, the Officer Candidate School Barracks. After his basic training at Fort Sill, Oklahoma, he was shipped here and given his chance to successfully finish officer candidate school and be commissioned a 2nd lieutenant. He could still hear the Training, Advising, and Counseling Officers, or TAC Officers for short, screaming at him. He chuckled as he passed the chow hall, remembering how they yelled at him to eat faster and get out. *It seems funny now, but it sure as hell was not funny then*, he mused.

The days passed slowly, and there were times when he was sure he would fall out, but he didn't. Instead, he ended up being among the distinguished graduates of his class. John still recalled walking across the graduation stage in Building Four and receiving his commission. But what he most remembered was looking into the crowded auditorium and seeing his mother shedding a few tears of pride for her son. He never forgot that moment.

John then stopped and turned back to see Building Four or Building Snore, as some had called it. Building Four was the main building on post where he had received his training first as an Officer Candidate and then later for both his Infantry Officer Basic and Advanced Courses.

He shook his head, thinking about the hours he had spent in that building. But the things he learned prepared him for war and were instrumental in making him the effective leader he became.

Yet as John recalled all of these memories, the ones of his buddies who he met in officer and infantry school stood most out. Tom, the athlete with whom he went through Officer Candidate School and who would eventually go on to a successful career in Special Forces. Matt, the comedian, and his wife Magen, two of his dearest friends. And Jim, the smartest of them all, graduate of West Point, and a natural leader. Of course, John made friends with other officers, but when these four men came together at the Infantry Officer Basic Course, they grew to be inseparable. Each was ready to give their lives for one another willingly, a vow not taken lightly, and throughout their careers, they stayed in touch.

But time had taken its toll. Today, Matt was dead, killed in an Army training accident. Tom had died of cancer a few years previous, and Jim, who made general, was still running his successful security agency. In the past, despite the distance between them, John knew they were never more than a phone call away. Now, only Jim was left, and that made John sad.

He smiled to himself. This place was his alma mater, Benning School for Boys, they had called it, home of the infantry.

"Can I help you, Sir? You seem lost," a young captain walking up to John asked.

John turned his head and realized he had been daydreaming. "Well, actually, you can, captain. My daughter was just commissioned and is here to attend the Infantry Officer Basic Course. I'd like to meet the officers and NCOs responsible for her training."

Surprised, the captain asked, "Sir, did you say your daughter is here to attend IOBC?"

"That is correct. She should have arrived two days ago for initial inprocessing."

"I see," the young man said. He then pulled out a small tablet from his cargo pocket on his uniform pants leg and punched on it. "We did get a new group two days ago. I have the list here. What is her name, Sir?"

"Lieutenant Sara Bradford."

The captain scrolled through his tablet until he came across Sara's file, which included her picture.

John noticed the young captain's eyes widened a bit as he studied the picture for a little longer than one would expect. He then turned to John with a straight face and said, "Yes, Sir. She's here. She's actually in my training battalion. I can take you to the commander if he is in, if you'd like?"

"That would be great. Please do."

The captain gestured the direction to go, and the two of them started to walk to the battalion headquarters.

As they walked by the airborne towers, John asked, "Those don't seem to be as in good a shape as when I jumped off of them. Do they still use them?"

"No, Sir. They haven't been used for a long time. Where you in the Army?"

"Yes. I was commissioned through OCS and then was put in the infantry. I retired as a colonel."

"Oh, I see, Sir. Then this must be like being back home again."

"Yeh, you could say that."

The captain paused and then, after a while, said, "We don't get a lot of women through here, Sir. Did your daughter request infantry or did she get put in it?"

"She requested it. She graduated at the top of her ROTC class at Texas A&M and was able to select her branch."

"I see."

John and the captain continued to chat until they reached the battalion headquarters. Then, the captain asked John to wait outside several offices to see if the commander was in.

John watched as the captain went office to office without finding the commander. He then went into another office and came out with a large master sergeant.

"Sir, I'm sorry. Unfortunately, the battalion commander is not in. This is Master Sergeant Butler. He conducts a lot of the hands-on instruction. I'm sure he could answer any questions you may have. Master Sergeant, this is Colonel retired Bradford, Sara Bradford's father."

As the captain explained to John about Master Sergeant Butler, John quickly assessed him. Butler stood a good six foot tall with a large pair of biceps squeezed by his rolled-up sleeves. He had a Ranger scroll patch on his right shoulder which told John he had been in a Ranger unit that had seen combat. When Butler extended his hand to shake, John saw scars on his hand. At that point, John knew precisely the kind of man he was talking to.

"I'm very happy to meet you, Sir," Butler said as he shook John's hand with a firm grip.

"I'm very happy to meet you, Master Sergeant, Butler."

John then turned to the captain and said, "Thank you, captain. I think you've brought me to the man I want to talk to."

John then turned back to Butler and said, "Master Sergeant, do you mind if you and I visit for a few minutes."

"Sure, Sir. Come on into my office."

As John walked into Butler's office, he scanned the walls covered with numerous awards and pictures. But one picture caught his eye. He walked over to take a closer look at it. It was a picture of Butler as a Sergeant First Class surrounded by what looked like a platoon of Rangers. Below it was written, "The Dirty Third, Masters of the Hindu Kush!"

John thought for a while and seemed to remember a news story from a couple of years ago. A Ranger battalion had been part of a raid into the heart of Afghanistan to capture several high-ranking terrorists. Since the withdrawal of American and NATO forces, the country had again descended into chaos and became a cesspool of trouble. He remembered the raid had been a success, but there were many casualties.

John turned around and asked Butler, "You were with the Ranger unit that went into Afghanistan a couple of years ago?"

"Yes, Sir. I was a platoon sergeant in Alpha Company, 1st Battalion, when we went in."

"I spent a year in Afghanistan back in 2002. I know what that place is like. Did you lose anyone on that mission?" Usually, John would not have asked such a question of another Soldier without getting to know him better. But there were a few more things he wanted to know about Butler before he settled down to talk.

Butler's eyes narrowed a bit at the question. Then he got a faraway look for a while, a look John had seen a thousand times before on the faces of combat veterans. Finally, he replied, "We lost seven men from the platoon that day, including the platoon leader."

John slowly nodded and said, "I'm sorry, Master Sergeant."

"Thank You, Sir." Then, Butler looked back at John and said, "Sir, would you please have a seat and let me know what I can do for you?"

Both men took a seat, and John began to speak, "Master Sergeant, my daughter, Sara Bradford, has been assigned to your unit for her infantry officer basic training. I understand you will be one of the primary instructors."

"Yes, Sir. I am the primary instructor for physical training, combatives, land navigation, and weapons training. Your daughter was in here the other day inprocessing. We almost don't get many women through here, so I remember her."

"Good. So, tell me about the basic course these days. What's the training like?"

"Well, Sir. It's probably similar to the course you went through. We've had some issues with the quality of officers coming through here in the past, and the Commanding General's Warrior Initiative has us going back to the basics, and standards are strictly enforced. We push the students a lot harder than in the past, and if they can't hack it, they get sent to other branches of the Army. We do a lot of training on the old ways, or I guess they call it analog, in addition to all the new high-speed digital technology. It seems nobody knows how to use a compass or a map anymore. Well, they do by the time they leave here. We also emphasize physical fitness and our combatives training. The CG said there will be no Task Force Smith's while he is in command."

"That sounds impressive. I think the CG is headed in the right direction."

146

"I looked at your daughter's file. Graduated from Texas A&M ROTC; that's usually a pretty good program. Top 5% of her class. She had some good evaluations from her TACs at A&M. Pretty impressive."

"I think she is. But I'm obviously biased, in my opinion. I want you to give her the best training possible."

"I intend to, Sir. That's my job. Texas A&M is a hard ROTC program, from what I understand. If she's as good as they say on her evals, then I don't see a problem here. Do you?"

"Master Sergeant, I don't know shit about ROTC. I graduated from Basic Training, went to OCS, and then straight to IOBC. I guess A&M has a good program. I really don't know for sure. But I do know this. Rote discipline, fancy boots, and traditions don't make combat Soldiers. Realistic and tough training led by battle-hardened NCOs makes good leaders. I don't know what she learned at A&M exactly, but I know what this place is capable of doing, and I think you are exactly the man she needs."

"Well, what exactly do you want me to do, Sir?"

"I want you to be brutal on her. I want you to put her in the toughest jobs there are. I want you to run her into the ground. I want you to push her to her limit and beyond."

"OK, but I'm not exactly sure what you are asking me, Sir. Do you want her to fail here?"

"NO! Not at all. I want her to excel. I know, just like you do, what kind of world she will be going into out there, but I don't know if she truly knows. That's why when she leaves here, I want her to be prepared to be the best infantry officer possible capable of leading Soldiers under the worst conditions that can exist. You know what combat is like. I don't need to tell you about that. I want her to be better than any man out there, and if she can't, then I don't want her in the infantry."

Butler thought about it for a while. Then he said, "OK, Sir. I'll do my best."

"Your best won't cut it, Master Sergeant."

"Sir?"

John gestured toward the picture on the wall he had looked at earlier. "Your platoon leader you lost. Was he a good man?"

Butler's eyes narrowed sharply. "He was a great young man, Sir. One of the best I ever served with."

"Good. I know what it is to lose Soldiers in your command. Think about it this way. If you could turn back time, knowing what was about to happen, and you had the opportunity to train your platoon leader and all of the men you lost before you went into combat that day, how would you train them? I want you to train her like you would train them so they

147

would have made it. I want you to train her as though she is your own child."

Butler paused and then said, "I understand, Sir. I'll do it. But just understand, it will be up to her to meet the challenges. I will not guarantee she will graduate."

"I understand."

Then John stood up and put his hand out to shake. "I appreciate you taking the time to talk to me, Master Sergeant."

Butler stood up, shook John's hand, and replied, "Any time, Sir."

John squeezed Butler's hand a little harder than before as they shook and said, "I will come back here either when she graduates or if she doesn't, and will ask you if you are satisfied with the outcome. I will expect an honest answer."

Butler nodded his head. "And I'll give you one, Sir."

John released Butler's hand, and then he smiled and said, "Before I go, I think I should warn you that she takes a lot after her mother. I think you are going to have your hands full."

Butler gave John a questioning look before he returned his smile and said, "I will heed your advice, Sir."

John then left Butler's office confident Butler was the right man for what he had asked.

After talking with Butler, John left the training battalion headquarters in search of Sara. He called her, and she told him to pick her up in front of the Bachelor Officer's Quarters. These quarters were on post for officers who did not have families and were not permanently stationed at the base.

John picked Sara up and took her to a nearby fast-food restaurant so they could visit before he left.

"You all settled in?" John asked.

"I am. Since I got here a couple of days ago, I was able to get my quarters set up. But that wasn't too hard. My room is tiny. I'm glad I won't be in it for long. That place seems like it's as old as the hills, Daddy."

John chuckled. "It is, sweetheart. I lived in that place several times, and it doesn't look like it has changed at all."

"You stayed in that same building when you were a lieutenant?"

"Yep. Sure did."

"But that was like back in the time of dinosaurs, wasn't it?" Sara joked. She loved to poke fun at John and see him laugh.

John gave her the raised eyebrow right before he broke into a smile.

"Daddy, you should have seen the master sergeant who is going to be our trainer. His arms are the size of my legs!"

"Really? Well, the Army usually assigns some pretty tough and very professional officers and NCOs to jobs like his. Are you worried?"

"No. They had some tough trainers at A&M. I should be good."

John was a bit worried about her answer. "Sara, don't underestimate what you are about to get into. ROTC is one thing. The real Army is something else."

"I won't, Daddy. But I'm ready to get started."

John nodded, and they continued to talk about the post and Sara's upcoming training.

After about forty-five minutes of visiting, Sara told John she needed to get back to her room.

When they got in John's 4 Runner, he pulled a bag out of the back seat. Then he said, "Hey. Before I forget, I wanted to give you this," as he handed her a plastic bag with something in it.

Sara took the bag from John and opened it up. She pulled out a portion of a lightweight camouflage blanket and said, "Oh, wow, Daddy! This is nice! And it feels so soft! Where did you get this?"

"It's my woobie."

"Your what?"

"My woobie. When I was in the Army, they issued us these as poncho liners. These things go back to the Vietnam days. It's a lightweight, soft blanket that will easily fit in your rucksack. Guys loved those poncho liners and would take them everywhere. Everyone had them"

"Why do they call it a woobie?" Sara asked as she examined the soft blanket in her hands.

"I don't really know, but some guy said it was because without it, you would be or woobie cold. I guess they kinda joined the words together in a slang term. I've had this one since basic training. I took it on every one of my combat deployments. It was a little dirty, so I washed it. It should be clean and fresh now."

As Sara looked at the blanket, she found a dark spot and looked at it closely. "Daddy, what's this stain on it here? It looks kinda dark red."

John did not answer.

Then she realized what it was. She looked at John, who was looking down at his steering wheel and seemed to be in deep thought. "Daddy, is this a bloodstain?"

John hesitated a bit. The memory of his first deployment to Afghanistan as a company commander flashed through his mind. By the second night, after he had taken out the machine gun emplacement and had led the defense of that critical hilltop, he was exhausted. His First Sergeant demanded he sleep at least four uninterrupted hours that night. John remembered laying on the bare ground and shivering from the cold as he wrapped the poncho liner tightly around him, trying to get warm. The cold kept him awake until exhaustion finally won out, and he fell asleep. He did not realize the bandage from the wound on his arm had come off until he woke up the following day. But he remembered that it was one of the nights he dreamed of Lisa, and that dream brought him the comfort he so desperately needed then.

Finally, as John returned from his memory, he said, "Yeh. That was from my first deployment to Afghanistan."

"Daddy, I can't take this from you. It's yours. It must hold a ton of memories for you."

John smiled sadly. "It does, baby girl. But I want you to have it. It did a great job of bringing me comfort when I needed it most. And you're right; it does have a lot of memories for me, but that's exactly why I want you to have it."

Sara tilted her head and tenderly smiled at John. She could see in his eyes that expression he would often get whenever he thought back to his days in the Army. She knew enough of his stories to know that his career in the Army had been not only an exceptional one but one filled with both great joy and sadness. Seeing his old bloodstain on the blanket he wanted her to have made her dream of being a successful officer like her father even more special. She saw it as an endorsement of his confidence in her and the road ahead.

That thought brought a beaming smile to Sara's face. "Thank You, Daddy. Whenever I use it, I promise to think of you." Sara then leaned over from her seat and gave him a quick kiss on his cheek.

"Hey! No displays of affection while in uniform. You're on duty! You've got to be strait-laced the whole time," John jokingly chided her.

Sara raised her eyebrow. "Why do I get the feeling you weren't that way with mom when you were in?"

"Well, that was different. Your mother wouldn't have it any other way. Plus, she was the prettiest woman around, so I had to make sure guys knew she was mine."

Sara rolled her eyes a bit at John and settled into a grin.

Then John said, "Funny. I'm still with the prettiest girl around even after all these years."

Sara felt a tingle of warmth, knowing he honestly believed what he said.

After John dropped Sara off at her quarters, he drove by the Infantry Museum next to the post entrance. In front of it stood "Iron Mike," the stature of the Soldier urging his subordinates forward that previously stood in front of Building Four. It had been moved to now stand in front of the museum.

John got out of his car and walked up to the statue gleaning in the sunlight.

He stared at it for a moment and then pulled a picture up on his cell phone. It was an old picture he had scanned in from his days at Benning. It was graduation day from the Infantry Officer Basic Course, and in front of Iron Mike stood John, and his dear friends, Jim, Tom, and Matt. John had asked his mother to take a picture of them as they left the graduation ceremonies.

He reflected on the men in the photo, young and strong with handsome uniforms and huge smiles on their faces, a genuine band of brothers. He remembered the sadness of bidding each other farewell and the excitement because they were ready to start their Army career. The anticipation of the unknown enthralled them all.

As John looked closer, he saw all of them had almost no ribbons on their dress uniform. He thought about how that changed by the time they retired and when Matt died. Courtesy of the War on Terrorism and numerous deployments, each of them would leave the Army with a chest full of medals and countless memories, some of which would be forever burned in their minds as reminders of what they had endured. Many being things they would wish they had never seen or done.

But none of them knew anything about that on that day. Despite their military training, they still retained the innocence of youth, and that picture showed it.

Looking at the picture, John wondered if Sara had any real idea about the path she was embarking on. He knew he didn't at that time. But most of all, he prayed she would live long enough to one day be able to look back and reflect on it all like him.

Chapter 14

Monday morning, physical fitness training came early on a brisk Georgia morning as Master Sergeant Butler called the formation of young lieutenants to attention and present arms as revile started playing.

The moment he gave the command of order arms to drop salutes, Sara came running up to him. She stopped beside him, presented a salute, and then breathlessly said, "I'm Lieutenant Sara Bradford. I'm sorry for being late. I went to the wrong field this morning. I won't let it happen again."

Butler eyed the young lieutenant with the death stare he had perfected over the years, pressed his lips together, and then returned her salute. "You're an officer, lieutenant. I salute you first, and then you salute me."

Still panting and very nervous because of her mistake, Sara said, "Your right. I'm sorry."

Butler looked her over. "Are you sure you're in the right formation? This is IOBC class 31-06."

"Yes, Master Sergeant. I'm in the right place. I'm slotted to be in this class."

"Are you sure? You're a woman?"

By now, Sara had caught her breath, and she replied. "Yes, I am. And I'm slotted for this class."

As Butler and Sara talked, Butler noticed all the male officers in formation behind her had their eyes glued to her. He didn't need to guess what they were thinking.

"Very well, Lieutenant Bradford. Fall into the rear of my PT formation so we can get started."

Sara nodded and quickly ran off and took a position to the rear of the formation as instructed.

As she made her way to the rear, Butler noticed several other male offers tracked her movement until she was behind them. Their eyes seemed locked on to her, and a few of their mouths were open.

That's fucking all I need. Every hard dick in the class trying to nail her. Just great! Butler thought.

"Fall In! Extend to the left! March!" Butler yelled out as he began his physical training class for the morning. He had them stretch, do some calisthenics, and then went on a four-mile run that he deliberately led at an exceptionally fast pace. By the time he returned, half of the class was spread out, some several paces behind him.

He patiently waited for the group class to fully assemble, then he spoke. "Gentlemen," he yelled at the top of his lungs. Then he paused and looked over at Sara. She was half bent over, trying to catch her breath but looking over at him. "And lady. That was pathetic! As officers, you need to be in superhuman physical fitness shape. Your little display this morning tells me we have a lot to work on," Butler bellowed out.

He then looked over at Sara and yelled. "Lieutenant Bradford. What is the primary mission of the infantry?"

Sara stood up and yelled back, "Master Sergeant, the primary doctrinal mission of the infantry is to close with the enemy by means of fire and maneuver and defeat or capture him or to repel his assault by fire, close combat, and counterattack."

"Bullshit," Butler screamed.

"I'm sorry, Master Sergeant," Sara replied.

"That's bullshit. Tell me in two words what the mission of the infantry is!"

Sara thought, "To defeat or capture the enemy?"

"That's more than two words, Lieutenant. Certainly, a college graduate like yourself can count!"

Butler then looked around. By now, he had everyone's full attention.

"Gentlemen and lady, the mission of the infantry is To Kill! To kill the enemy, plain and simple. You must kill him before he kills you. That is the absolute bottom line here. You must be willing and able to kill the enemy and to lead men and women to do the same before the enemy can do that to you or your Soldiers. If you can't do that, then you do not belong here. It's my mission to train and evaluate you in the areas of physical fitness, land navigation, combatives training, and small arms weapons training to do your mission of killing the enemy. You will receive additional training in doctrine, tactics, communications, logistics, and other subjects with other instructors. But when you are with me, you are mine. This is not college. This is not a prep course. This will not be easy. You will either meet the standard and become an infantry officer or not and be moved to another branch. I can see we have a lot to work on before any of you are given command of Soldiers.

There are NO questions. When I give the order to fall out, you are
released to begin your first class at 0830 hours in room 34 in building 4.
Class, Attention! Fall Out!"

After Butler released the class, the officers began to disperse.

Butler looked over and yelled, "Lieutenant Bradford."

Sara looked over at Butler and walked over to him.

"Are you sure you are in the right class, Lieutenant?"

Sara eyed Butler. "Yes, I am, Master Sergeant," she firmly said.

Butler stared back; his face still stone solid. "We'll see, Lieutenant.
I'll be watching you."

Sara remained silent, and Butler indicated she was dismissed.

As Sara walked to her car to go back to her room and get cleaned up
for class, she kept thinking to herself, *You asked for this, Sara.*

On day two of training, Butler took the class to a gym on post he
had reserved for PT that morning. He had each officer assigned to a
different exercise and was rotating them around in a circuit every three
minutes.

Sara was lying on an exercise bench with a free weight bar and
weights doing a bench press. She felt pretty confident in the amount of
weight she could bench press and had added a few more pounds than
what she usually had done in the past. She had just completed her tenth
repetition and her arms began to shake as she strained for the eleventh
rep. She was halfway through the repetition when she realized she was
not going to make it and began to panic because she did not have anyone
present to catch the bar before it lay on top of her.

The bar began to descend, and she was about to yell out for help
when suddenly a single giant hand grabbed the middle of the bar, lifted
it up, and placed it on the pegs of the bench press stand.

Sara sighed a breath of relief. She then sat up on the bench and saw
it was Master Sergeant Butler who had helped her with the bar. "Thank
You, Master Sergeant."

Butler gave her his usual glare Sara was becoming used to and said,
"How about we put some weight on that bar, Lieutenant. Then maybe
you'll get something out of it."

Sara was not off to a good start that morning, and she was quickly
becoming annoyed at Butler's almost constant berating. After he walked
past her and had his back to her, she stuck her tongue out at him.

Without looking back, Butler said, "Officers do not do childish
things like sticking tongues out."

Sara's eyes got wide. *How did he see me do that?*

As if reading her mind, he pointed to the wall, and Sara saw the mirror he was looking at her in. "The enemy is always watching, Lieutenant," Butler said before yelling at another officer for his poor form while doing a squat.

One of Sara's classmates, Lieutenant Bowen, walked over to Sara to start his turn on the bench press and said, "I think he has your number, Sara."

Frustrated, Sara said, "I know he knows how to punch them. That's for sure."

By mid-morning, the sun was already turning the heat up on the training fields located on Fort Benning as the new lieutenants of class 31-06 stood in a circle making last-minute preparations for their first training event of the day, pugil stick fighting. The days of intense training for hand-to-hand combat had returned as part of the infantry officer basic training program, and the first part of the combatives program was pugil stick fighting.

Each officer wore an old-style football helmet to protect their face and protective gloves for their hands. Once called into the center of the circle, they were paired with another individual, handed their pugil sticks, which looked like quarter staffs with pads on each end, and told to fight it out until one of the individuals was on their feet.

"Lieutenant Bradford! Front and center," Master Sergeant Butler yelled out.

Hearing her name called, Sara nervously walked to the circle's center.

As Sara was walking, 2nd Lieutenant Bryant, a former West Point linebacker, smiled and slanted his eyes to his buddies standing next to him. He quietly told them, "So whose gonna be the lucky guy to pop that sweet cherry?"

One of his buddies quietly replied, "I sure hope it's me."

Bryant then said, "Well, if it's me, I won't need any pugil stick for what I want to do to her. I got another stick I'll use."

When Sara walked up to Butler, he thrust a pugil stick in her hand. "You know how to use this LT?" he barked.

"Yes, Master Sergeant!" She cried out

Butler cut his eyes to her and said just loud enough that only she could hear him, "We're gonna see. Put this helmet on and stand by."

He then turned to his left and yelled, "Lieutenant Bryant! Front and center!"

155

Hearing Bryant's name called, Sara grew anxious. *He's got to be kidding. Me against that gorilla?*

The smile on Bryant's face doubled as his buddy next to him quietly said, "Don't be too hard on her. I'd like to use my stick too when you're done."

Bryant walked over and stood next to Butler, who then thrust a pugil stick and helmet in his hand.

Bryant stood over six feet and outweighed Sara by a good 90 pounds. As he stared down at Sara with a satisfying gaze, Butler said, "OK, you two. When I say on guard, you will get in your fighting stance. When I give the signal, I want you to engage the enemy until one of you is on the ground. I should also tell you I don't want any blood spilled here today. But blood is what I use to grow my grass here on Fort Benning, and this grass right here needs some good nutrients today to help it grow. OK, get ready!"

Sara and Bryant took their pugil sticks in their hands and got in the ready position.

Bryant stared directly into Sara's eyes and never blinked. He had been waiting a long time to show up Sara, who he thought should never have been allowed in the infantry. He also figured if he played his cards right, he just might be able to get his hands on some of her assets, which he found very enticing.

Sara could smell the anticipation and combination of hate and lust in Bryant, which scared her. Then, in a flash, an idea came to her mind.

As she bent forward in her fighting stance, and gave Bryant her best "come hither" look she could muster, and took her tongue and slowly ran it around the outside of her lips.

With the helmets on their faces, only Bryant could see Sara's face. His eyes exploded, and the smile on his face was now one of pure lust. He could practically feel her breasts in his hands.

Just as Butler yelled, "On Guard," Sara pressed her lips together and sensually blew Bryant a kiss.

Bryant's eyes widened even more.

"GO!" Butler yelled.

Suddenly and using all of her strength, Sara swung the part of her pugil stick closest to the ground in an upward motion and hit Bryant square on his lower jaw where there was no protection from his helmet.

Two of Bryant's teeth flew out as his limp body fell to the ground with a hard thump.

Stunned by what he had just seen, Butler's mouth flew open, and in the background, Bryant's buddies' faces matched Butler's as they exclaimed, "Holy Fuck!"

Seeing Bryant had been knocked out cold, Sara stood up. She then walked over to Butler and thrust the pugil stick in his hand. "Here, Master Sergeant. Next time, give me someone worth fighting. I'd like to at least get a little training out of all of this."

She then turned and walked back to her former position in the circle, taking her time and ever so slightly swiveling her hips.

Butler's head turned slightly to the side, watching her walk back. When Sara stopped at her spot in the circle and turned, she caught him watching her hips and smiled.

Butler shook his head, firmly shut his mouth, and then yelled out, "What the fuck was that, Bradford? Didn't I tell you no blood?"

"Just helping the grass grow, Master Sergeant," she replied.

Butler looked down, and Bryant was slowly coming to. "Bryant! Get your fucking ass up! Go get yourself to the troop clinic and get back here ASAP!"

He then turned to Bryant's buddies and yelled, "Help him get his ass up and to the clinic! Move!"

Then he looked at two other officers and yelled, "Lieutenant Hernandez! Lieutenant Smith! Front and center!"

Two of Bryant's buddies ran over and helped him get on his feet. Bryant wobbled as he cleared the cobwebs from his head, and one of his buddies whispered, "I guess she used her own stick on you, dumbass." They then started to walk while holding Bryant under his arms to the troop clinic.

As Bryant walked past Sara, he scowled at her. *I'll get you bitch before this is all over!*

Sara returned his look with a stone face, but there was no doubt in her mind he was furious with her. She heard the Lieutenant standing next to her whisper, "Way to go, Sara. That asshole deserved that a long time ago. Where did you learn that?"

Sara turned to the officer and replied, "My father always said to try to distract the enemy so he has no way of knowing what you are about to do. I just followed his advice," and then proceeded to bat her eyelashes at him.

Chapter 15

WEEK 10, IOBC Class 31-06. It was six p.m., and Sara sat on the ground with her back against a tree near the designated land navigation training area, taking a drink of water. She had just successfully completed the day land navigation course and now waited for the night portion to begin.

Of all the tasks at IOBC, land navigation was the major discriminator between who would make it and who would not. It was a skill set required for commissioned as an officer, and until recently, it did not have to be retested after commissioning. However, because the skill was so crucial to the combat arms branches and so many young officers struggled with it, officers were now required to recertify on land navigation, and for the infantry, that meant using a map and a compass and no GPS.

The night portion would not begin until well after sunset, so Sara decided to open up an old Meals Ready to Eat packet, or MRE, that she had for her supper meal.

A few moments later, one of her classmates, Lieutenant Bowen, walked over to her, sat down near her, and started to eat his MRE. A little on the heavy side, Bowen had an easy-going demeanor, unlike most of the other lieutenants who seemed to have more of their share of testosterone. He turned to her and said, "Man, I'm starved. I think I could eat three of these things."

Sara looked over at Bowen in disbelief. "Are you serious? This stuff must be a hundred years old. I didn't even think they still had these things in the Army."

Bowen tore open one of the food packets inside his MRE and poured the contents into his mouth.

"Bowen, what did you just put in your mouth?"

Bowen chewed a bit, swallowed, and then replied, "It was the dehydrated chocolate pudding. I think."

"But aren't you supposed to put water in it first and mix it up?"

Bowen started opening up another packet and said, "Yeh, but I figure when I put it in my mouth, it's gonna get wet then, so why waste my water." He then proceeded to pour the contents of the second bag he opened into his mouth.

"I bet you'll eat anything."

Still chewing the food in his mouth, he said, "Yeh. Pretty much. You gonna eat yours?"

Sara handed her MRE to Bowen and said, "No. You can have it."

Then she sheepishly asked, "How did you do today?"

"Well, I made it, but it was close. I only had about 20 minutes to spare before time was up. How about you?"

"I finished with 30 minutes left. It wasn't so bad. But I'm really worried about tonight."

"Why?"

"I checked, and there is almost no moon showing tonight. Plus, lots of the points are in the forest. I just don't know if I can do it."

Bowen finished taking a drink of water and said, "Sure you can, Sara. You're one of the sharpest officers here. You'll probably be back with plenty of time to spare."

Sara grinned at the compliment and asked, "You really think so Bowen? I mean, no foolin?"

Bowen took another drink and replied, "Of course I do. I wouldn't lie to you about that."

Sara smiled. Bowen had always been genuinely nice to her. Several other lieutenants were nice to her also, except their intentions seemed to be linked to their groin. "Thanks."

Bowen then looked at her hands and wrists and asked, "Where did you get those scratches?"

"From these stupid vines that hang off the tree. They have these little thorns, and they grab on to you when you walk by them. My father called them "Wait a Minute Vines," because it would be like they were trying to grab you and hold you up."

"Yeh, they tore me up too."

Bowen then pulled off his boot and started rubbing his feet. "Damn. I got a tear in my hose."

"What did you say?" Sara asked.

"My pair of pantyhose under my pants has a tear in it."

"Bowen, are you really wearing pantyhose?"

"Yeh. Stops the chaffing of my pants against my legs on these long marches, especially when I sweat. Aren't you wearing them? I figured you would cause you're a girl."

At first, Sara couldn't believe what he was saying. But then, she thought about it, and it made sense to her. Her legs were all torn up from her pants, rubbing against them after walking all day. "Where did you learn to do that?"

"I was enlisted before I got picked up for OCS. An old Sergeant taught me to do that when we went on those long road marches. Lots of guys do that. They just don't tell anybody they do."

Just then, they heard Master Sergeant Butler yelling for the lieutenants to assemble and receive their test sheets.

Bowen started putting his boot back on, and calmly said, "Well, Godzilla is yelling. We better go see what he wants."

Sara shook her head. "You're crazy, Bowen."

"Yeh, pretty much. Good luck, Sara."

"Thanks! You too!"

Two hours later, Sara was once again making her way slowly through the land navigation course in the middle of near darkness. There was just a sliver of the moon showing, and what little light it cast was quickly absorbed by the forest trees Sara had to contend with along her path. Nevertheless, she had already found her first point and felt good about finding her second one soon.

As she walked into a section of heavy brush, she felt a sting from the vines she complained to Bowen about earlier. "Dammit!" she quietly said to herself as she showed her light with a red lens on it to preserve her night vision onto her hand and looked to see if there were any thorns in it from the vine.

While she stood looking at her hand, she heard a twig snap and quickly turned around and listened. She heard what sounded like the flapping of bird wings and frogs singing from a nearby pond. In the far distance, there was the sound of a large truck driving on main post. The combination of darkness and quiet gave her an eerie feeling and got her imagination going. She knew the training area was full of her classmates, and she had run into a few twenty minutes ago but hadn't seen anyone lately.

She suddenly got a creepy feeling she was being watched. She shined her light around and called out, "Is anyone out there?"

No answer came.

Sara sighed and decided it was just her imagination running wild.

She then pointed her light in the direction she wanted to go and continued on.

She took five steps toward a pile of brush, and then suddenly, her head violently jerked as a large cloth wrapped around it, gagging her, and she was thrown to the ground on her back. A large man wearing a ski mask straddled her while another man held her arms down over her head. From what little she could see, both men were in T-shirts but had what looked like Army camouflage pants on.

Sara tried to scream, but the cloth tightly bound against her mouth prevented her from doing so. She struggled to free herself, but both men were very strong, and the one holding her arms strengthened his hold on her the more she struggled.

"Well, look what we found tonight. One of those Army officers walking around," the man on top of her said. It seemed he was trying to disguise his voice because it sounded familiar to Sara.

The man looked her over with fire and lust in his eyes. "You don't look like no Army officer to me. You look like a girl who's ready to party. Are you ready to party, sweetheart?" he asked.

Sara was deathly afraid, and her whole body quivered from her fear of what the two men were going to do. She struggled again, even harder this time, but to no avail.

It looked to Sara as if the man was smiling as she thrashed while the other man silently held her. Then the man on top said, "Mmm, you sure smell nice."

He then bent his head down next to hers and inhaled deeply through his nose.

When he was close enough, Sara headbutted the man hard, and he quickly snapped his head and body back.

The man holding her said, "Maybe she doesn't want to party with you. Why don't you let me try?"

The man on top of Sara rubbed his forehead and then shook his head.

He reached behind him and pulled out a large knife and held the sharp edge next to Sara's neck.

Sara felt the cold blade on her throat and the slight sting from the edge against her skin. She tried to settle her breathing as her heart rate exploded so the knife would not cut her.

The man on top of her said in an angry tone, "We can do this the easy way where you leave here still pretty, or we can do this the hard way, where you leave ugly if you leave at all. Do you understand?"

Sara swallowed. She slightly shook her head, with the knife-edge stinging her with each nod.

"Good," the man said.

He then pulled the knife away from Sara's throat and put it back where he had gotten it from.

He then took his right hand and grabbed Sara in the crouch.

Sara's eyes got big, and her breathing pulsated.

"I've been looking forward to this for a long time. You know?" The man said as he squeezed her crouch and rubbed his thumb on her genital area.

"Does that feel good?"

No longer able to control her emotions, Sara's eyes teared up.

"Come on. Get it over with," the man holding Sara's arms said.

"Oh, no. I'm going to enjoy every second of this," the other man said as he moved his hands from Sara's crouch to her belt and started to unbuckle it.

Sara closed her eyes, trying her best to suppress the tears.

Just as the man was unbuttoning her pants, a large combat boot slammed square into his face throwing him off her.

She then heard another sharp wallop, and suddenly her arms were free.

Not wasting any time, she jumped up and yanked the cloth around her mouth off.

She spun around and saw the two men were laid out on the ground, unconscious. She then looked, and standing in front of her was Master Sergeant Butler looking at her.

"Are you alright, L T?" Butler asked.

Sara took a second to catch her breath and said, "Yes, I'm OK."

She then buttoned up her pants and buckled her belt as Master Sergeant Butler walked over to the man who had been on top of her and pulled his ski mask off. It was Lieutenant Bryant.

He then went to the other man and pulled his mask off. It was a man Sara had never seen before.

Butler pulled his radio out and called back to the base for three of his sergeants to come to his location and for an MP patrol to meet them at a nearby road.

Once Butler finished talking on the radio, Sara turned to him and said, "What were you doing out here? Did you know something like this was going to happen?"

"It's my job L T to always know what is going on with the Soldiers and officers I train. I had a sense Bryant might try something like this with you. I was hoping I was wrong. Unfortunately, I wasn't"

Sara nodded. Then she humbly said, "Thank You."

Butler said nothing at first as he stood looking at her with his usual glare. Then he said, "I'm disappointed in you, Lieutenant Bradford."

"What? Why?"

"You made two major mistakes. First, you underestimated the enemy. Bryant's actions tonight were not unpredictable to anyone paying attention. You know how much he hated you humiliating him during the combatives session several weeks ago. You failed to consider the worst-case scenario of what he was capable of doing. Second, you let your guard down, and the enemy took advantage of you. You're a woman. You already know you can't match a man Bryant's size in strength, so you have to be vigilant constantly and have a plan. The moment you are in combat and let your guard down, the enemy will capitalize on it, just like they did tonight. If I had not been here, the outcome would have been very different. It's your job as an officer to consider what could happen and have a plan to deal with it. That's what your Soldiers will expect of you, and if you can't take care of yourself, how do you expect to take care of them. You failed tonight, but better you make this a learning moment so you don't fail again in the future."

Butler's words hit Sara hard. He was right. She knew Bryant was angry with her, but she had never considered he would try and harm her. She had underestimated him. And she never even contemplated the danger of being raped in the middle of the training area at night. Yet, in hindsight, everything Butler said made perfect sense to her. She had failed in her duties as an officer.

Sara lowered her head. "You're right, Master Sergeant. I'm sorry."

Butler then said, "Make your way back to the base camp and don't worry about finishing the course tonight. Stay there until I return with the MPs."

"WILCO," Sara said. Then she slowly turned to start walking back to the base camp. She took a few steps when she heard Butler say, "Lieutenant Bradford."

Sara turned. "Yes, Master Sergeant."

Plan on meeting me at the gym this Saturday at 0800 sharp in PT uniform. We will refine your combatives skills."

Sara slightly smiled. "Thank You, Master Sergeant."

Butler nodded but remained stone-faced.

Sara turned around and walked back to camp. The whole time she walked, she promised herself she would never make the mistakes Butler had pointed out again.

Several weeks later, Sara had one of the proudest moments of her life when she walked across the stage at her IOBC graduation ceremony.

John watched in the audience as she received her certificate and his heart burst with pride. Previously, he had briefly met with Master Sergeant Butler, who had assured him Sara had earned her infantry branch certification. He was satisfied.

After the ceremony, Sara and John walked outside the auditorium and waited as several lieutenants congratulated Sara on her certification.

When the crowd had thinned out, Sara asked John if he would wait for her for a few minutes while she went and did something. She then walked over to where Master Sergeant Butler stood alone, looking over the crowd. It was the first time she had seen him in his dress uniform, and his chest was filled with ribbons, including two purple hearts.

Sara stopped in front of Butler, and he saluted her and looked at her with his familiar glare.

Looking at the vast array of ribbons on his chest and reflecting on the sole ribbon she wore on her dress uniform, Sara felt very humble in his presence. She said, "Master Sergeant, I want to thank you for everything you've taught me. I've learned a lot from you."

"You did very well here, L T. You should be proud of what you've accomplished."

Bashfully, Sara replied, "Thank You."

There was a moment of silence as Sara wrestled with what to do next. By the end of the course, she had grown fond of his relentless poking her to do better. He had both challenged her and taught her how to meet those challenges. And she reflected that had he not looked out for her the night of the land navigation incident, she might not be alive.

Breaking Army protocol, Sara walked up to Butler and gave him a warm hug.

She then released him, took a step back, and saluted him, holding it until he saluted her back.

For the first time, Sara saw the ends of his large mouth curl up into a heartfelt smile as Butler sharply saluted her.

"I won't forget you, Master Sergeant Butler."

"Neither will I forget you, Ma'am. Good luck."

Sara smiled, turned, and walked back to John.

Watching Sara walk over to her father, a thought floated into Butler's mind. *I wonder what this place would do if she ever becomes a general officer?*

PART FOUR

LAST BRIDGE ACROSS
THE HAN RIVER

Chapter 16

12 JUNE, 2036; 0814 LOCAL TIME. Major General Shawn Davis, commander of the First Cavalry Division, scanned Seoul, South Korea's smoldering ruins as the UH-80 Pawnee he rode in bounced between the tall buildings. It was dangerous for him to fly in a helicopter so close to the front, but time was very short, and if he wanted to make sure his orders were absolutely understood, he had little choice. Every major road in the city was clogged with traffic jams, refugees, and the debris of their exodus. It would take precious hours to move around the city on the ground to move forward, a luxury he did not have.

As the helicopter jumped over the shorter buildings, the general was able to look out north across the city out of the open doors and saw large plumes of smoke rising in the distance. He could see the tops of the flames of whatever was burning in some places. The wash from the rotor blades brought in a toxic burnt smell that filled the helicopter cabin and stung Davis's eyes. As the general looked below, burned wreckage of vehicles and trash littered the streets. In several spots, there were still bodies lying about, twisted, torn, and misshapen. What a few days ago had been a bustling modern city had been reduced to a burning hulk of wreckage and chaos.

The opening barrages of the artillery buried in the mountains opposite Seoul in North Korea had done a brutal job of raining down hell upon the city once the war started. With the help from Chinese long-range missiles adding to the destruction, not a single part of the capital was spared. It was hard to believe anyone was still alive in many parts of the city, but Davis knew better. Despite the massive traffic jams and endless lines of refugees walking south, Davis knew there were still people left in the city, buried in basements and bunkers while the fighting continued. As he looked north, the visual evidence of explosions and the occasional aircraft swooping low gave him a good idea of where the current fight was.

Having deployed early from the states, he initially felt good about being ready for the upcoming war. That was until he saw how little supplies he had, how little equipped the other US units on the ground were, and the unpreparedness of the South Koreans. It only got worse after that. Higher command kept telling him a diplomatic solution was in the works, and they were only there for show. Davis wasn't buying it. But other than fighting for scarce ammunition and fuel for the division, there was not much he could do.

When the fighting started, it caught everyone by surprise, and they sent Davis and his division straight into it. No plan, no real guidance other than to stop the Chinese from coming south. That was impossible, so he issued his own guidance to his troops – "Give ground grudgingly, and kill as many of the bastards as you can along the way."

That was a week ago, and since then, he hadn't slept more than three hours in a stretch. He was tired, hungry, and bewildered at the gullibility of the current US leadership. Their diplomatic solution had gone nowhere, and it seemed to him there was still no strategy other than to react to what the Chinese were doing.

Yesterday, Davis's Republic of Korea Army liaison officer, a man that Davis had come to trust, told him there were closely-held rumors at the highest levels in the ROK Army that they might surrender and try for a negotiated settlement with the Chinese. When Davis questioned his US higher commander about such rumors, he was told that was not true. However, he watched as the ROK Army units north of the Han river withdrew south even if they were not under attack by the North Koreans or Chinese. If the ROK Army would not fight anymore, there was little Davis could do to stop the Chinese, and every time Davis thought about that, he got angry. He couldn't shake the belief his Soldiers might be dying for nothing.

With the possibility of the ROK Army units north of the Han capitulating, he decided to do what he could to save what remained of the division. The 1st Brigade had been reduced to a third of its strength within the first two days of fighting and was trying to secure what remained of the artillery and aviation brigades, both at half strength. The 2nd Brigade had had its nose beaten hard, losing a full battalion, and was limping across the last bridge still standing across the Han River, while the 3rd brigade fought its way to the same crossing and temporary safety.

Despite pressure from his higher headquarters, Davis was determined to keep the bridge open until he could get 3rd Brigade across. He was not going to needlessly sacrifice a single Soldier of his. The Chinese had figured that out as well, and they were doing their best to get to the bridge before 3rd Brigade so it would still be up. The Han River had always been the primary obstacle preventing them from quickly rolling through the city to the south. Once across, the North Koreans and Chinese could race south and capture as many of the imperialist Yankees as possible. Prisoners in large numbers would make great bargaining chips for the immediate future, and they had their eye on 3rd Brigade.

But Davis was not going to have any of that. He was personally going down to the bridge site and give his orders face to face, so there was no doubt about what needed to be done. He told his staff to task organize the battalion at the bridge site to the division so he could run the fight directly if he had to. He knew and trusted the battalion commander but still acknowledged it might take a small miracle to pull off what he needed them to do.

The Pawnee helicopter barreled in and quickly touched down at the landing site next to the bridge. In no time, Davis, followed by four other Soldiers, jumped out of the helicopter and started walking toward the group of officers huddled next to a JLTV, the Army's replacement for the Humvee as most called it. Davis moved quickly and walked with authority. He was a man on a mission.

As he approached the group of officers, the battalion commander, Lieutenant Colonel Campos, called the group to attention, and they all straightened and saluted. Davis returned their salute and then walked directly to Campos and shook his hand. "Larry, it's good to see you again. How are you?"

With the same bloodshot eyes that Davis had, Campos said, "Fine, Sir. A little tired, but we're OK."

Sensing the division commander was in a hurry, Campos immediately started making introductions. "Sir, I'd like to introduce you to my company commanders. This is Captain Levi of Alpha Company, Captain Mendez of Bravo, Captain Sara Bradford of Charlie, and this is Major Benson, my S3. The other company commanders are still moving their units currently."

As Campos made his introductions, Davis looked at each officer in the eye and nodded to them. When he looked at Sara, he paused for a second more than with the others.

Sara wasn't sure what that meant, and she suddenly became nervous but did her best to hide it.

As soon as Campos finished his introductions, Davis called out to one of his men to lay out a map on the JLTV hood.

"Gentlemen," the general said, then slightly paused and looked at Sara, "and lady, we don't have a lot of time, so I'm going to lay this out very simply. As of ten minutes ago, you're working directly for me. Your brigade will consolidate at an assembly area ten miles from here, then establish defensive positions to the south in the next couple of hours. I've got a full brigade fighting the Chinese house to house, trying their best to slow them up so they can get across the Han River and reconstitute. A half-hour ago, we dropped the next to the last bridge across the Han River. The only bridge left is this one."

"Your job is to hold this bridge until the last of 3rd Brigade can get across, then destroy it. We selected this bridge to be the last one because it is old enough that it is prechambered for explosives. The engineers are rigging it now. We will also try to hit it with air and missiles, but the Chinese are bringing some pretty lethal ADA stuff forward that will hamper that effort, so I need your battalion to make sure the bridge is destroyed. Now I want every possible effort made to give the forward brigade the chance to get across, but under absolutely no circumstance are the Chinese to capture the bridge intact. You will blow the bridge on my order, or as soon as the brigade gets across or if you have no coms with me and the North Koreans or Chinese show-up, you blow it even if the brigade is still not across. Got it?"

Campos was about to say yes, sir, until he thought about what the general had just said. He was willing to sacrifice a whole bridge to stop the Chinese from crossing the Han. After taking a second to let that thought set in, Campos replied, "Yes, Sir. You can count on us."

"Good. which company do you think you will put on the far side to hold the bridge open?" Davis asked, knowing that would be the company ultimately responsible for holding the bridge and possibly blowing it at the critical time.

Without hesitation, Campos said, "Sir, Charlie company is my one company still up to strength, so I'm putting Captain Bradford on the far side. I will position myself next to her headquarters and run the fight from there."

Sara's blood pressure exploded at the news.

Davis looked at Campos, then Sara, and back to Campos and finally said, "Alright." Then he followed up by saying, "Look, I'm not going to sugarcoat this. This is going to be a shit sandwich the whole way. The Chinese want this bridge intact, and they will do everything they can to get it. But I think they want 3rd Brigade more. Parading a whole brigade of American prisoners on a TV screen would be a great victory for them. We can cover you with some artillery and air support, but you folks are in for one hell of a time. But whatever happens, give 3rd Brigade every opportunity to get across. OK? I'm not letting over four thousand of our troops fall into the hands of those bastards. But! And this is a big but.

Don't let the Chinese get that fucking bridge, no matter what you have to do." As the general finished his sentence, he looked straight at Sara as though he was talking directly to her. He then turned away to look at the rest of the officers as they all replied, "Yes, Sir!"

"Questions?" Davis asked as he scanned the group of officers.

"None, Sir," Campos replied.

Davis then turned toward Campos and shook his hand. "I know you'll do a good job, Larry. I wouldn't have given you this mission if I didn't trust you."

"Sir, we will not let you down."

"Alright, I need to get back. Keep me updated on exactly what's happening. Good luck."

The officers quickly stood straight and saluted.

Davis returned the salute and then turned to walk away. But when he took his second step, he stopped and then turned around slowly and looked at Sara. "Captain Bradford!"

Sara's heart stopped. "Yes, Sir!" Sara snapped.

The general paused as if he was trying to decide what he wanted to say. Then he finally asked, "Is your father, Colonel John Bradford?"

"Yes, Sir, he is."

The general stared at Sara for a moment, and then his eyes shifted slightly to the right as if he recalled an old memory before looking back at Sara. "Your father's a good man, Captain. You've got big shoes to fill."

"Yes, Sir."

Then for the first time since he arrived, the general smiled at Sara. "Good luck."

"Thank you, Sir."

Sara watched as the general boarded his helicopter and took off. There was a lump in her throat as she realized that her company had just been selected to hold what was now the most critical piece of terrain for the entire division.

As Sara turned, she saw her battalion commander standing next to her. Looking at him, she sensed he knew what she was thinking.

"Don't worry, Sara. You got this. Go get something to eat and meet me back here in the next hour. I'll move my TOC over to that building a few blocks away, and you and I will layout the defensive perimeter."

Sara saluted and walked back to her JLTV she used to transport her around when she was not in her armored personnel carrier.

When she arrived at the vehicle, her driver, Sergeant Thompson, and First Sergeant Dixon, the Charlie Company First Sergeant, were standing beside the JLTV waiting for her.

"So, what did we get this time?" Dixon asked.

"Well, Top. We get to hold the far side of the bridge until 3rd Brigade can make it across. But if the Chinese get here before that can happen, we blow it."

Dixon looked at her without the faintest hint of emotion. This was the second time in his career he had been a company first sergeant. He was experienced, dependable, filled with endless energy, and ruthless with his Soldiers. One look from him and even the most confident of Soldiers, NCOs, or junior officers melted. He was not afraid to tell a senior grade officer what he thought. Tact was not something he had very much of.

When Sara had taken company command, the former battalion commander assigned Dixon to be her first sergeant because he had his misgivings about her abilities. He trusted Dixon would pick up the slack if Sara floundered in company command until he could find a replacement.

Dixon was not an initial fan of having Sara as his company commander. He also did not think she was up to the task. But that all started to change when he happened to be walking by her office the first couple of weeks she was in command and overheard her chewing out the platoon leaders for a severe lack of discipline on their part during a recent training exercise.

Dixon himself was appalled at the company's overall disregard for discipline when he first arrived as well. The previous company commander and first sergeant had a long record of poor leadership. Dixon had his hands full of improving the company's NCO leadership and had not had time to talk to the platoon leaders about their lack of leadership.

Even though two of the platoon leaders towered over Sara, she was brutally laying into them. Dixon himself winced a few times as he overhead her through the closed door, scolding them. But what made his day was when one of them smarted off, and Sara answered him with a barrage of curse words, several of which even Dixon had not heard. That platoon leader was out of the company by the end of the day.

When the door opened, and after the platoon leaders left, Sara emerged from her office. She looked over and saw Dixon standing a few feet away, smiling at her. It was the first time she had ever seen him smile.

"Ma'am, I think you and me are going to get along just great," he told her.

From that day on, they became a dynamic team. Between the two of them, they promptly transformed Charlie Company from a problem child to the best company in the Brigade in a few months.

Additionally, Dixon became Sara's most ardent supporter. Many of the male captains that were in line to take command of the company made many quiet complaints about Sara taking command. Some of them even alluded to Sara sleeping her way to company command. But Dixon made it clear he would not tolerate any talk of that nature from anyone. To Dixon, not only was Sara his company commander, but she was the best one he had ever served under.

"And just how long before 3rd Brigade gets here?" Dixon asked.

"I don't know, Top. They didn't say. I'm supposed to get with the battalion commander in an hour, and we will work out the details."

"What we need to work out before then is how many vehicles we got operational, especially that damn tank platoon they gave us. I think all of their shit is still down."

"I know. I need to light a fire under the maintenance guys to get everything we can of ours up and operational. I just want to get a quick bite from the field kitchen. I've got to eat something besides those field rations before we get started. Then I'll run over to headquarters company and talk to the commander."

"I'll go get you something to eat from the BK, Ma'am," Sergeant Thompson said.

Sara turned to Thompson and smiled. At the ripe old age of 19, Sergeant Thompson was one of the youngest Soldiers in Sara's company. Having joined the Army at age 17, Thompson had taken to the Army's discipline and made rank quickly. He had just pinned on Sergeant stripes and couldn't be prouder. His sandy blond hair, boy next door good looks, and innocent nature promptly endeared him to Sara.

"That's OK, Thompson. I'll get it."

"No problem, Ma'am. I'll run over, grab you some chow and meet you back here at the vehicle and then I can drive you to see the battalion commander for your meeting."

Seeing Thompson was insistent, Sara decided to relent. "OK. Thank You."

Thompson then grabbed his rifle and walked over to the field kitchen to get a hot meal for Sara.

When Thompson was out of earshot, Dixon said, "You need to be careful with that one, Ma'am."

"What do you mean, Top?"

"He really likes you."

Sara questioningly looked at Dixon. "Oh, come on, Top! I'm almost ten years older than Thompson. I doubt he has any kind of romantic feelings for an old lady like myself."

Dixon tilted his head and arched an eye.

"Top, I've never given Thompson any crazy ideas at all about anything like that. And you know I go to extremes not to show any kind of favoritism toward any of my Soldiers."

"I know, Ma'am. And I'm not saying that you show Thompson any favoritism or give him any other ideas. I'm just saying he is a highly impressionable young man. You know both his parents died from COVID when he was very young. Since he left that orphanage, you are probably the first person to show him any real attention. He's very young, and he really looks up to you."

"I understand. I'll make sure to keep an eye on him. I'd send him down to a platoon to take a squad, but I can't afford to trade out drivers right now. When this operation is over, we can look at reassigning him."

"Sounds, good."

"OK, well, I'm going to go and talk to Captain Carlson about our maintenance stats. I'll meet you back here in about 25 minutes and tell you what he says."

"Yes, Ma'am."

Sara then walked over to one of the deserted buildings that Headquarters Company temporarily occupied. Numerous buildings in the area were vacant or so severely damaged they were uninhabitable. Despite a steady flow of refugees across the bridge, the civilians seemed to sense a local battle was in the making, and they continued moving south instead of stopping in the area.

When Sara entered the building, she looked around and saw several Soldiers unpacking equipment to set up shop for the company TOC. Before she could ask, Captain Mark Carlson, the Headquarters Company Commander, walked out of a hallway and looked over at her. Blue eyes met brown, and a discreet heartfelt greeting was exchanged.

"Captain Bradford, do you have a minute to review your vehicle maintenance status? The boss just told me to make your vehicles priority, and I need to make sure I've got your stats accurate," Carlson asked.

"Yes, I do. Actually, that's why I stopped by."

"Great, can you come to my office? I've got the latest maintenance report from the maintenance chief on my desk."

Sara's tired blue eyes looked at Carlson as the slightest hint of a smile came to her face. She nodded and walked with Carlson into his makeshift office in a room further down a hallway.

Once they entered the room, Carlson slowly closed the door, turned, and pulled Sara into a tight hug.

Sara responded by placing her arms around Carlson and burying her face in his chest. If there was ever a time when she needed a hug from Carlson, it was now. They hadn't seen each other in several days, and with the burden of the mission ahead now weighing so heavily upon her, she desperately needed a moment of relief. Carlson's arms brought the sanctuary she needed.

Holding Sara in his arms, Carlson breathed in the scent of her hair. Even without the expensive shampoo she usually used, it still smelled like heaven to him.

After a moment, he released her and said, "I'm sorry, babe, it's just been so long, and I just needed to hold you."

Sara's disappointed face softened at his words. She wanted so much to linger in his hug just a few seconds more.

From the moment they both met several months ago, they were smitten with one another. While on duty and in public, they were strictly professional. But away from prying eyes, their relationship flourished. Finally, Sara had found a man who respected the Soldier she had become and loved the woman she was. She had decided the moment they made it home, she would introduce him to John. She just knew John and Carlson would get along well. Although he had not formally proposed, Carlson let Sara know he wanted a lifetime with her, and Sara felt the same.

Hearing Carlson's words of love tugged at Sara's heart to think of him, but she couldn't. This was not a time for love. The fear in her over what she was about to do had taken deep root.

When Sara did not say anything, Carlson softened his smile and said, "Honey, it will be alright. I know you will do a good job. I believe in you."

Sara's sad smile became a genuine one. "Thanks, Mark. I needed to hear that. Especially from you."

Carlson kissed her forehead and said, "You better go get something to eat. I've got to meet with the boss and make sure your stuff is fully working. Will you stop by if you have time tonight?"

Sara's smiled then turned to a "come hither" look that let him know how much she loved him. In a seductive tone, she said, "I promise, sweetheart." Then she turned and left.

Carlson watched as Sara opened the door and walked down the hallway. When she was out of his sight, he shook his head, blinked his eyes, and quietly said to himself, "God, I love that woman!" But immediately upon speaking, he felt a ping of fear. The woman he loved so dearly would soon be in the midst of mortal combat in a matter of hours. He vowed he would do everything humanly possible to help her. He didn't want to imagine a life without Sara.

Thirty minutes later, Sara had finished eating and was sitting in her armored vehicle, going over a map of the area with her first sergeant, trying to decide on initial positions for her platoons just before meeting with the battalion commander.

Suddenly an alarm went off inside the vehicle on one of the command-and-control screens. She quickly looked at it and saw that a high concentration of artillery fire had just been fired. Before she could complete her thoughts, a series of massive explosions started happening a short distance from her location. The armored vehicle she was in shook, and she could hear the horrible screams of some of the Soldiers outside who were hit. Dixon jumped up, grabbed the massive door on the closed ramp, and pulled it shut. Then both Sara and Dixon jumped on the vehicle's floor, and she heard Dixon call out, "Hold on Ma'am and stay down! We just need to ride this out!"

Explosion after explosion hit, and Sara's heart skipped every time the armored vehicle shook from a blast. She felt her stomach tighten and pulled her hands over her head as if to try and shield it from any shrapnel that might penetrate the hull. She couldn't tell the difference whether her body shook from the massive high-pressure concussions or from the fear that gripped her. Either way, there was nothing she could do but wait and pray. For Sara, the next couple of minutes turned to hours.

Chapter 17

12 JUNE 2036; 10:10 LOCAL TIME. "OK, we all need to just settle down and focus, dammit! I want only one person to talk right now, and that's Captain Jenson!" Sara firmly commanded. Her tone left no doubt she had had enough of the bickering that had started the meeting.

She turned and scanned the haggard faces of the sergeants and officers sitting around a table in a subway station near the bridge. Around it was what remained of the battalion leadership after suffering a massive artillery attack one hour before. The toxic stench of gasoline and smoke that hung in the air was only slightly stronger than the fear within Sara. As the only surviving company commander, she now commanded what remained of the battalion.

"Captain Jenson, please continue."

"The strike took out the commander, sergeant major, almost the entire battalion staff, and pretty much what was remaining of Alpha company. I'm not exactly sure what our operational vehicle count is or current manpower strength. We're still counting. Your company is in good shape. It looks like maybe half of Bravo Company is left, and the maintenance section from Headquarters Company was also spared. They were in a position that gave them pretty good protection from the blast."

"I told the SIGO not to put those damn antennas so close to the TOC. That is what they probably keyed on to find it," Sergeant First Class Woods, the platoon sergeant of the Electronic Warfare platoon, blurted out.

"Shut the fuck up, Conehead!" Staff Sergeant Pickford yelled. "Why the fuck didn't you assholes give us a heads up that they were tracking us? What the fuck do you do all day in the shelter on the back of your truck? Pull you pud?"

"OK, I said that's enough!" Sara yelled as she jumped up and turned to Pickford. "One more outburst and I'll personally pistol whip the next son-of-bitch!"

All the sergeants and officers around the table winced, and total silence ensued. Sara was usually very professional in her exchanges; however, her temper was legendary when riled. Despite her fear, she was determined not to shy away from her command responsibilities. Everyone now got the message she was firmly in charge.

Sara turned to Staff Sergeant Cole, the senior communications sergeant remaining, and said, "Cole, how long before I have coms with division? I need to give them an update immediately, and I'm sure they're wondering why the hell we have not reported in lately."

"Ma'am, we're trying our best. We had a lot of equipment destroyed, and the jamming and electronic interference the Chinese are hitting us with is affecting everything. It's like being back in the stone age."

"Cole, I don't give a fuck how much equipment was destroyed or what the Chinese are doing. You get me comms now! Do you understand?"

Cole ducked his head a bit. "Yes, Ma'am."

"Alright, we will take a 15-minute break, and I want everyone to return back here with facts and figures. I don't want any more, "I think" crap. I want exact numbers on operational vehicles and personnel."

Sara then turned to Cole and continued, "By then, I expect to have comms with division. I will update them on our situation and see if our mission has changed. Now, move out, gentlemen."

As the sergeants and officers stood up and walked away, First Sergeant Dixon walked over to Sara.

Sara remained tense after releasing what was left of the battalion leadership and then looked at Dixon when he stopped in front of her.

Dixon had that hard, impassive look that Sara never knew what he was thinking until he spoke. He then smirked and said, "We seem to be putting a couple of new expletives in our orders this afternoon, Ma'am. You doing alright?"

Sara released a heavy sigh and said, "I'm sorry, Top."

"Don't be. These dickheads are walking around in a daze, and they need to snap out of it. The Chinese will be here in a couple of hours and we've got a lot of work to do."

"Do you really think division will not release us from this mission? We're down to maybe two companies in strength at best. How the hell can we hold off the Chinese with that?"

"Ma'am, I don't know all that high-level operational art bullshit that you officers do. But I do know this. If we got hit this hard, they probably hit the rest of the division just as hard. I don't think the division commander is going to have much of a choice. We are it by my way of thinking."

Sara nervously replied, "Well, Top. This is one time I hope you are wrong."

"I understand. I'm going to check on 3rd platoon and light a fire under their platoon sergeant. I'll be right back. And you need to drink some water."

Sara smiled at Dixon. At times, he could be argumentative, stubborn, foul-mouthed, and a general pain in Sara's ass. But if there was one man in her company who was unquestionably loyal to her, it was him. And as her First Sergeant, he always took it upon himself to watch after her regardless of her wishes.

Just as Dixon turned to walk away, Sara murmured, "Top."
Dixon turned back.

Sarah struggled to ask her question. *Am I doing the right thing taking command? Should it be me? Should I turn this over to someone else better than me? Is there someone here better than me that should take charge? I'm afraid! I'm not ready for this!*

But Sarah needn't say anything. She and Dixon had been together long enough he could almost read her mind, and this was one of those times. Before she could speak, Dixon said, "Yes, you are! Look, Captain, we don't get the option to choose when we're called upon to do the tough shit. We're never ready. But you are. I don't know how this shit is going to all turn out. The only thing I know is it's going to get a lot worse, and there's not a swinging Richard around that I want in command presently. I want you, here, in charge, now. No one else. So, for the remainder of our time here, don't expect me to pump your ass full of sunshine. We've had the conversation. You got this. Am I clear enough?"

Just as Sara hoped, Dixon's insubordinate little speech was the tonic she needed. Although her fear remained, the doubt within her was whisked away by the resolve that now filled her.

A smile brimmed her face. "Thanks, Top," she whispered.
Dixon nodded and walked off.

Feeling better, Sara walked outside. The fresh air and warm sunshine on her face were a welcome surprise. But the dim light of hope that had just broken through was soon to be extinguished.

As Sara walked outside, Captain Foster, one of the few sole surviving officers from the battalion staff, walked up to her. She had asked him to search the TOC's debris ever since the attack to try and recover whatever he could and give it to the officer who would assume command. She had also asked him for a personal favor that she begged him not to tell anyone.

When Foster stopped in front of Sara, he bowed his head to hide the expression on his face momentarily. Sara's heart beat rapidly, waiting for what he would tell her.

Finally, he looked up with a look that gave Sara the answer she did not want to hear and refused to believe.

Sara said nothing. As long as Foster did not speak, she could hang on to hope.

In a low tone, Foster said, "I'm sorry, Sara. They just dug up what was left of Mark. I confirmed it was him."

Sara felt her new resolve buckle, although she still managed to steel herself for a few minutes more. She whispered, "Thank You, Harold."

She then turned and slowly walked behind her armored personnel carrier in a location where no one could see her. She placed her hand against the hull, buried her face against her arm and silently sobbed as her heart broke. The emotional rollercoaster had just begun.

Thirty minutes later, Sara pulled out her tactical tablet and set it up on the ping pong table inside the meeting. The key officers and sergeants of what was left of the battalion staff and the other surviving units now under Sara's command sat around the table. Having glanced at them before opening her tablet, Sara saw most of them were clearly either tired or scared or both. That didn't bother her too much. At this point, you'd have to be sub-human or a fool not to realize the situation was grim. What worried her most, however, was maybe they could see the same in her.

A large tablet was the modern-day replacement for the old paper maps and overlays commanders used to plan and conduct military operations. It was hardened against the expected rough treatment, ran off of a combination of solar cells and batteries, and was linked to the battle command system that could retrieve information from all of the world via a global communication system. Commanders could display maps that showed the terrain they were fighting over, the units' locations under her command and adjacent, and the control graphics that allowed her to control her subordinate units. Touching on the various unit icons would pull up their latest status reports or open a communication link to the appropriate person depending upon who you had selected. All known information on enemy units could also be displayed in addition to reports of current units in contact with the enemy. When it worked, it was a miracle of technology. When it didn't, it was a three-pound rock that fit in someone else's rucksack.

Sara touched the division headquarters icon and opened up a channel to General Davis via the radio embedded in the tablet. Within seconds, General Davis's face appeared on the tablet, and Sara began updating him on her situation since the destruction of the battalion headquarters and the death of her battalion commander.

"Sir, we have a combat strength of 4/15/207. We have established defensive positions on both sides of the bridge. I have taken what is left of Headquarters Company, all the attached units, and the remainder of the battalion staff and placed them under my command," Sara explained. She went into as much detail as she could about what she knew about the destruction of the battalion headquarters and the other infantry company the massive Chinese artillery attack had destroyed. When she finished her report, there was a long pause on the other end.

"Standby, Cobra 6," the division commander said. He then turned to his G3, who had an anxious look on his face. Davis muted the open channel to Sara as he talked to his G3.

"Well, Stan. What do you think?"

"Sir, they're going to be hanging on by a thread. It looks like the Chinese will try and take the bridge before the 3rd Brigade gets there. If they get there before 3rd Brigade, Charlie Company could be facing about a six to one ratio in combat power against them," the G3 answered.

"OK, so what can we beef them up with?"

"Sir, the whole division got hit hard by that artillery attack. Right now, we don't have anything to give them."

"Stan, you're not giving me any options here. I'm not sacrificing a whole brigade. You get those fucking Jedi Knights of yours to pull something out of their ass in the next 30 minutes. In the meantime, they hold. Got it?"

"Yes, Sir!"

General Davis unmuted the channel to Sara, and spoke. "Cobra 6, this is Pegasus 6. I understand your current situation. There is no change to my intent I gave you during my visit. We'll see if we can send you any reinforcements as soon as possible. We will provide you an update in about 45 mikes on any changes in the priority of division fires or other combat multipliers. Continue mission. Six out."

After the general's last transmission, he closed the comms channel, and the screen went blank. That the general had not allowed her to ask any questions meant only one thing to her. Their mission stood regardless of whether they received any help at all. They were it!

Sara turned to Dixon, whose stone face revealed nothing of whatever was going through his mind.

She then turned to the other officers and sergeants sitting with her. "Well, you heard what I did. No change. We hold."

"They've got to be crazy! The Chinese will be all over us in a matter of hours, and we're gonna need all the help we can get!" Lieutenant Bolton, the platoon leader for 2nd platoon, blurted out.

Sara looked over at Lieutenant Laura Bloom, the sole survivor from the battalion S2 section, and asked, "Laura, what are we looking at?"

Laura turned to Sara and replied, "Ma'am, the latest intel we have shows the 3rd Chinese Regiment of their 24th Division on its way to capture the bridge before 3rd Brigade can get across. I've currently got the scout drones covering the avenues of approach into our sector, but they haven't recorded any ground movement. The ADA guys shot down three Chinese drones a moment ago, so it's safe to assume we are already under at least partial observation. Overall, we could be looking at a six to one ratio."

"Six to one! There's no fucking way we can hold against that!" Bolton yelled out.

Sara snapped her head toward Bolton and firmly said, "Look! No one said this was going to be easy! We've got our orders, and we're holding on until 3rd Brigade gets across. If you can't handle that, Bolton, then let me know now, and I will find someone who can!" Sara's eyes told everyone at the table any further discussion about whether they could do the mission or not was over. It was now only a question of how.

Sara then turned back toward Laura. "Laura, I want you to give me your best guess on how the enemy will approach this. I want their recon effort, attack routes, artillery timing, the works. Then get with the scout platoons and lay out a surveillance plan for those attack routes."

She then turned to her platoon leaders. "Charlie Company will hold the far side. What's left of Bravo will hold the near side. Layout a defensive sector for your platoons based on your current locations, get your folks digging in, and then get back here. We're gonna consolidate your defensive plans and review a couple of battle drills. You've got one hour. Any questions?"

Lieutenant Dan Clark, the tank platoon leader, raised his hand. "Yes, Ma'am. You didn't give my platoon a mission. I guess then we will be the reserve and pull you out of whatever you can't handle."

Sara had only recently received the tank platoon to be a temporary part of her infantry company, which had no organic tanks. Clark had been an NCO before he was commissioned as an officer and actually had more time in the Army than Sara. Although Sara had to admit he seemed very competent, his self-confidence in himself and his unit irritated her to no end. He appeared to be the typical armor officer, brash, self-confident, capable of making decisions on the fly, and with little sympathy for the infantry who did not have the luxury of fighting mounted.

Sara raised an eyebrow. "Well, Lieutenant Clark, I would gladly give you a mission if you could tell me when the three of your four tanks will become operational. I'm getting tired of pulling those things around the battlefield. I didn't realize those pieces of junk you call a tank sucked so bad on maintenance; otherwise, I would have asked the battalion commander to give them to someone else."

"Excuse me, Ma'am. But those incredibly lethal death-dealing machines you call pieces of junk have more firepower in them than a whole enemy company. And besides, I don't mind you guys pulling them around. Saves my fuel expenditure," Clark said with the hint of a grin.

"Yes, but when will they be operational?"

Clark looked over at the maintenance chief. "I'm sure Chief Gray will have them up in no time. Right, Chief?"

Sara then looked at Chief Warrant Officer Two Gray, who squirmed in his chair. "Ah, well, Ma'am. We've got the 3d printers making the parts I need, and I'm trying to download the latest software update for them now. I should have them back up in about four hours."

Sara then alternated between looking at Clark and then Gray. "You two have exactly three hours to get those pieces of shit . . . I'm sorry, lethal death-dealing machines up and operational. Otherwise, I will strip the crews from your tanks and use them to fill in for the infantry soldiers I'm lacking. Got it?"

Chief Gray quickly acknowledged, but Clark gave Sara his trademark smirk and answered, "Yes, Ma'am. We'll be glad to show you guys how it's done."

Sara was about to say something back, but realized she was wasting valuable time. "OK. No more questions. Get moving."

Soon after the meeting broke up, Sara heard a ding on her tablet, notifying her she had received a message. She hoped it was from the division commander telling her of what additional forces she could expect. When she saw the title was labeled "From a friend,' she grew curious.

Sara touched the icon and opened up the message. It read, *Sara. We know what your orders are from the division commander. In just a few hours, we will have a tremendous force at your location. 3rd Brigade has already been cut off and is unable to move to your area. They will never arrive at the bridge you are to guard. There is no need for anymore useless bloodshed. We simply ask you remove your forces from the far side of the bridge and then pull back approximately one mile from the river. We will not interfere with your movement. Do this, and you will be saving the lives of your Soldiers from dying to hold a bridge for American Soldiers who will never show up. I promise if you do this, we will not harm you are any of your Soldiers.* It was signed, *A Friend.*

Sara blinked her eyes in disbelief. She yelled out for Sergeant Woods and Lieutenant Bloom to come over to her. When Woods walked over, she handed him her tablet and said, "Read this."

When Woods finished reading, he looked at Sara. "This is not good. I think the Chinese have infiltrated the network. No wonder our comms have been so clear the past couple of hours. They're reading our traffic."

Sara looked down at the tablet and said, "Which means anything we put on the network, they will know about."

"Yes, Ma'am, defensive locations, plans, statuses, they could get the whole thing."

Bloom then said, "This is also probably how they were able to pinpoint the location of the battalion TOC."

"OK, let's think this through," Sara said as she turned to Bloom.

Bloom thought for a while. "Well, Ma'am, we don't know for sure they've infiltrated the network. This could just be an email they managed to get through."

"But they called me by name," Sara said as she interrupted Bloom.

"That's true. They've got a good read on what's happening. And it's obvious they want the bridge and to cut off 3rd Brigade."

Woods added, "They might not be as strong as they say, and this could be an attempt to catch a break when they attack, that is if we do what they ask. But no matter what, you've got to assume they have infiltrated the network and can see whatever we see. They might even be able to send us false information or orders. We need to notify division."

Bloom asked, "Ma'am, do you want me to tell the platoon leaders not to use their tablets to update their defensive graphics on the network?"

"No. Let them do it. This gives me an idea on how we can alter our defense. Woods, I need a way to set up a secure line to the division commander and let him know what is going on."

"We have a secure chat line between us and the G2, Ma'am, we test every six hours for infiltration. I'm pretty sure it's still secure," Woods said.

"OK. Get a message to the division commander right now that I need to talk to him on it."

Twenty minutes later, General Davis was sitting in the division intelligence communications van waiting to talk with Sara.

"What the fuck is this all about, Gene?" Davis asked his G2. "Why is Captain Bradford asking to talk to me on this chat line and not the normal operations comms links?"

"I don't know, Sir. We just got this message to get you down here to talk to her. Based on what's going on in that sector, I figured this was pretty important."

Sitting on the other end of the channel, Sergeant Woods handed Sara the keyboard and said, "OK, Ma'am. The CG has arrived and is waiting."

"Are you sure it's him? Are you sure the Chinese are not either listening or are the ones on the other end? I've got to be sure I'm actually talking to the CG and not some Chinese intel guy."

Woods squirmed in his seat. "Ma'am, I'm pretty sure. But I can't guarantee anything right now. This is the best I can do."

It was Sara's turn to take a deep breath. This was her one chance to let Davis know the Chinese had infiltrated the network without tipping the Chinese off about what she was planning to do about it. She thought a while about how she could verify it was General Davis on the other end. Finally, she had an idea and started to type. *Sir, I wondered when you were stationed with my father at III Corps if you remembered his secretary's name. It's been so long, I've forgotten. She took care of me as a child, sometimes when my father was working late. Do you remember her name?*

When the message appeared back at the division intel center, Davis's and the G2's heads jerked back as the G2 said, "What the fuck is this? Secretary's name? What kind of bullshit is this?"

But Davis immediately picked up on the significance of the message. "Wait, Gene. I think I understand. First, this is definitely Captain Bradford. She did not even know I knew her father until I told her at our meeting on site. I think she is trying to confirm that it is me she is talking to. But why and why on this channel?"

The G2 blurted out, "Sir, you don't think the operations network has been compromised? Sir, if that's the case, they could have access to all of our information, especially everything associated with defending the bridge and our effort to recover 3rd Brigade."

Davis sat back in his chair and folded his arms. "Fuck!" He thought for a while, then said, "We've got to get to the bottom of this and fast. I've got to know what she thinks is going on."

"Sir, if she's trying to verify it is you she is talking to, you're going to have to answer her question first."

Davis shook his head. "That was a hell of a long time ago. I don't think I remember her name."

Sara waited for a reply, and when one did not come, she asked Woods, "Are you sure they got the message?"

"Yes. I got an electronic receipt. They got it."

Sara was about to ask what was taking so long, but she realized even if she was talking to General Davis, he might not remember. But she couldn't think of any other question to ask. So, she sat and waited.

Back at division headquarters, Davis sat in deep thought for a moment. Then he said, "I can't fucking remember exactly. I thought I could. Maybe I can say something else that might verify the comms link for her. Tell her I remember her father listening to old 70s and 80s music, that he liked that stuff a lot."

The G2 questionable looked at Davis.

"Just send it. It's the best I can do right now."

The G2 typed in the response.

At Sara's location, Sergeant Woods said, "I got a response, Ma'am. They say he can't remember, but the general remembers your dad liked to listen to 70s and 80s music. What do you think?"

"That's not good enough. My father has that on his social media page. They could have easily pulled that off the open internet."

"You're right, Ma'am! That's a good catch!"

Sara did not know what to do. She had to know if this was General Davis or not. If she alerted the Chinese that she knew they had penetrated the network, it would put the whole division in even greater danger. Her insides started to roll with despair, but she wasn't ready to give up yet.

"Tell them I still need her name."

Sergeant Woods typed in the response and waited.

At division headquarters, the G2 said, "Sir, they acknowledge receipt but still want her name."

"Goddammit! OK. Just let me think for a moment."

A door opened into the small room, and a female civilian contractor poked her head inside. "Oh, I'm sorry, Sir. I thought there was no one in this room. I need to send a status report to the states, but I will come back later."

The G2 nodded and said, "That's OK, Amanda. I'll let you know when we're finished here."

Suddenly General Davis yelled, "That's it! Her name was Amanda! Amanda Simpson! Send that name to her immediately!"

As Sara and Sergeant Woods sat inside the shelter on the back of the vehicle loaded with military intelligence gear, they began to hear rumbles in the distance. They both listened and then looked at one another. Before Sara could say anything, Woods said, "Artillery. It's getting closer."

Just then, he looked down at his console and said, "Amanda Simpson. Is that her name?"

Sara exhaled. "Yes! Thank God! Open up a video feed for me."

As soon as the video chat came up, the screen filled with General Davis's face, who immediately said, "Captain Bradford, what the hell is going on?"

"Sir, the Chinese have penetrated our command-and-control network, and I believe they can get information off of it, specifically our tactical plans."

"Shit!" Davis responded as he turned and looked at the G2.

"Sir, we don't have a lot of time. I've got an idea that I want to run past you on how we will defend the bridge."

Davis knew she was right, and time was short. He glanced at his watch. The last intel report put the lead Chinese column at her location in a matter of hours. With nothing else he could do with the little time he had left, he said, "OK, Captain. Tell me about your plan."

When Sara's subordinate commanders assembled to back brief her on their defensive plans, she adjusted her C2 tablet to review their defensive graphics. They had done what she had hoped and had set up a relatively static defensive line on both the far and near sides of the bridge. Her three platoons were positioned on the far side and what little remained of Bravo Company was on the near side.

After taking a moment to look at the plans, Sara looked up and said, "OK, Gentlemen, I see your graphics. Now, forget them. We are going to implement a different plan."

Confused, all of the commanders looked at her.

"The Chinese have infiltrated the C2 network. From this point on, we will assume anything on our C2 network has been compromised. That means they probably have access to all the graphics that currently exist on the network, and they have access to our plan."

"Holy Fuck!" one of the platoon leaders blurted out. "What are we going to do now?"

"In a nutshell, we're going back to old school. First, from now on, don't put any graphics at all on your tablets. You can use them for navigation purposes, but even then, you better double check. Second, we're going to conduct an area defense."

Turning to Lieutenant Bloom, Sara said, "Laura, please give us the latest."

Laura stood up and pointed to a large blown-up photographic map of the area lying on the table in front of everyone. "The latest intel reports show the advance guard of the 3rd Regiment/24th Mech rapidly moving toward us. We assume they understand it's a race to grab the bridge before 3rd Brigade gets here so they can prevent their withdrawal across the Han River. I've reviewed the avenues of approach coming into our AO. With the destruction and debris laying around, it boils down to three major roads that could support a regimental size unit coming in mass into our AO. I've labeled them Dog, Cat, and Bird."

Sara rose and pointed to the map. "If the Chinese are racing to get here, we should be able to catch them in these narrow roads where they can't deploy. We've laid engagement areas that correspond to each avenue of approach. Each platoon will cover one of the three avenues of approach. Phase line Windy crosses each avenue and is along the end of the EAs. The engineers will position explosives to create obstacles at the end of each EA. When we see which one they are coming down, we will blow it, stopping the column. Once the column is stopped, we will have hunter-killer teams simultaneously move to the rear of the EA. They will destroy the trail vehicle resulting in the column trapped in the middle of the EA. At that time, we will initiate an artillery attack from division artillery and destroy the column. Our armored personnel carriers will move up and cover the streets to the left and right of the EA to destroy any enemy forces that manage to escape. If they use more than one avenue of approach, we will use the same method to attack each EA."

Lieutenant Harvey, 1st Platoon Leader, interjected, "Excuse me, Ma'am, but that position your pointing to where the team needs to engage the column is pretty for forward. How will those guys get back once all this goes down?"

"It's going to be risky, no doubt. But we can't think in linear terms. We must constantly move from position to position, using the tall buildings as our cover and concealment. Also, we need to use the subway tunnels as much as we can to move throughout the area. We can't allow the Chinese to mass their fires on us at any one point, or they will pulverize us. We have to keep moving."

"So, what happens after we take the first column out?"

"That should bring them down to a strength we can then deal with and destroy so we can get 3rd Brigade across before the main body gets here."

"But, Ma'am. We're still gonna be outnumbered six to one," Harvey said.

"Yes, but they can't effectively get a six to one ratio if we have them canalized in the relatively narrow streets of the EAs. It's the one opportunity we have to attack them before they can spread out and concentrate their fire on us. Plus, if we are constantly moving from position to position and attacking them, we will hold the initiative."

"That's a good plan, but what are you going to do if they get through the obstacle at the front of the EA before you can hit them with artillery?" Lieutenant Clark, the tank platoon leader asked.

It was a good question, and Sara didn't have a good answer. She had already spread out what little forces she had, and the engineers did not have anything that could fight off a determined tank attack.

Sara paused and looked over to Dixon. He was always her sounding board for the plans she came up with. Dixon was silent.

"I got you covered. I'll have three tanks in hide positions across the river and one on the near side to kill anything that we don't want to come across the bridge. As soon as you tell me which EA you are going to hit, I'll move them to backstop the engineers and cover the obstacle," Clark said.

Sara liked his answer, but as of now, Clark still had three tanks nonoperational being repaired. "I could really use your help here, Lieutenant, but you only have one tank operational."

The confident grin Clark had perfected appeared again. "Ma'am. Please. Have a little faith. They'll be up in an hour."

Sara narrowed her eyes. "You better hope so, Lieutenant."

Then she followed up. "OK, I want everyone to go and update your defensive positions. Do not post them on the C2 network. Update the TOC using point-to-point comms or send a runner. Gentlemen, you have one hour to be ready."

As soon as Sara finished talking, Sergeant Thompson yelled from outside the building, "Ma'am! Someone's driving up."

Sara gestured to her platoon leaders and sergeants, and said, "You've got your orders, gentlemen. Good luck." Then she grabbed her helmet and walked outside, followed by Dixon.

As they walked to the road to meet Thompson, several wheeled armored vehicles with ROK Soldiers pointing their guns out of the windows drove by, followed by several large SUVs with South Korean flags. The lead vehicles moved quickly with almost no regard for obstacles or personnel onto the bridge. When the last SUV approached, it drove up next to Sara and her Soldiers and stopped.

The door opened, and an American lieutenant colonel in an immaculate duty uniform stepped out of the SUV and smartly walked up to Sara. "Who's in command here?" he brusquely asked.

"I am, Sir," Sara confidently answered.

The lieutenant colonel's eyes betrayed a look of disbelief. "I mean of the defense of this bridge. Who is the field grade officer in charge?"

"I am in command here, Sir. All of the field grades are dead."

"I see. I'm Lieutenant Colonel Rollins of the US Embassy. That was the Deputy US Ambassador and the ROK Deputy Defense Minister in those SUVs. We got out just in time. The Chinese are right behind us. You need to blow this bridge right now."

"But, Sir, I have orders from Major General Davis, 1st Cav Division Commander. I'm to hold it open until 3rd Brigade gets back across or until he orders it."

"Davis has no idea what he's talking about, Captain!" Rollins angrily said, his hands in fists now as one of them rose. He yelled, "If he were a half-ass decent commander, he wouldn't have lost half of his damn division already and left a captain in charge of this bridge!"

Sara's head jerked slightly back in reaction to Rollin's violent outburst. It was then that she got a whiff of alcohol from his breath.

"Captain, I'm ordering you to blow this bridge right now."

Sara tensed as she contemplated what he was ordering her to do – a direct contradiction to General Davis's orders. She vividly remembered Davis's last words to her right before he left her. *But whatever happens, give 3rd Brigade every opportunity to get across, but don't let the Chinese get that fucking bridge, no matter what you have to do.*

"Sir, my scouts have not reported any Chinese activity in the area yet. I have to give the brigade across the river time to get back."

"Captain, I don't give a damn what your scouts have reported. I just told you the Chinese are right behind us. The US brigade across is lost. They're probably all dead by now anyway. Blow the bridge!"

Sara understood she had to make a decision immediately. Was he telling the truth? Were her scouts wrong? Was the brigade lost? She had heard nothing about this from division, and General Davis's intent was clear to her. Save the brigade, but don't let the Chinese get the bridge intact. If she blew it now, any US Soldier on the other side would be immediately cut off. But if the Chinese captured it intact, they would be flying down south right into retreating US troops. She had Davis's order, but Rollins was a superior field grade officer. What should she do?

"Captain, do you not understand my order? Blow the Goddamn bridge!" Rollins screamed at the top of his lungs.

"Sir, I have my orders from my commanding officer."

"I am with the US Embassy! We exercise authority over all military action that happens in this country! Your commander takes orders from the ambassador, and I am relaying his intent now. Blow the Goddamn bridge!"

Sara's face tightened. She felt her hands tighten into fists as her body straightened. "No, Sir. I will not blow the bridge now."

Rollins's face swelled once he heard her response, and his whole head was beet red with pulsating veins. He took his finger and shoved it in Sara's chest SAPI plate as he screamed at the top of his voice, "Listen, you little bitch! You will blow this fucking bridge now, or I will take command of this unit personally and have you arrested!"

The next sound both of them heard was the unmistakable clanging of a charging handle of an automatic rifle being pulled back and released, indicating a round had just been chambered in the rifle.

Both Sara and Rollins snapped their heads toward the sound's source and saw Sergeant Thompson pointing his rifle directly at the lieutenant colonel. "Sir, my commander's name is Captain Sara Bradford, and I think it's best if you leave now."

Rollins' expression went from surprise back to anger. "Are you threatening me, Sergeant?"

Without hesitating, Thompson answered, "Yes, Sir."

Rollins then turned to Dixon. "First Sergeant. Are you just going to stand there and let one of your Soldiers threaten a superior officer? Have that man removed immediately!"

Dixon's stone look didn't flinch. But his eyes slid over to Thompson, then looked over and met Sara's who was looking at him. He finally said, "Sir, I think it's best you leave as my Sergeant has asked."

Rollins quaked with anger. He looked at all three. When it seemed as if he was going to move toward Sara, Thompson raised his rifle to his shoulder and firmly said, "Sir, please leave now!"

"Fucking idiots! All of you!" Rollins belted out. "I will see every one of you before this is over court-martialed and in prison! I swear it!"

He then turned and jumped in the SUV. Seconds later, the SUV raced off across the bridge and out of sight.

As soon as the SUV drove away, Dixon roared to Thompson, "Put that fucking rifle down, Thompson, and get your ass back to the TOC! And don't you ever fucking do that again!"

Thompson, who moments before had been so determined, lowered his rifle and sheepishly nodded his head. "Yes, First Sergeant."

He then turned and ran into the TOC.

Dixon turned and looked at Sara, who was still tense over the exchange.

"Thanks, Top," she quietly told Dixon.

"Well, Ma'am. We're committed now. I hope you made the right call."

Dixon then turned and went back into the TOC as he yelled at a nearby Soldier to put his helmet on.

Sara sighed. *I hope so too, Top.*

Chapter 18

12 JUNE 2036; 13:27 LOCAL TIME. At 13:25 exactly, another large barrage of artillery fire hit Sara's defensive positions on both sides of the riverbank, but the results were much different this time. They fell on empty foxholes, and only two Soldiers were slightly wounded.

When Sara realized the Chinese were targeting the positions marked on the US command and control network, it confirmed they could read whatever was posted on the network, and she had wisely decided to move her troops to other positions not shown. She had also anticipated the Chinese would send aerial drones to try and evaluate the results of their strikes. To prevent the Chinese from seeing their attack was ineffective, Sara had ordered several air defense teams to take up positions in the tall buildings surrounding the area. As soon as the artillery attack began, the drones arrived, and the teams destroyed them. Finally, things were looking better, but the real test was still to come.

Sara figured because the Chinese did not have much time, they would not hold up the advance of their lead regiment regardless of their drone coverage. With the artillery attack complete and the counter reconnaissance fight underway, all Sara could do was wait and see if she was right about the Chinese ground attack and hope she could stay one step ahead of them. It was not long before she got her first report from her forward-positioned scouts.

"Cobra 6, this is Snake Eyes 6. I got movement on Alpha Alpha Dog. Switching to our tactical UAS feed to you now," the scout platoon leader radioed Sara. As soon as he finished talking, a window appeared on Sara's C2 tablet as she sat in her armored personnel carrier. It showed what looked like a column of armored vehicles moving down a street. But the picture was unfocused, and it occasionally froze.

Captain Foster, who was sitting next to Sara, looked at the screen and asked, "Do you think they are jamming the signal?"

Sara replied, "I think they're trying to send a fake signal. I don't think that's actually video feed from our tactical drone."

"Well, let's find out. I'll contact the scout team near that location and see what they see," Foster said. He then switched frequencies on his radio in his helmet and said, "Snake Eyes 13, this is Mustang 3 Alpha. What do you see?"

"3 Alpha, this is 13. It's all quiet."

Foster arched one eye and then said, "Look to your nine and three o'clock. What do you see there?"

There was a moment of silence, then the scout leader reported back. "Nothing at the three, but I got some sort of activity over at the nine. I'm looking at the UAS feed, and I don't see anything showing over there. But I definitely hear something."

Foster looked at Sara as he replied to the scout, "Can you move your position and get actual eyes on Alpha Alpha Cat?"

"WILCO. Stand by."

Both Foster and Sara waited patiently. What was only about two minutes seemed like thirty.

Then the scout reported, "3 Alpha, this is 13. Roger, multiple armored vehicles steadily moving down Alpha Alpha Cat. Tanks and APCs. I can see dismounts riding on top. They will be at Phase Line Windy in about fifteen mikes at this speed."

Sara replied, "Roger, maintain eyes on and report when at Phase Line Windy. Break, Snake Eyes 6, move teams 11 and 12 into place for eyes on Alpha Alpha Cat and Bird."

"WILCO 6."

Sara then stood up and started to strap her helmet on as she told Foster, "That's it. They are feeding us fake drone video to believe they are coming down Dog. Thank God we put those actual scouts in place. I think the S2 is right. Their advance guard is trying to quickly move to grab their end of the bridge until the main body can catch up. I'm moving with first platoon to ambush them in the rear. Have the mortars start firing into Dog in a few minutes. I want them to think we took the bait. The moment they hit Phase Line Windy, blow the obstacle. Don't wait on my attack."

Foster ordered the driver to start the vehicle up and prepare to move. "WILCO. I'm going to reposition back to the alternate TOC position now that we know which approach they're attacking on. I'm going to move second platoon to cover Bird because whatever comes out of Cat will go into Bird. But I'm holding back third platoon until the last moment in case we need to backstop you."

"Sounds good. And tell Clark to get off his ass and get his tanks in gear."

"WILCO."

As soon as Sara finished speaking, she grabbed her rifle and ran outside to get the first platoon moving.

Foster watched her move in a flash and said to himself, "Good luck, Sara."

Sara exited the armored personnel carrier and said to the Soldiers waiting for her, "OK, on me. Let's move!"

The platoon broke out into squads and moved with one squad in front of Sara, one squad with Sara and the platoon leader in the center, and another behind her to provide rear security. They moved quickly down the street, which was a block off the main road that the Chinese column was traveling on. In each squad, soldiers scanned their area as they pointed their weapons in the direction they looked and dodged the debris scattered all about. The streets and buildings appeared deserted as if the civilians knew something was about to happen.

Sara continuously scanned the area all around her. She could feel herself in overdrive now as the adrenaline poured into her. The radio net inside her helmet filled with traffic as her plan was put into place.

"Hammer 6, this is Mustang 3 Alpha. We've got contact, Alpha Alpha Dog. Multiple vehicles. Begin firing into EA DOG."

"Hammer to 3 Alpha. WILCO."

Foster used a radio frequency he hoped the Chinese were monitoring to order the attack into the engagement area to trick them into thinking their ruse had worked. But even if they had not intercepted his transmission, once the Chinese saw the mortar fire going into EA Dog, they would hopefully believe they had successfully fooled the US Soldiers as to their approach route. Foster then switched to a secure radio net he knew the Chinese could not intercept.

"Mustang 3 Alpha, Snake Eyes 13. I still got visual contact, multiple armored vehicles. Lead vehicle will be at Phase Line Windy in eight mikes."

"Mustang 3 Alpha, Snake Eyes 12. In place. Negative contact."

"Pegasus Thunder, Mustang 3 Alpha. Multiple armored vehicles moving into EA Cat. Stand by to initiate fire."

"Roger Mustang. Standing by."

"Sapper 31, Mustang 3 Alpha. Enemy column moving in EA Cat. Blow the obstacle as soon as they get to Phase Line Windy. Do not wait for the command."

"Roger 3 Alpha. We're in place. I can smell the bastards."

While listening to the radio's ongoing traffic, Sara continued to build the picture in her mind as she quickly moved down the street. *OK, mortars are firing, so they think we are attacking the vehicles we think are coming down Dog. I got 6 minutes to be in place for the rear ambush. Scouts are in place. Division artillery is set. Engineers are set to blow the obstacle and stop the enemy column from moving forward.*

As Sara moved faster and faster down the street, every fiber in her body was alive, every neuron in her brain was firing. She looked, listened, and moved simultaneously. She constantly reviewed the scenario, trying to anticipate every contingency. When the radio traffic stopped, she repeatedly asked herself, *What am I missing?*

In the distance, she heard explosions. *Good! The mortars are firing!*

Suddenly, Sara heard vehicle noises on the next block over. She looked down the road and saw they were still a block away from where they needed to be to get to the high rise overlooking what would be the end of the ambush zone. Without realizing it, Sara was now running with the rest of the platoon as they were too far away from where they needed to be.

She could feel her gear bouncing around her body as she ran, but the adrenaline in her had temporarily removed any fatigue that might have risen. Her breathing was steady.

"Recon vehicle upfront, maybe moving this way!" the squad leader in the lead squad several paces ahead yelled out. Instantly the lead squad fanned out and started to fall into an L-shaped ambush formation, taking up positions behind the destroyed and damaged cars on the side of the road and behind building corners.

Sara said over her radio, "Take them out but hold your fire as long as you can. Second and third squad, on me!"

She hurriedly looked around and saw a narrow alleyway off to her right. Without breaking stride, she turned and ran toward the alley.

The Soldiers near her followed as three of them ran ahead, and the rear squad fell in behind. They hurried through the alley despite the trash that clogged the way.

Sara was impressed with the speedy yet deliberate movement of her Soldiers. Everyone was on edge, yet maintaining the discipline needed to carry out the operation. The training she had stressed since taking command was paying off.

Inside the First Cavalry Division TOC, General Davis sat in his chair, watching the video feed from a US drone circling overhead on a large TV screen to his front.

"Sir, looks like the advance guard of the Chinese Mech Division is making its move to the bridge," one of the intel analysts said.

"I see dismounts running down the parallel street to the column. I think they're ours!" another yelled out.

"Zoom into the dismounts," Davis ordered.

Just as he gave the order, the picture became a distortion of snow.

"What the hell happened? Where's the video?" Davis asked.

"Sir, the Chinese are jamming our transmission. We can't override it."

"Fuck!" Davis sneered. Then he turned to the artillery officer and asked, "Is the artillery ready?"

"Yes, Sir. Cobra just called Hammer TOC to standby. Guns are ready."

"Good! Those bastards might be able to jam our comms and missiles, but they can't jam cold steel raining down on their ass. Let me know the moment you receive the order."

"WILCO, Sir."

The major acting as the battle captain turned to Davis and reported. "Sir, the Air Force is still holding off on CAS. They are pushing everything into counterair right now to try and gain air superiority. The aviation brigade is continuing their support of 3rd Brigade but reports heavy losses so far. They are working to give me accurate strength figures. Finally, the air defense battalion has reported destroying multiple aerial drones that seem to be looking for our artillery locations."

The Division G3 turned to Davis and said, "Well, Sir. At least we may be winning the counter-reconnaissance fight for now. It's up to Charlie Company to hold that lead regiment in the EA so we can kill them. We just might have a chance."

Davis was silent. *Come on, Sara. Nail those fuckers.*

Meanwhile, Sara and her Soldiers dodged garbage cans, old furniture, and various other obstacles strewn about as they ran down the alley. She could hear the armored vehicles' engines a block away as they sprinted parallel to them and prayed they were not seen.

After what seemed like an eternity, Sara called over her tactical radio to the two squads, "OK, let's go into that large building up ahead to the right. Second squad, follow me up the stairs. Lieutenant Harvey, take third squad and secure the first floor."

After running a few more feet, the three lead Soldiers rushed into the doorway of a large office building with Sara and the rest of the Soldiers following.

Inside, it looked like they were at a large apartment complex entrance. Broken furniture was strung around the floor, and no one was in sight. As soon as Sara entered, one of the Soldiers yelled out, "Stairs are on the right."

Sara motioned with her arm for the Soldiers with her to go up the stairs. "Go up as far as you can."

The lead Soldier rammed into the stairway door, and the rest followed.

Sara raced up the steps, and soon her leg muscles started to cramp under the weight she was carrying. Occasionally, she glanced behind her to the Soldiers carrying the antitank missiles to see if they kept up. Climbing the steps in the enclosed space, Sara could hear the soldiers' heavy breathing and felt her lungs beginning to hurt.

When she got to the top of the stairs and entered the adjacent hallway, she felt a hand grab her protective vest, abruptly bringing her to a stop.

She turned to see Staff Sergeant Reynolds holding her with one hand and his index finger from his other hand placed on his lips to signal her to be quiet.

She looked around and saw Soldiers on either side of them with their weapons up and scanning the hallway in total silence.

Reynolds silently signaled Sara to listen. She heard women's voices in a nearby room and now understood what Reynolds was trying to tell her. There were civilians nearby.

Reynolds motioned for two of the Soldiers to quietly move down one end of the hallway and check it out while he pulled out a tiny drone and threw it in the air to go down the opposite end of the hall. He then watched the video feed from the drone on the heads-up display on his helmet visor.

Weapons still pointed and ready to fire, the two men crept down the hallway until they came to an open door to one of the apartments and then disappeared inside.

Reynolds continued to watch the tiny drone video feed and concluded that there were no enemy Soldiers or civilians on that side of the hallway.

Sara and the rest of the squad waited. For Sara, it was a moment to catch her breath and reflect on what was about to happen. She was now only a few feet away from a massive Chinese armored column filled with combat troops. If they were detected, it would just be a matter of time before the dismounted Chinese troops would take control of the first floor, cutting them off. If not, there was still a chance they could pull off their mission and destroy the column, if the engineers could stop the lead vehicles, and if the division's artillery was ready. If, if, if. A lot of ifs she thought.

Sara's gaze was drawn to the faces of the men around her, bathed in sweat, mouths open trying to replenish their lungs, and eyes filled with a mixture of excitement and fear. No one looked at her. Instead, each man concentrated on their surroundings while several still stood on the stairs below, waiting for Sara's orders.

If there was ever a moment she felt the weight of command on her shoulders, it was now as the realization that whatever she decided, these men would do. Any mistake on her part now, and they would pay dearly. She could feel the doubts in her begin to gather as her hand started to slightly shake with fear.

For a microsecond, her mind ventured to that early Sunday morning run with her father as he pushed her to her limit to test her resolve. His words once again played in her mind. *Sara, there will be days when you are leading Soldiers, and everything seems against you, and it looks like there is no way out or no hope. Their lives will depend upon you, and they will look to you to lead them. You can never give up.*

Silently to herself, she whispered, "I won't let them down, Daddy," as she felt a resolve fill her spirit. She tightened her hand into a fist and gritted her teeth, forcing her doubts to leave.

Finally, the two Soldiers came out of the apartment and motioned for the rest of the squad to enter. The voices had come from a TV that was left on.

When Sara walked into the apartment, one of the Soldiers told her about two balconies extending from the far wall.

Then suddenly, an explosion in the distance went off.

Sara looked at Reynolds and said, "The lead vehicle of the convoy must have gotten to Phase Line Windy, and the engineers blew the obstacle. We don't have a lot of time. We need to attack the rear of the convoy and box them in now!"

She then ran to one of the balconies to look at the enemy convoy below as Reynold followed close behind.

As she got to the balcony, machine-gun fire sounded like it was coming from the street on the other side of the building, followed by another explosion.

Reynolds said, "That's probably first squad hitting the recon vehicle." He then turned and yelled, "Saunders, Martinez, bring the AT-8s up! Move to the balcony and attack the vehicles below like we talked about! GO!"

Sara cautiously walked onto the balcony to look around. She was thankful that what looked like some laundry was hanging on the exterior rails providing her some concealment as she poked her head just high enough to get a good view below. Armored vehicles were stretched in two parallel lines for several blocks toward the bridge. Many of them had Soldiers riding on top, looking around with their weapons drawn to defend against any attack from the surrounding buildings. Several of the armored personnel carriers were dismounting their Soldiers, who she figured were going to aid the recon vehicle that first squad ambushed.

She turned and saw several more lined up well past the point at which they were at. Her platoon had not gone far enough to catch the entire convoy in the engagement area, but she was satisfied if they could destroy what was forward of them, that would stop the initial attack.

She pulled back so she wasn't seen just as one of her Soldiers carrying a large tube antitank missile launcher and another with a large machine gun crawled out onto the balcony. Another Soldier carrying another anti-tank missile launcher walked onto the second balcony next to them.

All three looked at Sara, and she signaled for them to begin the attack.

The man in the nearby balcony wasted no time. He quickly took a position at the handrail and raised his antitank missile launcher. He steadied it for a minute, then suddenly there was a loud rush followed by an explosion below.

The two men with Sara were not as fast. As the other man with the launcher took a stance at the guardrail, machinegun fire rang out. The man's helmet flew off, and an explosion of red followed as he and his missile launcher fell to the floor.

The man with the machine gun had taken a position and fired at the Chinese below but jerked back and crouched on the ground as the balcony was covered in enemy bullets, steadily firing back at them. He looked around and yelled, "Martinez!" when he saw his buddy lying in a pool of blood.

An explosion hit just beneath the balcony, and Sara crouched on the ground near the dead Soldier.

"Cobra 6, Alpha 6. You guys finished up there. We got company down here, and it's getting ugly. You need to get back down soon before we're cut off. Over," the platoon leader on the ground floor told Sara on her helmet radio.

"Hold your ground, Alpha 6," Sara sharply replied.

She peeked over the balcony. The first missile had hit a tank that was now on fire, but there was ample room for other vehicles to turn around in the street and escape. If she could not prevent them from leaving, she would not be able to destroy as many as she could with the artillery attack. They had to destroy another vehicle to keep the convoy held up.

"Can you give me suppressive fire?" she yelled at the Soldier with the machine gun over the staccato sound of bullets flying up at them.

"In this shit? Are you joking?" he yelled back.

Sara reached over and grabbed the missile launcher from the dead Soldier on the floor. She saw the trigger mechanism was damaged from gunfire, and there was no way to fire it.

"Reynolds! Give me the other launcher!" Sara yelled.

Immediately, a pair of arms handed the third missile launcher to Sara through the door, and she took it.

She quickly broke the seal around the trigger and armed the missile.

Sara then turned to the machine gunner and yelled, "On the count of three!"

"They'll hit us for sure the moment we pop up over the rail!" the machine gunner yelled back as another explosion hit near the balcony next to them.

"Cobra, Alpha 6. What is taking you guys so long? Come on!" Sara's radio barked.

"Hold the goddamn line down there!"

Then Sara turned back to the machine gunner. "One!"

He shook his head no.

"Two!"

He shook his head again, then yelled, "Goddammit!"

"Three!"

Immediately, they both stood up, and the machine gunner fired on the enemy Soldiers below. He fired wildly, and to his surprise, the shooting at them seemed to lessen for just a second.

Sara firmly planted her legs and looked through the launcher sights. She saw another tank moving past the burning tank and fired. Instantly an explosion followed, and then a few seconds later, a massive blast ensued, followed by a plume of smoke. The ammunition from the tank had exploded, and the turret popped off and tumbled across the street.

Now the convoy was trapped between the wreckage from the two destroyed tanks and the engineer-blown obstacle ahead.

"Division Command Net!" Sara yelled to switch her helmet radio from her company tactical command frequency to the division command frequency. "Pegasus TOC, Cobra 6! battle king! I say again, battle king!"

Battle king was the code word for an immediate artillery attack on the engagement area where the Chinese armored column was now trapped. Over forty miles away, three divisional artillery battalions stood waiting to receive their orders. Fifty-four tubes of artillery armed with a full load of smart munitions designed to home in on their targets began to swing slightly to the left to align themselves with their targets. Once the first volley fired, the tubes were automatically reloaded and fired.

Three full volleys would be in the air before the first one hit their assigned targets.

Back at the Division TOC, one of the Soldiers listening to the radio, yelled to General Davis, "Sir, Cobra 6 is requesting battle king!"

Before Davis could say anything, his division artillery officer said, "Fire mission relayed, Sir. Outgoing in two mikes!"

Davis held his breath. It was going to be a long two minutes.

Back on the balcony, the machine gunner continued to fire until the explosion from the tank Sara had hit caused him to pull back for a moment. Then, as soon as the blast passed, he jumped back up and started to fire again.

Sara listened to Pegasus TOC acknowledge her fire request when she heard the machine gunner yell out, "I'm hit!" He fell next to the dead Soldier and tried to plug a bullet wound to his shoulder.

"Cobra 6, If you don't get down here now, we are going to be cut off!" the lieutenant below anxiously called out to Sara over the radio.

Sara crouched down next to the wounded Soldier. "Can you still move on your own?"

He nodded, obviously in pain but still conscious.

"OK, get going!"

Sara then turned inside the doorway and yelled over the backdrop of gunfire, "Reynolds, order your men to withdraw down the stairs. If I'm not down there in five minutes, pull back to our lines!"

"What are you going to do up here?"

"I need to observe the fire to make sure it is on target!"

"This whole fucking street is about to go up! We all need to get out of here now!"

"GO! I'll be right behind you. Now GO!" Sara screamed against the overwhelming noise of explosions and gunfire.

Both the machine gunner and Reynolds ran back into the apartment and began to rapidly make their way down to the squad defending the first floor below them.

Sara crawled back inside the apartment and waited for the artillery strike to hit. Waiting for the attack to begin, she glanced over at the dead Soldier lying on the balcony floor. It was not the first time she had seen a dead body, but it was the first time she saw one of her soldiers killed under her command. He lay face down in a pool of crimson red blood with his hand outstretched to her.

Sara tried her best not to be emotional, not to try and look at the man's face. But she could feel her insides starting to turn, knowing it was her orders that were the last thing this young man heard. It tortured her that she could not remember his name. *This man has given his life doing what I asked him to do, but I can't even remember his name*, she thought.

She reached out and held his outstretched hand. It was still warm. "I'm sorry," she whispered.

Then Sara heard the sound of incoming artillery fire, and soon explosions toward the front of the armored column could be heard.

Sara got up and looked just beyond the balcony rail as round after round started to hit.

Suddenly, massive explosions started near her location. She jumped inside the apartment, and just as she entered, several massive blasts hit, and the whole building shook. The explosives were so large Sara fell to the ground as debris from the ceiling fell on her.

Explosion after explosion rang out as Sara buried her head under her arms. She felt her hands shaking in fear; sure she was going to die.

Then the artillery fire stopped, and only the sounds of secondary explosions below continued.

It took a concerted effort on Sara's part, but she forced herself to stand up and look outside the door to the balcony and see the strike results.

Looking outside, she saw the balcony had collapsed to the street below, which was now a sea of wreckage, fire, and destruction. Even as high as she was in the air, she could feel the heat from the raging fires below.

"Cobra 6, Pegasus TOC. Fire mission complete. Report BDA. Over," a voice from the radio inside Sara's head requested.

Despite the massive destruction below, Sara could still hear gunfire and knew she had to get her platoon back to friendly lines.

"Pegasus, this is Cobra 6. Good mission. Standby for additional fire missions. Over." Sara reported.

Then she rushed out of the apartment, into the hallway, and down the stairs to the first floor.

When she arrived at the bottom floor, she looked around to see the chaos that filled the room. Every Soldier in the place was firing their weapons. Expended brass bounced as men yelled out to report targets and ammunition status. Two were on the ground, either dying or in severe pain.

Someone yelled out, "Grenade!" followed by an explosion that hit the doorway. The man firing from the door was thrown to his back while blood gushed from his stomach.

The concussion threw Sara back into the stairway, but she managed to keep standing. She blinked her eyes, trying to regain her senses, and clear the ringing in her ears.

She stumbled back into the room. Despite the continued confusion that remained, her world had suddenly become quiet except for the intense ringing in her ears. Scanning the room, she seemed detached from reality as men screamed yet made no sound, their movements slow and jerky.

She looked toward the door that had been blown open as three men dressed in Chinese uniforms burst through.

Without thinking, she raised her rifle and emptied her magazine into all three. The bullets found their mark as each man violently jerked and twisted before they fell lifeless to the ground.

Suddenly full-motion returned as she heard Sergeant Reynolds yell out, "I'm out of ammo! They're coming up again!"

Again, several Chinese Soldiers rushed inside the room, and again Sara raised her rifle, but this time when she pulled the trigger, nothing happened. She was out of ammo.

She released the magazine from her rifle and yanked on her vest to pull another one out, but before she could finish her movement, she felt a hard strike to her head, and she fell to the ground.

Lying on the ground face down, she felt a sharp pain in her head, and her mouth filled with the taste of copper as spit and blood dripped from her lips.

She turned to get up but was violently thrown on her back by someone who kicked her in the front of her vest.

She opened her eyes, and sitting on top of her was a large Chinese Soldier. Sweat dripped from his face onto her, and she could smell his foul breath and feel the droplets of spit on her face as he spoke. He breathed hard from the fight, and hate flowed from his body onto hers. His eyes narrowed with lust, and when Sara felt him force her legs open with one of his legs, she knew what might come next.

She felt weak, barely able to breathe. She raised her hand to him, but he effortlessly swatted it away and laughed.

The enemy Soldier then put his hand around her neck and brought his face to hers.

Sara's mind raced with thoughts, and a terror she had not known before absorbed her. Then, she heard Master Sergeant Butler's words, *"I'm disappointed in you, Lieutenant Bradford. . . . It's your job as an officer to consider what could happen and have a plan to deal with it. That's what your Soldiers will expect of you, and if you can't take care of yourself, how do you expect to take care of them. You failed tonight, but better you make this a learning moment so that you don't fail again in the future."*

She gritted her teeth and spit in the Chinese Soldier's face. Then she reached inside her vest, summoned every single bit of strength within her she could muster, pulled out a knife, and shoved it into the Chinese Soldier's neck.

Blood spurted out of his neck onto Sara as he screamed and fell off of her.

The moment she was free, she sat up, grabbed a rifle lying near her, and shot the enemy Soldier three times.

After her last round had fired, she heard a scream and turned to see Sergeant Reynolds about to be stabbed by a Chinese Soldier he was wrestling with.

With the last of her strength, she pointed her rifle at the enemy Soldier and fired. One round hit his side, another hit his head, and it burst. The man lifelessly fell to the ground.

Firing the rifle had exhausted the last of Sara's strength. She dropped the gun and rolled over on all fours as she tried to catch her breath. She had no more in her. Certain the enemy had successfully overrun their small stronghold, and it was only a matter of seconds before she was shot, she waited on her hands and knees.

However, after a few seconds, she realized the shooting inside the room had stopped.

She raised her head and looked around. Several bodies of US and Chinese soldiers were scattered around the room, either dying or dead.

She looked over toward Reynolds. He staggered, then stood slightly bent over, trying to catch his breath. He called out, "Juarez! McDonald! Stafford!"

"Here, sergeant!"

"Over here, sergeant!"

"I'm OK."

Then Reynolds walked over to Sara. He crouched down and asked, "Are you OK, Ma'am?"

By now, Sara had caught her breath. "Yes. I'm OK. Please help me up."

Reynolds took hold of her arms and helped her stand up. When he looked at her, his eyes widened.

"What's wrong?" Sara asked.

"That's a hell of a shiner you got there, Ma'am. You sure you feel OK?"

Sara touched her face below her left eye and felt a sharp sting as soon as she touched skin. "I'm fine. Just a little shaken, I guess."

Reynold nodded. He looked around and saw her rifle. He walked over, picked it up, and gave it to Sara. "Here, you go, Ma'am. You're gonna need this."

Sara smiled at his gesture. "Thank You."

Then she unintentionally looked over at the Chinese Soldier she had just killed. His body lay contorted in a death spasm of pain. The blood from his body had pooled underneath him.

Sara's eyes glued to the body. She could feel his hand on her neck and his weight on top of her from moments ago. Her right hand started to tremble, and she could feel a terror inside of her start to grow.

"Captain Bradford?"

Hearing Reynolds call her name, Sara's eyes flinched as she caught herself having slipped away for a moment. She turned and silently looked at him.

Reynolds knew what was going through Sara's mind, and because of that, he deliberately chose his next words very carefully. "If you had not come down and shot those Chinese when you did, they would have overrun us. And if you had not shot the guy on top of me, he would have killed me for sure. You pretty much saved us down here today. Please don't ever forget that."

Sara heard his words and took a moment to process them. The memory of the last 15 minutes quickly replayed in her mind; attacking the convoy, the dead Soldier on the balcony, rushing downstairs, shooting the enemy Soldiers running through the door, and fighting off the man on top of her.

She looked around and saw the five remaining Soldiers still standing, all looking at her. Their faces were sweaty, dirty, bloody, and bruised. But there was resilience in them, and if she could dare say, a pride as they looked upon her. Slowly what Reynolds said sank in. Had she not done what she had, these men would not be standing here now, and their unspoken gratitude and respect spoke volumes. They were forever united in a bond of brotherhood born of battle that neither time nor space could ever remove from this moment on.

Sara looked back at Reynolds and understood now why he said what he did. His words would forever temper these memories and give her a pathway to the solace she would forever need when the demons from these days would come haunting her. She smiled at Reynolds. "Thank You."

Suddenly a voice from outside the doorway yelled out, "Three armored vehicles moving this way, sergeant! Looks like ours."

"Roger. Be ready just in case they're not."

Sara loaded a fresh magazine in her rifle and walked outside. When she exited the building, Lieutenant Harvey came running up to her. Harvey looked at her closely and hesitated to speak just as Reynolds had done.

"Give me a SITREP, Lieutenant," Sara said, not giving the young man a chance to ask her about her condition.

"I've got second and third squad consolidating the wounded and dead now, Ma'am. First squad took out the recon vehicle and is making their way back to the lines. I've also got our APCs coming up with tank escort to carry us back to our defensive positions. I'll have a strength count for you as soon as I can. As far as I can tell, the Chinese have backed off for now. Looks like we destroyed the dismounted platoon that tried to overrun us."

"Do you have coms with the Company TOC?"

"Negative. But we should have them as soon as the APCs get here."

"Good. Let's get the hell out of here as soon as we can."

"Yes, Ma'am," Harvey said and went about his business.

A few seconds later, two armored personnel carriers pulled up with two massive tanks in the little convoy's front and back.

The lead tank pulled up next to Sara and stopped. The top hatch on the turret opened, and Lieutenant Clark crawled out and jumped down from the tank next to Sara.

He took one look at Sara and said, "You look like shit, Ma'am. You OK?"

Sara's lips curled downward, portraying her best display of being perturbed. "Thank you, Lieutenant Clark for your esteemed observation. I see that you finally got your equipment fixed. Maybe now you can contribute just a little to the fight. Hmmm?"

"Yeh, Chief got my babies finally up and running. You should have seen the tanks we shot up to get here. And look at this!" Clark said as he pointed to a large dent in the side of one of the armored panels on the turret. "One of those fuckers actually got a hit on me. Motherfuckers scratched the new paint job and all. Bastards!"

Sara stared at Clark, trying her best to show disdain and disinterest. But inside, she was thrilled to see him. She did not want to try and walk back to the company positions after going through what she and her Soldiers had just done.

"Well, I'll make sure you get a medal for your actions," Sara sarcastically said.

"Cool! Well, we need to load up and get going." Clark then outstretched his arm toward his tank and slightly bowed as he said, "Madame, your chariot awaits."

"I am not getting in that death trap with you. I'll catch a ride in the APC."

"Ma'am, they need the room for the wounded. It's best you ride with us."

Sara forced a deep breath. He was right, and she could not argue. "Oh, all right."

Then she grabbed hold of two handles on the side of the tank to pull herself up when Clark said, "Uh, Ma'am. Can I ask one favor?"

"What is it now?"

With a straight face, Clark said, "We just cleaned up inside. Looks like your' boots are a tad dirty. Could you take them off before you get in?"

Sara's eyes widened in disbelief. "NO!" she grunted and then proceeded to climb on top of the tank.

Clark's face expanded into a massive grin as he shook his head.

Staff Sergeant Reynolds walked up to Lieutenant Clark and said. "You need to be careful, Sir. Captain Bradford personally shot several enemy Soldiers and gutted one like a fish that was on top of her. She just might do that to you if you push her too far."

"Sounds like a hell of a woman. You all loaded, sergeant?"

"Yes, Sir."

Clark slapped Reynolds on the shoulder and said, "Good! Let's move out!"

As soon as everyone was loaded, the convoy moved out.

Back at the division TOC, General Davis waited and watched the big TV screens in front of him as the intel officers worked to reestablish the video feed from the drones circling the area where the attack on the Chinese column had just taken place.

"It should be on the screen now, Sir."

Before the young Captain had finished alerting Davis to the new incoming video, a picture emerged on the screen. All Davis saw was destroyed, and burning tanks and other armored vehicles through clear patches in the smoke.

"Holy shit," he said.

"Sir, we're trying to double-check the BDA now, but it looks like they destroyed the better part of the lead regiment. We're intercepting their comms now of what is left of their advance guard command group, and they are trying to regroup," the G2 reported to Davis.

"Is it safe to say that this unit is no longer a threat to the bridgehead?" Davis asked.

"Yes, Sir. But I don't have any information on blue casualties or strength numbers, so I can't say for sure."

"What do you think their next move is?"

"From what I gather, they're pretty pissed off about what just happened. I would not be surprised if the Chinese try another massive artillery strike on our forces at the bridge."

Davis immediately turned to the division fire support coordination officer and said, "I want the division artillery to immediately begin counterbattery missions on anything that fires at our forces at the bridgehead."

He then turned to the Air Force Liaison Officer and asked, "How long before we can have CAS on site?"

"Sir, the Chinese still have two large SAM batteries that we have not been able to take out yet. Corps does not want to release us any of the manned aircraft until they are destroyed, and all the unmanned aircraft are targeting the SAM batteries and associated radars."

"That's not acceptable. You get on the horn to Corps and tell them I want some CAS missions, now! I don't give a fuck if it is manned or unmanned, but they are going to need some help down there soon."

He then looked over at his G3. "What's the report from 3rd Brigade?"

"They are currently on the move again, Sir. They estimate they will be at the bridge in seven hours."

Davis shook his head. By the grace of God, Sara and her Soldiers had pulled off a small miracle by destroying the lead Chinese regiment that could have taken control of the bridge and cut off 3rd Brigade's retreat. But he knew the Chinese were far from finished. Until he could find some way to help Sara, anything could still happen in the next seven hours.

When Sara walked into her small company TOC, everyone in the room turned and looked at her. "We did it, Ma'am!" her XO enthusiastically cried out.

Then he stared at her and nervously asked. "Are you alright, Ma'am?"

"I'm fine. Just a few bumps on my head is all."

Still looking at her, he asked, "Your vest and shirt, ma'am?"

Sara looked at herself and, for the first time, realized her vest and part of her shirt were covered in bloodstains.

"I'm fine. Give me a SITREP."

"First platoon is at 85% strength and is manning their alternate positions, second and third platoons are still at 95% strength and are in their positions. They received direct fire contact from recon elements and remnants of the lead regiment and have successfully defeated them. We now have four M7 tanks fully operational, with two forming our reserve. The last report from division was that 3rd Brigade was seven hours from linking up with us. Finally, class three and five are amber after the attack."

"Thanks." Then Sara turned to Captain Bloom. "Laura, what do you have?"

"We've destroyed the majority of the lead regiment from what I can piece together from our tactical UAS footage and SIGINT reporting. The Chinese are regrouping, and I would expect them to attack again with whatever they can pull together and hit us hard with artillery and fixed-wing air soon. They know we know they have penetrated our C2 systems, but I would still recommend not using it."

"OK, let me know the moment you see any further movement and show me your current recon and surveillance plan as soon as you can."

"Yes, Ma'am."

"Sara felt a presence behind her, and turned to see First Sergeant Dixon standing next to her.

With no emotion, he said, "Looks like you were in the thick of it, Ma'am."

Sara sighed and said, you don't know the half of it, Top. I need just a few minutes to clean up a bit. Will you stay here until I get back?"

"Sure, Ma'am. But you need to visit the aid station first."

Sara looked at Dixon and knew he would not have asked her to do that unless there was a specific reason. She wanted to visit it anyway to see her Soldiers, but there had been no time with everything she had recently been through. She questioned him why with her expression.

"Thompson."

Sara felt her heart stop. She had lost many Soldiers that day, but the last person in the world she wanted harm to come to was him.

Without hesitating, she replied, "I understand. I'll go right away. Call me if you need me."

Trying her best to show courage and calm in the face of the news she had just heard, she walked to the aid station located in the subway station.

A few minutes later, Sara entered where the casualties were collected until they could be evacuated to the rear. The room was dim and filled with the smell of body odor, blood, and burnt flesh. She almost put her hand to her mouth to cover the smell but caught herself and stopped. Several Soldiers were lying on stretchers, with a few propped up against the wall. The room was quiet except for one Soldier who quietly moaned in pain.

Looking around, she walked over to a corner where she saw a medic
kneeling on the floor over a Soldier who seemed to be severely
wounded. She knelt next to the Soldier opposite the medic and saw it
was Thompson. His uniform was badly torn, with just a shred of a shirt
covering a large wound to his left chest. The bandages around the
wound were filled with a dark red, and each breath Thompson took
seemed to flush more blood into them. Both of his legs were gone with
tourniquets tightly tied above where they had each been severed. The
burn marks on his face marred the once innocent young face Sara had
come to enjoy so much.

She watched the young man struggling to stay alive and fought hard
the emotion that built within her. What was once the epitome of the
delightful young man next door was now a near lump of flesh. She
looked over to the medic who was administering a shot of morphine in
Thompson's left arm, and almost as if he could read her mind, the medic
slightly shook his head. Sara felt her chest tighten with distraught.

She gently took hold of Thompson's left hand that was shaking and
softly called his name, "Thompson."

Thompson slowly rolled his head, looked at Sara, and in a weak
voice, said, "Hello, Ma'am."

Sara forced a smile, but she could not suppress the tears forming in
her eyes. "How are you feeling?"

"Not too good, Ma'am. But I'll be OK. I just need to . . . . . rest a bit.
Really hard . . . . to breathe right now."

"Just relax. We'll get you out of here on the very next load out.
You'll be in a warm bed in no time."

Thompson's eyes looked deep into Sara's as if trying to understand
what she was saying. His breathing became even more labored. He
coughed a few times, and he turned back to Sara and said, "Will you
come visit me in the hospital?"

Sara took her other hand and now held his left hand with both of
hers and said, "Of course I will."

Then Thompson just stared at her for a while as if he was searching
for something to say. Finally, he said, struggling again, "I never knew
anyone as beautiful as you before. Would you take your helmet off for a
moment?"

Sara realized Thompson knew he was dying. He had thrown off all
pretenses and was doing his best to hang on for a moment more. Despite
the superior and subordinate relationship that required a necessary
distance between them, she could not deny his final requests. She had
always been careful to separate herself from her subordinates to
maintain the professional space needed to maintain good order and

avoid the ugliness of favoritism. But as she watched this young man, who for her had always held an air of innocence about him, struggle in the last moments of his life, she felt bound to give him the dignity he deserved—the dignity to live his final moments as a man in the way he wished. She owed him that.

Sara slowly undid the snaps on her helmet and placed it on the ground. Then she took her hand and gently brushed his matted hair from his forehead. She continued to look into his eyes and tried to be strong, but a tear slowly trailed down her cheek.

Thompson took his left hand and tried to wipe the tear from her face. "Will you miss me, Sara?"

Sara nodded and whispered, "Yes, I will miss you very much."

Thompson was silent as he continued to stare at Sara. She could only imagine what was going through his mind. She smiled at him despite the sorrow consuming her heart. She did not want him to die alone.

They stared at each other for a moment until Thompson finally said, "I'll miss you too."

Then his eyes dulled. He became anxious and called out, "Sara! Where are you? It's getting dark! I'm afraid!"

Sara grabbed his hands, and with tears dripping off her cheeks, replied, "I'm here, Andrew. I'm here. Don't be afraid."

Her soft words seemed to calm him. Then his breathing became very hard, as if he was struggling for every breath, and then it stopped.

Sara sat, watching him in silence. There was no dramatic background music, no commentary, no one else watching, just a young man whose life had just passed. Having been an orphan, no one would need to be notified of his death. The world would go on without Thompson. But to Sara, this moment would forever be a part of her life.

The medic who had been watching from a distance walked over and bent down opposite Sara. He gently took a towel and put it over Thompson's face. When Sara did not move, he quietly spoke to her. "Ma'am."

Hearing the medic, Sara looked at him with tear-soaked eyes. When she realized she was still holding Thompson's hands, she slowly placed them on his chest.

She then put her helmet back on her head, got up, and walked out of the room.

When Sara left the room, she turned into the stairway and struggled to come to grips with herself as the thought of an innocent young man who never had the chance to fall in love had just died rushed through her mind. When they first arrived in Korea, she had promised him he would be OK, yet she failed to deliver on that promise.

She hated the war. She hated the Chinese. She hated the division commander for giving her his orders to hold the bridge. But most of all, for that moment, she hated herself for making decisions that cost men and women their lives even if they were the right decisions. It took every bit of willpower in her body to pull herself together and not wholly break down and cry. Eventually, she managed to stay in control by swearing that Thompson's death and all of her Soldiers' deaths would not be in vain. Sara vowed to God and herself she would do whatever it took not to let that happen again.

Chapter 19

13 JUNE 2036; 0745 LOCAL TIME. "Ma'am. The lead elements of 3rd Brigade have linked up with the scouts," First Sergeant Dixon said as he gently nudged Sara on the shoulder. When Dixon saw she had fallen off to sleep in the chair near him, he decided to let her rest for a while. But she told him to make sure to let her know when the linkup happened.

"OK," Sara said as her eyes opened and blinked several times to try and make herself regain some sense of consciousness. Her head felt like it was filled with lead, and her whole body ached from being tired. It was now to the point she seemed to fall asleep if she stopped moving for just a second.

The seven hours to get to the bridge 3rd Brigade reported earlier had turned into eighteen grueling hours of almost nonstop combat. Soon after Sara returned to her company TOC after visiting Thompson, the Chinese began their artillery attack. Even without pinpoint targeting, the initial barrage was so large that they destroyed an entire platoon.

Division artillery began a counterbattery fight to destroy the Chinese guns, but that took time, and the Chinese continued to fire long after they came under fire themselves. Meanwhile, the Chinese had managed to infiltrate a dismounted infantry battalion and a tank company to reinforce what remained of the lead regiment on the ground. Upon arriving, they immediately attacked Sara's company positions on the bridge's far side during the artillery attack.

As soon as the artillery barrage ended, the Chinese started their attack before the US forces knew their presence. Still trying to pull themselves together after the artillery attack, Sara's company fought hard but was almost overrun several times. The fighting eventually became house to house and hand to hand several times. Lieutenant Clark had charged into the enemy positions with his tanks twice to push back the Chinese attempts, with Sara personally riding on top of the lead tank in the second attack. Finally, the division provided several air support sorties that finished off the last of the Chinese tanks hiding in large concrete parking garages.

By the time 3rd Brigade reported they were about to link up with Sara's company's lead patrols, it had been reduced to a third of the strength it had started the fight with. After over twenty hours since Sara assumed command, she had lost half of her Soldiers, yet they still held control of the bridge.

After talking with Dixon, Sara crawled out of the basement of what had been a small restaurant. She did not have the visor down on her helmet, and the sun stung her eyes. She went to wipe some fresh beads of sweat from her cheeks when she realized how filthy she was. Her uniform, soaked with sweat, had several salt stains in several spots in addition to blood stains from the first fight. She looked at her hands, darkened with dirt, blood, and sweat.

She laughed to herself for a moment as she looked at her jagged nails and remembered how she had always insisted on having them manicured and freshly painted when she was in high school. Her sweat-crusted hair was matted in the shape of her helmet. There were no mirrors around, so she could only imagine what she looked like.

She looked toward the road and saw a line of various armored and unarmored, military and nonmilitary vehicles crossing the bridge. It looked as though the 3rd Brigade soldiers had confiscated anything that could still run to get to the bridge site. A couple of guys riding motorcycles seemed to be herding the convoy. All of them had some sort of damage to them. The tanks looked like they had been hit multiple times and probably would not make it many more miles down the road. Most had splintered antennas and deep gashes in their sides from hits. All of the vehicles carried numerous Soldiers, with many riding on the outside of the tanks that passed by. Lots of those Soldiers had bandages on them, and several were lying across the back deck of the armored vehicles.

The lines of vehicles steadily moved along the road and across the bridge, but this was no route. The movement was deliberate and unhurried. Although their faces were tired and dirty, the Soldiers remained alert.

Sara heard the sound of a helicopter approaching from south of the river and watched as two attack helicopters arrived and hovered as a transport helicopter landed in an open field next to the river just a few feet from where she was standing. Several Soldiers got out and started walking toward her, but then they all stopped except one who continued in her direction.

As Major General Davis walked up to and looked at Sara, he didn't have to wonder what she had gone through. Her eyes alone told him.

In addition to her filthy uniform, there was a large bruise around her left eye that he was able to make out over the grime covering her face only because of the swelling and redness. Her blank expression of near-total exhaustion with a faraway look in her bloodshot eyes was one Davis was becoming accustomed to seeing in almost all of the Soldiers under his command. She was no longer the young woman he had seen when he first arrived at the bridge site, but a Soldier who had been pushed to her limit yet somehow had found the courage to hold on.

Sara saw Davis walking toward her, but it felt like she was in a dream state. She stood motionless as he approached and did not move until he stopped in front of her. She then pulled herself together and slowly saluted him.

"Good morning, Sir."

"Morning, Captain Bradford. What's your status?"

"Sir, 3rd Brigade made contact with my scouts 45 minutes ago and is in the process of crossing the Han. I spoke to their Brigade XO a few minutes ago. He said the Brigade Commander was bringing up the rear. I haven't seen him yet. We are still holding our positions on this side of the bridge, but I've only got one operational tank, six APCs, and an overall strength of less than 50%. I'm about to go black on Class 3 and 5. We've requested resupply, but nothing has come forward, and comms have been almost nonexistent the past few hours. The Chinese haven't attacked in the last hour, but I don't think we can hold out against another attack when they do. If there is no one to relieve us, do I have your permission to pull back across the river once 3rd Brigade is across? Do you still want us to blow the bridge?"

"Yes, as soon as 3rd Brigade is across, pull your units across the bridge and set up a defensive perimeter, but don't blow the bridge. A ROK battalion will relieve you in the next two hours. Once they are set, report back to us, and we will release you back to your brigade. We've had major comms problems too, but they should be fully restored soon. Coordinate with them and move back to Assembly Area Crystal to rejoin them."

"Yes, Sir," Sara said. After what seemed like an eternity, she hoped her and her Soldiers would get some rest. But she prayed the Chinese would not attack before they could get back across the bridge themselves.

"Sir, I just hope the Chinese don't attack us before we can get across." Then a thought came to Sara. "Sir, isn't it dangerous for you to be so far forward right now? I would expect the Chinese to start pounding us at any minute."

"No, there's very little chance that will happen. South Korea has called for a ceasefire, and the US and Chinese have agreed to one for the next 96 hours."

Hearing what Davis said, Sara suddenly became more aware. "That's good news! What happens after the 96 hours, Sir?"

Davis took a deep breath before he spoke. "We have that long to get off the peninsula."

"Sir?"

"The South Koreans are trying to negotiate peace with the Chinese before their whole country is destroyed. The Chinese are willing to negotiate, but the price is all US forces leave the peninsula in the next 96 hours."

"But, Sir! I can't believe this! Why is this happening?" Sara exclaimed. She couldn't believe what she was hearing.

"We've done some damage to the Chinese, but not as much as we needed to. The South Koreans have taken things into their own hands. Looks like they would rather live under some sort of Chinese hegemonistic government than have their country destroyed again. They're calling the shots right now, and we're going to have to comply. When you get to your brigade, they'll make arrangements to get you and your Soldiers out of here."

"But, Sir, what about all of our equipment? We can't get all of it to ports and loaded on ships in the next four days."

"It will all be destroyed before you leave. You'll get further guidance."

Sara took a moment to try and comprehend what she had just been told. The United States Army was being forced to leave Korea. The Chinese had won.

She looked toward the line of vehicles approaching the bridge entrance and saw the line was coming to an end. Sara watched as the convoy's last vehicle, an armored personnel carrier, pulled up and stopped a short distance away from Davis and her.

The back ramp dropped down, and a lone Soldier stepped off the ramp onto the ground. He hesitated as he looked around until he spotted Davis and Sara standing nearby. He then slowly made his way to them.

The Soldier stopped in front of Davis and Sara and saluted them both. Sara could barely make out his rank on his uniform, but he was a command sergeant major. She assumed he was 3rd Brigade's Command Sergeant Major. Unlike the usual immaculate appearance sergeant majors present, this man sported a week's worth of growth on his face.

That, along with the pronounced bags under his eyes and his dirty uniform, told Sara he had been through as much if not more hell than she. But there was a determination in his eyes Sara not only saw but could feel. He might be exhausted, but he was not defeated by any stretch.

"Sergeant Major, it's good to see you," Davis said.

"Good to see you too, Sir. I just wish it was under better conditions."

"Me too. Where is Colonel Shelton?"

Upon hearing Shelton's name, the sergeant major's determined eyes got misty. He paused and then turned and pointed to the armored personnel carrier. "He's over there, Sir, in the bustle rack on the back of the turret."

Davis and Sara looked and saw a body bag inside the bustle rack on the back of the turret, securely tied.

"He told me he would be the last man across the bridge after making sure we all got across. I owed him that honor."

The command sergeant major then turned back to Davis and said, "Colonel Shelton was shot in an ambush just as we approached the river an hour ago. He was personally commanding the rear guard. Sir, we would not be here right now if it weren't for him. When all of this shit is over, I'm going to make sure everyone else knows that," the sergeant major firmly said.

Davis nodded. "Let's get you across the river. As soon as you get to the assembly area, let me know, and I'll have an aircraft pick up Colonel Shelton's body."

"Yes, Sir," the sergeant major replied. He then saluted and walked back to his armored vehicle.

Again, Sara found herself in silence with Davis and trying to comprehend what was going on entirely. *We've lost! I can't believe this! After everything my Soldiers have done! The sacrifices they've made! The lives that have been lost! I can't believe this! How could this happen?*

"Captain Bradford," Davis said to regain Sara's attention.

Sara turned and looked at Davis.

"Sara, you and your Soldiers did a hell of a job here. I want you to know how proud and impressed I am."

Sara heard what Davis told her, but she was beside herself with what he had previously said about pulling out of Korea. "But what was it all for, Sir? Just so we could be told to leave and let the Chinese have this stinking country? We've lost! What did my Soldiers die for? What did Colonel Shelton die for? How can I look my Soldiers in the eye and ask them to fight any more if the people we are fighting for are asking us to leave? What the hell . "

"Captain Bradford!"

Hearing the firmness in Davis's voice, Sara realized she had overstepped her bounds in her tirade to him. A sharp feeling of regret and fear filled her as she realized she was talking to the division commander.

"Sir, please forgive me. I didn't mean to go off like that."

Davis was not happy about her outburst, but just looking at the bruises on her face and thinking about what she had just been through tempered his mood. "I understand, Sara. If it makes you feel any better, you just fought one of the most critical battles in this fight. We may be forced to leave, but there are no large groups of American POWs for the Chinese to use against us because of your actions. And every one of those Soldiers in 3rd Brigade owes their lives to you and your Soldiers. Don't ever forget that. I understand why you are angry. I've lost well over a third of the division, and I'm angry about the same things. But those big decisions are not up to us. We follow the orders given to us as best we can. That's our job."

Sara felt selfish for not considering what General Davis had also gone through. "I understand, Sir."

"Good. You better get your troops positioned on the other side of the river. The South Koreans will be on the way. The Chinese should not attack you anymore, but be ready just in case."

Sensing the meeting was over, Sara straightened herself and saluted.

Davis returned her salute, turned, and walked back to his helicopter.

As Davis was walking, First Sergeant Dixon walked towards him to talk with Sara. When Dixon met with Davis, he stopped and saluted. "Good morning, Sir."

"Good morning, First Sergeant. How are you holding up?"

"We're still alive, Sir. It hasn't been easy, but we're still in the fight."

"You and your Soldiers did a great job here. You should feel very proud of them and yourself."

"Thank you, Sir. I am very proud of my Soldiers. But I have to tell you I am immensely proud of my commander. She's the reason we held this bridge. Not sure we could have done that without her."

Davis nodded and made a mental note to have someone get the full story about what had happened here at the bridge site over the past 24 hours. He figured he owed some special recognition to the men and women who had just fought such a vital battle as this one.

"I'll remember that, First Sergeant."

"Sir, if you don't mind me asking, I understand you know her father. Is that correct?"

"Yes, I do. But I haven't talked to him in years."

Dixon reached inside his pocket and pulled out a piece of paper and handed it to Davis. "I met her father when she took command of the company, Sir. He gave me his phone number and asked me to call him if I was ever concerned about her or needed to talk to him about her. I'm sure he's worried sick about her right now. I think he'd liked to know what just happened. I also heard a rumor we are headed home. If that is true, I know he'd want to be there when she gets off the plane. I can't get word back to him, but it would mean a lot to me if you could let him know these things, Sir."

Davis took the piece of paper from Dixon. "Consider it done, First Sergeant."

"Thank you, Sir."

Dixon and Davis then saluted one another and parted.

Still standing motionless and alone, Sara's mind wandered back to think about what Davis said about their pulling out of Korea. Despite her fatigue, Sara's anger rose again, thinking of all her Soldiers who had died and how their lives had been uselessly sacrificed. She thought about her battalion commander, whom she always held in high esteem. He had been an excellent mentor to her, and now he was gone. She thought about all of her friends in the unit who had died. She thought about the heart-wrenching moment she was told of her love, Captain Carlson's death. She thought about the last moments she had spent with Sergeant Thompson and the look on his face just before he died. She squeezed her eyes shut to stop the memories, but they kept coming.

She trembled at the onrush within her mind. It was almost too much. It was then she realized her whole being inside had changed. Whatever innocence, love, or hope that had been in her seemed to be gone. Only anger remained. Her world would never be the same. These past few days would forever mark her future. The Sara she had known lay dead in the ruins on the far side of a bridge on the Han River.

When she opened her eyes, she saw the armored personnel carrier carrying Colonel Shelton's body begin moving across the bridge. She then felt the humiliation of being part of an Army that had failed. *I don't understand! What happened? Did we fail in our mission? I know my Soldiers did not fail! They went beyond what I expected them to do. Did I fail them? I don't think so. Did the division fail? Did General Davis screw things up? I don't think so either, but I don't know. I was not at his level or the division TOC. Did our politicians fail us, the Soldiers on the ground here? Did they not have the nerve to follow through with this*

219

war? Is there something that happened that I don't know about regarding our security as a nation? I just don't understand! My Soldiers did what I asked them to do, and now, over half of them are dead and injured. If we are just going to pull out, what did they die for? Why did we stay and fight? This is all bullshit! I just don't understand! Why?

The more Sara questioned what had just happened and why, the more she felt anger and humiliation as her hands tightened into fists. She watched the armored personnel carrier with Shelton's body until it left her sight. It was then she made a promise to herself. *As long as I stay in the Army, I will do whatever I can to never allow this to happen again! This will NOT happen again on my watch!*

Chapter 20

John sat at the edge of the couch, watching the news out of Seoul, Korea, in the same position he had been in for the past two hours. The reports were incredibly vivid as aerial drones from several major news networks broadcasted live footage of the fighting on TV. They panned over the city at times, and all John could see from their position to the horizon was smoke, flames, and destruction. At other times, they zoomed in on the ground and showed civilians fleeing the area, and in a few rare cases, troops engaging in combat. However, since several drones had been shot down, most kept their distance from the fighting.

The news reporters on the ground tried their best to dodge the fighting and simultaneously provide coverage. However, the battle had been so intense that several embedded reporters had been killed and wounded. As a result, all but the most dedicated kept a safe distance, allowing the drones to provide the actual coverage.

Supposed military experts provided their commentary about what was shown, but John tuned them out. He didn't need someone to tell him about what he saw. He had been in those situations too often not to have a good idea. His heart went out to the men and women doing their best to fight off the invasion, and he did not have to imagine what they were going through. He knew.

He watched the images flashing on the screen, but his mind was often not paying attention. Memories of his little girl sitting on his lap, laying against his shoulder and chest as they watched TV together, or her smiling face covered in birthday cake and icing as a new three-year-old filled his thoughts. He closed his eyes and remembered those precious few months of the three of them together before Lisa was sick.

It wasn't good enough for them to take Lisa from me, he thought. *Now they want to take Sara too.* Sara was down there, somewhere, leading Soldiers trying to stop the Chinese invasion, and every time that thought crossed John's mind, a cold streak of fear shot through his body. He felt helpless. Once again, he remembered how powerless he felt sitting next to Lisa's bed, watching her slowly succumb to cancer and agonizing in the knowledge that there was nothing he could do about it. Those thoughts chilled his entire body as again he realized there was nothing to do but watch what was happening and pray Sara was not taken from him now too. *God, you can't do this! You can't take them both away. Please! You took Lisa. Please, don't take Sara! Not yet!*

He tried to call a few of his old Army buddies who still had contacts within the Army to get information on exactly what was happening but could find nothing. Finally, he tried calling Jim, but there was no answer. Even though Jim had retired a few years ago, John hoped at least he could get him some inside information.

All John's efforts came to nothing, so he tried to talk to the one person that might be able to help. He closed his eyes and silently thought. *Lisa. Lisa, if you can hear me, please be with Sara. Please help her. I know she needs you. Lisa, you have to help her like you helped me. Please, baby, do this for me. Do it for Sara. Please!*

Deep in thought, John felt a soft hand on his shoulder. He opened his eyes, looked up to meet another pair of concerned eyes looking at him.

Jennifer sat down next to John and gently ran her hand through his thick gray hair. "John, honey, are you OK?"

She had become a Godsend to him. Years ago, after returning from his mission with Jim, he went to her and said he wanted to start a relationship with her. She was thrilled. They took it slow, and in time, Jennifer found fertile ground in John's heart. Despite her flaws, being together brought them the warmth, companionship, laughter, and love they both had been without for so long. Even though in the deepest confines of John's heart, Lisa remained as she would forever, his mind had finally succumbed to a chance to live the rest of his life in the company of someone he loved and who truly loved him.

Once they were together, it did not take Jennifer long to fall deeply in love with John. She adored the time they were together, especially alone. Just as for Lisa, John was a man unlike any man Jennifer had known, and despite being nine years older than her, he somehow did his best to remain young at heart. At times, she could still see the boy in him.

Still, she understood that ultimately, she was a caretaker of John's heart while he remained alive. She knew John's love for Lisa would never end. However, John never talked about Lisa to Jennifer. When they were together, his love solely focused on her. And because Jennifer knew she owned a part of his heart, she accepted him for who he was.

Despite being together for several years, they still owned their own houses, but they never slept alone, taking turns at whose house they would stay at for the evening. John kept his home in the country. He just couldn't bring himself to live in the city, and his house on the outskirts of town gave Sara the sanctuary she needed at times when she would come to stay with him.

"I'm fine, Jen. I'm OK," John answered.

She knew he was lying. She knew what he was worried about, and she was concerned too. "Sweetheart, I'm sure she will be OK."

He tried to smile but couldn't. He simply exhaled and nodded.

Just then, Jennifer's cell phone rang, and she went to the kitchen to answer it.

John heard Jennifer talking and realized she was talking to Mary.

A moment later, Jennifer handed John the phone and said, "It's Mary. She'd like to talk to you."

He took the phone from Jennifer's hands, and said, "Hi, Mary. What's up?"

"Have you heard any news about Sara?" she timidly asked.

"No, nothing."

Mary waited for John to continue to talk, but she only heard silence after giving his short answer. She knew John was very worried about Sara. She'd been over to visit him at Jennifer's house a few times, and she didn't remember a time when he wasn't sitting in front of the TV since the war started. "I don't know what to tell you. I've been in your shoes several times, worried sick, every time you were deployed. But there is one thing that is different between then and now. Sara had the best teacher there ever was for what she is doing right now, you. That will make a huge difference. I know she's going to be alright. I just know it, like I knew it when you were gone."

Again, John tried to smile but failed. He knew Mary was just as worried as he was about Sara and doing her best to cheer him up. But he also knew there are no guarantees in war. "Thanks, Sis."

"If you hear anything, will you call and let me know?"

"Sure, Sis."

With that, Mary wished John a good night and hung up.

John set the cell phone down on the couch next to him and turned back to the TV. He listened as the news anchor announced the President was considering a complete withdrawal from South Korea.

He shook his head in disgust. He could hear the words of Garcia's mother echoing in his mind when he visited their house, and he offered his condolences for the death of their son, who had been his driver in Iraq. "Was my son's death worth it?" he remembered Garcia's mom asking him. Never in a million years had he thought it would be him now that might be asking that same question.

Jennifer walked over and turned the TV off with the remote. Before John could look at her, she grabbed his arm and pulled him up from the couch. "Come on, honey. You're not going to sit here another hour and worry yourself sick. You need to eat something, and then let's go to bed."

He knew she was right. He needed a break. "Jen, I'll eat something, but then let me watch a little bit more before I turn in."

"No can do, handsome. The heater in the back of the house is acting up, and I need a nice warm body next to mine to keep me comfortable tonight. You'll do just fine," she replied with a mischievous smile.

For the first time all day, John cracked a grin. "So that's what I am now? Just a bed warmer?"

Seeing John grin made Jennifer's smile widen. "Well, amongst other things." She brought her hand up to his face, gave him a quick kiss, and led him to the kitchen.

When John finally climbed into bed, Jennifer snuggled close to him and put her arm around him. He concluded it was colder than usual, but he knew Jennifer was trying her best to put his mind at ease. He alternated between looking at the ceiling and turning to see the time on the clock on the nightstand as sleep never did come.

Suddenly as if he had willed it, his cell phone on the nightstand started to ring. John jumped up in bed, and answered it without looking at the caller id. He instinctively seemed to know it had something to do with Sara. "Hello!"

"Sir, are you, Colonel John Bradford?" Hearing the person on the other end calling John by his rank immediately sent chills through his whole body. It could only mean one thing.

"Yes, I am Colonel John Bradford."

"Sir, please stand by. Major General Davis would like to talk to you." John's body froze, and his stomach tensed into one big knot. *Oh, my God! No! Please, no!*

The man on the other end did not wait for John to reply, and John felt as if his life depended upon the next words he heard.

"Colonel Bradford, I'm Major General Shawn Davis, Commander, First Cavalry Division. I don't know if you remember me, but I worked for you at III Corps Headquarters when you ran the lessons learned section back at Fort Hood in 2010."

John had to think for a while, then it hit him finally, "Yes! Shawn! I remember you! Oh, my God! It's great to hear from you!"

"It's great to get a chance to talk to you too, Sir. I'm sorry for calling in the middle of the night, and I don't have a lot of time, so I will get right to the point. I wanted you to know your daughter, Sara, is alive and well."

The moment John heard and understood Sara was OK, his heart exploded with emotion. Tears immediately filled his eyes. His hand trembled, and he tried to say something, but his throat choked as the words tried to make their way out. Finally, he was able to stutter, "Thank You."

John felt a soft hand on his shoulder and turned to see a very worried expression on Jennifer when he turned around. He shook his head to indicate to her it was good news.

"I can't go into details," the general continued, "but I want you to know you can be very proud of your daughter. She is an extraordinary officer, just like her father; however, I need to tell you she's been through hell. Physically, she's fine, but it might be best if you could meet her when she returns soon if you understand what I mean."

John read through the lines of what Davis was saying. "Where will you send her?"

"She will land in Hawaii in a few days for some rest."

Before Davis could say anything else, John immediately said, "I will meet her when she lands in Hawaii."

"I was hoping you would say that. I'll have an officer contact you so you can gain entry to the airfield."

"Thank You, Shawn. I can't tell you what this means to me."

"No need to thank me, Sir. When I realized Sara was your daughter, I figured you'd like to know if she was OK. I can't do this for all my officers, but I needed to finally repay the officer who taught me what it was like to be a good leader."

"You don't ever need to repay me for anything. You're a good officer, and I'm so glad to know you became a general officer. Congratulations! I'm very proud to have served with you."

"Thank You, Sir! I should also tell you I don't know if you remember that time you gave me a three-day pass, but that young lady I was with has been my wife for the past 25 years."

"I'm happy to hear that. Please take care of yourself and stay safe, Shawn. God bless you."

"Thanks, Sir. The same to you."

The moment John hung up his phone, he turned to Jennifer and said, "We need to get packed. We're leaving for Hawaii tomorrow morning."

Soon after the flight from Guam landed at Wheeler Field in Hawaii, Sara started disembarking. Everything had happened so fast she struggled to keep her mind straight. Only a few days ago, she and her Soldiers were in some of the war's most intense combat, and now she was walking off of an airplane in "Paradise." The war was essentially over for the US with their pullout of South Korea, and the Army wanted to get their units as far back as they could to reconstitute them quickly. But it would take several months to reequip Sara's company with the equipment they left behind, and the Army figured the best thing to do in the short term was to give her unit some rest.

Sara slowly made her way through the plane and to the top of the ramp. When she emerged from the aircraft, the cool Pacific wind blew some loose strands of hair around her face, and she squinted her eyes in the bright sunshine.

Before her, the calm airport scene was in stark contrast to the almost chaotic activities on the military airfield at Guam. No burning wreckage, no ground crews running to receive and quickly turn around aircraft for missions, no collection of tired and dirty Soldiers, Marines, and Airmen waiting for flights out. It seemed there was no organized process as to who was selected to fly out when. Once onboard, she looked around the aircraft and did not recognize anyone on it. Most were Marines. She was told the Soldiers from her unit would be consolidated at the barracks on Schofield, and she would meet them in a day or two. Her orders were to link up with the 1st Cavalry Division officers who would meet the plane, and they would direct her to the local Bachelor Officer Quarters on base for temporary housing.

Walking down the steps of the ramp, Sara still felt the intensity of being in a combat zone. She had not yet exhaled or come to believe she was out of harm's way. Despite being exhausted, she was still on edge, as were the rest of the Marines on the plane. What normally would have been a very joyful and rambunctious mood on a military aircraft returning from a deployment, was instead a very subdued one. The memories of what had transpired the past couple of weeks kept trying to appear in her mind, but she would push them out, thinking of nonsense, if nothing else. But she realized once she was alone in her room in a couple of hours, she would no longer be able to push them out. She thought maybe she could volunteer to help receive the incoming personnel from her brigade, but she felt drained. She desperately needed a couple of hours of full horizontal sleep.

When she stepped off the ramp, she saw in the distance the rally point where the line of military personnel from her plane were gathering and started to walk that way. From her peripheral vision, she saw a civilian man and a captain standing alongside the line of Marines walking to the rally point, but paid them no attention. With each step, her mind grew numb.

She had walked past the two men when she heard someone call out her name, "Captain Bradford."

She stopped, turned, and looked directly at the man's face. For a short moment, she tried to remember. Then a voice she had known all of her life called again. "Sara."

That was when it hit her, like a tidal wave. It all came flooding back - the orders to hold the bridge, the constant artillery barrages, the hand to her throat, the sight of her Soldiers, twisted, torn, dead, the division commander shaking her hand, the news Carlson had been killed and being with Thompson as he died. It all rushed through her mind so fast it overwhelmed her.

She looked into the eyes of the one man who loved her like no one else ever would. And she knew. She could see it in his eyes. He understood what was in her mind. She did not have to say a thing. He completely understood. And she saw within his eyes fear for her, sympathy, understanding, but most of all, his love for her.

Tears streamed down her cheeks as she began to relax for the first time since she had gotten on the plane bound for Korea that started her deployment months ago. She let go. She threw her hands up and rushed toward the man and hugged him as tight as she could. Through her sobs and broken voice, she cried, "Daddy!"

John tightly hugged Sara as if placing a wall between her and the outside. He felt them, all the demons now circling and trying their best to stalk her. But John would never let them in. He knew their game. He knew what it was to return from a combat deployment only to find yourself in a room alone, and he swore he would not let that happen to his daughter. Not on his watch.

Sara buried her head beside John's neck as he gently rubbed her back and let her cry.

John turned his head to the captain near him and quietly asked, "Is there any problem if she stays with us for a night or two?"

"No, Sir. You've got my number if you need to contact me. I'll get her bags and have them delivered to your hotel."

"Thank You. And please pass on to General Davis, my deepest thanks."

When Sara got back to John and Jennifer's hotel room, she took a long shower. Jennifer lent her one of her robes, and when she dried off, she told John she wanted to take a nap before they went out to eat.

Sara laid down on the bed in the second bedroom of John's hotel and was soon fast asleep. When it was time to get ready for supper, John checked on Sara and saw she was in a deep sleep. He decided not to wake her.

Standing next to her bed, he got a better look at the bruises on her face. He hadn't asked her how she got them. Looking down at Sara, John saw his little girl, the one who would give him precious little smiles that melted him. Then he saw a strong woman, a Soldier, and a fearless leader. From what Davis had told him, John could almost not believe what she had done.

Yet, he also felt fear and guilt. Fear for her life in the profession she chose and for what John knew she was in for. Guilt that in some way, he was responsible for her current situation. Had he not been a Soldier, she would probably not have decided to follow in his footsteps.

But the one thing John saw the whole time he looked at her soundly sleeping was how beautiful a woman she was and how proud he was of her. He smiled to himself and thought, *Oh, Lisa. You would be so proud of your little girl right now. How I wish you could see her.*

He resisted the temptation to lean down and kiss her on the forehead as he had countless times as a little girl as he wished her good night. Instead, he turned and silently walked out of her room.

When John and Jennifer went to bed later that night, Jennifer thought it odd John left the door to Sara's room and their bedroom door open. Later that night, she found out why.

In the middle of the night, Jennifer felt John quickly get out of bed as she heard Sara cry out.

Jennifer got up, put on her robe, and walked into Sara's room. She found John sitting on the side of her bed, calmly talking to Sara as he held her.

"I've got to get to them, Daddy! They're in trouble!"

"Shhhh. It's OK, baby girl. Everyone is safe. You are safe. There is no threat here. I'm right here with you. No one is going to hurt you. I promise," John quietly told Sara.

Jennifer watched John until he nodded to her that he had everything under control and she could go back to bed.

When John later crawled back into bed and laid on his back, Jennifer turned on her side and softly said, "You knew she was going to have nightmares tonight. Didn't you?"

"Considering what she's been through, I thought she might. I know what it is to come home after a combat deployment, and that's why I didn't want her to be alone this first night."

Jennifer then wondered about John. He hadn't told her a lot about his time in combat. She asked, "Who took care of you that first time you came home?"

There was a long silence following Jennifer's question as the painful memories of coming home to an empty room after his first combat deployment to Afghanistan returned to John. Suddenly, he felt the emptiness and loneliness of that first night back. Despite how long it had been, he could feel his eyes welling up. Finally, John simply said, "No one."

Hearing John's answer, Jennifer felt a profound sadness. She reached and placed her hand on his chest. "I'm sorry, sweetie."

John placed his hand on her hand and replied, "It's OK, sweetheart. It was a long time ago."

But Jennifer knew better. She heard the pain in John's voice despite his words otherwise. She drew him close, placing her head on his shoulder and her leg over his. "I promise you won't be alone again, baby, as long as I'm here."

"Thank you, sweetheart," John replied as Jennifer's loving voice and gesture removed the pain he was feeling. He turned his head and kissed her on hers to let her know how much he appreciated what she said.

John stayed awake for the next hour, listening to hear if Sara had any more bad dreams. She remained quiet the remainder of the night. Finally realizing his little girl was safe, John succumbed to the warmth of Jennifer's body next to his and drifted off into a restful sleep.

Three days later, the officers and Soldiers of the 2nd Brigade, 1st Cavalry Division, stood at attention in a gym on Schofield Barracks, Hawaii, as the awards for valor were given to those who had distinguished themselves in Korea. Major General Davis gave a short speech, then began the individual presentations of which Sara was the last Soldier called forward. She walked up to the stage, sharply turned, and stood at attention, facing the crowded gym. General Davis stood to her left, and the sergeant, holding her award for presentation, stood next to him. Her Brigade Commander stood to her right.

General Davis took a step forward and spoke. "It is my great honor and privilege to present these awards for valor to the men and women standing on this stage and who have distinguished themselves in combat. But in this one instance, I must relinquish this honor to another very distinguished former Soldier of the 1st Cavalry Division. Colonel

Bradford, would you please step forward and present Captain Bradford her award?"

Dressed in civilian clothes and sitting in the front row before the stage with Jennifer, John stood up, made his way up the stairs, and stood at attention in front of Sara.

Davis turned to the officer at the podium and said, "Major, please read the orders."

"Attention to orders. Captain Sara Maire Bradford is awarded the Distinguished Service Cross for her extraordinary heroism in the performance of her duty against overwhelming odds in the face of the enemy. Captain Bradford distinguished herself by . . ."

As the officer read the orders, John looked at Sara, who was staring straight ahead just below his eyes. He thought for a moment about the little girl he held in his arms the day Sara was born and the glow of joy on Lisa's face when told she had a daughter. He thought about the journey Sara had taken, initially against his desires, only to now stand before him and her contemporaries, unmatched in what she had done. The little girl, the woman, the Soldier Sara had become, was beyond anything John could have imagined. He prayed Lisa was looking down upon them so she could see the incredible woman their daughter had become.

When the officer finished reading the orders, John turned and took the Distinguished Service Cross medal from the sergeant and pinned it on Sara's pocket. Then, he put his hand in his pants pocket and pulled out another medal – his own Silver Star awarded to him years ago. As he was pinning the medal on Sara, he quietly told her, "When General Farmer pinned this on me, he said he was very proud to have men like me in his division. But now I get to have the chance to pin this on you and tell you I could never be more proud of you, my daughter, than I am right now."

When John finished pinning his Silver Star on Sara, he stood at attention and saluted her, holding it until she returned the gesture.

Hearing John's words, Sara's eyes got watery as she returned his salute. She mouthed the words, "I love you, Daddy," and John smiled. He then stood to the side as General Davis and the Brigade Commander congratulated Sara, followed by applause.

For Sara, it was a bittersweet moment. On the one hand, she was overcome with pride in having received such an honor, and hearing her father's words meant the absolute world to her. She never forgot that moment.

However, her heart and mind were forever scarred by memories of those Soldiers who did not return, and the bitterness defeat brings.

Regardless of the decisions of those above her, this Korean war had been fought and lost on her watch. The Army she served in had lost. They had failed the nation, and she was a part of that failure. Her passion for never letting that happen again had just begun.

PART FIVE

THE LAST VACATION TOGETHER

Chapter 21

JUNE 2037. "Dad, I can't just fly off to the Virgin Islands right now! We've just gotten back from our NTC rotation. I need to help the S3 update the Battalion TACSOP," Sara said over the phone to John.

"But you did get Jack's wedding invitation. Didn't you?" John asked.

"Yes, I got it a week ago. I just haven't had time to sit down and read it. You know what it's like in a Battalion 3 shop. Constant chaos."

"Yes, I remember. Sweetheart, we haven't seen you in almost a year, and I don't know when the last time you've seen your Aunt Mary and the boys. You know, Jack personally asked me to make sure you would come. He still sees you as his baby sister. We're all going. It will be a great chance to see everyone again."

"I know. I can't believe it either that he finally decided to get married after all these years. But we've got the TACSOP update, then a relook at our METL. Oh, yeh, we're supposed to field the new upgrade to the Bobcat APCs starting in two months. That will be a nightmare in itself. I just can't leave the three shop hanging right now. I promise I'll call Jack and explain it to him. I'm sure he'll understand."

When Sara finished talking, there was silence on the other end of the phone for a while before John said, "I'd really like to see you, Baby Girl."

"I know, Daddy. I miss you too. I tell you what. I promise to come home this Christmas, no matter what. OK?"

This time there was an even longer moment of silence. Finally, Sara said, "Daddy, are you still there?"

"Yes, I'm here. I understand. Well, I love you very much. I'll talk with you later."

"I love you too, Daddy," Sara said before hanging up. It was clear from the sound of John's voice he was disappointed she wasn't going to take leave and attend Mary's oldest son's wedding. But she knew it wasn't the wedding as much as that he missed her.

WHEN LOVE PERSEVERES

After talking with John, Sara pulled out the frozen dinner from her microwave and sat down in the recliner in her apartment's tiny living room. It had been an extra hectic day at the battalion operations section, and she needed a moment to clear her mind. As the assistant operations officer, it seemed she got all the taskers the battalion S-3 didn't want to mess with in addition to her regular work.

Sitting in the chair with her meal on a small tray on her lap, Sara suddenly realized she heard nothing for the first time all day.

She took a bite of her dinner and quickly spat it out as it burned her tongue. The meal still needed time to cool off. She grabbed her glass of water from the small table next to her recliner and took a drink to cool the fiery sensation still in her mouth. The silence continued.

At first, it was welcome. There were no ringing phones, no constant interruptions by others for help, and no bellowing by the battalion S-3 for yet another status report on the countless projects she was working. However, soon the silence brought an uneasiness within her that robbed her of her earlier peace. She asked herself why.

Looking around the bare little room, Sara reflected on where she was in life. Her tiny apartment was nothing more than a place to lay her head. It seemed she spent almost all of her time on post at work. She was approaching 30 in a year, and while her Army career was going well, other things were not. She hadn't had a real date in years, it seemed. Silently laughing to herself, she thought, *I don't know how I could even fit a boyfriend in right now.*

All of her friends from college were married, and most had families. She was forever getting invitations for weddings, baby showers, and various other social events that come with this point in one's life. But she'd throw down the Army work card and bow out after sending a gift. She'd lie to herself and say those things were not important to her. She was a Soldier; duty came first. But that excuse was wearing thin.

Remembering her cousin Jack swearing he'd never get married brought a mental smile to Sara. He was so adamant the last time they'd visited. *He must have found someone very special. I wonder if I will one day?*

Sara found herself staring at an old picture John had given her of him and Lisa when they had first brought Sara home from the hospital as a baby. She treasured it because it was one of the very few pictures she had of the three of them together before her mother got sick. John held Sara in his arms, and Lisa had her arm around him with a loving smile on her face. If there was one man who was always there for her, it was her father.

They had spent a lot of time together when she was young. She laughed out loud at the thought of John having the daddy-daughter talk with her about sex. He was so nervous, and she didn't have the heart to tell him she already knew.

Suddenly she missed him dearly. When she realized he was already 70, she felt worried. What would she do when he died? She didn't want to answer that question because she wasn't sure. Even though she hadn't seen him in a while, he was always a phone call away, just within reach. One day he wouldn't be. Focusing on that thought, Sara decided somehow the battalion S-3 shop would just have to get along without her for the next two weeks. She had a wedding and a well-deserved vacation she needed to attend to.

Sara picked up the phone and called her father. The joy in his voice alone when she told him she was coming made it all worthwhile.

When the driverless car Sara rented pulled up in front of her Aunt Mary's house in the Victoria Country Club, she was surprised to see so many cars parked in front of it. By looking at the different vehicles, she could determine who was there. The BMW was Mary's and Jason's Mercedes was in the garage. The older 4 Runner had to be her father's. Jennifer hated that thing, but he refused to give it up. The sparkling new Ford pickup truck had to be her cousin Ed's, and the Maserati was definitely her cousin Jack's.

She knocked on the door, and when it opened, there stood Jack, as handsome as ever with his 6'2" lean frame towering over her with a brotherly grin. "Wow! Who do we have here! You must have the wrong house, lady. The pool party for the centerfolds is a block over."

Sara rolled her eyes and said, "Oh shut up," as she playfully slapped his arm.

Jack laughed and gave Sara a big hug. "I'm so glad you could make it, Sara. You look great!"

"Well, I had to come to see who this woman is who could convince the life-long bachelor to give up his ways."

"Oh, I can't wait for you to meet Dana. You're going to love her. But come on in! Everyone is dying to see you." Closing the door behind Sara, Jack called out, "Hey everybody, the prodigal daughter has finally returned!"

Sara made her way into the kitchen, and already everyone was standing up to come and greet her. Her Aunt Mary had bolted out of her chair the moment Jack announced her arrival and threw her arms around

Sara. "Oh, baby, it is so good to see you! I've missed you so much." Her embrace was a tight one filled with love.

"Hi, Aunt Mary. I've missed you too."

"OK, sister-in-law, don't hog all the hugs," Jennifer said, walking up to them. As soon as Mary released Sara, Jennifer jumped in and squeezed on Sara. "Hello, baby. Welcome home," she told Sara.

"Thanks, Jennifer," Sara replied. After the rocky start to their relationship, Sara realized how much Jennifer loved her father, and she couldn't deny he was much happier with her around. Though never having children of her own, Jennifer had gone out of her way to make Sara feel like her daughter, and Sara welcomed it, although no one could take the place of her Aunt Mary, who she was still very close to.

Standing behind Jennifer stood Ed. She loved his boyish dimples, and he was still as handsome as ever, even with his receding hairline. "It's about time you come home and see us, Wonder Woman!"

"It's about time you got a haircut," Sara joked back as Ed hugged her. "It's great to see you, Sara."

"Where's your wife Linda and the herd?"

"They'll be here soon enough. Stan wants to visit with Aunt Sara again so you can teach him how to drive a tank."

Mary's husband, Jason, was next. "Hi, Sara. It's great to see you."

"Good to see you, Uncle Jason."

Feeling a little delirious from all the hugging, she looked around and instantly found the person she wanted to hug most.

Standing near her, patiently waiting his turn, was John. It'd been almost a year since she last saw him, and there was a tiredness about him. His hair was all gray now, and the lines in his face a bit deeper than she last remembered. Age was slowly taking its toll. But there was no denying the gleam in his eye and his bright smile that showed forth for her.

Sara walked over to John, and before she could say anything, he pulled her into a warm embrace and quietly said, "It is so good to see you, Baby Girl."

"Oh, Daddy! I've missed you so much!"

She felt his embrace tighten, and when he released her, she saw the mist in his eyes, her heart warmed, and she felt her eyes moisten.

John's smile never left as he said, "Come on and sit down. We just started lunch! You must be hungry after all that traveling."

Ed grabbed Sara a chair, and Jennifer made a place for her at the table next to John.

"OK, just a little. I got something at the airport and ate it on the way here."

"You ate while you drove?" John asked. He then handed Sara a bowl of pea salad and said, "Here, try this pea salad. Jennifer made this, and it's delicious!"

"Thanks, Daddy. No. The car drove itself, so I just rode and ate."

"I thought you were going to parachute in like a commando," Ed teased.

"They waved the mission off. Unfortunately, the glare from your bald head interfered with their visual guidance," Jack interjected.

"Oh, my God! You rented one of those kinds of cars?" John asked.

"Yes. It's all I could get. Most of the tactical vehicles I ride in now are self-driven anyway, like the new armored personnel carrier we're fielding next month. You should see the sensor package on it!"

"What's the armament?"

"OK, NO Army, talk you two!" Mary proclaimed. "This is family time! You can talk about how you two are doing, what everyone is up to, what's the latest gossip, blah blah blah. You can talk about sex as far as I care. But you're not going to talk that Army lingo that no one else understands!"

John pointed his head at Mary with a raised eyebrow.

Jennifer, who was sitting next to John, reached over and interlaced her hand with his. "Yes, sweetheart. Let's not get started with that. OK?"

Turning from Mary to Jennifer, then back to Sara, John acknowledged his defeat.

Biting her lip to keep from smiling, Sara mouthed, "Later," to John with a grin.

"I saw that young lady," Mary said.

John winked at Sara, then turned to Jason, and innocently asked, "So, bother-in-law, how is your sex life these days?"

"John!" Mary yelled out.

"Well, you said we could talk about that."

"I know what I said! Jennifer, please get that husband of yours under control."

Watching the playful banter between the people she loved the most, Sara realized how much she'd missed it. As a teenager, she thought it was sometimes corny how everyone in her family would tease one another, especially John and Mary. But today, it was music to her ears.

"So, what's the timeline for the wedding?" Sara asked.

"We fly two days from tomorrow. We'll get to the islands before most of the wedding party so we can enjoy some family time. Then the wedding is on Saturday. Sunday to recover, and then fly out on Monday," Mary explained. Sara could tell she was enjoying her role as the groom's mother. She looked a little thinner than Sara last remembered.

"I've told Dana all about you, Sara. Her parents can't wait to meet you. They will arrive a day after we do," Jack said.

"Sara, I can't wait to see the dress you're going to wear. I bet it's stunning," Mary said.

"Well, Aunt Mary. I didn't have time to pack much. I brought my class A uniform along to wear for the wedding."

"What? Oh, heavens no, my dear!"

"Did you see those new dresses at that new fancy shop in the mall the other day? They would be perfect for her. I bet they'd fit her straight off the rack," Jennifer interjected.

"Oh my God, Jen! I know the ones you're talking about! Yes! They would be perfect for her! And what about that French bikini they had in the lingerie store next to it?"

"Oh, yes! It would fit her like a glove!"

Sara's eyes bounced from Mary to Jennifer until she said, "Uh, I appreciate your enthusiasm, but . ."

"Don't worry about anything, sweetheart. We girls are going shopping tomorrow. Oh, I can't wait to get you all dressed up!" Mary said.

Worried about what she was being volunteered for, Sara glanced at John, who grinned and hunched his shoulders.

"And don't worry, sweetheart. Your father will pay for it all," Jennifer said.

John's face went from grin to horror as he blustered out, "What?"

Sara giggled. "Ohhh. Thanks, Daddy. It's so great to be home!"

Chapter 22

Taking inventory one last look in the mirror before Sara headed down to the resort's beach, there was no denying there was not a lot left that was covered. Shopping with her Aunt Mary and Jennifer had been a blast. They gave Sara the royal treatment, bringing clothes to her so all she had to do was try them on. After being a little resistant at first, Sara finally gave in and decided it was time to ditch the uniform for a while and be a woman. When Mary and Jennifer brought some full one-piece bathing suits for Sara to try on, she asked if they could get her something a bit sexier, and the two women grew giddy. Sara realized that, among other things, the two older women were going to live vicariously through her on this vacation, and she was more than willing to play the part.

Sara couldn't remember the last time she cut loose or put the military behind her so she could be a normal woman again. She slept in late and enjoyed being unencumbered to a daily schedule, although Mary ensured they met the travel deadlines.

A trip to Jennifer's and Mary's favorite spa the day before flying was Sara's introduction to the art of the bikini wax. Looking at her bottoms, she was glad she decided to get a lot trimmed off. Sheer skin was much better than stubble. The nails, exfoliation treatment for her skin, facial and massage alone made her feel like a whole new woman. She loved the aromatherapeutic effect and smell of her lavender oil.

After Sara left the spa, she and Jennifer had lunch at a little Mexican restaurant nearby. She could feel almost every male eye in the place on her, giving her confidence the girls at the spa had done a great job. The waiter must have stopped by their table every five minutes, checking on them, always talking to Sara. When they left, Sara smiled at him and waved goodbye with her lashes, causing him to drool practically.

She struck a final pose, eyed herself in the mirror, and thought, *Hmm. Not bad.* The daily physical training was showing its dividends. Her legs were tone, and her rear firm thanks to the hundreds of leg exercises she did almost daily. Carrying around a rucksack filled with all the things an infantry Soldier needed even in the 21st Century was not easy.

She adjusted her top to make sure everything was snug. She'd inherited her mother's full breasts, and the girls were in full display today. The only thing that might obscure their view was her long, shiny, brunette hair that hung well past her shoulders. The stylist at the spa trimmed her hair, and Mary told Sara she was included on the list for a complete hair and make-up treatment before the wedding.

Yep! Not bad for twenty-nine, she mused.

There was a knock on her door, and Sara grabbed a wrap to cover herself before she answered it.

Mary came in, and seeing Sara dressed for a day at the beach, she asked with a smile, "So, how does it fit?"

Sara's face blushed as she said, "Well, it covers everything it's supposed to. But that's about it."

"Mind if I take a look before you venture out to the wolves?" Mary asked.

Still blushing, Sara opened her wrap.

Shaking her head, Mary said, "Sweetheart, you look beautiful!"

"You think so?"

"Oh, I know so. You know who you look like?"

"Who?"

"You look just like your mother."

Sara's face turned into a sad but grateful smile. "Thanks, Aunt Mary. That's so nice of you to say. But I know Mama was a lot prettier than me."

"Oh, I don't know. But it doesn't matter. Somewhere right now, she's smiling with all the pride in the world at her beautiful daughter. May I escort you down to where everyone is at on the beach?"

"Absolutely!"

Mary took Sara down to the beach where John, Jennifer, and Mary's son, Ed, were camped out under a large umbrella shade. Ed's wife and children were playing in the water.

Walking up to the shade, Sara heard a loud whistle just before Ed gave her a goofy smile.

Playfully chastising Ed, Sara asked, "Will you cut that out?"

"Well, at least you're not in some Army commando outfit. Hey, come on. The kids want their favorite aunt to go swimming with them!"

"OK!" Sara said. She threw off her wrap, and Ed and her went running toward the kids in the rushing waves.

John had just finished taking a sip of his fruity, alcohol-induced drink when he looked up and saw plenty of Sara's cheeks dancing as she ran.

He jerked toward Mary and Jennifer and said, "What the hell! I thought you two were supposed to get some clothes for her. What the hell is that?"

"It's a swimsuit, John," Mary casually said.

"Swimsuit, hell! She can't wear that! She's an officer!"

"She's also a woman, John. Let her be. This is a chance for her to forget the Army for a while."

"I bet you two put her up to this."

"Actually, sweetheart, Sara picked that bikini out herself," Jennifer said.

John just shook his head and stared at Sara.

"I'm going to get another drink. Anyone else need a refill?" Jennifer asked.

When both John and Mary answered no, Jennifer walked off to the nearby bar on the beach.

Mary noticed John had not stopped staring at Sara and that he'd gotten a faraway look as though he was in deep thought. She knew what he was thinking. "She looks just like Lisa. Doesn't she?"

Still looking at Sara, John answered, "Yes, she does. She looks just like her."

When John turned to look at Mary, his eyes had that familiar mist whenever he thought about Lisa.

Feeling the tug in her heart at always seeing her brother sad over the loss of his beloved, Mary said, "Come on, brother. No sadness this week. We have a lot to celebrate. Your beautiful daughter is home, and I get a new daughter-in-law for me."

John smiled and nodded.

A half-hour later, Sara walked back to the covered area where her family had been and found only Jennifer sitting there. She picked up a towel and started drying herself off as she asked Jennifer, "Where did Dad and Aunt Mary go to?"

"They decided to take a break from the sun and go up to the rooms. You look like you had a lot of fun out there with the kids and Ed and Linda."

"I did! Those boys are something else. They just about wore me out. Ed and Linda also decided they needed a break. They went up to the room to get ready for lunch." Sara then put her wrap back on and took a seat in a chair next to Jennifer. Despite the time they'd been together shopping and at the spa, Sara hadn't had time to have a one-on-one visit with Jennifer, and she thought this would be a great chance to do so.

"I can't believe how much the boys have grown. Linda told me Cheri is already dating, and Dan is so tall. He must have grown five inches since I saw him last."

"Well, I think you have a perpetual admirer in Stan. He really looks up to you."

"Oh, my God, Stan is such a sweetheart. He's got Ed's dimples."

"You'll make a great mother one day, Sara."

Sara smiled despite the sadness she suddenly felt. "Thanks. I would love to have children one day. But I don't know if I'll get the chance any time soon."

"You'll find someone. A beautiful girl like yourself. When you're ready, you'll have no problem."

Being almost thirty with no family of her own was one of the things Sara did not want to talk about.

Changing subjects, Sara asked, "How is Dad doing?"

"He's doing fine."

"He looks tired, and I've noticed he's walking slower."

"I know. I think his body, especially his leg, is finally fully feeling the results of everything he did. Sometimes he has bad days, but mostly good ones."

"You do a great job taking care of him. I know you keep him young."

"Thanks, sweetheart. He's such a wonderful man, and I love him so."

"And I know he loves you too. A lot."

John's feelings for Jennifer were always a sensitive subject for Sara. Sara knew the one woman who would forever own John's heart was Lisa. Although Jennifer accepted this fact, it wasn't pleasant for her. But she loved John anyway and understood he did love her despite not asking her to marry him.

"Thanks. I appreciate you telling me that. It means a lot coming from you. But I have to admit there is one woman he holds very dear to his heart," Jennifer said.

Worried she had opened up that old wound, Sara asked, "Who?"

"You. Your father is so proud of you, Sara. I wish you could hear how he talks about you."

Glancing down into the sand, Sara bashfully said, "Thanks."

242

"You made him so happy when you called and told him you'd come. And especially, your Aunt Mary and Jack. We all love you very much, sweetheart. Please don't ever forget that."

Sara felt a tremendous warmth from Jennifer's words. Already three days into her vacation and she was dreading having to leave her family.

Chapter 23

After lunch, Mary and Sara were walking through the resort's lobby when they ran into an excited Jack pulling the arm of a petite, auburn-haired woman. "Well, here come the soon-to-be newlyweds," Mary said as she called out and waved to them across the way.

"Hi, Mom. We just got off the plane with the rest of the party in tow. Dana's mom and dad and some of the groomsmen and bridesmaids are in the taxis pulling up now."

Jack looked over to Sara and said, "Sara, I want you to meet Dana. Dana, this is my cousin, Sara Bradford, who I told you about."

Dana extended her hand with her freshly painted nails sparkling and said, "Hi, Sara. I'm glad to meet you. Jack has told me so much about you. I'm so happy you could make it to the wedding."

"I'm glad to meet you too, Dana," Sara said as she quickly summed Dana up. She was a small-framed woman with a nice figure for someone she assumed to be in her early thirties. Dana was dressed in the latest name-brand summer fashion shorts and top, with light skin and pearl white teeth smile. Knowing Jack was a perfectionist, Dana physically met Sara's expectation of the woman that might finally catch his eye. She was surprised Dana appeared much younger than Jack.

"I'm going out to the entrance to grab everyone and bring them over," Jack said.

"You two wait here, and I'll go help Jack," Mary said.

Sara felt a bit uncomfortable standing alone with Dana, having just met her. She wanted to make a good impression for Jack's sake. "How was your flight?" Sara asked.

"It was alright. We had to herd everyone on a commercial flight. My friend offered for us to take her husband's private jet, but we had too many people. But at least we got everyone in first class, so it wasn't so bad."

"I see." *I wonder who her friend is that has a private jet? I already get the feeling that she comes from money,* Sara thought.

A tall woman, looking to be in her late twenties, walked into the lobby, and Dana waved to her. "Crystal!" Dana then turned to Sara and said, "That's my maid of honor, Crystal. We've been friends since high school."

Crystal strolled over to Dana and said, "Can you believe we finally made it! Oh God, I'll never take another commercial flight again! I told James we should have found a way to fly everyone over here on our plane."

"Do you think it really was so bad?" Dana asked.

"Yes! And the food was terrible. My dogs eat better than that," Crystal snapped.

Judging by the scent of alcohol from Crystal's breath, her spray tan, shorts that were tighter than what they should be, overpriced designer handbag, store-bought picture-perfect breasts that were in clear view from her deep V blouse, and thick use of makeup, Sara had already pegged Crystal - *Fake, rich, bitch.* Silently listening to Dana's conversation with Crystal, Sara began to worry about Dana's character.

"I'm sorry, Crystal. We just got a late start on planning all this. You know how it is?"

"Honey, you know I'd do anything for you and that hunk of a man of yours."

As Dana and Crystal were talking, Crystal's husband walked up behind her with Jack and Mary.

Sara blinked twice to make sure she wasn't seeing things. It was her old flame from college, James Beachman looking as handsome as ever. Sara averted her gaze from James and forced herself to look at Dana and Crystal instead. But she knew he saw her.

"Did you get our room information?" Crystal asked James.

"Yes, honey. We're facing the beach, just as you asked."

"Hmmm, that will be great. Gives us a chance for some foreplay with no one able to see," Crystal purred.

"Oh, you two need to behave," Dana joked. Then she turned to Sara and said, "Sara forgive my poor manners. This is James and Crystal Beachman."

Now, Sara had no choice. She looked at Crystal first and extended her hand. I'm very glad to meet you, Crystal."

Crystal half-smiled and shook Sara's hand. "I'm glad to meet you , Sara."

Then she looked at James and found his blue eyes locked on hers. Sara did not extend her hand when she said, "Nice to meet you, James."

Despite her hint, James reached out, and Sara hesitantly extended her hand. "I'm very pleased to meet you, Sara."

When their hands touched, Sara felt that familiar tingle but maintained her best neutral face. James's stronger-than-expected squeeze of her hand and the devilish grin on his face told her he recognized her.

"I had no idea Jack had cousins as beautiful as you," James continued.

Crystal slanted her eyes toward James, not happy with his comment. She then put a proprietary hand on James, looked at Dana, and said, "Well, honey, I need to freshen up after that flight. Maybe we can get together for supper tonight?"

"Yes, let's do that," James said. "Sara, would you have dinner with us tonight?"

Hold it together, Sara. "Well, I'm having dinner with my father, his girlfriend, and Jack's parents tonight. I'm afraid I can't."

"Perfect. Bring them along. I'd love to meet them," James interrupted. "I'll make reservations here at the resort for all of us."

"Well . "

"Please. It will be my treat."

"Oh, that would be wonderful," Mary said. "We'd love to have supper with all of you tonight."

"Good. Then we'll see you tonight at 6:30," James said.

Sara nodded as her stomach tightened.

I can't believe this! Of all the people to meet now it has to be him! Dammit! Sara thought, sitting in her room, hesitating to go to the resort's restaurant for supper. Since James hadn't acknowledged they had previously known each other, Sara decided to follow suit. Drama was the last thing she wanted, especially when it could take away from Jack and Dana's wedding. But her mind and heart had been in a tug of war ever since she saw James.

On the one hand, Sara believed James looked as handsome as ever. Age had only improved what God had initially bestowed. She was embarrassed to admit just the snippet of his blues eyes staring at her in their short visit pulled her to him like a magnet. His soft touch sent her pulse into overdrive, bringing memories of the rapture of their lovemaking. It had been a long time since she had been with a man, and James had been much more than just a man in the bedroom.

However, on the other hand, she still felt hurt by his decision to choose his inheritance and money over her. She would never forget the way she had been cast aside. *And Crystal!* she thought. *That bitch is the kind of person you marry instead of me?*

But what hurt Sara even more was that nine years after being dissed, she didn't have a husband or a family. She didn't even have a boyfriend. In contrast, James still had his looks, money, and now, a family even if Crystal wasn't Sara's ideal model of a woman. Sara saw herself coming up short on the balance sheet of life. And the thought James might pity Sara's status filled her with despair and hatred. Yet, no matter how much she disdained his life decisions, she was ashamed to confess that deep within her, she desperately wanted James's loving hand, even if only for a moment to make her feel like a woman again.

This tug of war had played a role in the dress she had selected for tonight's dinner. It was provocative enough to show off her hourglass figure and tone body. Her legs would be on full display, and just enough cleavage showed that would draw interest without being gaudy.

Part of Sara wanted to show James what he had given up. From the attention she'd already gotten from the male population since she arrived, Sara felt comfortable in her looks, and in her assessment, that was one area she held the advantage over Crystal. She wanted James to squirm in his seat in pain, wanting her. But a part of her also wanted James to look at her lovingly. She wanted James to come to her, to repent, and beg for her forgiveness. She wanted to feel his arms around her, even if for just one more time.

Sara glanced at her watch and decided she needed to head downstairs. It was a few minutes early, but her military-inspired habit of never wanting to be late got her on her feet and moving.

When she entered the dining area, she paused at the entrance to survey the room.

She spied Jack, Dana, James, and Crystal at a table near the window overlooking the beach. As she looked across the room, she saw James look up and see her. Even at the far distance, she could see the smile on his face. Knowing he would be watching her every move, Sara looked away from him and sauntered along the path that led to their table.

Soon, a very handsome young man looked up from a nearby table and saw Sara.

The man caught Sara's eye, and she waved to him with her long lashes and a slight seductive smile that captured his complete attention. As if on cue, he stood up from his table, intercepted her halfway to her table and did his best to entice her to join him for a drink.

Sara smiled the whole time she talked to him and lightly touched his arm during their short tryst. Only when she promised to have a future drink with him did the man finally release her.

Wanting James to know she was still a very desirable woman, she concluded she couldn't have choreographed her interaction with the good-looking young man any better. When the young man walked away, and she continued her short walk to the table, the look on James's face told her she had gotten her message across to him. She mentally tallied the score at Sara 1, James 0 so far for the evening.

Standing up to pull her chair out and seat her, James told Sara, "Please, allow me, Sara."

Sara gestured her OK and allowed him to seat her while noting Crystal's facial agitation towards James's attention to her.

Sitting back down, James said, "Jack, there is no doubt in my mind we have the most beautiful ladies in this entire resort sitting with us tonight."

"I would definitely agree with you on that one, James," Jack said.

"That's a beautiful dress, Sarah. You look stunning in it," Dana said.

"Thank you, Dana. You look great tonight, too," Sara said.

"Would you like something to drink, Sara? The margaritas are exceptional here. Or perhaps a glass of wine?" James asked.

Having decided she would not avoid looking at James tonight, Sara looked straight at him and said, "No, thank you, James. I'm not a big alcohol drinker. I'll stick with water for a while."

Once again, despite her mental protest, James's blue eyes were calling out to her.

"As you wish," James said.

Agitated she was no longer the center of attention, Crystal asked James, "Sweetheart, would you be a doll and get me another margarita?"

"Sure, honey, but you haven't finished this one yet."

"The ice has melted, and I need a fresh one. Please?"

"Of course."

"Dana, I'm so glad you and Jack decided to take our offer up to visit us at James's parent's house in the Bahamas after your honeymoon. You'll love it. We always enjoy our time when we go," Crystal said.

The memory of James flying Sara off to that same house for a long romantic weekend during her college years flashed in Sara's mind. After a night of making love, waking up to a flawless white sanded beach was pure heaven for her. She'd even allowed herself to dream about being James's wife and living a life of luxury. She wondered if Crystal had purposely mentioned the Bahamas' house, that maybe she knew about her and James's past.

Sara made a passing glance at James as she turned her head to look at Dana.

James was looking away for a waiter, and Sara couldn't see his reaction.

"You know I just love your mom and dad. They've always been so sweet to me. They're my second set of parents as far as I'm concerned," Dana said.

About that time, John, Jennifer, Mary, and Dana's parents joined them for supper. After everyone made the appropriate introductions, they took their seats.

John looked at Sara and said, "Sweetheart, you look beautiful tonight."

Sara heartfully smiled. "Thank you, Daddy."

"James was just saying before you got here that we have the most beautiful ladies at the resort sitting with us, Uncle John," Jack said.

Still looking at Sara, John said, "I totally agree with him," and winked at Sara.

The smile on Sara's face couldn't get much bigger. She could feel her father's pride in her.

Dana's parents appeared to be younger than John and Mary by at least ten years. Dana's father was a financial lawyer at a prestigious firm in New York. Dana's mom had never worked, and she had two other sons.

Sara remained quiet for most of the meal. She enjoyed watching the interaction between everyone. Most of the attention was placed on Jack and Dana as expected, and Sara was pleased with Dana. She had an engaging and down-to-earth manner about her Sara believed would suit Jack perfectly. She noted the almost giddiness in their faces when they looked at one another.

Dana's father prided himself, boisterously at times, on his extensive knowledge of the financial markets and world affairs that impacted them. On the other hand, Dana's mom didn't talk very much and seemed pleasant enough.

Despite his earlier attention paid to Sara, James mostly talked with Dana's parents and Jack and John. Sara was disappointed he hadn't asked her any questions during the evening. But she knew he was thinking of her.

Once when Sara looked up from her meal, she caught James looking directly at her. He did not avert his eyes, and for the moment they looked directly at one another in silence, she swore she saw a genuine longing for her in them.

Much of the evening, Crystal had been dominating the conversation with stories of her and James's exotic travels when she said, "We had a trip all planned to visit Seoul to do some shopping when all that nastiness started."

Sara had not been paying much attention to Crystal, but her ears perked up when she heard her mention Seoul.

"I know it was horrible what the North Koreans and Chinese did," Dana's Mom said.

"Well, what was more horrible is we just let them walk right in and take it," Dana's Dad declared.

"What do you mean?" James asked.

"We did nothing. We stood by while the Chinese simply marched in and took what they wanted. It was pathetic the little fight we put up to stop them."

"But that's not what the news showed."

"Fake news, that's what that was. Nothing but fake news."

Did nothing to stop them! Fake news! Sara thought. She felt her stomach clench with each hubris statement Dana's dad said. The last thing she wanted to think about was what had happened to her in Korea. Sara slightly bowed her head and stared at her plate.

Knowing in detail what Sara had gone through in Korea, John felt very uneasy about what was being discussed.

Dana realized Sara and John had become subdued over the last few comments. She sensed something was upsetting to them about the discussion and decided she needed to change it. "Would we like to order dessert now? Mom, they have an excellent pastry selection."

Oblivious to Dana's attempt, her father continued, "The news video, especially from the aerial drones was all fake. An investigative reporter on the Real Truth channel showed how the major news networks edited their video footage before it aired. I only watch the news on The Real Truth channel anymore. All the others are just fake news."

"Is that true? I'd read a conspiracy theory that the Chinese and US President had secretly made a deal so we wouldn't have to keep Soldiers in South Korea anymore. They were just milking us for more money." Crystal said.

"That's no conspiracy theory, young lady. I believe it. There are several good articles about how the Chinese paid us off to just leave, and the war was just one big show. This country needs some decent leadership," Dana's father said.

Sara closed her eyes. The memories were coming too fast - Lieutenant Colonel Campos orders, Captain Carlson's loving touch, Sergeant Thompson's last words to her. She felt the Chinese Soldier's hands like daggers at her throat.

John looked over at Sara as Crystal and Dana's father were talking. She'd lowered her head as to hide her face, but John saw the agony and fury in her eyes. He felt her pain and dropped his right hand so no one could see it start to shake.

Jennifer immediately picked up on John's actions and knew what was happening. She reached under the table and grabbed his hand as if to keep it from shaking.

"It was all just so stupid," Crystal said. "Well, at least it made for some interesting TV for a while."

With that comment, Sara could take no more. She placed her napkin on her plate, stood up, and said, "I'm sorry. I'm really not feeling well tonight. I need to go to my room for a while. Please excuse me."

"Sweetheart, do you need me to go with you?" Mary asked.

"No, Aunt Mary. I'll be fine. Thank You," Sara said as she walked away.

"You know, I felt a little nauseous too this afternoon. I wonder if it's the water?" Dana asked.

"Probably just your premarital jitters," Dana's mother said.

"John, I understand you were in the Army. What's your evaluation of our troop's performance in Korea?" Dana's father asked.

John felt Jennifer squeeze his hand to remind him to restrain himself.

John turned to Jennifer and grinned. It was his signal to her to let go.

Reluctantly knowing there was no stopping whatever he was about to do, Jennifer released his hand.

"Well, Sir. That's a good question," John said.

He then stopped a waiter walking near their table with a bottle in his hand and asked, "May I have a shot of that tequila, Sir?"

"Of course, Sir," the waiter said as he poured a shot into his glass.

"It just so happens the Commander of the 1st Cavalry Division was one of my subordinate officers when I was still in the Army. Bright lad with a good head on his shoulders. He happened to call me up after they had redeployed to Hawaii as part of the withdrawal," John explained.

"Really? That's very interesting. What did he say?"

"He said my daughter and the company she commanded of about two hundred Soldiers had held a bridgehead against a reinforced Chinese regimental attack for over 48 hours. He said they probably had about two thousand Soldiers attacking them. Overall, they ended up having a kill ratio of about ten to one. That included the one motherfucker she killed herself with her knife. I'd say that was damn good killing," John said just before he downed his shot of tequila.

An awkward silence hung in the air.

"I remember General Miller telling me people who have no clue about a subject should know when not to speak. I find his advice still very valid today," John said with a grin.

Quickly, James spoke up, "Sir, please forgive our foolishness in our comments about the armed forces. Sara is clearly an exceptional officer, and we owe her our deepest gratitude."

John locked eyes with James and said, "She's the best there is, young man. You should remember that. Apology accepted. Now, how about some dessert?"

Sara sat in her room with her head between her hands. There were no tears, yet she trembled from the aftermath of the rush of memories from those horrible days. Her breathing was slowly returning to normal as she chastised herself for attending the wedding. *I knew I shouldn't have come! I knew it! Fucking stupid idiots can't even begin to understand what happened over there! They have no clue! No fucking clue!*

There was a knock on Sara's door, and she hesitated to open it. She was in no mood for company. But when the knock came a second time, she heard Dana ask if she could enter.

Sara reluctantly opened the door.

"May I come in, Sara?" Dana asked.

"I'd rather not have company right now, Dana."

But Dana was persistent. "Please?"

Seeing Dana was not going away, Sara relented and let Dan in.

"Sara, please accept my deepest apologies for our tasteless comments, especially my father and Crystal. They didn't mean what they said. Sometimes my father just doesn't know when to shut up, and neither does Crystal when she has had one too many."

"That's alright."

"No, it's not. Your father said at the table, and later, Jack explained to me what you'd been through in Korea. I didn't know, or I would have shut them both up immediately. I can't even imagine what it must have been like, especially as a woman. I know my father was looking for you to apologize, but I warned him to leave you alone for tonight."

"Thank You, Dana. I appreciate everything you've said. But you didn't do anything wrong. So, there isn't any reason for you to apologize."

"I understand. I just hope you don't hold any of what was said against us."

"No, I promise not to do that."

"Thank you. I see why Jack and the rest of your family think so much of you. I know we haven't gotten to know one another very well yet, but I hope that will change soon. I'd love for us to be good friends."

Sara believed Dana was sincere in her words and appreciated her effort. "Thank you. I'd love to do that."

"Great. Say, the girls and me are all going shopping in town tomorrow. Would you like to come with us?"

"I think I'm going to pass on that. But thank you for asking me."

"I understand," Dana said and then bid Sara goodnight.

Sara was very thankful Dana had come by. It confirmed for her Dana was a good person, worthy of Jack. Her visit had softened some of the blow from the evening's events, but not them all. Sara did not understand why James allowed Crystal to say the things she did. *Is James utterly unaware of what I've done since we last saw one another?* Sara wondered. *Or did he take pleasure in seeing Crystal hurt me?* She didn't know the answers to those questions, and the thought of James's lack of genuine interest in her only made her feel worse.

Chapter 24

Pounding away on the treadmill, Sara pushed herself faster and faster. She kept replaying the previous night's conversation in her mind, which only made her madder and quicker. Each stomp of her foot on the racing belt brought a release of the energy building up within her, and she felt her heart pounding. She'd lost track of the miles, calories, and other statistics the display panel tallied. All she wanted to do was to run until she was out of breath.

Jack rounded the corner to the resort's gym and saw Sara running at an incredible pace through the glass wall. It didn't take him long to see that between her shorts showing off her super-tone legs and the bouncing of her full breasts, despite her sports bra, Sara was garnering a lot of male attention. Several men acted as they were working out but kept a close eye on her. One man had stopped working out and stood by his machine in awe with his towel over his shoulder. But Sara was in high gear, oblivious to their stares as her ponytailed hair bounced from side to side.

Jack, too was in amazement of her. Even as a young man, he couldn't dream of matching her current speed. The little girl he remembered long ago was not just a beautiful woman but a phenomenal athlete.

When Jack opened the door to enter the gym, Sara had finally slowed down and began her cool down. He went searching for a towel, and when he returned, a man was standing next to Sara, talking to her as she brought the treadmill to a stop. Jack watched Sara get off the treadmill and try to wipe herself off as the man continued to talk to her. Judging from her expression, Sara did not appear interested in talking to the man, but he persisted and looked as if he had her trapped.

Jack walked closer to Sara, and when she saw him, her arched eyebrow glance told him she needed assistance. Jack nodded and walked up to Sara.

"Hey, babe!" Jack said as he approached her, gave her a quick kiss on her forehead, and slid his arm around her. "Looks like you got here before I did. Man, you really worked up a sweat! Where did you get all that energy? I thought I wore you out last night."

Picking up on Jack's game, Sara smiled at Jack and replied, "I didn't want to wake you this morning, Honey, when I got up. I figured you'd need more rest than me."

The man looked at Jack and then looked back at Sara. "Oh, hey, ah, ah, I didn't know. I mean, it's been nice talking to you, Sara. I need to get to my room and clean up. I'll see you guys later," the man said, then turned and left the gym.

Sara looked up at Jack and said, "Thanks, Jack. He seemed like a nice guy, but he just wouldn't go away, and I wasn't in the mood."

"No problem. I figured if I'd better come to his rescue before you backhanded him through the wall."

Sara laughed.

"Hey, Dana's having a spa morning, so how about I take you to breakfast? Just watching you on that treadmill has worked up my appetite."

"Sure, why not? I'd love to get a good breakfast with my boyfriend, especially after he wore me out last night," Sara said with a wink.

"Come on, you!" Jack said as they both laughed.

After they were seated and ordered breakfast, Jack asked, "I hope you're OK from last night. Please don't let what Dana's father and Crystal said bother you."

"I'm fine, but thanks for asking. Dana came by last night and apologized, but I told her she didn't need to because she didn't do anything wrong."

"She was pretty upset with what happened. I have a feeling she let her father and Crystal know that in no uncertain terms later in the evening. Especially after your dad told everyone what you had been through."

"Dana's a wonderful lady, Jack. I think you made a great choice. I know how parents can be. It's just that Crystal, I . . well, never mind."

"I know. She can be a bitch."

"Well, yes."

"She and Dana were best friends growing up, but even Dana admits she's changed, especially since she and James married. Sometimes she does and says things that make me cringe. James seems nice enough. But I've never spent much time with him. He seems to like you a lot."

Jack's last comment worried Sara. She did not want to disclose their previous relationship. "He's just being polite," she said.

"Well, like I said. Please don't think that what was said last night in any way reflects what we think of you. I don't know if I've ever said it directly to you, but I want you to know how proud I am of you, Sara. You are an incredible woman. I don't know much about the Army, but I know if you decide to stay, you'll be wearing stars one day, and the only question will be how many."

Sara blushed at Jack's compliment and looked at him with an endearing smile. "Thank you, Jack. Coming from you, that means a lot to me. But I'm sure I won't be wearing any stars. I don't think I could ever handle that kind of responsibility."

"Well, I beg to differ."

Sara' blush grew a little redder. She enjoyed speaking to Jack, one on one and decided she wanted to open up to him too. "Well, since we're being honest with one another, I want to tell you how proud I am of you. Not just because you've been like a big brother to me through the years and because of how successful you've been, but also because of your patience and wisdom."

"Patience and wisdom?"

"Yes, I know you've dated a lot of good women over the years. But you waited for the right one to finally come along. You didn't just settle or give up looking. I can see Dana loves you a lot. I think it was well worth the wait to finally find that very special someone."

Now it was Jack whose face turned a slight shade of red. "Thanks. What you said means a lot to me too."

Before either one could say anything further, the waiter showed up and served them their breakfast.

"Wow! This looks wonderful! I'm really hungry now," Sara said as she placed her napkin on her lap and went to pick up her fork.

"Hey, before you dig into that food and blow your girlish figure, I want to tell you one last thing," Jack said.

"What's that?"

"I know there is a very special man waiting for you too. Someone who will love you as much, if not more, than Dana loves me. And I'm sure when you find him, he'll be worth the wait."

Jack's sincere words touched Sara's heart. It was exactly what she needed to hear, and she wondered if he had somehow read her mind these past few days. Looking at him with a bright smile that thanked him for his kind words, Sara prayed, *I hope you're right, Jack.*

The next day, Sara watched as the wedding ceremony took place on the beautiful resort grounds. Seeing Jack and Dana exchange vows, Sara couldn't help but think what it would be like to be standing in Dana's shoes and have a man as wonderful as Jack by her side. Of course, she was very happy for them both, but that bittersweet taste of seeing her life pass by her without love kept poking at her.

She'd snuck a few glances at James, but his attention was focused on the ceremony. He hadn't paid any attention to her since the supper, and she figured he had finally just chalked her up as an old girlfriend and moved on.

She felt embarrassed at even thinking about him and putting on her fancy dress the other night to draw his attention. She started reminding herself she was a decorated officer in the Army with an outstanding career, and she should be proud of that. He was the past, and she didn't need to think about him anymore.

Sara had reassured herself and was ready to have fun the last few days of her vacation when it happened.

After the ceremony, she was walking to talk with John and Jennifer when suddenly, James appeared in front of her. Looking up, she was caught off guard by his beautiful smile. He then softly said, "Meet me on the beach in front of the resort tonight at midnight."

Sara was speechless. After just talking herself out of thinking about him anymore, here he was asking to meet her.

When she didn't answer, he whispered, "Please."

The want in his eyes and soft tone in his voice plunged her back to where she had been when she first saw him again. She couldn't resist his request. She whispered back, "OK."

Then before any other words could be exchanged, James left.

Sara looked at her watch, and it was five minutes to midnight, and anticipation was getting the better part of her. Standing alone in the darkness, she was hypersensitive to being surprised. But the butterflies in her stomach were from more than just normal fear. They were also from the anticipation of waiting for a man, whom she knew she still had feelings for. She dared not dream what their rendezvous would be like.

She saw someone in the distance walk toward her and soon, James stood before her. Even in the pale moonlight, she could see the intense desire in his face.

"Hello," she said, but before she finished the last syllable, James took her in his arms and pressed his hungry lips against hers. His body pushing against hers removed the last vestiges of her resolve, and she threw her arms around him, pulling him into her. She felt his visceral need for her in his embrace, which only made her want him more. Once again, she reveled in the taste of his mouth and felt those old familiar feelings.

After what had seemed like an eternity, James pulled back with Sara still in his arms. His face still inches from hers, he said, "I've wanted to do that ever since I first saw you here."

Without reservation, Sara said, "So did I."

Sara saw James's eyes grow as he said, "I want you so bad right now."

Sara smiled. Feeling his manhood pressing against her leg, she knew he was telling the truth.

Unable to control himself, James kissed her again, and Sara did not stop him. She didn't want the rapture of being in his arms to end. She felt his hand make its way down her back to her rear, and her body electrified with sensations.

James then escaped her lips and kissed her neck, causing Sara to moan.

But her bliss was mentally interrupted by the unpleasant fact that James was a married man. Her pride also reminded her he had chosen something else over her, and no matter how much she wanted him, that sin had not been forgiven yet. Reluctantly and with all of her strength, she took a deep breath and slightly pulled back.

Puzzled, James looked at her.

"We need to talk," Sara said.

"OK. But why do we need to stop and talk?"

Still struggling with the desire within her, Sara paused. "Well, I'm sure Crystal would not find any of this to be amusing."

James laughed. "Why the hell are you worried about her?"

"She's your wife, James."

"Some wife. Do you know where she is right now?"

"No."

"She's shacked up with the guy across the hall for the next few hours. How else could I get away from her like this?"

"Why don't you go and stop her?"

"Why? This isn't her first time?"

Surprised, Sara couldn't tell if he was hurt or being cynical.

"She's done this before? Why don't you divorce her?"

James sarcastically said, "She gives me what I need when required."

Sara wasn't happy with his answer. It led to too many questions, some of which she didn't want to know the answers to. But before she could go on, she had to ask them.

"Have you cheated on her before?"

James was silent.

Sara released her embrace of James and gently pushed him away. "I asked you a question?"

"You see the kind of woman she is. What am I supposed to do? Live with that for the rest of my life with no recourse?"

"Isn't that the vow you made?"

Not happy with the course their discussion had taken, James softened his voice. "Sara, Let's not talk about all of that. Please? I've missed you so much, sweetheart. I've dreamed about our days together for years. I couldn't believe it when I found out who Dana was engaged to. I prayed you would come to the wedding. And here we are."

James reached out and held her hand. "God, I've missed you."

Moved by the genuine tone in his voice, Sara said, "And I've missed you too, James. I remember how we were together. I could never forget those nights in the Bahamas." Then she felt that familiar sting. "But you were the one who chose money over me. You were the one who left me. And you replaced me with a bitch like Crystal?" Then, with watery eyes, Sara asked, "Why, James? Why?"

"There were so many things going on out of my control. We were both young, my parents, the future, hell, Sara, I wasn't sure what the right answer was then."

"So, tell me. What's the right answer now?"

Puzzled, James looked at her. "What do you mean?"

"You talked about then. But what's the right answer now?" Then, pausing because of her fear over what his answer might be, she added, "Do you still love me?"

"Yes, I do!"

Sara's heart skipped. He'd said the answer she prayed for, but she wasn't done.

"Are you willing to then come to me?

"I'm here, aren't I"

"I don't mean for a single night. I mean for a lifetime."

"I can't do that right now, Sara."

Sara felt her throat choke. She'd risked opening her heart to him again, praying he loved her. But the love she sought after was not just physical. Concluding she'd already opened herself to more hurt, she had nowhere else to go. She had to find the final answer to the question of his love for her once and for all. Quietly, she asked, "Why not?"

"Because it's just not that easy."

Suddenly, Sara saw her dream becoming a fantasy and that fantasy fading. "But why?"

"Sweetheart, I just can't right now."

Two tears dropped from Sara's eyes. Emotion had grabbed her as she mouthed the word, *why?"*

"Because I can't just up and divorce Crystal! She'd kill me in the settlement, and my mother would have a meltdown leaving her and going to you. Not to mention . "

"You haven't changed. Have you?" Sara blurted out. She straightened her spine as she found her resolve again.

Sensing her change in attitude, James begged, "Look, sweetheart. I understand how you feel. I know I fucked up a long time ago. Look, just give me some time. I can work it all out. I promise. You know I love you. You know what it's like when we make love. We can be together starting tonight, but it will all just take time. Come on. Give us a chance."

Sara shook her head. "A chance to do what? To be your weekend whore while you play the role of James Beachman, President of Beachman Enterprises, committed family man, and business tycoon? No James. I don't want that. I want real love, now. I want the kind of love that's fully committed. I want the kind of love Jack and Dana have." Then, her voice trailing off, she said, "I want the kind of love my parents had. That my father still has for my mother."

James stood silent.

"I'm sorry, James. I shouldn't have come here." Sara turned to walk away, but James grabbed her arm and spun her around.

"Wait a minute! I love you, Sara! I need you! Don't just walk away! You know what we can have together. It will just take time. Do you think you will find what we can have together in the Army? Come on! Be real! You'll never have all the things we can have if we just take our time. I promise you. You'll never want for anything. Just be with me on my terms for now."

"But there will be things I can never have with you. I can see that now."

"Like what?"

"My self-respect and the respect of the people around me. My freedom to do as I want, grow as a person, and be the kind of person I want to be. But most of all, my chance to find someone who loves me above all things. I can see now I can never have those things as Mrs. Beachman." Sara paused. Without tears, she shook herself free of his grasp and said, "Goodbye, James," and left. Walking away, Sara decided she would never look back.

She made her way back to the resort and rode the elevator up to her floor.

After leaving the elevator, she started walking to her room, and when she turned the hallway corner, she suddenly came face to face with Crystal, who seemed to be rushing down the hall.

Startled, Crystal stopped and fidgeted with her dress and hair that appeared out of order. Then she placed her hand on her hip and said, "Well, did you and lover boy have a good fucking? I didn't expect you two to be finished so fast."

Sara grew angry. "I didn't fuck your husband, Crystal! We talked, but that's none of your business." Sara then tried to move past Crystal, but Crystal jumped in front of her.

"You want James? Go ahead! Take him, bitch. But don't think that either one of you will get one red cent of his money. You'll both be wishing you'd never seen my lawyers by the time I'm finished, not to mention his mother."

"You don't have anything to worry about. I don't want James or his money. You can have them both. All I want is to go to my room. Now please step aside."

"And if I don't? Then what?"

Sara narrowed her eyes, and said, "Then you can decide if you need a doctor or a mortician by the time I'm finished with you."

Crystal's defiance suddenly melted in the wake of Sara's threatening tone, and she stepped aside.

As Sara walked by her, she heard from behind Crystal say, "Army Barbi Bitch!"

Although she wanted badly to turn around and yell back at Crystal, Sara didn't.

When Sara got into her room, she slammed the door, tightened her fists, and started to cry. She was ashamed of herself. She'd let her guard down, and in doing so, she felt she had compromised her values, and herself for a man she saw was so shallow, she couldn't stand.

When she finally calmed down, she lay on the bed on her stomach, clutching a pillow. For some unknown reason, she felt a warmth come upon her, and then she swore she heard a voice softly say, "I love you so much, Sara."

Sara sat up in bed and looked around. There was no one there. She felt she should be afraid, but she wasn't. Then she realized the voice she heard sounded exactly like Lisa's voice from the old video recordings she had seen of her, but much clearer.

She quietly called out, "Momma?"

There was no answer, but the warmth she felt earlier returned, easing her pain.

Smiling, Sara whispered, "I love you too, Momma."

Chapter 25

John was walking to the door to his room when he heard a tired, soft voice call his name.

"John, honey."

He turned and saw a sleepy, squint-eyed Jennifer looking at him from just above the bed covers. The early morning sunlight was doing its best to get through the closed curtains giving the room just enough light to see her charming face.

John walked over and sat on the edge of the bed next to Jennifer. Despite her 61 years, she was still a beautiful woman. The stylist had dealt with the random strands of gray, and her lush blond hair lay splattered all over her pillow. Even without makeup, she looked to be in her early 50s. John found himself enjoying one of his favorite past times, looking into Jennifer's eyes and soon found himself mirroring the simple smile that appeared on her face. "Did I wake you?"

"No, I just opened my eyes. Where are you going, sweetheart?"

"I thought I might go to the beach and take an early morning walk to get the morning started. You know, get a little exercise before breakfast."

Jennifer's smile turned seductive, and she said, "Well, if you'd woken me up, maybe we could have found another opportunity to get your exercise in."

John's smile turned into a slight laugh. Then the curve in his mouth reversed as he continued to gaze into two sparkling emeralds, reflecting her love for him. He loved her very much. It wasn't that she was beautiful or sexy or smart or successful. No, while she was all those things, it was something else that eventually won him over. She loved him with all of her heart. Despite knowing Lisa would forever have a hold on him, Jennifer still wanted him, and her love was genuine. John was 70, and age was beginning to keep him from being the man he'd always been, but she didn't care.

In retrospect, John could see her love had kept him young. Had it not been for her, he might have fallen victim to age's pessimism and disengagement from life. But she had saved him from all of that. In the face of such genuine love, John could only surrender to the tenderness in his heart for her. In the almost ten years they had been together, he could honestly tell himself he loved her.

Staring deep into Jennifer's eyes, John said, "I love you so much."

Jennifer's seductive look now gave way to a warm smile that thanked him for his words, which she were honest.

"I love you too, sweetheart."

Feeling the fortune of Jennifer's love in his heart, John paused before he said, "Jen, I don't know what I would ever do without you."

Jennifer continued to smile, soaking in his love, as she raised her hand and ran it through his thick salt and pepper-colored hair.

"I'd dare say yesterday's bride had but a rival for her beauty, and I'm the lucky man to be in her company now."

"Thank you, my love. That was very sweet of you, even though I may disagree. Several young ladies looked much better than me yesterday, with your daughter being at the top of the list."

"Well, I can't disagree too much with you on that last one."

"Honey, I think you might need to talk with her. I got the sense something has not been quite right with her, beyond that supper discussion about Korea. Today might be a good time for a daddy-daughter talk."

"I was thinking the same thing. Maybe I can catch her for breakfast. She's an early riser too, like her father. You know, Army living and all."

"That sounds like a good idea."

"OK. And I have another good idea."

"What's that?"

"Sometime today, I'd like to take a nap, and I'd love it if we could share some preliminary activities just before the nap starts."

"Hmmm, I think that can be arranged. I'd love to spend some special time with you today."

John bent down and tenderly kissed Jennifer on the lips. Then he tucked the covers in around her and left the room.

When he got downstairs, he walked out from the resort to the beach where the sun was just beginning to rise from the ocean. He surveyed the covered spots on the beach and saw a woman sitting in a chair under one of them. She seemed to be deep in thought. Looking closer, he realized it was Sara and decided this was the perfect time to have their talk.

John walked out onto the sandy beach, and when he walked underneath the cover where Sara was, he asked, "Deep in thought?"

Broken from her trance, Sara looked up and said, "Hi, Daddy."

"May I sit with you for a while?"

"Sure."

There were several minutes of silence as they both watched the rolling waves of the ocean hitting the beach in front of the rising sun. Their minds relaxed with the sound of the sea and the occasional seagull calling out to their friends. There was no hurry to their visit as each pondered what to say.

"If you could do it all over again, what would you do differently?" Sara asked.

"That's a deep question. I'd have to think about that for a while."

"But I'm sure there are some things you wish you could have changed, aren't there?"

"Yes, I supposed."

"I mean, if you would have known what was going to happen to you and mom, wouldn't you change that. Wouldn't you have tried to get her back earlier or something?"

"Maybe."

"Why do you say, maybe? I mean, she was the one. Right? You two loved one another like you've never loved any other person before. You two were soulmates. So why would you not want to change the past so you could have spent more time with her?"

John pondered her question. It was one he'd thought about many times. "That summer, when we met, yes, we fell deeply in love. I know I thought then she was for me. I believed it then, but I did not know it. I couldn't. We can't know the future. Only once in the future can we look back at the past and see if what we believed was true. And only in hindsight of everything that happened to us did the reality come to the point I saw she was the one. And your mother, God love her. I don't think she really saw it then either. No, she had to go and find out things for herself, like we all have to. We were both so inexperienced in life, then. It's experience and failure that bring us wisdom, and we both had our share of that to finally discover the truth, that we were soulmates after all."

"You don't think that all those years apart were wasted, especially since she left us so soon? You two could have been together."

"Maybe, in a way. But you're asking her and me to have known the future at such a young age, and we just can't do that. Humans are imperfect beings. We are prone to make mistakes. Don't get me wrong. I'd love to have spent my life with your mother. Don't think I don't think about the happiness we missed out on. But I have to believe things happen for a reason, and I think, maybe, what happened to us had to happen to us for both of us to see what we really meant to one another. Not just for your mother, but for me too."

"It just seems like a big waste, the time you two lost out on."

"Maybe. But, you know, good things did come out of it."

"Like what?"

"Like you."

Sara lowered her eyes in silence.

"Sweetheart, you were the product of all that wasted time, and that made it worthwhile. I know without a doubt, your mother would have told you that if she were here right now. I will never forget the look in her eyes every time she held you. Even when she was near the end, she would ask to hold you, and I could see that spark of life within her want to hold on a little longer just so she could be with you. Honestly, I don't know if your mother ever wanted children before you. But that all changed the moment she asked me to give her a child and later when she had you. There's no doubt whatsoever in my mind she would have said it was all worth it the moment she held you in her arms for the first time."

When Sara did not speak, John remained silent. He felt her questions were not the actual ones causing her despair. But he resolved to let her decide for the moment what she wanted to talk about.

"I guess you two were blessed after all. At least you found one another and then had a second chance to make it work," Sara said. "But why can't I do that, Daddy? Why can't I find that special someone and have a chance to be with them, if even for a little while?"

"I don't know, sweetheart."

"I've tried. But I can't find him. Or when I find him, he leaves before we can have something, or he turns out not to be the one."

"James?'

"Yes. How did you know?"

"I remembered the name. And I remember the twinkle in your eye when you were in college, and you talked about him. I just put two and two together."

"I feel like a fool. But I couldn't help how I felt about him."

"Sweetheart, I don't think we get to decide who we fall in love with. If we did, that would be too simple. Whether you like it or not, love is messy. It doesn't want to conform. It comes when it wants and not to some schedule. It puts demands on us in ways we don't want. But maybe, that's part of what makes it so special in the end."

"I just want to have what you and mom had. That's all. Why can't I have that?"

"I don't know, baby girl. Maybe it's still to come. Or maybe you were meant for something bigger. Or maybe both. I don't know. But what I know is you are here for a reason. God has his plan, we just don't know what it is right now. A buddy of mine once told me dying is easy. It's living that takes courage. But I think it's more than that. Life is chaos, unorganized, and filled with chance. Love is messy, and never comes easy. It requires sacrifice and effort. Otherwise, none of it would be worthwhile. You have to find a way to balance living each day as though it was your last, yet retain the faith that what you seek will come to you. In your case, it is the love you seek. Don't take the easy way out and give up. Find the courage to live."

Sara thought about John's words. He'd given her a lot to think about.

"There they are!" a voice from behind yelled out.

John and Sara turned to see Ed and his three children walking through the sand to see them. "Hey, we're headed to breakfast, and the boys wanted to visit with Aunt Sara before we leave this afternoon," Ed said.

"Yeh, come on, Aunt Sara. Let's go eat. I want to ask you when we can come visit you at an Army base," Ed's young son Stan said.

"Yeh, that would be so cool. I want to see one, cause I want to be like you when I grow up," Daniel said.

Then young Cheri bent down and whispered in Sara's ear, "Aunt Sara, before you leave, can you and I talk? I want to know how to get boys to look at me like they look at you."

Sara looked at Cheri and whispered back, "Sure, sweetheart. I promise just you and me will talk before you leave."

"Come on, kids. We need to meet your mom in the dining room cause I know she's starving, and she'll kill me if we're late. You guys coming?" Ed asked.

"Two minutes behind you. Save three seats for us. I'll call Jennifer to meet us there too," John said.

"OK," Ed said and then herded the kids to breakfast.

When Ed was out of earshot, John asked Sara, "We good, or do we need to talk some more?"

"I think we're good for now, Daddy. Thanks."

When John and Sara got up, and Sara started to walk off, John touched her shoulder, and she turned around and looked at him.

"Just a parting thought," he said.

"OK."

"Listening to those kids, I'd say Aunt Sara is a pretty special lady who they hold in very high esteem. High enough they want to be like her. That's important. Something you might want to keep in mind."

Sara looked at her father and smiled. But the smile was for more than letting her cry on his shoulder or for sharing a bit of wisdom with her. It was her recognition of the one man in her life that loved her like no other. "Thanks, Daddy. I promise to keep that in mind."

A few days later in Victoria, Sara was packing the last of her bags into her rental car to take her back to the airport and fly home. She'd told Jennifer goodbye earlier in the morning before Jennifer had to unexpectedly go to her office. So, it was just Sara and John standing together as she slammed the hatchback to the car shut.

"Here's a little money for the trip back," John told her as he handed her some cash bills.

"Three hundred dollars! Daddy, I'm not a poor college student anymore. You don't need to do this," Sara said.

"I know, I know. Well, just buy yourself something special when you get the chance. You got everything packed?"

"Yes, it surprisingly all fit. I didn't realize how many clothes I bought while I was here. Or, more accurately, you bought me."

"Well, I'm glad you got what you wanted. How long before you have to report back to base?"

"Probably the very next day after I return. The battalion S-3 texted me today and asked when I would be back, even though he has my leave dates. Apparently, we will be part of the Rapid Deployment Brigade force starting in three months, and we have to start our trainup. After relaxing in the sun for so long, I have to admit I'm not looking forward to that."

John nodded. That awkward silence when two people feel the sadness at leaving one another fell into place as John and Sara looked at one another.

"I wish I could stay longer. I had such a good time, Daddy. It was wonderful to forget about the Army for a while and just be with my family. I didn't know how much I missed everyone until I came back home."

"I'm glad you came home, baby girl. We all missed you so much. I missed you a lot. Please don't make it so long before the next time you come home."

"I won't. I promise."

John reached out and gave Sara a big hug, kissing her on the top of her hair as he usually did before his final goodbye.

Sara felt his embrace tighten a little longer than usual. When he finally released her, she saw his watery eyes. There was a sadness about him that was more than she'd expected, and for a second, she felt a slither of fear that maybe something would be different the next time she saw him.

"You better stick around a long time, Daddy. I got a feeling I'm going to need a lot more of our sessions like we had that last day at the resort."

"I'll always have time for you, baby girl. All you have to do is reach out."

Sara sadly smiled, and they said their final goodbye.

She watched John as the driverless car took her away until he was no longer in sight. She felt that slight feeling of fear again and prayed it was nothing more than the normal departure blues, but she didn't seem to be able to convince herself.

Chapter 26

SEPTEMBER 2037. John stood in water just above his waist about three hundred yards off the shore in Espiritu Santo Bay, patiently waiting for his prey to arrive. The wonderful fall day was in full bloom with temperatures in the relatively comfortable mid-80s, and just a hint of southwest wind. The ubiquitous puffy clouds he loved to see filled the sky, with a ring of them running parallel to the surrounding horizon.

John stood still, holding his fishing pole with his left index finger, lightly touching the fishing line for the slightest hint of a bite. A few taps on the fishing line on his finger would indicate a trout had found his croaker on the end of the line and was subduing him before eating the tasty morsel. He could smell that watermelon aroma his grandfather said was an indicator of trout nearby in the air.

He had done this drill many times. His grandfather taught John decades ago the patience of waiting for the taps and letting the fish run with the bait a while to ensure it was in his mouth before setting the hook. He loved those memories of his grandfather. He remembered the smile on the old man's face whenever John would reel in a trout. It was as if his grandfather was happier than John himself when that would happen. He missed his grandfather, especially on days like today.

Suddenly he felt a short series of taps on the line. His mind returned from reminiscing and focused sharply to see if the line would begin to stretch. It did not. Eventually, he eased his pole upward and tightened the line. He felt the wiggling of the croaker, indicating whatever had tried had failed to take it, leaving the bait alive and well. John lowered the tension on his line and relaxed again.

It was then John realized there was not a breath of air moving. He looked around and saw the entire bay had smoothed out and had almost become a mirror image of the sky. The only sounds he heard were the occasional splashing of the mullet disturbing the water surface and a boat in the far distance going by. This stillness brought a feeling of presence and serenity to him and everything around him.

WHEN LOVE PERSEVERES

As John looked in the distance, he saw something he had never seen before. In some areas on the horizon, he could no longer distinguish between where the water ended and the sky began; it all seemed to be one seamless picture. He focused in amazement at the scene before him. It occurred to him it was as if a door had opened between this world and another one. He felt if he started walking, he could eventually walk through that door and wondered what he might find on the other side. Deep in thought, there was one name that came to mind. Lisa. She had been gone twenty-eight years, and those days seemed a lifetime ago. He hadn't thought about her in a while. Yet there were still moments when he would see something or smell something that would trigger her memory, and if he thought about it, a tear or two would gather in his eye. His mind had done its best to move on, and in several ways, it had. His heart, however, could never forget.

Just then, the fishing line tapped again. John's deep thoughts quickly left, and his attention sharpened on the line and the pole in his hands. But this time, the line started to pull slowly. He deftly pushed the lever on his reel to allow the line to release slowly. After a few seconds, he clicked the lever to hold the line and yanked on the pole. Success! A robust and continuous tug on the other end confirmed he once again fulfilled his grandfather's coaching and he was soon rewarded with a large trout he scooped up in a net.

For the next couple of minutes, he maneuvered the hook out of the fish's mouth and put it on a stringer. Although he had done this many times before, it was never easy to hold the pole out of the water simultaneously, and age affected his efficient movements.

When he finished putting the fish on his stringer, his buddies, who had brought him fishing, yelled out for him to meet them back at the boat. It was time to head back home. He waved back with a good feeling that he would have bragging rights today for bringing back his trout limit.

John looked back to the horizon and saw the wind had picked up just slight enough that the seam between water and sky was now visible. He imagined the door that had been open was now closed. He felt a little sad, wondering if he had missed an opportunity. But he started to feel silly about the whole thing and made his way back to the boat.

As his buddies helped him crawl back into the boat, he felt silly as they pulled him up out of the water. How many times as a younger man, he effortlessly jumped into and out of armored vehicles, helicopters, Humvees, aircraft, and numerous other vehicles. But at age seventy, those days were long gone.

John took a seat on the boat as his buddy took his trout off his stringer and put them in the cooler.

"Damn, John! You put it on us today, buddy. They're all over 20 inches. What the hell were you using for bait?"

John wiped the sweat from his forehead and sarcastically replied, "The same thing you were using. I just know what the hell I'm doing!"

His two buddies started laughing.

"Hey, you guys see the horizon when the wind stopped blowing a minute ago? I couldn't tell where the water stopped, and the sky started. Looked pretty weird to me. Did you guys see that?" John asked.

"No, I didn't see anything like that. What the hell has Jennifer been giving you that you see weird shit like that?" his buddy asked.

The other jumped in and teased, "I think she's trying to get rid of her old man and get a new one who doesn't need those little blue pills before you head to the bedroom. She's still got some good mileage on her and is probably looking to upgrade."

Both men laughed, and then one of the men turned and looked at John. "Hey, you're sweating like a pig and look red in the face. Let me get you a tea or some water from the cooler." He then moved over to the cooler with the drinks in it, pulled a large can of ice tea out, and handed it to John.

"I'm serious. You guys didn't see the horizon?" John asked again as he took the tea from his buddy's hands.

"No, I didn't see anything like that."

John took a swallow from his can, and the cold liquid cooled his throat as it went down. He then finished his sip and wiped the sweat off his face again. "Yeh, it's hot today."

He happened to look toward the horizon again, and saw the scene was the same as before; the water and sky had become seamless.

John stood up and pointed to the horizon in front of him. "Hey, do you guys see it now? The sky and the water, it's like it was before."

Suddenly, John felt dizzy as his sense of orientation became hazy. His legs grew weak, and before he knew it, everything grew dark.

When John became conscious again, he opened his eyes and saw a ceiling rushing by his vision. He felt the sensation of laying on a bed being quickly rolled along a hallway, and could hear the voices of several people walking beside him.

"Get the IV started on him immediately, and have the anesthesiologist meet us in the operating room as soon as we arrive! We don't have a lot of time!"

John felt weak and was having trouble breathing. He tried to say something to the people beside him but could not speak. As he listened to their discussions, he became afraid as he determined they were talking about him. He began to understand he was in a hospital and dying.

Again, he struggled to talk but could not. He became more afraid. He did not want to die. He had always been afraid of dying. But what made him even more afraid was that he was alone. He knew no one around him. It was as it had been all of his life. In those desperate minutes, as he neared death so many times in the past, he felt he was always alone.

Finally, they entered a room, and a very bright light shined down upon John, blinding him. He felt hands on him, removing parts of his clothes, and inserting needles into his arm.

He marshaled all of his strength and finally reached out and took hold of the nurse's arm to his left.

She looked down upon him and brought her face closer to his. "Mr. Bradford, are you alright?"

John finally found the ability to talk. "Where is Jennifer? Is she here?"

"She is not here yet. She and your sister are on their way."

"I want to talk to Sara. Please call Sara for me."

The nurse thought for a second and then remembered Sara was his daughter. "I'll try and have her called as soon as your sister gets here. I need you to try and relax now. We are going to operate on you, and you need to relax. Everything will be OK."

Her words brought no relief to John, only more fear. He was alone. He closed his eyes as a tear ran down the side of his face. He desperately thought of what he could do. Then the last words Lisa had spoken to him came to him. "I will never leave you." If there was ever a time when he needed her since she had been gone, it was now.

John called out, "Lisa. Lisa, please hold me. Baby, I need you! Please."

The nurse took John's hand as she adjusted some equipment next to her. She then looked down upon John and said, "I don't know who Lisa is, Mr. Bradford. Tell me who she is, and I will try to find her."

But as John waited for Lisa to call out to him, there was no reply. He could not feel her presence as he had at times in the past. He now the utter desolation of loneliness.

He squeezed the nurse's hand and said, "I'm afraid. Please don't leave me."

"I'm right here with you. We're just waiting for the anesthesiologist to arrive."

John heard someone call the nurse's name and ask her to help them in the next room. He squeezed her hand harder, and she looked down at him. "I'm just going to leave for one minute, and I promise to be right back. I will stay with you until we begin the operation. You're going to be OK."

John did not want to let her hand go. He did not believe her.

"Mr. Bradford, I promise I will be back in less than a minute. I have to get another IV bag for you. OK?"

John did not want to let go, but she had promised him. He released her hand. A second later, the darkness returned.

Mary walked to the operating room entrance and stopped just as a nurse closed the door to it. "Ma'am, where is my brother, John Bradford? I'm his sister, Mary."

The nurse looked at Mary and realized that she already knew by the expression on her face. She did not have to tell her John was dead. "Ma'am, I'm very sorry for your loss. Yes, your brother is in there. You can see him in just a moment."

Mary's eyes welled up. She had always imagined John would outlive her somehow despite what he had done in his life. Instead, his death had taken her by complete surprise.

"Was anyone with him when he died?" Mary asked.

"Yes, Ma'am. I was."

Mary then anxiously asked, "How was he? Did he say anything? Did he ask for anyone?"

The nurse hesitated. These were complicated questions folks would ask at times like these. She was never sure what she should and should not say, being ignorant of family dynamics and the ongoings of the deceased. She thought for a second and then finally said, "He asked for you, and Jennifer, and his daughter Sara. I tried to tell him you were on his way and I would get a hold of Sara as soon as we could."

Mary lowered her eyes and said, "I see."

Then the nurse said, "And he also asked for Lisa. I remembered Mr. Bradford from some of his previous visits here. I know who you, and Jennifer, and Sara are. Who is Lisa? He called for Lisa to help him."

Mary closed her eyes. Only because she could imagine the pain John must have felt at being without his family in his final hour. She was sure it was because he must have felt totally alone that he had asked for Lisa.

He knew her memory often compounded the loneliness and pain he usually felt. He would not have asked for her unless he was desperate.

Mary opened her eyes and sadly said, "She was his wife. She died many years ago. He never stopped loving her."

The nurse simply said, "I see."

Then Mary closed her eyes again and prayed. *Lisa, if you can hear me, and if you can. Please help John. I beg you! Please!*

John awoke to a sudden massive explosion off to his left as he found himself crouching low behind the wreckage of a car. He put his head to his chest and became aware of the helmet on his head, his sweat-soaked uniform, a full load of combat gear on him, and an M16 rifle in his hands. Crouching low, he felt dirt and debris from the explosion rain down upon him and onto his helmet.

A long burst of machine-gun fire bouncing off the car in front of him immediately followed the explosion. The cracking of the bullets told him they were shooting at him, and he dared not raise his head, or he would die. His pulse raced, and his hands trembled. They had him pinned down with nowhere to go.

The sound of the ongoing battle all around him drowned out all other sounds until John became aware someone was calling his name.

"Bradford! Bradford!" someone yelled out.

John looked to his right and saw an officer crouched behind a stone wall looking at him. John shook his head to indicate he heard him.

"Bradford, you need to move to that house across the street and give me some suppressive fire!" the officer yelled.

Another explosion hit, and John crouched again. He was deathly afraid, but his Soldier instincts were kicking in. The officer was trying to tell him something, and he couldn't hear him. "What?" he yelled to the officer.

"I said, get to the house across the street and get the motherfuckers to put their heads down!"

This guy's crazy! I'll be hit the moment I move out from behind this car! John did not move. Fear had frozen him like never before. He looked down and then looked back toward the officer as another round of machine-gun fire raked his position.

"Goddammit, Bradford! Get your ass across that street! I'll call you on the radio as soon as the birds arrive. Now MOVE!"

John did not want to move. He knew for sure he would be hit. Just as so many times before, his whole body was shaking with fear. But he had to find a way to overcome it. He couldn't let fear stop him. He had his duty to perform. Yet, he struggled.

"Bradford!" The officer yelled even louder.

John took a deep breath, tensed his body, and jumped up from his position in a flash, spraying the enemy position to his front with rifle fire. He ran as fast as he could as bullets pinged the ground inches behind him, and his helmet bounced on his head with each step.

He saw a door to the building he was moving to and, running as fast as he could, barreled into the door with his shoulder crashing it open. The door flew open, and he saw three men dressed in black turn toward him with rifles in their hands. But John had the drop on them, and in a flash, he shot each one before the last could level his rifle on him.

Suddenly, he heard voices yelling out that seemed to be speaking Arabic in the next room. He instinctively reached for his chest and grabbed a grenade. He pulled the pin, held it for a few seconds, and then threw it in the next room as he quickly went to the floor. The deafening explosion filled the room with dust and noise.

When the dust settled, he did not hear any more voices. He quickly got up and surveyed the room. It was clear. He pulled the magazine out of his rifle and put in a new one. John's heart was racing, and he took a moment to try and catch his breath. Sweat stung his eyes, and his mouth was dry.

"Good job, Bradford!" a voice over John's headset underneath his helmet said. "I've got another squad moving to your three o'clock. You need to cover them and once they're in position, let me know, and I'll give you the LZ to meet back up with us."

"Hey, where the fuck am I?" John asked.

"Goddammit, Bradford! Don't ask stupid questions. Just do what you're told, and you might make it out alive. Got it?"

John took a deep breath. "OK."

He cautiously moved to a window and peeked out to see. The street before him was littered with trash, pieces of cars, and a single body alongside a sidewalk. He looked to his left and saw a Soldier peak around the corner of the nearby building. *OK, there's the squad moving up.*

John then looked to his right and saw a machine gun barrel poke outside the window of a second-story building. *Fuck!*

"Hey, tell the squad to hold up! There's a machine gun position about to engage them to their twelve o'clock!" John called over his radio headset.

"What? Say again. You came in broken."

"I said tell the squad to hold up! They're walking into an ambush!"

"I can't understand you! Say again!"

Goddammit!

John looked again, and the squad was making their move. He saw the machine gun barrel move as it tracked the squad's movements waiting for the perfect time to fire. He knew it was only a matter of time before the enemy opened fire on them in the open. He had less than a second to make a decision.

John jumped out of the window and started to run to the house with the machine gun as he yelled out to the squad to take cover. But it was too late. The enemy opened fire, and several men dropped as bullets hit all around them.

A rage exploded within John as he watched small explosions of red hit the Soldiers' bodies caught in the open street, screaming for help. He ran as fast as he could and into the house. Quickly moving through the house with no regard to stealth, he seemed to know instinctively which room the enemy occupied.

When he got upstairs to the room at the end of the hallway, he rushed in and found three men, again dressed in black, operating the machine gun. He raised his rifle and shot two of them. As he turned to shoot the third, his gun jammed. Before he had a chance to clear it, the third man jumped him.

They violently wrestled on the ground, each one trying to grab the throat of the other. Finally, the enemy Soldier had managed to pin John and took a knife from his belt. He swiftly went to stab John in the throat, but John managed to grab his arm and hold it. Both men strained as hard as they could to overcome the raw strength of the other. John smelled the putrid breath of the man lying on top of him and saw his eyes, filled with black hate. An expression of joy was on the man's face as he slowly overcame John's strength inching the knife ever closer to his throat.

Finally, the rage John felt earlier returned to him, and he threw the man off of him. John rolled along the floor, grabbed the pistol from his side holster, and emptied an entire magazine of bullets into the man just as he was attempting to stand up.

The man's body violently jerked, and then it fell lifeless to the ground.

Fatigue from the struggle filled John as he lay on the floor and tried to gain his wits about him. His headset crackled, and a voice said, "Bradford! You were supposed to cover the squad moving up. What the fuck are you doing? They're all dead!"

Breathing hard and still not clear-minded from the struggle, John replied, "I tried to warn them, but they didn't listen. I cleared the enemy position as soon as I could."

"Well, you failed, dammit! Get your ass to the clearing around the corner in the next five minutes. I have a bird coming in to lift us out. Get moving!"

John felt horrible. Several Soldiers lay dead because of him. But he had to keep moving if he wanted to get extracted from this hell hole.

He slowly got up and found his rifle. He worked the bolt back and forth several times to clear the jammed round and then reloaded the chamber.

Looking around the room, John got a familiar feeling until he finally realized this was his room when he was a boy! The bed with the small bookcase headboard was against the wall, and his books were thrown about the ground, which by now had become splattered with drops of blood from the dead men. He gradually made his way through the house, watching every corner to ensure he was not attacked again by someone hiding in the shadows. Finally, as he walked into the living room, he realized he was in his old house from his childhood.

He stooped down and picked up a picture with broken glass of his parents, sister, and him. He looked around and saw other pictures of his family. *Why am I here? I can't be home? What the hell is going on?*

"Bradford! Where the fuck are you?" the voice on the radio yelled.

"I'm moving now," John replied.

When he reached the front door, he once again looked around the buildings surrounding the house he was in. The sounds of the fighting seemed to have moved several blocks from his location. Scanning the scene and seeing the items scattered before him brought a flood of memories. Laying all about the front yard were his toy Soldiers, model airplanes, fishing poles, and other things from his childhood. A carcass of what was once a red, white, and blue Honda racing bike lay in the street, still smoldering. John looked all around but could not see anyone moving.

He stepped out of the house and started to walk to the LZ while he deliberately looked around, rifle in hand, ready to engage anything that looked like enemy movement. Walking across the street, he came upon more debris. Looking closer, he saw broken records, torn album covers, cracked cassettes, and broken CDs strewn all about. He stopped and picked up an old Barry Manilow album cover. When he turned it over, he saw the song "Somewhere Down The Road" circled in red. He had played the song numerous times, thinking about and wishing Lisa would return to him after she left him that summer of 89. *This is my music collection! What the fuck?*

"Bradford! What are you doing? We've got to leave soon!" the officer on the radio demanded.

John threw down the album cover and started to walk quickly again, still scanning the houses around him.

As he crossed the street, he heard a weak voice call out, "Help me . . . Please."

He turned toward the voice and saw one of the Soldiers from the squad that got ambushed earlier trying to reach out to him. His shirt was covered in blood, and sweat and grime covered his face underneath his helmet.

John ran over and knelt next to the Soldier. "Where are you hit? Are you bleeding?"

The Soldier's eyes tried to focus on John, but it was as if a film covered them and the man couldn't see. "Please help me. I think I'm hit in the chest and leg. I can't feel my leg anymore."

John ran his hand along the Soldier's chest and felt several entry wounds with blood slowly oozing out with each breath. He glanced down and saw the man's leg was almost in shreds.

The voice in the headset called again. "Goddammit, Bradford, I'm not going to wait all fucking day!"

"Look, I got a wounded Soldier from the squad you sent. He's in bad shape, but I think I can get him to the LZ. You need to give me a few more minutes."

"Leave him."

"I'm not fucking leaving him!"

"Please don't leave me," the Soldier begged.

"We don't have room for him on the bird."

"Well, you're going to fucking make room for him on the Goddamn bird!"

"You need to just shut up and follow orders, Bradford. Get moving!"

"You listen here, motherfucker! I've had enough of your shit! You fucking better hold that bird for the two of us. Out!"

John did not wait for a response. He reached down and pulled the Soldier up off the ground. "Hold on, buddy. I'm going to carry you to an inbound helicopter."

John struggled to balance the man on his back, and as soon as he got him positioned, he stood up and started to carry him to the LZ slowly. As soon as he started walking, gunfire erupted, and John realized they were firing at him. The crack of bullets passed by him, and several bounced off the ground near him.

"They're shooting at us! Hurry!" the wounded man pleaded.

"Hold on, buddy! I got you!" John said as he tried his best to move quickly. The man's weight made it awkward to move, and John could feel his strength beginning to fail him.

Suddenly, he felt as if something had hit the body of the Soldier on his back as the man cried out. He ran over to a nearby concrete planter and laid the Soldier down.

A bullet hole was centered on the man's forehead. His lifeless body became just another corpse littering the street.

Dammit!

Another round of gunfire erupted, and John ducked his head. When it stopped, he popped his head up to determine where it was coming from. He realized he was in the middle of the street, totally cut off from any other cover, and needed to get out of there before he was caught in a crossfire.

He grabbed his rifle, jumped up, and started to run as fast as he could to the nearest house. Then a sharp sting hit him in his left leg, followed by another in his shoulder and back. An explosion occurred, throwing him several feet into the air and crashing his body onto the nearby sidewalk.

John lay face down on the concrete sidewalk, exhausted and in pain. He used the minute strength he had left to fight for breath that never came. The hot concrete burned his face, but he didn't have the strength to lift his head.

"You failed, Bradford. You failed the squad. You failed that wounded Soldier. You couldn't even save Lisa. You're a fucking failure!" the voice over the radio said.

John could feel his eyes closing as he struggled to reply to the voice on the radio. "I tried my best," he said. "I . . . tried . . ." and then nothing.

A second later, he felt himself standing, facing the open ocean with the warm breeze blowing in his face and the sound of the waves crashing into the seashore. Birds were hovering just above the waves, occasionally diving into the water, searching for a meal as small fish scattered about breaking the surface. The puffy clouds with the blue underbellies he loved to see in the sky slowly inched toward the horizon as the warm sun reflected off his face.

There were no explosions, no gunfire, and no death and destruction, yet, John was afraid. He did not understand what was happening to him and prayed he would not return to the battlefield he just left. His breathing was still hard from the fear and anxiety he had just experienced. Yet, his mind was alert, and his body poised to move at a second's notice. John felt he could not allow himself to be seduced by the serenity around him. He was too afraid of what might happen next.

Then from behind, he heard a voice he had not heard in years call out to him. "John."

He turned and looked into a pair of beautiful blue eyes, full red lips, and clear skin on a face he had almost forgotten how beautiful it could be. The woman's long, brunette hair blew in the wind and danced around her face as a smile crept upon her. She slightly tilted her head and said, "Hey."

He stared at the beautiful face before him, a masterpiece of God's work, unmatched in his memory. Her simple gesture removed all memory of the desperation he had just experienced. His mind could only hope and pray what he saw now was real. He slowly reached up with his hand and touched her cheek with his fingers. The sensation of supple flesh tingled his fingertips as he felt the love, longing, passion, and desire of her expression. He held his breath, afraid to ask the question that eventually escaped his lips. "Lisa?"

"Yes, baby. I'm here."

He asked again, but with tears welling up in his eyes this time. He had to be sure. "Lisa?"

She raised her hand and caressed his face as her expression filled with love. "I'm here, baby. I told you I would always wait for you."

His heart sprang with joy as he took in the sight before him. His eyes feasted upon the woman he could never forget. The one woman who he loved and had loved him like no other. The one woman in his entire life that was his soulmate.

But once again, he became afraid. Afraid, like several times before, she would leave him after only being with him for a few precious seconds. He could not let that happen again.

John put his arms around Lisa and pulled her into him, and hugged her tightly so that nothing could take her away from him. "Please don't leave me, Lisa. Not this time. Please. I need you so much. Please, baby."

John felt Lisa's arms squeeze him as she softly cooed into his ear, "I have never left you, baby. And I promise I will never leave you again. Never! My heart has ached for this moment for so long, my love. And finally, it has come."

John felt Lisa's arms rub his back and the sensation of her body next to his. He felt her soft face and the edge of her lips pressed against his cheek. The sound of her gently breathing next to his ear was music to him.

John began to cry as he released the pain of being without her for so long. Soon his cries became sobs, his body trembled, and his heart shuddered. He had heard her words, and he believed her. Lisa was here, with him, in his arms as they had been in the past.

Lisa felt John releasing his pain and continued to whisper to him, "It's OK, baby. I'm here now. It's OK. We're together now."

For the next few moments, John felt his heart finally heal. The emptiness that had been inside of him for so long eventually filled with the love that only Lisa could give him. When he felt the last of his pain go, he stopped crying and pulled back from Lisa's hug to look at her again.

Once again, he gazed upon the most beautiful woman he had ever seen, and finally, a smile of love and happiness came to him.

But then the voice that reminded him of his failures came to his mind. The memory of trying to save her from the terrible cancer that killed her came to him. He thought if he could have done better, she would not have had to leave him as soon as she did. She would have lived a full life. Instead, his failure had prevented Lisa from having the joy of watching their daughter, Sara, grow into the wonderful woman she became. The smile on John's face and the joy in his heart at seeing Lisa again left him replaced with watery eyes and regret.

"But Lisa. I failed you," he said.

Lisa's smiling face turned serious as her eyes penetrated deep into John's soul. "No, my love! You have NEVER failed me! I never want you to say those words ever again. You are my heart. You are the man God made for me. You have not failed me any more than you have failed them," she said as she pointed toward a crowd of people who now stood beside John.

He turned his head to look at the crowd and recognized many of the faces. Specialist Feldman, the first man John lost in combat, smiled at him. Specialist Garcia, John's driver, killed in the roadside bomb attack on his Humvee, waved to him and greeted him. Several of the Soldiers from the platoon he saved from the murderous crossfire in Afghanistan looked at him and smiled. He turned as he heard his buddy Matt call out his name. Sergeant Major Sanchez, Jefferson, and so many more all stood off to the side, their faces full of smiles and nodding their heads as they looked at John. General Bartley called out, welcoming John. Chief Carter, who he had comforted in Iraq after their dangerous mission, called out, "It's about fucking time, Sir!"

John laughed. Her foul mouth was still the same.

Many other faces he could not remember also filled his vision. They all smiled, nodded, or called out his name.

When John turned back toward Lisa, she was smiling at him once again. She reached up with her soft hand and touched his cheek. "Do you understand now, my love? You have never been a failure. Not to them or me. You are a success in every sense of the word. You are my hero, my knight in shining armor, my husband, my soulmate. You are a part of my heart just as I am a part of yours."

With Lisa's touch, he finally understood and believed. He had not failed her, nor the countless men and women he had served with. The fear in him from the voice on the radio disappeared forever, and he felt a peace come upon him as never before. The demons in his mind that had tortured him for so long left, never to return. The loneliness he had felt all of his life was gone, replaced by the warmth of the woman whose hand caressed his face.

Then John looked around and saw the crowd that had surrounded them was gone. Once again, it was only he and Lisa.

Lisa took John's hand. "Come with me, babe."

"Where are we going?"

"Home. To a place where nothing will ever separate us again."

John smiled.

But as Lisa turned to take John with her, she felt him tug back on her hand. She turned with a questioned look on her face. "What is it, sweetheart?"

John's smile grew. "First things first," he said. And with that, he pulled Lisa into his arms and drew his face inches from hers. He stared into Lisa's eyes that darkened with desire and love. He closed his eyes and gently brushed his lips against hers. He slowly opened her lips to his, taking his time to allow the passion to build. Years of desire and need for the woman of his dreams to be back in his arms slowly unleashed a love that could not be contained. The sensation of her warm body next to his, her ample breasts pressed against his chest, her legs positioning around his as they stood together grew to an explosion of hunger within them both.

John could feel Lisa melting in his arms while the heat of her yearning for him built within her. Her arms now started to pull him into her tightly. Her heavy breathing filled his ears as much as her wonderful scent filled his nose.

John released his kiss and placed his lips along the side of Lisa's neck, softly kissing her.

Lisa could not hold back any longer. She moaned as the ecstasy in her built, anticipating what was to come, her fingernails now digging into John's back.

John whispered into Lisa's ear, "Make love to me now, baby. Do it like never before."

Lisa moaned again, doing her best to keep her desire at bay, knowing her the effort was useless. She pulled back to look at John, whose expression took her breath away. Then, after catching her breath, she said, "Maybe we could go home tomorrow. Or the next day, depending upon how long you think this will take."

John said before he pulled her lips back to his, "It will take me forever."

PART SIX

GENERAL BRADFORD

Chapter 27

23 May 2058, 5 MILES WEST OF ALYTUS, LITHUANIA. Twenty minutes after a violent battle between US and Russian forces had ended, three lightly armored wheeled command vehicles made their way up to the front lines.

What a few weeks before had been a thriving small city was now an urban shell of rubble and destruction. Fires raged, and smoke billowed around the command vehicles as they wound their way through the devastation to the US Army unit manning what remained of the forward defensive positions. They stopped when they came upon a wrecked Russian armored personnel carrier that blocked their path.

The doors from the middle vehicle opened, and a slim figure of a woman dressed in a US camouflage uniform, combat gear, pistol holster strapped to her thigh, and helmet got out, followed by a man dressed the same but with a rifle. From the vehicles in front and behind, several heavily armed men exited and formed a perimeter around the woman.

The woman scanned the area around her as she walked with authority toward what appeared to be a company tactical operations command center. She seemed unphased by the carnage around her and only intent on finding her Soldiers who had survived the battle.

The man following the woman did his best to keep up and stay close to her as he dodged the debris, a combination of human bodies, tactical military robots, and various vehicles from both sides, and the remnants of civilians who were unfortunate to be caught in the middle. The smell of burnt flesh and electronics assaulted his nose as bad as the sight of torn limbs that lay about. In an era when robots and drones were supposed to do most of the fighting, this battlefield was more reminiscent of the 20th century than the 21st.

As the man found himself walking around a large destroyed armored vehicle, he heard a radio transmission come over his headset inside his helmet.

"Pegasus 61, this is Pegasus TOC. Ski, what the fuck are ya'll doing?"

"Roger, Sir. We've stopped, and Pegasus 6 is trying to find a command post to get a SITREP. Battalion comms in the area are either being jammed or are down."

"Goddammit, Ski, do you know where the fuck you guys are?"

"From what I can see, Sir, looks like we're pretty far forward."

"You're on top of the fucking Russians!"

"I'd say from the collection of bodies lying around here, Sir, your tactical assessment is right on."

"Listen, Stalanski! I don't need the fucking division commander dead or sitting in some fucking prison camp. She won't answer my calls. You go get her and tell her to get her ass out of there ASAP. Got it?"

Major Stalanski silently chuckled to himself. The only person in the whole division that could get away with talking about Major General Sara Bradford in that tone of voice was the division chief of staff, Colonel Jack Eddington. Despite their difference in rank, he was the one man in the division that equaled her in experience, and because of it, General Bradford allowed him broad authority within the division. She always consulted him about any major decisions and valued his input. But even Colonel Eddington had his limits with her. If he pushed her too far, she would let Eddington know in no uncertain terms who was in command, and it wasn't him.

"Ahh, Sir, last time I checked, she outranked me by quite a bit. What exactly would you like me to do to influence the general? I'm pretty sure she knows exactly where she is and what the situation is."

"I should never have allowed you two to go touring around the battlefield right now. It's just too damn hot."

"Yes, Sir, but you know how she is about her Soldiers."

There was silence on the radio, and Stalanski knew Eddington was trying to calm himself down. It seemed he took it upon himself to look out for General Bradford, although to Stalanski, General Bradford could more than take care of herself.

"Yes, I know. Look, Ski. You just make damn sure nothing happens to her out there. Because if something does, I'll have your balls hanging from the mirror of my LTV. Got it?"

"Yes, Sir."

"And make sure you radio me the moment you exit the area!"

"Yes, Sir."

"Pegasus TOC, out."

Despite replying to Colonel Eddington's inquiry, Major David Stalanski, Sara's aide, kept her in sight to ensure her safety. Knowing Eddington as he did, he did not doubt if anything did happen to Sara, Eddington would follow through on his threat.

As he watched her walk toward several Soldiers, he thought about what an incredible woman Sara was. He remembered when he told his buddies he would be her aide de camp, several of them laughed at him. They teased that he would become one of "Bradford's Bitches," as her staff was sometimes referred to.

But in the little over a year Stalanski was with Sara, he not only learned a great deal but was also able to separate myth from fact.

The first time Stalanski met Sara, he was amazed at how beautiful she was for her age. He remembered the first time he saw her with her hair down and in a pair of PT shirt and shorts that highlighted the contours of a well-defined woman. Years of hard physical training had molded her hard body into a shape envied by women half her age with long chiseled legs. Her lavish blue eyes, lush brunette hair, and supple lips momentarily lured Stalanski into lascivious fantasy.

It took him a few minutes to remove the sexually explicit thoughts that had come into his mind after he realized he was thinking about his boss in a less than appropriate manner. And for a moment, he fell into the trap some men initially did, in thinking she was an empty-headed floozy who had slept her way to the top. Some said there was no way someone as attractive as Sara could be a professional Soldier.

That instantly changed the first time she threw him to the ground in a combatives training session. Her flawless timing and technique amazed Stalanski in addition that she even participated in such training. Other generals never did.

Stalanski quickly learned the talk of her merely being a fake military Barbi was far from true. General Bradford knew her business cold. When male officers briefing her took her to be "dumb," they learned the hard way how wrong they were the moment she opened her mouth and educated them on combat tactics. One look at the number of ribbons on her dress uniform, and any man less than comfortable with his skills would indeed shrink in her shadow. Stalanski found very few men or women that could match her knowledge or exploits.

No, General Bradford knew warfighting and had a reputation for being tough, both on her staff and her Soldiers, pushing them to their limit. Merely meeting the standard was not good enough in the First Cavalry Division. You had to do better.

She also pushed herself hard. Stalanski was astonished at her energy and the standards Sara held for herself. She did physical training with troops half her age and outran most of them. She was faultless in all the basic Soldier skills. She kept abreast of the latest Army doctrine, understood the capabilities and limitations of all of the major equipment in her division, and always took the time to educate young officers and Soldiers on leadership.

But of all the things Stalanski learned, what stood out most in his mind was the loyalty General Bradford's Soldiers showed to her, and she showed them. Despite the high standards Sara held for them, they also felt her care and compassion for them. General Bradford had a complete lack of tolerance toward leaders who failed to take care of "her" Soldiers. She was relentless in her attention to their training, living conditions, and overall well-being. When she visited with her subordinate units and following the standard "dog and pony shows" that leaders felt obliged to give, she would always sit and talk with Soldiers. Stalanski would invariably end up sitting next to her, writing out a laundry list of things that need to be addressed on their behalf and then sending those items out as taskings to her commanders and staff that needed to be fixed immediately.

During one of their computer simulation exercises for the division staff, Stalanski remembered when one of the civilian contractors walked up to Sara and introduced himself to her. Before he had finished, she realized he had been one of her Soldiers in Korea when she was a company commander. She threw her arms around him and gave him a warm hug. For the remainder of the exercise, she always stopped and talked with him whenever they happened to meet, and they shared several hearty laughs about the old days.

It was moments like those when you understood why her Soldiers loved and respected "The Queen of Battle," as some of them liked to call her. She had earned their respect. Once you had worked directly with General Bradford, there was a good chance you would want to stay with her.

By now, even Stalanski felt strongly about her in that way. Despite her relentless schedule, she would take time out to talk to him and genuinely ask him about his family and his career. Watching her as he did, Stalanski had received an exclusive education in leadership and warfighting he couldn't have gotten anywhere else.

However, very few saw a side of General Bradford that Stalanski did, completing the paradox she was to him. There were those rare moments when Sara appeared to let her guard down, and the strong, professional Soldier gave way to the woman held captive in a uniform. Sara was unmarried, which Stalanski believed to be a combination of her lack of free time and her high standards for a man. He believed few, if any, male egos could accept a woman of her stature.

But that did not mean Sara wished to be single. There were even rarer moments when Stalanski dared say he saw envy in Sara's eyes as she looked upon a happy couple exchanging the silent language of love. Although she was always very discrete about it, Stalanski remembered one time when Sara turned and realized he had seen her as she gazed at a handsome man eating dinner by himself. She smiled at Stalanski as if caught in the act of some nefarious schoolgirl transgression before bowing her head.

He also never forgot when he took Sara to visit her parents' graves. They were traveling to a conference when General Bradford scheduled a short detour to the small town of Victoria.

After she got out of the car, she asked Stalanski to wait for her and give her a few minutes alone. He watched her walk to the graves and silently stand before them for several minutes after she had laid flowers next to their tombstone. Watching her as she was deep in thought and reflection, Sara did not look like a Soldier, but a very sad woman whose past had been influenced by the two people she now visited. Stalanski knew her father had been in the Army, a decorated colonel, but he knew nothing of her mother other than the pictures of them both she kept in her office.

When Sara returned, Stalanski swore her eyes were wet with tears, but he dared not ask, and she remained silent for most of the remainder of the drive to the conference.

This was the enigma of Major General Sara Bradford, two-star general, the first female to commander an Army combat division, the First Cavalry Division, deployed to war. A woman who commanded the respect of the harshest of men under her command, who had defied death and never shied from danger, yet whose undeniable beauty encased a true woman full of feminine emotions that she kept well hidden.

Looking around as she walked, it was apparent to Sara the fighting had just finished only a little while ago. The smell of death was very prevalent, a scent Sara was well familiar with.

Sara saw US Soldiers moving about, a good indicator to her they had prevailed. The enemy attack had come quickly, but her staff had anticipated it, and she had ordered a tank company to be moved to reinforce this sector. As she looked around, she was surprised not to see any tanks in the vicinity.

Sara approached what she determined to be a young captain giving orders to a master sergeant and a lieutenant.

"Get over to first platoon and get me a status. I haven't heard from them in over thirty minutes," the captain told the lieutenant. He then turned to face Sara. Surprised, the captain strained to straighten to attention and raised his hand to his bloodshot eyes in a shaky salute.

"Hello, Ma'am. I did not know you were in this area," the young man told Sara.

Sara returned his salute and replied, "We've been trying to get in touch with your brigade TOC for the past twenty minutes to notify them of our presence in this area and have not been able to raise them. Are you in contact with them?"

"No, Ma'am. We lost contact a while ago. I'm not sure what happened."

Looking at the young man's filthy uniform and exhausted state reminded Sara of those desperate days in Korea when she was a captain. She felt empathy for him yet dared not show it too strong. Then her eyes gravitated to a dark red stain on his pants leg. "Are you wounded, captain?" she asked.

Stuttering as he spoke, he said, "No, Ma'am. . . . . not that I know . . . . I think," he answered. Then the captain tilted a bit, and the master sergeant standing next to him grabbed him and guided him to a large piece of broken concrete to sit on.

Once the captain sat down, the master sergeant yelled for a medic to come and look at him.

"I'm fine, Ma'am. I really am. I just need to sit for a minute," the captain told Sara.

"Can you give me a SITREP on exactly what happened here?" Sara asked.

"Yes, Ma'am," the captain answered. But he did not continue and seemed a little disoriented.

Stalanski walked up to the group just as a medic also joined them. When the medic saw Sara, she quickly came to attention and saluted.

"Let's dispense with all this saluting in a forward combat area. Specialist, please take a look at the captain." Then she turned to the master sergeant, whose uniform was as dirty as the captain's, and said, "Master Sergeant, please step over here with me for a moment."

Sara then indicated to Stalanski to walk over and join them for the conversation.

"Master Sergeant, tell me your job here and explain to me what's going on here."

"I'm Master Sergeant Ronald Dupree, Ma'am. I'm the acting First Sergeant for Bravo Company since First Sergeant Steed was killed two

290

days ago, and this has been the biggest cluster fuck I've been on in my twenty-five years in the Army!" Dupree belted out.

Sara stood unphased. "OK. Please explain."

"Well, Ma'am. We occupied this sector five days ago from Delta Company, 2nd Brigade. We were told to set up a defensive perimeter and stop any enemy penetration beyond Phase Line Stan, which is the street running north and south two blocks behind us."

"OK, I understand. Please continue."

"We were told not to expect very much if any enemy activity in this sector. Well, that turned out to be bullshit. We'd hadn't been here two hours when we got drone reports of a massing of enemy units two miles to our front. Right after that, we started taking sniper fire. They killed our First Sergeant before we were able to clear most of the snipers out. Then we dug in and requested additional support prior to any further contact with major enemy forces. We got nothing. Not long after that, we started taking incoming artillery fire. Then the first wave hit us. Those bastards played rough, but we played harder and kicked their ass, but only after we'd lost more than we should have. But by then, the scouts and drones confirmed we had at least a battalion headed our way, maybe more, supported by robotic heavy tanks and engineer equipment. So, we requested reinforcements. Still, we got nothing!"

"OK, wait a minute. Why did your battalion not provide any additional resources to you? They had to have had a reason," Sara asked.

"It wasn't battalion. It was brigade. They moved our battalion out to set up in another location and put us under brigade control until the battalion finished moving."

"So, your requests went straight to 1st Brigade, then?"

"Yes. But they kept getting denied. They kept saying our scout reports were wrong and we could handle whatever was in front of us. Well, that was bullshit, and the captain told them so. By now, we had been hit by a full battalion plus. That was yesterday. We reported black on ammo and class one last night, hoping to get a night resupply. We got one fucking truck with less than half the ammo we needed and no class one."

"What about tank support?"

"Tanks? Haven't seen any of those around, but we sure could have used them."

The medic walked up to Sara and Dupree and said, "Excuse me, Ma'am. The captain will be OK. He's just dehydrated. I've got him set up with an IV, but I can't stay here. I've got to get to the aid station and help out there."

"Get going, Specialist. I'm combat lifesaver qualified. I'll take the IV out when it's done," Dupree said.

The medic looked at Sara, and Sara gestured for her to leave. The medic then ran off.

"The captain hasn't had more than two hours sleep in the past four days. None of us have, but he's had it the worst. I don't know how he did it, but he got a hold of an attack helicopter squadron, and they moved in three birds early this morning. If we hadn't had them, we wouldn't have made it. We're sitting at about 50% strength in personnel, and lots of them are walking wounded."

Sara acknowledged the master sergeant and then turned to Stalanski. "Ski, I don't understand. This attack should not have been a surprise. We monitored the two enemy battalions' movement headed this way and OPCONed a tank company to 1st Brigade to beef them up. I'm not aware of any other engagements with 1st Brigade. Those tanks should have been sent here."

"Yes, Ma'am, you're right. I checked with the TAC right before we arrived, and this was the only sector within the 1st Brigade AO that had contact in the past forty-eight hours."

Sara nodded, then asked, "Since you've been placed under brigade, when is the last time you've seen the brigade commander?"

"We haven't."

Sara nodded again.

While they talked, Sara saw several JLTVs drive up. An officer dismounted the first JLTV and walked up to Sara just as the sergeant finished talking. Sara recognized the officer as Lieutenant Colonel Ron Driscoll, the 1st Brigade Executive Officer. She knew Ron well and liked him. A former battalion commander, Ron was a good officer who knew his business. She was surprised at what the sergeant had just told her, and was anxious to hear Ron's explanation.

"Good morning, Ma'am. I wasn't aware you had made it here yet."

"Good morning, Ron. We've been trying to get in touch with your TOC all morning. What's wrong with your comms?"

"Our network hardware took a hit last night, and we've been trying to reestablish it all morning."

"Ron, I've gotten a SITREP from Master Sergeant Dupree. I don't understand what's going on here. The way he describes it, they've been in contact for the better part of four days, yet haven't received any support. I'm not aware of any other engagements 1st Brigade has had in the last forty-eight hours. Where are the tanks we sent you? What in the hell is going on here?"

Driscoll's face suggested a conflict in his mind in trying to provide an answer.

Sara never knew him to withhold information or cover up bad news deliberately, so she was surprised by his silence.

As the two officers talked, yet another set of vehicles arrived on the scene, and an entourage of officers and Soldiers emerged.

Before Sara could press Driscoll again to answer her questions, he glanced over to the new arrivals, turned back to Sara, and said, "Ma'am, the brigade commander has just arrived. I'd rather he answer those questions."

Sara remained calm, yet her eyes narrowed at his request. She knew under normal circumstances, he would have never deflected her questions, so her concern about what was going on grew. Then, seeing the brigade commander walking directly towards them, Sara waited.

Colonel Jeffery Parker, the Brigade Commander and son of General Jim Parker, the former Chairman of the Joint Chiefs of Staff, came from a family with a long and distinguished history of service within the Army. Because so many had made it to general, the Parker name had become royalty within the Army. However, the only problem was Jeffery Parker used that distinction to his advantage every opportunity he could. Despite what many would consider average evaluation reports, Parker was consistently promoted ahead of his peers. Three months before the combat deployment, when the 1st Brigade Commander became ill, Personnel Command pushed Parker into the newly vacant slot.

Knowing several more experienced officers than Parker should have been considered for the command, Sara began to smell the old "ticket punching" game being played. Officers were rushed to key positions just long enough to get the required time needed to qualify for promotion. Once they reached the minimum time, they were moved on to a different assignment, usually less stressful, to await their next rank. Being a brigade commander during wartime would be a significant achievement under Parker's belt and would put him at an advantage to promotion to general.

Sara assumed Personnel Command had a good reason for giving Parker the command slot, but she was less than impressed since his arrival. Under his command, 1st Brigade's rating dropped considerably. When Sara asked about the poor brigade performance, Parker's response was always to blame his predecessor and explain he had left him a mess and Parker was doing the best he could with what he had. Sara knew the previous commander and did not believe Parker's excuse.

Additionally, Sara began to hear some disturbing things about Parker's lack of knowledge concerning the employment of crucial equipment and a lackadaisical attitude toward preparation for the deployment. Parker acted as though his brigade would only have to show up, and the enemy would take one look and run away. He frequently talked about how close combat was a thing of the past. He believed with the technology his brigade possessed, the battles would all be over by the time Soldiers arrived on the scene.

Sara had been down that road before and knew better. Wars would never be as bloodless as Parker believed, and his lack of performance was putting Soldiers at risk. In her mind, she was rapidly coming to a point where she might need to take action. However, several senior officers warned her about the long reach of the Parker family arm and how it wasn't a good thing to make them your enemies.

To try and rectify the situation without ruffling feathers, Sara took it upon herself to put Driscoll in as the brigade executive officer right before the deployment. She knew he would bring a lot of experience to the job and hoped he could counter his boss's limitations. With what Driscoll had just told her, she now thought she might have been wrong.

Just before Colonel Parker reached Sara and Driscoll, he called out to the young captain who was sitting down with the IV in his arm, "Captain, why are you sitting down? Do you not know the division commander is standing a few feet from you? On your feet, Soldier!" Parker's aristocratic tone matched his sharp-pointed features that gave the impression of privilege.

The captain had regained his senses and stood. Parker paid no attention to the IV in his arm.

As Parker walked up to Sara, her eyes went straight to his uniform. It was immaculately clean. Despite the privileges of being a general officer, even Sara could not maintain her uniform that clean. While not filthy, her attire attested to the harsh conditions of living in a war zone. What she saw spoke volumes about Parker, and none of it was good.

"Good morning, Ma'am. Welcome to 1st Brigade. I'm sorry for being late, but we did not know you were coming to visit us," Parker said as he snapped off a salute without giving Sara the option to return before he dropped his as is custom.

"Good morning, Colonel. I was moving through this area and decided to see what was developing with the fight here. We called your TOC several times but got no response."

"We've been having a few problems with comms, but we've been back up for a while now. You might need to check your equipment," Parker answered.

Knowing Sara demanded her communication equipment be in perfect working order at all times, and she would kill him if it were not, Stalanski forced himself to cough to keep himself from calling bullshit on Parker's accusation.

Sara glanced at Stalanski and got his message. Their communication equipment had no such issues.

"Colonel, I've received a SITREP from the captain and his first sergeant. They say they've been in contact for four days and haven't received adequate support. Can you expound upon that for me?"

"Yes, Ma'am. Their contact has been light. We resupplied them with ammunition the other day, and they are green on Class one and three."

"I don't know if I'd classify a company being attacked by two battalions as light contact."

"I'm not aware they have been in contact with any enemy battalions. The last report I got from them was they were receiving sniper fire. If they were in contact with such superior forces, they should have told us. The company commander and his first sergeant are weak leaders. I'll talk to their battalion commander about replacing them as soon as possible. I won't tolerate such incompetence!"

While Parker and Sara talked, Sara occasionally looked over at Driscoll for his reaction, but his downward cast eyes hid any. Usually, an executive officer would add things to the conversation the brigade commander might not be aware of to defend his actions. But Driscoll said nothing.

"I see. But certainly, you should have known about this attack. When we published CONPLAN Pluto a week ago, the G2's most probable course of action was a two-battalion attack in this area. That's why we gave you the tank company to reinforce this sector."

"Yes, I saw that. My S2 said he disagreed with the division assessment. So, we adjusted that plan and moved the tanks elsewhere."

"Where are they?"

"They are sitting at my headquarters, guarding it."

Sara blinked her eyes a few times and wasn't sure she'd heard correctly. "I'm sorry. Where did you say they are?"

"The tank company is sitting at my TOC, guarding it. There is a strong probability of a commando attack against the TOC, and I need to ensure its survivability."

Sara was having a hard time believing what she was hearing. She'd heard nothing to indicate an imminent commando threat to any of the major headquarters in her division, including her own. Even if that was true, the tank company was overkill for such a contingency based on the brigade's available forces.

Up to this point, Parker's performance was much less than what she expected and considering what she had just heard, Sara was seriously beginning to question his tactical proficiency as an officer. Sara's woman's intuition kicked in, and she started to wonder if the reason the tank company was at Parker's headquarters was to protect him more than his tactical operations center.

"Colonel, this is the first I've heard of any commando threat to any of the major headquarters' locations. We specifically gave you that tank company to support the fight in this sector. I'm not sure I understand your reasoning for placing the tank company at your TOC location."

"Excuse me, Ma'am, but once again, my S2 disagrees with the G2 regarding the commando threat. We've had several signal intercepts indicating it will happen at any time. I can't afford to lose my TOC. I need all the ISR and fire support connectivity I can get. If my TOC goes down, we're sunk. I understand you gave us that tank company, but I am the brigade commander, and I have the authority to use my assigned assets as I see fit. Wouldn't you agree?"

Major Stalanski trembled at the tone Parker ended his answer with. Although technically correct in his final statement, no one got away with talking to Sara like that, and even Eddington would only go so far behind closed doors. Never in public. Stalanski didn't have to look at Sara to know she was probably steaming right now. But just to be sure, he slanted his eyes her way.

Sara was expressionless. But then Stalanski glanced down at her hand and saw it in a fist. He'd seen that fist before, and it was always a clear indicator she was on the edge of losing it.

Sara was doing her best to keep from exploding. It was true she wanted commanders who could think for themselves and were not afraid to take risks. But Parker's risk-taking had resulted in losing half a company and if the acting first sergeant's assessment was right, what was left was combat ineffective.

She had continued to glance at Driscoll to gauge his response, and he never said a word and had yet to look at her the whole time Parker was talking.

"Yes, Colonel. I expect you to command your brigade as you see fit. But losing half a company to an enemy attack we expected and gave you additional forces that were not allocated as we saw fit is not the results I expected. I need you to clean up this mess and ASAP!"

"Yes, Ma'am. I'll have it fixed before I leave."

"Very well. I need you to excuse me for a moment while I speak to my staff."

"Of course, Ma'am."

With that, Parker, Driscoll, and the other officers in the area saluted and left Sara.

Sara turned to Stalanski, and the glare on her face foretold what she was feeling.

Before she could ask, Stalanski said, "I've contacted the G2, Ma'am. She'll be calling you momentarily."

He'd read her mind. She liked that about him. Sara slightly smiled, and the next thing she heard was a call on her helmet-based radio from the G2. "Pegasus 6, Pegasus 2. Over."

"Laura, I've just talked with Colonel Parker. He's telling me there is a major commando threat to his headquarters. Is this true? You've never mentioned anything about that before."

"No, Ma'am. There is no commando threat. First Brigade's S2 called us a few days ago asking about that possibility, and we told him it was extremely low. Whatever commando forces the enemy had were destroyed early in the fight. I can't guarantee the possibility is zero, but it's highly improbable, and we've seen no indicators at all to warrant any change from that assessment."

"Did the S2 tell you he disagreed with your assessment?"

"No, Ma'am. He said he agreed. He said the only reason he asked was because his brigade commander wanted to know and seemed convinced of the threat."

"Thank you. Pegasus 6, out."

Now Sara was very angry. She felt for sure Parker was lying to her. Sara looked over at Stalanski, who she knew had listened in on her conversation with the G2.

Stalanski bit his lips to keep from saying anything that would make Sara even angrier.

"This is bullshit," she told him.

"Yes, Ma'am."

"Come with me," Sara told Stalanski, as she turned and rigidly walked straight to where Parker and the other officers were standing.

As she walked up from behind Parker, Sara saw he had the company commander, who still had an IV in his arm, the acting first sergeant, and Driscoll all standing at attention. The closer she got, the more she could hear.

"This is unacceptable! The division commander shows up and sees how fucked up all of you are," Parker was saying. "Driscoll, I told you to keep this shit straight!"

297

"Sir, I told you about the attacks three days ago and we needed to move the tank company to this area and send a resupply convoy," Driscoll interrupted.

"I don't remember you informing me of any of this. As a former battalion commander, I expect more of you than what I've seen so far. We'll talk about this later."

Then Parker turned to the company commander and his acting first sergeant. "You two are pathetic. You can't hold off a fucking little attack with all the firepower you have. Effective right now, you are relieved. I won't have cowards in my brigade!"

Stalanski did not need to wonder what was about to happen. The red color filling Sara's face told him in no uncertain terms what was about to unfold. He'd only wished he could put some distance from Sara when she reached Parker because the blast wave was going to be a big one.

"Colonel Parker," Sara firmly called out as she stopped directly behind him.

Parker turned with an expression and voice dripping with irritation at being interrupted. "Yes, General."

Stalanski winced.

"You're relieved of command!"

Now it was Parker who jerked. "What did you say?"

"I said you are relieved of command. Get the fuck out of my division!" Sara said, with both her hands on her hips.

"You can't do that, General!"

Sara stepped forward and beat Parker's chest squarely with her index finger. "I am the division commander, and until someone relieves me, I run this fucking outfit. You have no clue what the fuck you are doing, Colonel. Your tactics are infantile. Your priorities are more personal than professional. You display the worst qualities of toxic leadership. You consider yourself omnipotent and do not listen to others who are more experienced than you are. You put Soldiers at risk, needlessly and do not provide them with the resources they require to do their jobs. . . ."

Stalanski held his breath as each sentence Sara spoke was a direct body blow with no holding back. Speaking from a position of strength in both experience and knowledge, Sara forcefully and systematically destroyed Parker's incalcitrant demeanor. Stalanski felt himself wanting to backtrack and had to remind himself he was not the target, just an innocent bystander.

"But most of all, you are more concerned with your own Goddamn safety than you are for the safety and well-being of my Soldiers! And that, Colonel, is unacceptable in my command. You have 24 hours to get the fuck out of my AO, and if you are not out by then, I will have the MPs escort you out by force!"

Parker opened his mouth, but before he could talk, Sara yelled out, "Colonel Driscoll, get over here!"

Standing a few feet away from Sara and Parker, Driscoll almost ran over to Sara.

"Yes, Ma'am."

Now, Sara's rapier finger pressed against Driscoll. "Colonel, Driscoll, you will assume command until further notice. I'm running a war, and I don't have time to deal with leadership failures of this nature anymore from this brigade. You will do the following things immediately. Number one, you will replace this company with a fresh company. Two, you will move the tank company you have from your command post and place it with whichever subordinate unit you deem necessary based on your tactical situation. Three, you will assist Colonel Driscoll in procuring transportation out of my area of operations. And four, I will be at your TOC in 48 hours for a complete rundown of your brigade. I want an update on all ongoing combat operations and an accurate assessment of your capabilities."

"Yes, Ma'am!"

"No more ass clowning around, Driscoll. You get this brigade in shape, or I will fire you and find someone who can do this job. And there are no questions!"

"Yes, Ma'am!"

"You two are dismissed, gentlemen," Sara announced.

Colonel Parker simmered, but he dared not speak. To engage Sara now would edge on insubordination, and he had friends in high places that should be able to fix his dilemma. Whereas Colonel Driscoll immediately saluted Sara, Parker slowly raised his hand.

Sara stared both men down, but her eyes focused on Parker. She waited for his salute, and his slow movement infuriated her more.

Finally, after both men had their hands up and waiting for Sara. She hesitated and then quickly saluted and gestured for them to leave. She wanted Parker to know she was standing her ground regardless of what he might try to pull.

Both men turned, and as they walked away, Parker quietly said for only Driscoll to hear, "She'll regret this."

Driscoll smiled, slanted his eyes to Parker, and replied, "No, she won't."

After Driscoll and Parker left, Sara, still fuming, finally turned to Stalanski.

Stalanski stood still, still hoping to avoid any residue of her wrath.

Finally, she said, "Let's get back to the TOC, Ski. We'll finish this there."

When Sara and her team returned to the division main command post, she told Stalanski to have the G1, and the senior Judge Advocate General Officer meet with her in two hours at her makeshift office in an abandoned school house. She also told him she did not want to be disturbed before her meeting just before she left him.

Stalanski acknowledged her "do not disturb" order but suspected that was not going to happen. He then decided to run to get a bite to eat before being present for the upcoming meeting. He had taken only a few steps when he heard a gruff voice call out to him, confirming his suspicion.

"Major Stalanski, when did you get back and why the hell didn't you let me know?"

Stalinksi turned and saw Colonel Eddington standing, hands on his hips, waiting for an answer. With fiery red hair and a temper to match, Eddington was a force to be reconned with regardless of rank. Not an attractive man, he had that rare ability of ruthlessly getting results, but not at the organization's expense or his subordinates, one of the many facets Sara greatly respected about him.

A graduate of officer candidate school, Eddington had been a staff sergeant with the Rangers before being commissioned, and not even Sara matched his combat experience. With two Silver Stars, three Purple Hearts, and various other awards for valor, Eddington was the epitome of a combat Soldier invariable finding himself in the heart of the action, exactly where he wanted to be. Sitting at some headquarters was not his way of fighting a war. However, the problem was it wasn't Sara's way either, so it fell to him to stay behind and keep things running in her absence, which irritated him to no end.

Sara met him when she was a brigade commander, and he was her executive officer. Together, they formed a good team, dubbed "Beauty and the Beast," by some, although with no hint whatsoever of any romantic scenes. When Sara was given command of the 1st Cavalry Division, she requested Eddington by name as her Chief of Staff, despite his career having peaked years prior, and he was on his way to retirement.

Their professional bond was created by mutual respect for each other's professional abilities. Sara would seek out Eddington's advice on most major decisions, and even if she disagreed with him, she respected his point of view. Sara looked at Eddington in the same way she thought of her former company first sergeant, First Sergeant Dixon. They were proud men and extremely capable, who were not afraid to stand their ground. Yet, they recognized and highly respected her professionalism and capabilities, which created an atmosphere of strong mutual respect and loyalty. Their support also helped her overcome the obstacles of being seen by some as just a woman, and she was very grateful.

"Hello, Sir. I was just coming to let you know we were back," Stalanski answered.

"Bullshit, Stalanski. You were going to feed your face. What the fuck did you two do out there? I told you to keep an eye on her while you were both dicking around. You're gone a few hours, and I got half the damn Army calling me about Parker being relieved. What the hell is that all about, although I have a pretty good idea."

"Well, Sir, I would just say General Bradford was less than impressed with his progress and command style."

To Stalanski's relief, Eddington chuckled. "You don't say. I told her from day one he was a dumbass, and his command time was going to be one big turd circus. She should have fired his ass way before we got over here."

"Yes, Sir."

"Where is the General?"

"She went to her office for a rest. She's meeting with the G1 and Senior JAG Officer in two hours."

"Good, that gives me enough time to talk to her about this."

"Sir, she asked not to be disturbed."

"Right," Eddington grunted and walked off toward Sara's office.

Sara entered the small room that looked like it had been the principal's office. She threw her helmet and protective gear onto the cot off to the side and took a seat in a cushioned chair next to it.

While many commanders of her rank routinely had two separate and grand locations to work and sleep, Sara usually accommodated both in a single modest room. When the division was moving, she often slept in her command vehicle. She could get most of the information she needed from her command-and-control network interface inside her command vehicle that could also be dismounted into a room.

But unlike her peers, Sara did not rely solely on her command-and-control network interface. Instead, she was constantly moving around the battlefield, getting the majority of her information firsthand. She used her office/quarters room most of the time just to sleep.

Sara had just sat down when there was a sharp knock on the door. She knew exactly who it was and knew the only reason he knocked was to make sure she was fully dressed before he entered.

"Yes?" she said, then Eddington walked in.

"So, I see my order to not being disturbed doesn't seem to concern you, Colonel Eddington."

"We need to talk about your latest escapades, Ma'am."

"Colonel, I'm in no mood for that discussion at the moment."

"Do you know in the last hour, I've had two generals call me and share with me their displeasure over Colonel Parker being relieved?"

Just great, Sara thought. *It's already started.* "Well, what did you tell them?"

"I told them to go fuck themselves. That way, the next phone call they would make is to you about me. If they have any balls, that is."

Knowing Eddington was probably telling the truth and tact was an alien concept to him, Sara was actually relieved. "Well, I haven't gotten any phone calls, so I suspect your question about their genitalia is a negative."

"Most generals I know don't have any."

"Well, Colonel, I certainly don't have any. Where does that put me?"

Eddington smirked. She was one of the few people who could match his sharp, insolent humor. "My only concern is what will the Corps Commander, General Fredricks, say. He does have a pair of balls."

"As a matter of fact, I talked to him on the way back."

"What did he say?"

"Officially, he acknowledged my request. Unofficially, I can't repeat what he said, but he's no fan of Parker. So, we should be fine."

"I wouldn't be so quick on that, Ma'am. Parker's family has deep roots in the Army. He'll bring some significant supporting fire to overcome this."

Sara arched her eye. She said, her tone dripping with mirth, "Excuse me. Did I hear you correctly? Do I hear fear in the voice of the "Irresistible Force?" I expected to be harangued for not handling the affair more succinctly, like just shooting him myself and be done with it."

Eddington grinned. "Well, you certainly had the chance. Could have said it was an enemy sniper."

He then waited for her pointed reply, but it did not come. Instead, Sara rested her elbow on the arm of her chair and tried to rub the fatigue from her forehead with her hand. She closed her eyes and, in a highly uncharacteristic moment of doubt, softly said, "Jack, I'm worried."

Eddington sensed the sudden change in mood, the free-wielding give and take moment was over. "About what, Ma'am? Certainly not about Parker."

"I'm not worried about any consequences regarding Parker. If the Army doesn't agree with my decision, they can relieve me and send me home."

"OK."

With her eyes still closed, Sara continued, "We lost a lot of Soldiers this past week. I should have been paying more attention to what was going on. How could I have let such an idiot stay in command for so long? I should have done more. It's just that I'm tired, Jack, really tired."

The first thought entering Eddington's mind was how ridiculous it was for Sara to blame herself for the casualties they had suffered. No one worked harder than Sara. She was in constant motion, pushing her commanders and staff to consider every detail, working contingencies, and personally checking on operations regardless of the danger. The failure resulting in the losses she regretted was not hers but the brigade commander's.

Sara's sullen behavior caused Eddington to realize he needed to be careful about what he said next. Despite his rough exterior and almost blatant insubordination at times toward her, he had the greatest respect for her.

Eddington remained quiet as Sarah remained deep in thought with her eyes still closed.

A moment later, she spoke as if talking to herself. "I wonder, sometimes, what it would have been like to have found someone. Someone very special who loved me, maybe have some children and raise them, see them go off to school, get married, have grandkids. I sometimes wonder what that would have been like."

Hearing her questions, Eddington realized Sara was exhausted. She had never spoken to him like this before. He softly replied, "That's not what you were meant to do, at least not in that simple a manner."

Sara's eyes opened at the atypical tenderness in his voice. "What do you mean?" she asked.

Eddington folded his arms, and thought. "You were meant to do something more."

Then pausing to choose his words carefully, he captured Sara's complete attention. "I'd like to think we were all put on this earth with a chance to serve some purpose, although we may not know what that is. And that purpose comes from how we live our lives. We take what's naturally given to us, learn from our experiences, and serve that purpose. Your purpose is to lead troops into combat at a time when our Army needs you most. You're very good at what you do. You're dedicated to a way of life that is beyond simply existing. You push the boundaries.

You excel. You do things others are incapable of doing, despite the boundaries in front of you. And you do it in a manner that develops the Soldiers and leaders of tomorrow's Army. That is your purpose. To do anything less would be a waste of the talent you have, and if you had taken that road, you would always have wondered what you could have been. And that would have haunted you the rest of your life."

Sara was amazed as she listened to a man who usually couldn't say more than three words without cursing speak in such a sincere manner. Her eyes grew appreciative. Despite their verbal antics over the years, she knew he had great respect for her. He had just never said it as eloquently as he just did.

She lowered her gaze in reflection upon what Eddington had said. His wisdom and insight surprised her. Then a hint of a smile spread on Sara as she asked, "So when did you suddenly become such an articulate warrior scholar?"

Eddington grinned. "Since I was given the job to take care of a crazy commander who puts herself in needless danger to relieve numbnuts, well-connected brigade commanders while I run the Goddamn war."

Her smile in full array now, Sara replied, "Well, I'm sure it has something to do with your observation about the lack of genitalia in most generals."

Appreciating the moment's seriousness was passed, Eddington was glad to see Sara back to her usual self. It was now time for him to do the same.

"Well, I wouldn't worry about that, General. You have a pair of balls, which catches most men by surprise. Especially when they realized yours are bigger than theirs."

"I see," Sara said, laughing.

"Now that we've gotten all of that cleared up, I need to get back to running a war. And you need to get some rest. I'll handle the G1 and JAG folks regarding Parker while you sleep. I'll have someone come wake you before tonight's BUB."

Having returned to his warm tone, Eddington's commitment to Sara almost brought a mist to her eyes. Instead, she simply nodded, preferring not to show emotion that would ruin the moment.

However, when Eddington turned to leave, Sara decided she could not let him go without letting him know how much his words had touched her. "Jack."

Eddington stopped and turned. "Yes, Ma'am."

Sara dropped her guard with a heartfelt smile and softly said, "Thank You."

Eddington returned her smile. "Yes, Ma'am." He then turned and left.

Sitting by herself now, Sara reflected again on her Army career up to that point. She had been a Soldier for many years now, and this was her third war. Hoping everything Eddington said was correct, she wondered how much longer she would serve and what would happen to her when she finally left the service. Was she destined to spend the rest of her life alone?

Chapter 28

SOMEWHERE OVER THE ATLANTIC OCEAN, FEBRUARY 2061. Sitting in her seat in the rear of the small executive passenger jet taking her to Egypt, Sara listened closely to the briefing her staff officers were giving her and tried to find an answer to the central question in her mind. Why did the Queen of Egypt request a meeting with her?

Sara's position as the three-star general in charge of all Army forces in the US Pacific Command meant she focused her attention on those countries and hot spots that lined the Pacific Ocean. Egypt was not on her list of places to be concerned with. That was the responsibility of the officers in charge of Central Command. Consequently, when Sara was told to meet with the Egyptian leader, she ordered her staff to give her a crash course on what was happening in the middle east, so maybe she had some idea of what the meeting was about.

Sitting in the seats to her front and rotated to face Sara was an intelligence officer from her G2 shop, and two planners from her G3 shop. Her chief of staff and the US Ambassador to Egypt sat next to her on either side. Sara sat holding a tablet in her hand with a picture of the queen and some key facts as the intelligence officer continued with his briefing.

"Queen Farood has led Egypt for over ten years now. In that time, she's consolidated her power by ruthlessly eliminating her competitors. She had one of her two brothers killed for his attempt to overthrow her and remove her from her office. She rules with an iron fist but is highly respected and popular with her people," the intelligence officer said.

"I still don't understand why she wants to see you, General Bradford," the Ambassador interrupted. It was clear from the irritation in his voice that he was not happy about Sara's visit.

"I don't understand either, Mr. Ambassador. I was hoping you could shed some light on that," Sara replied. S he was as irritated with the Ambassador as he was with her. He seemed always to be complaining to her about something.

"What about her personal life? What can you tell me about that?" Sara asked the intelligence officer.

"Educated in Oxford, speaks fluent English and several other languages. Previously married, but terrorists killed her husband in 2051. She's had two attempts on her life. Both failed, and everyone connected with those attempts is dead. She has two sons. One is in the Army, and the other is in the Air Force. She appears to be close to both of them and uses them to keep the military loyal to her."

"She's very pretty," Sara said, almost absentmindedly.

"They call her the Cleopatra of the modern age," Brigadier General Jack Eddington said. Eddington was still with Sara, primarily because she trusted him implicitly. He had also mastered the art of managing her staff and all the moving pieces within her command exactly how she wanted to provide her with the information she needed to make decisions and get things done. After serving as her chief of staff at 1st Cavalry Division, Eddington was headed for retirement. However, Sara told him she wasn't finished with him, managed to get him promoted to a one star general, a minor miracle, and pulled him along with her when she took her current position. He remained her definitive right-hand man.

"Yes, Ma'am. But don't let her looks fool you. She is a ruthless but effective leader who has kept her country intact against the insanity of the fundamentalists that have taken over the region since the war between Turkey, Saudi Arabia, and Iran in 2057," the intelligence officer continued."

"Colonel Dillon, explain to me again about the latest Chinese moves in the region," Sara asked her G3 Plans Officer.

"Ma'am, there is a move afoot by the Chinese to take full control of Karachi in Pakistan. They're doing it under the guise of assisting Pakistan with the latest pandemic that has sprung up in the region, but the implications are much more significant. If they take control of Karachi, they will have succeeded in outflanking India with a major port from which they can interdict Indian shipping should a war begin between them. Second, they currently control the port of Gwander in Iran, Jask in Pakistan, and Duqm in Oman. Although these are very small ports, they have been heavily fortified, giving them control over the Persian Gulf entrance. They can shut down all oil flow coming from the region if they want. With their almost global control over the renewable energy technology and now control over oil for which several major countries still require, they can exercise control over the world's major sources of energy."

"Not a very good situation for the United States or the West at that point," Sara concluded out loud.

"No, Ma'am. Not in the least."

Sara looked over some more information on her tablet and then asked, "What is this sentence about her being rescued from terrorists when she was 20? What details do we have on that mission?"

The Ambassador answered, even more irritated than before. "We have no information. It seems our friends in that three-lettered agency will not disclose what that was about."

"Do you mean we were behind that? And they won't give us any information on it. I'm a damn three-star general on her way to talk to the leader of Egypt. I think I have a need to know."

"Well, I'm the Ambassador, and I have an even bigger need to know, but they won't tell me either!"

Suddenly, Eddington spoke up. "Gentlemen, I think we've got the picture. I strongly suggest we call it a night and let General Bradford get some rest before we land in the next 5 hours."

"Yes, I agree. Thank you, gentlemen. You can go back to your seats for now. Jack, please stay for a moment. I have one item I need to review with you."

"I'm going to get some sleep myself as well. Just let me know if you have any questions, and I need an outbrief from you after your meeting," the Ambassador said.

"Yes, of course, Sir," Sara said as the Ambassador got up from his seat and walked to the front of the plane, where there were much better accommodations.

After the staff officers and Ambassador returned to their seats, Sara looked at Eddington and exhaled. "Thanks, Jack. I don't think I could take much more of our friend, the Ambassador, anymore."

"Ma'am, don't worry about him. He's just mad because he thinks you are usurping his power. He wants to be the sole person to talk to the queen for the US government. Plus, he's a pompous assclown."

Sara grinned. "Never one to mince words, Jack. That's what I like about you."

But then Eddington got serious. "We need to build a coalition with them for the region and especially get access to their ports, Ma'am. If the President is serious about his intent to reverse the power of the Chinese in the region, this is the last place we have. I have a feeling that is what the queen wants to discuss with you."

"I think you might be right. I would have bet for sure we would have done more to save Israel years ago when they were attacked. I couldn't believe our lack of resolve."

"Different president, different sentiment at the time. That was then, and this is now. The present administration is ready to push the Chinese out and take back the US's sole superpower status, and they're not afraid to do things to make that a reality."

"That's all nice, Jack, but my responsibilities are on the other side of the world, not here. Why does she want to talk to me of all people?"

"I don't know, but you'll find out soon enough."

The following day after Sara entered the presidential compound, she was led, alone, into a large office by a man in an immaculate silk suit. The man told her because the queen spoke fluent English, there was no need for an interpreter.

He then escorted Sara to a small room inside the compound with a commanding view of a large garden. The sun shined brightly through the large windows Sara assumed were bulletproof. There were two chairs seated close together within the room, separated by a small end table, and Sara surmised that this was strictly a meeting between her and the queen.

Once inside the room, the man turned to Sara and said, "General, please wait here, and her majesty will soon arrive. She has been momentarily detained and asks for your patience. Is there anything I can get you while you are waiting?"

"No, Sir. But thank you very much."

The man then slightly bowed his head and left.

Still standing, Sara looked around the room adorned with multicolored Persian rugs and several pictures. Her eyes were soon drawn to the large oil painting on the nearby wall of the queen's father and former King of Egypt. It was an impressive rendition of what Sara had read was an exceptional man. His uniform was adorned with many medals, and his expression was that of a determined leader.

Sara was lost in the painting's details when she heard a voice behind her say, "I have always loved that picture of my father. He was a great man and a good leader to our country."

Sara turned, and standing a few feet from her was Queen Farood. The pictures Sara had seen of her on the plane ride did not do her justice. She was even more beautiful in person. Her dark olive skin was flawless, and her brown eyes were both alluring and strong. She had a traditional headscarf halfway on her head, giving a front view of her elegant, shoulder-length black hair. She wore a tailored fit black jacket with a stylish cream blouse paired with a black velvet skirt that came to just below her calves. Her gaze toward Sara was warm, although she maintained an air of authority.

Knowing it was improper etiquette for Sara to show her back to the queen, she said, "Please excuse me, Your Majesty. I did not hear you come in."

"That's quite alright, General. I try to make it a point to move stealthily. The position I occupy comes with many enemies."

"I understand."

The queen motioned toward the two large chairs positioned facing one another. "Please, sit down."

"Thank You."

A servant walked in with a silver tray with two steaming tea cups of chai with several sugar cubes on a separate saucer with a spoon, placed them on the small table between the two chairs, then left.

As the queen took her seat, she said, "I have taken the liberty of having a cup of chai poured for both of us. Have you ever had chai before?"

"Yes, Your Majesty. I have."

"Good. I hope you enjoy it. I prefer it instead of coffee. Please sit with me," the queen said. She then took her cup and took a sip.

Sara took her cup and also took a sip. She was surprised by the bitter taste and did her best to hide her displeasure.

Watching her, the queen smiled and said, "You should have added the sugar."

"I'm sorry. It is a bit stronger than I've had in the past."

"I understand. It is an acquired taste without sugar. Much different than your sweet ice tea my late husband developed a great love for after visiting your country."

"I'm very sorry for your loss of your husband, Your Majesty."

"Thank you. You are very kind," the queen said, then her expression turned business-like. "I appreciate you accepting my invitation to meet, and I would love to visit with you at length, however, I assume you have many questions of me, of which the first is why I have requested this visit. Am I not correct?"

"Well, yes, Your Majesty. Usually, the Commander of Central Command would be your US military contact for this region, so it is unusual for any other US general outside of Central Command to communicate with you on matters of high military importance," Sara politely said.

"Yes. That is true. And I know General Shaw very well. He is an idiot."

Sara suddenly felt the urge to laugh as she had never heard a head of state say such things about an American general, but she did her best to stay straight-faced and silent.

"Your face betrays your thoughts, General Bradford. You know, General Shaw?"

Sara knew General Shaw very well. He was a master of playing politics to get what he wanted, and Sara despised him. There was no doubt in Sara's mind the queen spoke the truth. But not knowing what this meeting was about, she decided to be politically correct in her comments. "Yes, I know him, Your Majesty."

"Then you agree, he is an idiot?"

"He is a colleague of mine, but we have had our disagreements on things in the past."

"I see," the queen said. Then she took another sip of her tea and spoke again. "General, the first thing I ask of you is that we are honest with one another at all times when it is the two of us. I understand that one must be careful what one says in front of an audience. However, I can assure you that no one here can listen to you and me now. Therefore, I plan to speak honestly to you, and I ask the same of you."

Sara contemplated the queen's request, but again, being unsure of the reason for her visit, she was hesitant in agreeing. "I would never knowingly lie to you, Your Majesty. I may not answer all of your questions, but I will not tell you untruths. I can assure you of that."

The queen sensed Sara's concerns and acknowledged she would have the same apprehensions in Sara's situation.

"You and I are similar in several ways. We have succeeded and advanced in power in what has been traditionally male-dominated worlds—me in politics and you in the military. I know of you, General Bradford. I know you have succeeded because of your bravery and competence despite the challenges you faced from being a woman."

"Thank you, Your Majesty. Your words honor me."

"But there is another thing we share. The love of a particular man who was instrumental in both of our lives."

Sara frowned. "I'm sorry, Your Majesty, but I do not know what you are talking about. Who are you referring to?"

The queen reached into her pocket and pulled out an item Sara could not see very well. The queen seemed to hesitate as she held the object in her hands, treating it as a precious memento from her past. The memories from that night so long ago came back to her. Her fear, hopelessness, and overwhelming joy as her prayers to Allah were answered by a man she had never known before then but would never forget afterward.

The queen reached out to Sara and placed into her hands an old pair of dog tags.

Sara took the pair in her hand and looked at them. Her eyes grew, and her brow raised as she read the name stamped on them, Colonel John Bradford.

Sara looked up at the queen, amazed, and said, "These dog tags belonged to my father. How did you get them?"

"It was a long time ago. I take it you do not know."

"Your Majesty, I do not know what you are talking about. Please tell me. Did you know my father?"

Once again, the queen seemed lost in memory for a moment. Then she began. "When I was 20, my uncle betrayed my brother and me. He believed we were threats to his succession to lead Egypt. At that time, I cared not about taking power. I wanted only to find the true love of a man. In exchange for influence over the fundamentalist in our country, my uncle had me and my brother kidnapped and told my father we were dead. For several weeks I was held, beaten, and violated by animals that called themselves men. I believed I was to die soon. One night, I heard fighting. I dared not think it was anyone coming for me, but I prayed. My captors threw me in a vehicle and took me to what they thought was a safe place away from the fighting. After what seemed like an eternity, a Soldier came into the small building they had hidden me in. It was your father."

The queen paused in what Sara believed to be an emotional moment for her. "I saw your father fight off three of the worst of these men. He and the others fought off several more before returning and took me to the aircraft that took us to safety. I know from later details they could not find me at first and were about to leave, but your father would not go until he found me. He did all of this for someone who he did not know. I can only imagine what he would be capable of doing for someone he loved."

The queen hesitated as the memories wore heavy on her. Her watery eyes conveyed the deep feelings that accompanied her memory. Sara could see the emotion on her face and hear it in her voice.

"I was in the presence of your father for only a few moments during the rescue and then later for the aircraft ride back to their base. But in those precious hours, I saw a man, unlike any man I have ever known or been with. You might say I fell in love with him."

"When he walked off the aircraft that brought us to safety, he stumbled and fell to the ground because of his wounds. At that time, these dog tags fell from him. I bent down and comforted him. I could see the toll that night had taken on him. I helped him stand and regain the strength to continue. By then, it was time for us to part. My father had sent a trusted group of men to return me to him safely. Before I parted with him, I kissed him and thanked him. For what he had done for me, my gift was insignificant. But it was the least I could do for the man who had saved my life. Knowing I may never see him again, I picked up the dog tags and kept them. I dreamed maybe one day, I might meet him again. I dreamed maybe one day, we could . . ." The queen did not finish her sentence.

Instead, she sat in silence for a while, trying her best not to revisit a dream she knew even then was impossible.

Sara was amazed at the story she heard. She had no idea her father had gone on such a mission. She scanned her memories for when he might have done this. Then it came to her. Her first semester in college, he had been strangely absent in calling her. She assumed he simply wanted her to be on her own. Then she also remembered when he finally did come and visit her, he had injuries he claimed were caused by a boating accident while fishing. But now, she understood what had really happened.

"Is this why you asked me to come here, Your Majesty? To share this story with me?"

"No, not entirely. I called you to discuss the UN Security Council resolution to stop the Chinese from claiming Karachi."

"Very well, your Majesty. I'm listening."

"Your country is putting great pressure on my country to help them stop the Chinese control of the Middle East. Since the war between Saudi Arabia and Iran and the world's lack of need for oil, the middle east has been thrown into chaos. The fundamentalists, aided by the Chinese, have taken control of many of the oil-producing countries. Egypt now stands alone as the last major Arab country to remain against the fundamentalist movement. Should we fall to them, they will have complete control of the Middle East. Then, once the Chinese control access to the Persian Gulf, they will dominate both oil flow and clean energy resources through their technology, giving them control of the planet's major energy sources."

"Yes, that does seem to be their goal, Your Majesty."

"General Bradford, I hate the fundamentalists. These are the same animals that kidnapped me when I was young. I have seen them taking power throughout the region, removing women's rights, and pulling the middle east backward, robbing us of opportunities to grow to be great powers. They threaten me, but more importantly, they threaten my people. I will not allow what has happened in Iraq, Iran, Turkey, and Saudi Arabia to happen in Egypt."

"I understand, Your Majesty. It would seem Egypt and the United States have a common goal to stop the advancement of both the fundamentalists and the Chinese in the middle east. Perhaps we could help one another obtain this goal."

"Perhaps. But first, we must have an understanding."

"What exactly did you have in mind, Your Majesty?"

"I am well aware of recent policy by the United States. When your country withdrew from the international community years ago, several of your allies suffered due to your lack of commitment to them. This lack of commitment worries me significantly. I have remained in power as long as I have because I only deal with people I can explicitly trust."

"I understand. I am sure the US Ambassador and General Shaw will convey your thoughts to the President to arrange an acceptable solution. It would benefit us both greatly to have Egypt as the cornerstone of a coalition within the region to dislodge both the fundamentalist and the Chinese."

"I agree. However, I do not trust either of those men. I will not deal with them on the matter of a joint Egyptian and US strategy for the region."

"I see. Did you have someone in mind?"

"Yes. You."

"Me?"

"Yes. Your father was one of the very few men I trusted unconditionally. You are very much like him. I am sure you made him very proud of you. Certainly, the daughter of such a man as your father, who has brought great honor to him and her family, would emulate his qualities. To do otherwise would bring great dishonor to you and especially your father. I do not believe you would do that. Therefore, I believe I can trust you. I believe you will tell me the truth in our negotiations and operations, even if it is something I do not wish to hear."

"I sincerely thank you for your confidence in me, Your Majesty. But I cannot override the Ambassador or General Shaw in these matters. I am not even assigned to this region. Those matters would have to be decided by the Pentagon and State Department."

"Then I will tell your President I will only work with you and no one else."

"May I ask a blunt question, Your Majesty?"

"Yes, of course."

"Why do you believe I would be interested in pursuing this endeavor? I do not have any significant experience in the middle east. There are others much more qualified than me for this mission."

"Because, General, I know you have a dislike for the Chinese as much as I have for the fundamentalist. I know what it is to have experienced the disgrace of losing a war as you did in Korea. This is an opportunity for you to right that wrong and re-establish the United States' honor amongst the world community. But more importantly, this is an opportunity to justify your Soldiers' sacrifices made so many years ago at the bridge in Seoul."

Sara pondered the queen's words. She was right. Sara never forgot her Soldiers from those days, especially those that died. She recorded all of their names in a diary she kept for herself, never to forget them. She also never forgot the sting of defeat and humiliation she felt after suffering such casualties, only to be pushed out of Korea by the Chinese. From then on, Sara focused her entire Army career never to let the Army or the nation suffer such a dishonor again. Sara concluded the queen had done her homework well.

"Very well, Your Majesty. If I am presented with the opportunity to serve my nation and you in the capacity you wish, I will do it."

"Thank You."

It was then Sara realized she was still holding her father's dog tags in her hand. She looked at them, feeling the deep love she had for him.

But as Sara looked at the dog tags, she realized they meant more to someone else than they meant to her. She saw the expression on the queen's face as she talked about John. Remembering what the queen had told her earlier about men's failures toward her, Sara imagined the depth of the queen's love held for John despite it not being returned. The two simple metal pieces Sara held in her hand were all the queen had other than the feelings in her heart.

Sara reached out to the queen with her hand holding the dog tags and said, "Your Majesty, I believe these belong to you. I am sure my father would want you to have them."

The queen looked at Sara and sadly yet gratefully smiled. She reached out and gently took the dog tags from Sara. "Thank You."

After placing the dog tags in her pocket, she turned back to Sara and asked, "You look very much like your mother, Sara. I imagine she was an extraordinary person, like your father."

Sara smiled. "Yes, she was, Your Majesty. She brought great joy and love to my father."

"Good. I am glad to know your father found the happiness with a woman he deserved."

The queen and Sara visited for a few more minutes, and then their meeting concluded.

Sara returned to the US Embassy grounds and briefed the US Ambassador regarding her meeting with the queen. He was even more irritated than before, but she paid him no mind. The more she thought about the matter, the more she believed she would not be returning to the region.

Early the following day, Sara walked out onto the balcony to the room she was staying in her silk robe. The robe was a present to herself when she made three-star general and a reminder she was still a woman despite her wardrobe's austerity.

The call to morning prayer was being played throughout Cairo, putting Sara in a reflective mood. She first thought about her father. It was as if he never ceased to amaze her. She wondered if he knew the last mission he conducted was saving the future leader of Egypt. Furthermore, it was only because of her father's exploits that Sara was able to sit with the most powerful woman in the middle east and discuss a conflict that could determine the United States' future as a world power.

Then Sara thought about both her father and mother. Only because of a love for one another neither her father nor mother could escape was Sara born. It seemed she owed her destiny to that love between two very special people. She wondered if they would ever know all the things they had influenced in their lives. Sara concluded she would never know.

Suddenly, she heard a knock on the door to her room.

When she opened the door, it was General Eddington.

"Good morning, Ma'am. Sorry for disturbing you so early, but I believe you would want to see this message on paper for yourself. It just got transmitted to the Embassy."

Sara took it, and by the time she finished, she couldn't believe it. It was a notification to her from the Secretary of Defense that she had just been nominated for her fourth star and she would replace General Shaw as the new Commander of Central Command.

Sara shook her head and said, "Well, Jack. It looks like we will be staying."

"We, Ma'am? This message is for you."

"Considering what I know is getting ready to happen, I need the best officers I can get, and you're at the top of my list."

Eddington smiled, "Thank You, Ma'am. I take that as a great compliment coming from you."

"You should. Now get some paper and a pen because I have several other names we are going to add to the list of folks coming with us. We are going to be very busy and need all the help we can get."

Chapter 29

21 OCTOBER 2073. Looking out over the pasture land on that mild Texas October day, Sara found great peace in the serenity around her. She scanned the ground before her, an uneven carpet of green grass with various sized huisache trees and a few live oak tree motts scattered about. The sky had a few of what her father had called wispy clouds that slowly moved across the sky, but not enough to block the warm sun's rays she loved to feel on her face. Gone was the unrelenting humidity that kept her from enjoying her summer walks, and now, more than ever, she enjoyed being outdoors.

But of all the things she loved most about this time of year in Texas was the stillness. No wind blew, and with the open pasture around her, only the smallest of sounds occasionally interrupted the silence. She could easily hear an occasional dog barking in the distance, a cow mowing, or a solitary car going down a country road far away. It was as if time slowed to a crawl.

It had been a few weeks since Sara retired from the Army, and she decided to move back to the property her father had left her in Victoria when he died. It was the same house and acreage where she grew up as a young girl with him after he retired from the Army. She remembered taking walks alone back then, which gave her the peace she needed to reflect on what was going on in her life and think about the days to come. When she returned, she often found her father waiting for her. He was careful not to intrude on her time alone and would tell her he just wanted to make sure she was alright.

Taking her walk today, the first after many years, brought many memories. It seemed a million years ago since she was a young girl living in Victoria. Life was new then, and she found herself filled with the anticipation that comes with youth. But she also remembered the angst she felt at not having a mother to share it with. Then after finally finishing her long and distinguished military career, the innocence of those days seemed far away. She had seen and done things she never even dreamed of back then. Some of those things she'd wished she'd never had to do. However, in the end, there were no regrets, as the good times of her life so far way outnumbered the bad, and for the moment, she loved thinking about the days of her youth.

As she neared the old house, she saw a man waiting for her. Sara was still reminiscing, and a part of her hoped, in some fantastic way, the man was her father. She missed him. She wished she could talk with him again and share her exploits over the past years. She knew he would be very interested in how everything had turned out. But she knew that was not to be. He had been dead for many years now. Yet she sensed, he did know what she had done all these years, and most of all, he was proud of her.

Yet, despite her disappointment, she smiled as she walked closer to the man waiting for her. She had waited many years for him, and finally, her dreams had come true. Finally, her heart had found the one. It had taken a long time, and their relationship had not been an easy one over the years, but he was indeed the one. He loved and respected her like no other, and she was head over heels in love with him. The years of loneliness were finally taken away when she accepted his marriage proposal. Falling in love these past years kept her young and heart, and even at age 64, she felt like a schoolgirl again.

"Did you have a good walk, Sweetheart?" the man asked.

"Yes. It was very good. A lot of brush has grown up in the back pasture. We'll need to clear some of that."

"Sure. I don't think that will be a problem. So, what is on the agenda for the rest of the evening?"

"Well, I thought I would cook you some supper tonight. Maybe grill some fish on the patio. How does that sound?"

"That sounds fantastic! I mean, who else can say that a former five-star general of the US military will be cooking them supper tonight. Considering there hasn't been a fives star general since General Bradley from World War II, I'd say I feel pretty important. That is if you know how?"

Sara rolled her eyes. "Yes, my dear. I know how to grill fish."

Then that mischievous smirk Sara had grown to love appeared on the man's face as he then said, "By the way. I read the first draft of your biography from that pesky author. I think there might be a few errors."

"Really? I bet it was in the part that talks about our campaigns in the middle east when I was the CENTCOM Commander. No, it was probably in that chapter when I was the Chairman of the Joint Chiefs of Staff. Is that where you found them?"

"No, that looked alright to me. It was failing to mention it was me and my tanks that saved you at the Battle of the Han River bridge."

"I see. Well, I'll make sure to remind the author how obnoxious Lieutenant Dan Clark was and how much I couldn't stand him then," Sara replied with an equally mirthful smile. Her initial disdain for him then had been a running joke with them for years.

"As you wish, my love," Dan replied. "What do you plan to do tomorrow?"

"I thought I'd do some unpacking. There are still several boxes I need to go through in the spare bedroom. I'll work on that tomorrow. But the rest of tonight, I just want to cook my husband supper and be Mrs. Dan Clark-Bradford for the rest of the evening, whatever that may entail," Sara replied with another hint of mischief.

Dan loved it when she talked like that. No longer were they two active-duty generals with the weight of the world on their shoulders. No, they were now just man and wife.

He reached out to her and pulled her close to him, with a look that suggested their night would be filled with things lovers often did.

Sara lingered in his look, her eyes gleaming in anticipation. Playfully, she asked, "What if we delayed supper for a while?"

"I was hoping you'd say that."

The following day, Sara sat in a chair in the spare bedroom surrounded by unopened cardboard boxes that remained unpacked after her move from her Washington D. C. quarters. There were so many. Some of them were still packed from several prior moves. She'd never seemed to have had time to go through them. Consequently, they remained closed and got a new sticker from the movers as they traveled from house to house. She'd tell herself after each move that one day, she would get a chance just to sit and go through them all. She'd decided today was that day.

Opening them was like opening a time capsule. She found clothes she hadn't worn in years and had forgotten she even had. In one, she found the tiny bikini her Aunt Mary and Jennifer had urged her to buy and she wore for her cousin Jack's destination wedding vacation. Holding it up, she chuckled to herself in disbelief she actually wore it. Confident the days of wearing something so revealing were long gone, Sara was about to toss it in the pile of things to get rid of, but at the last minute, decided not to. Instead, she got a devilish idea. Laughing to herself, she thought. *I wonder what Dan would think if he found this lying around the house one day.* She loved playing little tricks on him.

She moved on to the other boxes, and each one held other little treasures reminding her of the various places she'd lived.

Then she came upon a box that looked very old. It had at least ten stickers on it from the movers indicating it hadn't been opened in a very long time.

Sara opened it up and saw it had been very carefully packed. Then, removing the packing paper, she pulled out what she realized was her father's old photo album. It had been decades she had looked at it and feared it had been lost in one of her many moves.

Sara sat back in her chair and opened the pages. She couldn't remember the last time she saw an actual photograph, and no one had photo albums anymore. There were pictures of her father as a young boy with his parents. He looked so young. Time was beginning to deteriorate some of the photographs, but others were still in good condition. There were some of her Aunt Mary as a young girl and others of her grandfather and grandmother, whom she never knew. As she turned the pages, she saw her father grow into a young man and thought he was very handsome.

Then she turned a page and saw a collection of pictures she didn't ever remember seeing. There were several with her father as a young man, probably when he was in college, sitting on a couch with a young woman. She was very beautiful. In one of them, they sat side by side with their arms around each other. Even though the photo was fuzzy, she recognized the young woman. It was her mother. Their eyes gleamed with happiness, and they were laughing like two young people deeply in love do. Looking at the photos, Sara could feel the joy her father and mother felt at that moment.

Sara sat in memory for a long time, thinking about her parents. Having never met her mother, she often thought about her when Sara was a young girl. She remembered her father's emotion each time he spoke of her, a testament to the deep love they had shared. She remembered the box with all the letters, photos, and videos from her mother to her and how all those things gave her insight into the struggles her parents had to overcome to be together. When Sara remembered the story the ER nurse relayed to her Aunt Mary about her father's last words calling out to her mother, she had no doubt what they meant to one another.

Looking at the photo in the album, Sara wondered if those two young people had any idea of the struggles for their love that lay ahead. Reflecting upon what they would go through together, she felt sad.

"You, OK, my love? You seem deep in thought."

Sara turned and saw Dan's loving eyes looking at her, and her heart filled with warmth. For in that look of love from him, she felt what her parents had felt, a deep true love from someone who loved her like no other. It had just taken her a little longer than she would have liked. But that did not matter now. She had found it, and she would spend the rest of her life with him.

"I'm fine, sweetheart. Just going through some old boxes," Sara replied as she met his look of affection with a loving smile. "I've come to a stopping point. Let me put this away, and I'll come be with you."

Dan returned her smile and left her to her work.

Sara turned back to the photograph. She thought back to her earlier question about them and decided she didn't feel sad for them after all. Instead, she realized it was their love that refused to die from that wonderful summer that had somehow sustained itself within them and, in turn, gave them hope for the future. Whatever happened after that summer ultimately didn't matter, for their hearts and souls had found the one, and while time and circumstances may have prevented them from physically being together, nothing on earth would ever break the bond they shared. Those things that had tried to destroy their love ultimately only made it stronger.

She closed the album, held it close to her chest, and closed her eyes for a moment. She wished her parents well.

And in a place far away, the young couple in the old photograph held hands and felt the deep love and youthful joy reflected in that photograph now and for all eternity.

GLOSSARY

AA – Avenue of Approach – A route for friendly or enemy forces.

ADA – Air Defence Artillery.

AO- Acronym for Area of Operations.

APC – Armored Personel Carrier.

ASAP – As Soon As Possible

BK – Battlefield Kitchen – A mobile kitchen to prepare meals for Soldiers.

BUB – Battle Update Brief.

C2 – Command and Control.

CAS – Close Air Support.

CASEVAC – Casualty Evacuation.

CENTCOM – Central Command.

CIA – Central Intelligence Agency.

CG – Commanding General.

Class One – Food.

Class Three - Fuel

Class Five – Ammunition.

CONPLAN – Contingency Plan.

EA – Engagement Area – the planned location where enemy forces are attacked.

ECM – Electronic Counter Measures.

Executive Officer – The executive officer's primary mission is to coordinate the unit's staff's work for the unit. That officer can also stand in for the unit commander in his absence.

G1 – Senior Personnel Staff officer at the division and corps level.

G2 – Senior Intelligence Staff officer at the division and corps level.

IOBC – Infantry Officer Basic Course.

ISR – Intelligence, Surveillance, and Reconnasaince.

JAG – Judge Advocate General.

JLTV – Joint Light Tactical Vehicle.

KIA – Killed In Action.

L T – Short for Lieutenant.

LTV – Light Tactical Vehicle.

LZ – Landing Zone.

MEDEVAC – Medical Evacuation.

METL – Mission Essential Task List.

MRE – Meal Ready to Eat.

NCO – Noncommissioned Officer.

NTC – National Training Center.

OPLAN – Operational Plan.

OPCON – Operational Control – a term used when placing a unit under another unit's control other than its parent unit.

PTSD – Post Traumatic Stress Disorder.

ROK – Republic of Korea.

ROTC – Reserve Officer Training Course.

S-2 – Intelligence Officer on a Battalion or Brigade staff.

S-3 – Operations Officer on a Battalion or Brigade staff.

SAM – Surface to Air Missile.

SAPI – Small Arms Protective Insert – bullet prove plates.

SIGINT – Signals Intelligence.

SITREP – Situation Report.

SP – Starting Point along a planned movement route. Also used to mean "begin movement."

TAC -Tactical Operation Center – This element is located forward of the TOC and helps the TOC control the subordinate units.

TACSOP – Tactical Standard Operating Procedures.

TOC – Tactical Operations Center – This element is centrally located and is the unit headquarters when it is deployed.

UAS – Unmanned Aerial Vehicle – aerial drone.

WARNO – Warning Order.

WIA – Wounded In Action.

WILCO – Will Comply.

CHARLES W INNOCENTI III

ABOUT THE AUTHOR

Charles W. Innocenti III, or "Bill" as his friends call him, retired from the US Army in 2008 as a Lieutenant Colonel after twenty-one years of service. He received his commission from Officer Candidate School in 1988, and started his service on the East/West German Border in Fulda, Germany in the waning days of the Cold War. He retired after his third deployment to Operation Iraqi Freedom in 2008. After retiring from the Army, Charles went on to work in Afghanistan as a civilian contractor working directly with officers and Soldiers of the Afghan military in support of Operation Enduring Freedom until 2011. All total, Charles spent six years of his life living inside combat zones giving him an upfront, personal, and unique perspective on war and life. Charles was born and raised in the small town of Victoria, Texas until he left for the Army and an adventure that would take him around the world with opportunities to work with and lead this generation's "greatest Americans." The day after he graduated Basic Training, Charles married an amazing lady named JoAnne, who was and is the cornerstone of their wonderful family with three children, Will, Jessica, and Rachel. He holds a B.A. in Business Administration from the University of Houston, Victoria, and two Masters degrees from the Command and General Staff College and the School of Advanced Military Studies at Fort Leavenworth, Kansas.

He can be reached at cwi3books@gmail.com.

Made in the USA
Las Vegas, NV
07 February 2022

43376301R00198